SQUARE ONE

L.A. WITT

Copyright Information

This is a work of fiction. Names, characters, places, and incidents are either the product of the author's imagination or are used fictitiously. Any resemblance to actual persons living or dead, business establishments, events, or locales is entirely coincidental.

Square One

First edition

Copyright © 2019 L.A. Witt

Cover Art by Lori Witt

Editors: Leta Blake & Jules Robin

All rights reserved. No part of this book may be reproduced or transmitted in any form or by any means, electronic or mechanical, including photocopying, recording, or by any information storage and retrieval system without the written permission of the publisher, and where permitted by law. Reviewers may quote brief passages in a review. To request permission and all other inquiries, contact L.A. Witt at gallagherwitt@gmail.com

ISBN: 978-1-07097-126-1

❦ Created with Vellum

ABOUT SQUARE ONE

Holden Russell let his job consume his life for too long, and it took his wife leaving for him to realize it's time for a change. His marriage is over, but he's determined to do right by his kids, starting with fewer hours at work and more with them. Except it's no longer the kids competing with his job for his attention. It's *Holden* competing for *their* attention... with their new live-in nanny. Their very hot *male* live-in nanny.

Porter Blake never saw himself becoming a nanny, but okay. After burnout and PTSD drove him from his job as a paramedic, he's desperate for something new, and it turns out the nanny gig isn't so bad. The pay is decent, the stress is manageable, the kids are great, and their mom is cool. It's the ex-husband he's not so sure about.

The situation is awkward enough when Porter and Holden are butting heads. When they find some common ground and their mutual attraction becomes too much to ignore, things are bound to get complicated.

And unless they want Porter to lose his job, they're going to have to fly under the ex-wife's radar. Except secrets like this have a way of coming out...

This standalone novel is approximately 115,000 words long.

CHAPTER 1

HOLDEN

"I can handle things here." My eldest son, Zach, shooed me toward the door of the mostly empty apartment we were moving into. "*Go.*"

"I can—"

"Dad. Come on." He threw me a look that reminded me of the *oh my God, Dad, why are you such a jerk?* faces from his earlier teenage years, but with a hint of playfulness. "I can sit here and play Box Bingo by myself." He held up the clipboard from the moving company. "It's pretty easy, you know?"

He had a point. At nineteen, he was mature and responsible, and I had no reason to believe he couldn't cope with the task of checking boxes off the list as movers carried them in from the truck. And I *had* been itching to go see his younger half-siblings now that we were all finally in the same state.

"Go." He made another shooing motion. "Tell Tiffany and the kids I said hi."

"All right, all right." I picked up my keys from the otherwise unoccupied counter. 'Give me a call or shoot me a text if you need anything, all right?"

"Will do."

"I owe you, kid."

"Oh, I know."

I rolled my eyes and laughed. "Of course you do."

Zach chuckled, then hoisted himself onto the counter and started thumbing through something on his phone. I left him to it and headed down to the car.

In the driver's seat, I texted my ex-wife to let her know I was on my way. She was working from home this week and had been the one to suggest me coming earlier than later; I might beat the kids home from school, but at least I wouldn't get stuck in traffic. Probably wouldn't hurt for the two of us to have a few minutes one-on-one before adding them to the mix anyway. Though we were amicable enough to be in the same room, there was definitely still some post-divorce awkwardness to contend with.

As I drove away from the new complex, I did feel mildly guilty leaving Zach to deal with the movers. Though I knew he could handle it, and I'd definitely make it up to him, was it really fair to leave it all to him while I took off to see my younger kids? Probably not, but he'd been insisting for days that I should go visit them as soon as we made it to town. Yesterday and the day before had been nonstop logistics—grocery shopping, coordinating with movers, meeting with my new boss and colleagues, and generally procrastinating because as eager as I was to see my kids, I was kind of dreading it too. Today, our things were arriving, which was a perfectly legitimate reason to stay home, but no, Zach had stepped up and said he could handle it.

No excuses, Holden.

It wasn't like I didn't want to see them. I adored them,

and I'd been missing them something fierce ever since they'd moved with their mother from Arizona to Everett, Washington, six months ago.

But at the same time, I was nervous. I didn't even know why.

It was entirely possible I was just a coward. Seeing them today would be a moment of truth I wasn't sure I was ready for. Starting now, for the first time in their lives, I wouldn't be on the road constantly. My new job had normal hours and required minimal travel. So I'd be close by instead of doing most of our interactions via phone, Facetime, and Skype like we'd done when we'd lived in the same house.

But is it going to be too little too late?

Ah, that was it. I'd had my wakeup call when Tiffany kicked me out a year and a half ago, and again when she and the kids had moved to Washington. After some long heart-to-hearts with my ex, I'd found a job here, and now I'd be able to actually see my kids on a regular basis for the first time in their lives. More than I had when I'd still been married to their mom. It felt like a good start, but I was worried sick that it had come too late. It wouldn't be enough. The damage was done and there was no fixing it. My ex-wife and I couldn't go back, so what if my kids and I couldn't either?

Keeping one hand on the wheel, I pressed my elbow against the window and rubbed the back of my neck. Tiffany insisted that the kids wanted to see me, and that they were excited about me living close by again. Every call recently had been full of "Dad, when are you moving?" and they'd been ecstatic a month ago when I'd told them I'd gotten the job and would be in town soon. Tiffany said it was all they could talk about, especially this past week.

I gnawed my lip as I merged onto I-5 and headed north.

My new place was three exits down from Tiffany's—a fifteen-minute drive in light traffic, probably much more if I got tangled in the daily Boeing exodus. Today I'd hit the road during one of the magic hours with minimal traffic, and before I knew it I was already nosing off the freeway toward her house.

But what if coming here had been a mistake? What if the kids and I couldn't handle being this close together all the time? I didn't want to continue being a distant—more like absent—father, but I was scared to death of being present and realizing they weren't interested in a relationship with me anymore. If that ship had already sailed...then what?

It didn't help that my entire world was in flux at the moment, which made me irrationally certain I was making a huge mistake. I'd left a well-paying job in Phoenix for one that paid slightly more here in Everett, but it may as well have been a pay cut thanks to the higher cost of living. Good thing my son and I had found a reasonably inexpensive apartment, and he would start contributing to the rent once he'd landed a job, too.

Tiffany had family here, but I'd only been to the area for brief visits during our marriage and for the odd conference. Besides my ex-wife and ex-in-laws, I didn't know anyone. I knew my way around some parts of Seattle and a few areas of Everett, but otherwise...nada.

New city. New job. New apartment. New arrangement with my kids. New life as a single dad. New...everything.

No, none of that was terrifying in the least. And what if it ended up being for nothing? What if the kids wanted nothing to do with me? What if the job didn't pan out? In the beginning this had felt like a leap of faith, but more and more it felt like diving in headfirst without checking to see how deep the water was, and now I was in midair, anticipating the paralyzing crunch at the end.

I shifted in the driver's seat and took a deep breath. I was way overthinking this. The new job would be fine. Navigating unfamiliar cities had become second nature thanks to my old job requiring eighty-five percent travel. Meeting new people would be a challenge, but as my son had helpfully reminded me—there were apps for that.

And my younger kids... it wasn't too late. It couldn't be. They were three, seven, and eight—young enough for me to get it together before we reached the resentful teenage years. Right?

Finally—and somehow all too soon—I was pulling into Tiffany's driveway.

The house was even nicer in person than it had been in the pictures she'd emailed. She'd rented a gray split level four-bedroom house on a quiet street a mile or so from I-5. Being in this part of the Pacific Northwest, the rent was sky-high, but we'd agreed on a higher child support payment so she could cover it. In part because of the astronomical cost of living, and in part because she needed enough space for our three kids, plus her daughter. An apartment was just too crowded.

Fortunately, in addition to my job and the one she'd started a few months ago, we'd made enough off the sale of our house in Phoenix to soften the blow of the expenses. We'd split the money three ways—a quarter to me, a quarter to her, and half into a fund specifically for child-related expenses.

Expenses which, in the last few months, had turned out to include the live-in nanny occupying the fourth bedroom.

I'd been a little surprised by that, but it made sense once Tiffany had explained the situation. Now that she was working full-time, she needed help, and even having her sister, Carly, nearby wasn't enough, so she'd made the decision to hire someone. The nanny wasn't cheap, but she kept Tiffany from losing her mind while she juggled working and single motherhood. That alone made her worth the price.

I got out of the car and, with no small amount of trepidation, started up the concrete walk to the front door. There were a few dirty plastic toys and naked Barbie dolls in the otherwise bare flowerbeds beside the neatly trimmed grass. That made me smile. The kids must have loved the mud instead of the more arid outdoors of Arizona. And Tiffany had mentioned more than once that letting them play outside was so much less stressful without the scorpions and snakes of the Southwest.

"We caught a gardener snake today!" my seven-year-old, Ethan, had excitedly told me a few weeks ago after a garter snake had apparently wandered into the yard. Instinctively, I'd panicked at the thought of my kids being close to a snake, never mind catching it. Tiffany had assured me that it wasn't venomous, though, and the nanny had carefully held it while the kids had taken turns gently touching its scaled skin. Then she'd let it go, and they'd all watched it slither off into the bushes. No freaking out. No frantic calls for snake removal.

Yeah, maybe moving them to this area *was* for the better, if only because I didn't have to freak out about them being bitten by a rattler or stung by a scorpion.

At Tiffany's front door, I paused for a deep breath. Then I knocked.

Footsteps inside the house thudded alongside my pounding heart.

The deadbolt clicked. The door opened. And for the first time in half a year, Tiffany and I were face to face.

The sight of my ex-wife made my breath hitch. It had been easier to get my head around our divorce when she'd packed up and left town. It wasn't hard to get used to the idea of her being gone when she was literally gone. Being in the same space again was... wow.

She didn't look nearly as tired as she had during the waning months of our marriage. Having a job outside the house had brought some life back into her, as had bringing in the nanny to help with the kids. Guilt hit me hard again —the nanny was doing all the things I could have done back then if I'd been around more, and the dramatically reduced strain was plain to see. For most women I knew, the transition to single motherhood left them drained and frazzled, but not Tiffany. The way she looked now made me realize just how exhausted and worn thin she'd been while we were married. No wonder she'd left.

You look amazing. How much was it killing you to be married to me?

"Hey." I smiled nervously. "It's, uh, good to see you."

"Yeah. You too." Jesus. We'd never been this awkward with each other.

She stepped aside and gestured for me to come in. I did, and immediately noticed the rack of shoes by the door.

"Shoes off?"

"Yes, please."

I toed them off, and as I did, realized the house was completely silent, which answered the question of whether the kids were here. There was never a quiet moment during the waking hours of three Tasmanian devils.

"Do you want some coffee?" she asked.

"Sure, I could go for some." I nudged my shoes up against the rack so they were out of the way. "Thanks."

I followed her upstairs into the kitchen, looking around

as I did. The house was definitely bigger on the inside, and it was quite nice. There was evidence of my kids everywhere—toys up against the wall beside the entertainment center, a bright orange bicycle helmet someone had left out, picture books, framed portraits on the walls, drawings taped to the refrigerator. The sight of it all brought a lump to my throat. I'd stayed in our house until it was sold, then moved into an apartment, and it had all seemed so empty and sterile without them. Even when I traveled, I always took a few of their drawings and some photos with me to make the hotel rooms feel less hollow. I missed the colorful chaos of a house full of kids.

In the kitchen, Tiffany took a couple of mugs down from a cabinet and set them beside the coffeepot. "Porter left half an hour ago to pick up the kids, so they should all be back soon."

"Porter?"

"Mmhmm." She glanced up from pouring our coffee. "The nanny."

Okay, so I knew there were some names out there that weren't gender indicative, but I was pretty sure I'd never met a woman named Porter. I cleared my throat. "Um, am I to assume that Porter is...a man?"

"He is." She pushed a mug toward me. "Just don't call him a manny. He hates that."

"I see."

Tiffany looked at me again. "What?"

"The, uh... Your nanny is a man?"

"Uh, yeah?" She quirked her eyebrows as if to ask if that was a problem, and, truth be told, it kind of was and I had no idea why. It hadn't crossed my mind until now that her live-in nanny could even be a man, and while I tried not to get hung up on things like gender roles, I wasn't going to lie—this rubbed me the wrong way.

As Tiffany put the coffeepot back, she said over her shoulder, "He's not negotiable, Holden."

I blinked. Was I that easy to read? "Okay, but can we, uh... Can we talk about this guy? You haven't said much about him since you hired him. I didn't even realize he was a guy."

She sighed, and when she faced me, I recognized that look of tired exasperation. "I have, actually. More than once."

"What? When?"

"When we've talked?" She shrugged and picked up her coffee. "Look, if I'd realized it would be such an issue, I'd have made a bigger point of it. But I think everything's just been so crazy for you the last few months, you probably didn't even notice when I mentioned him." She didn't sound mad about it. We both knew me—when my life was in turmoil, I could barely keep track of anything. During some of the really chaotic periods at my last job, she'd even casually dropped things into conversation like "I'm sleeping with your boss" or "I thought I'd start dabbling in meth" just to see if I caught it. Which I usually didn't. No wonder she'd gotten tired of me.

"Okay. So." I cleared my throat. "I assume he's, uh, good at his job?"

"Very." Her expression brightened. "They adore him. He's great with young kids. I guess he was the oldest of five, so he's kind of been there, done that." She paused. "Oh! And he was a paramedic for eight years. When he told me that, I practically hired him on the spot."

"Really?"

"Pfft. Are you kidding? Who better than a trained paramedic to take care of our wild animals?"

I couldn't help but laugh. She did have a point. Both of our respective older kids were pretty mellow, but the three younger ones? They were always finding innovative new ways to burn through our insurance's emergency deductible. So, okay, putting a paramedic on watch wasn't a bad idea. Neither was a male nanny in the first place, and I still didn't quite know why it bothered me.

She must have taken my silence for more uncertainty because she put her cup down and folded her arms loosely across her chest. "Listen, I hired him before I knew you were even thinking about moving to Washington. And yes, him being a guy was a point in his favor. The thing is, once the kids got here, they didn't have you or Zach in their world anymore. And let's be fair—they hadn't seen much of you at all." She shrugged tightly. "These kids need a male role model. Someone I can introduce to them without worrying he and I will break up and break their hearts. Porter is a positive, strong, constant, male presence in their lives."

I stared back at her, at a loss for what to feel, never mind what to say. My first instinct was to lash out that she'd unapologetically replaced me in my own children's lives. But almost immediately, the guilt set in, and...could I blame her? Had I really failed so much as a father that my ex-wife had to resort to *hiring* someone to fill in where I should have been?

Yeah. I kinda had.

I willed my voice to stay even and devoid of the resentment that wanted to bubble to the surface. "So, what happens now?"

"What do you mean?"

"I mean, I'm not in another state anymore, and the new

job will let me work from home a few days a week once I'm up to speed So I'll be able to spend more time with them."

"Right.' She inclined her head as if to ask, "*And?*"

"So does he...is he still going to..."

Tiffany blinked, then straightened. "Are you trying to ask if I'm going to cut him loose now that you're here?" There was a note of warning in her voice that I'd long ago learned to recognize as *"You better make sure you really want to go there before you put your foot in your mouth."*

"Do they still need a full-time, live-in nanny when both of their parents are around?" Our eyes locked, and I knew she heard what I was really asking: *"Do they really need a father figure now that their father is here?"*

Her jaw worked and her eyes narrowed just slightly. "How about this? When they all get home, you can be the one to tell them they won't be needing Porter anymore. Let me know how that goes."

The dare in her tone sent something cold prickling down my back. *"Go ahead,"* she wasn't saying out loud. *"See what happens. Then after it blows up in your face, we can talk about what happens next."*

"I'm not asking you to boot him out," I said quietly. "I'm just... I won't lie—I'm not sure how comfortable I am."

"Since when does it bother you if a guy is watching the kids? Zach used to babysit all the time, and so did the neighbors." Her eyebrow arched. "If you think he's going to do something he shouldn't, I—"

"No, no, it's not that." I shook my head. "I don't even know if it's rational. I've never met the guy, so I'm not going to accuse him of anything. I'm just not sure how I feel about it."

Tiffany studied me for a long moment before she spoke, her tone walking a fine line between soft and hard.

"Holden, I want you to be in their lives. You're their father, and they love you, and God knows I want you to spend time with them and have that relationship with them. The thing is, though, Porter has been good to them, and he's been good *for* them. Having him here has kept them happy and me sane. He's a constant in their lives where there hasn't been one before. He's consistent, which they need after all the change over the last two years. So yes, I absolutely want you to see them as much as possible and make up for lost time." Voice harder, she added, "But Porter isn't going anywhere."

I swallowed. What could I say? The kids had been through more than enough, so I couldn't justify suggesting that we add more turmoil by booting out the man who'd become a part of their new routine.

A car engine broke the stillness, and we both glanced toward the stairs.

Tiffany put her coffee cup down. "That would be Porter and the kids."

I took a deep swallow of coffee since my mouth had suddenly gone dry. Outside, car doors opened and closed, and I willed my nerves to calm down. I was even more nervous than I'd been when I'd left the apartment. Instead of seeing my kids for the first time in too long, I was also meeting Porter. The nanny. The man I had absolutely not expected.

Ever since she'd had me served with divorce papers, I'd wondered what it would be like when my ex-wife started dating. If I'd feel jealous or hurt, watching the woman I still loved with someone new. If my kids would like him. If they'd call him Dad. If they'd take a breakup hard or if they'd be glad he was gone. Zach's mother and I had had such a toxic relationship and nasty split, I hadn't felt a thing about her being with someone new. I'd just been concerned about how her new boyfriends—including the current one—would get along with our son. She and Andy had been together for almost seven years now, and he was still "Mom's boyfriend" or "Andy," not "Dad." Maybe my younger kids would be closer to their hypothetical future stepfather, maybe they wouldn't, but I'd always figured I'd cross that bridge when I got to it.

So how was I supposed to feel about a man who was in the picture specifically for them? Whose presence was not contingent on a romantic relationship with their mom, but focused solely on taking care of and being a role model—a *father figure*—for my kids?

I had no idea how to deal with that.

Downstairs, the front door opened, and over the sounds of jackets and sneakers, a smooth male voice said, "Shoes. Don't forget your shoes. Noah, hang up your backpack, please. Chloe, that's not where your shoes go."

Then, once the kids had apparently satisfied shoe and backpack requirements, thundering feet came up the stairs and—

Oh my God. I couldn't even breathe.

"Dad!" they shouted in unison and rushed across the kitchen to me.

"Hey!" I crouched, arms out, and the three of them bowled me over. They knocked me off balance enough that I smacked my shoulder against a cabinet handle, but I didn't care. It was a huge relief to see them, and an even bigger one that they were excited enough to tackle hug me. And they were big enough to do it, too. Wow.

I suspected—with no small amount of guilt—that Chloe was taking her cues from her brothers. She'd only been a year and a half old when her mother and I had split, barely two and a half when the family had moved here. All told, I'd probably been there for three or four months of her life, and that was being generous. Now she was three, and I was here. Did she even know who I was? Or was I basically one of many men she accepted as part of her tiny world, just like her eldest brother or her uncles, without her realizing I was her dad?

Fuck, that was a heavy thought. Especially as I realized that she'd probably started becoming more aware of the world around her in the last several months, during which time there'd been one constant adult male presence in her life, and it hadn't been me.

I tamped down my jealousy and guilt. Now wasn't the time. I just wanted to see my kids and bask in the relief that they weren't giving me the cold shoulder. Ethan and Noah were seven and eight, respectively, and they had a better grasp on my role in—and absence from—their lives. It was definitely a relief that they were happy to see me.

When they let me go, they bombarded me with questions. Was I really staying? When could they see my place? Could they have a dog at my house since Mom wouldn't let them? Where was Zach? Did I want to see their rooms? I tried like hell to keep up, but I could barely think straight because my God, I was actually with my kids. And I'd only be a few miles away from now on. I could see them just about *any* time. The fact that that was a novelty made me feel like even more of a failure, but I didn't let that linger because I was too thrilled about seeing them. Guilt could wait until I tried to sleep tonight.

"Hey, guys?" Tiffany broke in. "Why don't you change clothes, and then you can show Dad around the house and backyard, okay?"

I looked up, and whatever I'd meant to say got lost in my throat.

Tiffany stood at the top of the stairs the kids had come up. And beside her?

That... That was Porter.

Holy. Fuck.

I hadn't exactly had time to get my head around the existence of Porter the Male Nanny, so I also hadn't had time to conjure up what I thought he might look like.

Which meant it was safe to say that I absolutely wasn't ready for Porter, my kids' nanny who refused to be called a manny, their male role model in shining armor or whatever...

...to be *hot*.

I hadn't been with a man in years, and the last eighteen months or so had been so chaotic that I'd forgotten I even had a libido—bisexual or otherwise—and suddenly I was presented with this tall twenty-something in a flannel shirt and jeans, with sandy blond stubble and artfully tousled hair. He looked like someone who spent his summers surfing on the California coast. Judging by the fading tan, that might not have been far from the truth.

Unaware of me getting tongue-tied over their nanny, the kids reluctantly let me go and went down the hall to what I assumed were their bedrooms.

Leaving me alone with Tiffany and Porter.

As I rose, he and I locked eyes from across the kitchen. He studied me warily, as if he had no idea what to make of me. I just hoped I wasn't wearing my sudden attraction on my sleeve, though I had to assume that was tempered by the remaining mixed bag of emotions I had about him.

"So, um." Tiffany cleared her throat. "Porter, this is Holden. My ex-husband." She gestured at him. "Holden, Porter." Beat. "The nanny."

CHAPTER 2

PORTER

So I'd definitely been nervous about meeting Tiffany's ex-husband. I mean, it wasn't like I didn't want to —the man deserved to meet the dude who was hanging around his kids all day—but ex-spouses could be weird. No matter how much Tiffany insisted that Holden was totally cool and that they were amicable, that didn't necessarily mean he would be totally cool with *me*. I'd gotten plenty of side-eye from my own friends and family who couldn't believe someone would hire a man for this job. Between this and my brother working as an elementary school teacher, I was well aware of all the gross things people thought about a guy whose job meant being around kids all day. What would the kids' own father think?

A lot of things, apparently, but he was keeping a lid on them. Well, rather, he wasn't actually saying them out loud. His face was definitely involved in the conversation, and I could tell right away, as he rose from where he'd been crouching to hug his kids, that Holden Russell did *not* like me.

A few seconds of awkward silence passed before he

finally shook himself, cleared his throat, and extended his hand. God knew what had been going through his mind right then. I couldn't imagine it was good.

But in the interest of staying employed and avoiding a hostile work environment, I put on a smile and shook his hand. "It's nice to meet you."

"Yeah," he said a little warily. "You too."

And... hello, awkward silence.

I had no idea what to say, and if I stood here a minute longer, I was going to... I didn't even know. Physically unravel from anxiety?

"I'm, uh..." I gestured over my shoulder. "Going to go unload the car. I'll be back in a minute."

Tiffany nodded. Holden said nothing. Neither offered to give me a hand, and that was quite all right with me. The groceries were a convenient excuse to step outside and take a breather from all the tension. I needed a minute to collect myself. Thank God the kids had been too excited to unload the car before coming in to see their dad.

Outside, I opened the trunk and paused with my hand on the upraised lid. Glancing back at the house, I exhaled hard, as if I could finally breathe now that there was a little distance between me and the Russells.

From the moment Tiffany had told me Holden was coming to town, I'd braced myself for some weirdness. Maybe even some hostility.

Boss lady could've warned a boy that her ex was sexy as fuck, though.

His hair was dark and cut short—almost military short, but definitely longer on top. He was *just* starting to get the silver fox thing going at the edges of both his hair and his meticulously trimmed goatee. He had some lines at the corners of his blue-gray eyes, and everything about him was sharp and angular. Today he was in a pair of jeans and a snug Arizona Cardinals T-shirt, but Tiffany had mentioned that he traveled a lot for his job, and between that and the perma-seriousness of his expression, I decided that he must have had a job involving expensive suits. I didn't know why. He just didn't strike me as the khaki-pants-and-golf-shirt type, and I'd have bet my next paycheck he looked stunning in said suits.

And if I wanted to receive that paycheck at all, never mind bet it on my boss's ex-husband's wardrobe, I needed to do my job. Starting with bringing in the groceries I'd grabbed on the way home from picking up Chloe from her playdate and the boys from school. Good thing it was fall, so the air was crisp and cold enough to keep anything from melting during the two minutes I'd been inside ogling Holden.

"Be a nanny, they said," I muttered as I looped reusable shopping bag handles over my forearm. "It'll be an *easy* job, they said."

Okay, so it was easier by a mile than what I'd been doing before. Exhausting, yes, but I loved it, and the three Russell kids didn't run me through the wringer like riding in an ambulance had, so I couldn't complain about the job in that respect. I really couldn't complain at all. If the worst thing this gig had to offer was my boss's super hot ex-husband shooting daggers out his eyes at me, well, I could live with that. It was better than—

I shuddered before those thoughts could take over. I'd stepped off the ambulance for the last time ten months ago. All the mental aftershocks of that truncated career would wear off any time now.

Do your worst, Holden. I've been through hell—I can handle you.

I looped the handles of the last grocery bag onto my arm. Two trips? Pfft. I don't think so. With my elbow, I slammed the trunk, then headed inside with everything.

Tiffany was alone in her kitchen, sipping her coffee. When she saw me, she put the cup down. "Do you need help with any of that?"

"Nah, I got it." I shut the door with my heel and refused to let it show that I was gritting my teeth as I took off my shoes and went up the stairs. Not making two trips. No way in hell. When I reached the kitchen, I bit back a grunt of relief as I set the bags on the floor in front of the stove. I took out my wallet, slid the receipt free, and handed it to her. She tucked it away without looking at it, though she'd probably check it over later. Since I lived at the house, part of the deal was that my groceries were covered too, within reason. Any time I bought beer or something, I paid for that out of my own account. Otherwise, I used the debit card for the account she'd opened for kid and household expenses.

I picked up a bag and started pulling things out. "Is Holden with the kids?"

"Yeah. They're eagerly showing him their rooms." She smiled and picked up a bag as well. I didn't try to stop her—I could totally handle this, but she seemed nervous about her ex-husband being here, so I wasn't going to get in the way if she needed to keep herself busy.

While we put everything away, we caught up on things like we always did. How this afternoon's playdate had gone. If the boys' teachers had said anything she needed to know about (though they usually emailed both of us). Whether Ethan had taken his antibiotics for the ear infection he'd had last week. Any errands that needed to be run in the next few days, and whether she or I would handle them. It was almost enough to make me feel like things were normal.

Just business as usual while we divided and conquered to keep track of the kids.

As I was gathering up the shopping bags to take them back out to my car, Tiffany checked her phone and frowned. "Volleyball practice is over in twenty minutes. Do you mind running and picking up Ashley?"

"Not at all." I checked to make sure my wallet and keys were on me, then nodded toward the door. "I'll be back."

She smiled. "Thanks, hon."

I was admittedly relieved for yet another reason to escape the tension in the house, this time to go pick up Tiffany's oldest daughter.

The route from the house to her middle school was one I'd taken a million times, and I could easily drive it on autopilot. Which, of course, gave my mind plenty of opportunity to wander right back to the house, and to the unfairly hot man who had arrived today.

I was pretty confident Holden and I could eventually get past this awkwardness. It would be an adjustment, and he was probably as unsure about me as I was about him. The tricky part was going to be maneuvering through our interactions without openly drooling because, hello, what the fuck, Tiff? Couldn't have maybe shown me a picture of him or something? Let me prepare, for God's sake?

And Christ, did Tiffany *have* to let it slip a few weeks ago that Holden was bi? Did she just *have* to have a little too much wine with her sister so she could casually drop "Holden's ex-boyfriend" into the conversation while I was innocently trying to cook dinner ten feet away? I hadn't thought anything of it at the time because, I mean, what was I going to do? Start fantasizing about getting the guy into bed or something? Because that would be *absurd*.

Fast forward to today, and suddenly I'm blindsided by

the super hot, possibly-suit-wearing silver fox bisexual ex-husband, and just *what* in the holy hell was I supposed to do with that?

I groaned and thumped the wheel with my fist. I seriously needed to get a grip. It wasn't like I hadn't worked around hot guys before. My ambulance had been attached to a firehouse, so my world had basically consisted of EMTs and firefighters, not to mention cops and doctors, all the way through my twenties. This was nothing new. Even now, it wasn't all that unusual to encounter ridiculously hot dads at parks. In fact, I'd discreetly exchanged phone numbers with a few, and that jaw-droppingly sexy construction worker who sometimes brought his twins to the playground? Yeah. I fucked him. Don't judge me.

Hot men? Nothing new.

Holden Russell? Holy hell.

I shook myself and focused on the road. He was the last man in the world I had any business with, which was probably what made him so attractive. However, I really liked my job, and I especially liked that it came with groceries and a place to live, and if that wasn't motivation to keep my hands off my boss's ex-husband, I didn't know what was.

THE RIDE BACK FROM ASHLEY'S MIDDLE SCHOOL WAS mostly silent, as usual. She was fourteen, and really bristled at the idea of a nanny. It didn't matter that I was hired to take care of her younger half-siblings, and that sometimes it was just more efficient for me to pick her up. I was a *nanny*, and therefore it was *lethally* uncool for her to be seen with me unless the younger kids were there. Getting into my car in front of the school and her friends was *mortifying*.

So she sat in the backseat and played on her phone, and I drove us back while the radio played quietly in the background and her ex-stepfather wandered relentlessly through my mind.

It wasn't until I was pulling in the driveway that she spoke, startling me: "Oh, Holden's here?"

"Um." I cleared my throat as I parked beside the sleek blue Nissan. "Yeah. He showed up right before I came to get you."

"Oh." Of course her voice offered nothing to indicate how she felt about that.

I turned off the engine. "Do you get along with him?"

She shrugged as she unbuckled her seat belt. "He's okay. Isn't like I saw much of him, you know?"

"So I've heard."

We got out of the car and headed up the walk. "He's not a bad guy," she said. "He's just... I don't know. He wasn't around much." Ashley shrugged again. "I didn't even really notice when they split up."

"Wow." Yeah, wow. That was seriously sad. How absent did a father and husband have to be for one of the kids to barely feel the divorce?

After we'd taken off our shoes, we went upstairs. Ashley disappeared into the bedroom she shared with Chloe, and I hung up my keys beside the refrigerator. The house was quiet, but I could hear voices outside, so the kids must have dragged their father into the backyard.

I found Tiffany on the deck, which was attached to the second floor of the house and overlooked the fenced-in property. She had her arms folded on the railing as she watched Noah, Ethan, and Chloe dragging Holden all over the backyard.

She glanced at me as I stepped out to join her. "Was Ashley upset that you came instead of me?"

"She didn't say much." I picked my way across the deck so I didn't step on an errant pinecone with my bare feet. "But she had that 'oh my God, please let lightning hit me' look on her face while she was heading for the car."

Tiffany laughed. "Poor kid. She wasn't rude, though?"

'No, no.' I shook my head. "She's fine."

"Okay. Good."

We were silent for a moment, gazing down at the kids as they demonstrated how they used their Tonka trucks to move piles of mud around beside the swing set. Chloe had somehow already managed to get dirt on her face and in her curly blond hair, and one of Ethan's sneakers was completely coated in mud now. Good thing I'd grabbed an extra container of stain remover while I was the store. Tiffany was pretty chill about the kids being dirty—she didn't obsessively disinfect everything they touched or expect them to keep their play clothes spotless—but I at least tried to stay on top of things.

Holden glanced up at us. He'd been laughing at something one of the kids had said or done, but the instant he saw me, the amusement dried up and he cut his eyes away.

I shifted my weight. "He doesn't like me, does he?"

Tiffany's sigh wasn't exactly a *no*. "I think he's just feeling…elbowed out of his own kids' lives."

"What do you mean?"

"I mean, he's trying to turn over a new leaf with them. Be the dad he's never been." She met my eyes. "And he feels like he's got some competition."

"Competition?"

Nodding, she watched her family down below. "He's

supposed to be the primary male figure in their lives. The father figure. He, um, wasn't expecting them to have you."

"Oh." I gnawed my lip and absently flicked a couple of pine needles off the railing. "So what... I mean, how is this going to work?"

"What do you mean?" She turned to me, and she must have read between the lines because she jumped and shook her head. "Nothing's changing here. I'm not firing you. Don't worry about that. The kids adore you, and you've been a godsend for me."

I was way more relieved than I probably should have been, but considering how bizarre this situation felt, I wasn't making any apologies for that. "Okay. Okay good. Because I suck at job hunting."

She laughed softly. "No, don't worry about that. To tell you the truth, with everything they've been through since I left Holden, the last thing they need is more change. Just having him come into their lives like this is going to be an adjustment." She looked at me, brow pinched. "If anything, I'm going to beg you *not* to go because you've been such a solid, consistent presence in their lives."

I laughed, probably sounding almost as relieved as I was. "I'm not going anywhere."

"Thank God."

You're telling me.

CHAPTER 3

HOLDEN

As if I needed another reminder of how absent I'd been in recent years, I barely recognized my stepdaughter—former stepdaughter—when I came back into the house. She'd grown at least an inch and a half since I'd seen her last, and the long blonde hair she'd inherited from her mom was now a dyed black bob. And when had she gotten all those extra piercings in her ears?

When she saw me, she offered up a tired smile. "Hey, Holden."

"Hey, kiddo. How's it going?"

"Eh." She shrugged, and that was the extent of our conversation before she headed down the hall to what I assumed was her room. I tried not to read too much into that. Apparently she'd only emerged to get a drink, and anyway, while Ashley and I had never disliked each other, we'd never been particularly close either, especially when things had started going south between me and her mom. I didn't expect a tackle hug from my ex-stepdaughter; I just hoped this was some teenage *meh, I'm too cool to care about anything* and not the cold shoulder I probably deserved.

I turned to Tiffany, who was watching me with an unreadable expression, and I cleared my throat. "So, uh, how is she adjusting? To living up here?"

Tiffany half-shrugged. "Social media's made it easier for her to stay in touch with her friends in Arizona, so there's that. But... it's been an adjustment, and it hasn't been easy." Her eyes added a silent *"...for any of us."*

I winced and dropped my gaze to the kitchen floor.

Chloe and the boys had already shown me the entire house and the yard, and they were now playing quietly in the living room while Tiffany put something together for dinner. Silence hung between us as she opened up a bag of frozen vegetables. She was just pouring them into a casserole dish when Porter appeared in the kitchen doorway. He glanced at me, but we only held each other's gazes for a split second before we both broke away.

"Do you need me for anything?" he asked Tiffany.

"Could you make sure everyone's ready for dinner?" She glanced at the timer on the stove. "Should be done in about fifteen minutes."

"On it."

I watched silently as Porter went into the living room and herded the boys and Chloe down the hall. He was patient, but firm—not barking orders, but definitely conveying that he wasn't kidding. Noah got up and headed toward the bathroom to wash his hands. Ethan was a little slower on the uptake, but when Porter crouched and gently reassured him he could continue playing with his action figures after dinner, he got up and followed his brother.

Chloe tugged at Porter's sleeve, and he crouched again, let her climb on his back, and made a silly horse noise as he followed my sons. Chloe's giggles faded down the hall. I wasn't quite sure how I felt about any of that.

"He's really good with them." Tiffany's voice startled me, and when I turned, I realized she'd been watching me watch Porter. With a soft smile, she added, "Give him a chance. They love him and I think you will too."

I bit back a response of *we'll see about that* because deep down, I had a feeling she was right. And I didn't *want* her to be right. I wanted this guy to be awful at his job. Not because I wanted him to be terrible with my kids, but because I wanted him gone. How the hell was I supposed to get back on my feet as their dad when they had him?

I tried to tell myself supply and demand didn't apply to kids and parenting, but it was hard not to feel like I was showing up to interview for a position that was already filled.

I shifted my weight. "So, um, can I help with anything?"

"I think we've got it all under control." She flashed me a quick smile. "Just relax. I'm sure you've had a busy few days."

"You could say that," I murmured, pretending it didn't sting to be a pair of hands no one needed right now. "Uh, how's your new job going?"

"It's good. Really good." She paused to put the dish of vegetables in the microwave and set the timer. "It's been an adjustment, being away from the kids forty hours a week, but I can work from home sometimes. Plus I like the people I work with, and the job itself isn't bad."

Not bad? From the way she was beaming just talking about it, that was an understatement if I'd ever heard one. God, I wasn't sure how much more of this my conscience could take tonight. Every time she revealed a facet of her new life, it just drove home how unhappy she must have been with me. How the life we'd had in Arizona had been draining the life out of her, and I hadn't noticed until it was too late to go back.

"That's, uh, good to hear." I forced a smile. "I'm glad you've landed on your feet."

Her smile was genuine, but a little sad. "What about you? You haven't started at the new job yet, have you?"

"Not yet. I start a week from Monday."

"But you think you'll like it?"

A shrug had never taken so much effort. "I guess we'll see. It's similar to the sales I was doing before, but a different type of product. The main thing is that it pays enough for me to live up here where I'm close to the kids, and it's only ten percent travel instead of eighty-plus, so..."

"That's definitely an improvement. I really hope it works for you." Gesturing in the direction Porter had taken the kids, she added, "I know they're excited to have you close by again."

Having their dad in the same state shouldn't be a novelty.

Before I could respond, thundering footsteps came down the hall, and the boys appeared in the kitchen.

"What's for dinner?" Ethan asked.

"Food," Tiffany said.

He huffed and rolled his eyes. "Mo-om..."

She laughed and tousled his hair. "I need you and Noah to set the table. Set it for..." Her eyes flicked to me, and I could see the *"Are you staying?"* in her expression.

I lifted my eyebrows, hoping it conveyed, *"You tell me."*

To Ethan, she said, "Set it for seven. I'll have Porter add the extra chair."

"I can do it." I pushed myself away from the counter I'd been leaning on. "In the dining room?"

"Yeah, it's up against the wall."

Noah and Ethan both grinned.

"You're having dinner with us?" Ethan asked.

"Of course." I smiled and gave his shoulder a squeeze.

"Awesome!"

"Noah, honey," Tiffany said. "Could you fill drinks for seven?"

The boys got started on their respective tasks. Tiffany had put plastic cups in one of the lower cabinets, so Noah could reach them without straining, and there was a small step for Ethan to stand on while he pulled silverware from the drawer. They both took out everything they needed, and while Noah stood at the sink and carefully filled each glass, Ethan took the silverware and napkins into the dining room.

That was oddly breathtaking. Last I remembered, Noah was just old enough to be tasked with putting napkins at every place setting. I had no doubt she'd added gradually to their workload over time, but I'd been out of the picture long enough that it seemed like the change had happened overnight. Sort of like how Noah didn't need the step to fill water cups anymore.

Good thing I'd gotten my head out of my ass when I did. As fast as they were growing up, if I'd been a bit slower on the uptake, I probably would have come back into the picture just in time to watch Porter take Chloe to get her driver's license.

It isn't too late, I told myself for the millionth time. *I can do this.*

AFTER DINNER, THE BOYS RETURNED TO PLAYING WITH their action figures in the living room, and Porter went with Ashley and Chloe to take a walk around the block. Ashley always liked walking after she'd eaten—said it made her feel less like a slug afterward—and Chloe loved tagging along. I had to admit, Porter going with them let me breathe a bit easier. The neighborhood seemed safe enough, and it looked well lit, but I wasn't comfortable with them going out after dark. Tiffany trusted Porter to stay with them and keep an eye on them, so I didn't say anything.

About the time Tiffany and I had finished washing dishes and cleaning up the kitchen, Porter and the girls returned. Ashley and Chloe went to their room, and Porter appeared in the kitchen doorway.

"Looks like I'm a little late to the party." He surveyed the kitchen, which was spotless. "But, uh, can I help with anything?"

"No, I think we're good." Tiffany dried her hands on a towel and hung it back on the oven handle. "Maybe the three of us could sit down and talk for a few minutes, though?"

Porter and I locked eyes, and I immediately saw my own apprehension staring back at me. I wanted to get defensive and ask what the hell *he* had to worry about, but I kept my mouth shut. I supposed if I were in his shoes, having the ex-husband show up might be a little unnerving. I'd been nervous as hell the first time I'd met Tiffany's first husband, and that was *before* I'd realized what a dick he was. Though to be fair, I'd been dating Tiffany, not working for her, so who knew if the situations compared? Either way, Porter and I regarded each other uncertainly before he said, "Yeah. Sure. We can do that."

Yeah. Sure. Why the hell not?

First things first, Tiffany and Porter took the boys downstairs to the rec room and set them up with a video game so they would be out of earshot. I didn't expect this discussion to get heated, but maybe it was just as well the boys were in another part of the house so they didn't have to listen to everything.

With the boys occupied, the three of us sat down at the table where we'd just had dinner with the kids. Tiffany took the head seat, and Porter and I sat across from each other. Thank God, she didn't let the uncomfortable silence linger.

"To cut right to the chase," she said to me, "I was thinking maybe you could spend some time with the kids while they're with Porter."

"Come again?"

"Well, you said you don't start at your new job for another week. And I know you still need to get settled into your apartment, but..." She wrung her hands in front of her and stared at the table instead of looking at me or him. "I just think it would be, you know, a way for you to get reacquainted with them, and see what they're like these days." She glanced at Porter. Then me. "You know, their routines. That kind of thing."

"You think I need to shadow the nanny so I can get to know my own kids?" I exhaled hard. "It's not like I'm new to parenting."

Across from me, Porter shifted, his discomfort palpable.

Tiffany huffed and turned an impatient glare on me. "No, you're not new to parenting, but you're new to them." She must have seen that I was about to argue because she put up a hand. "Holden, for God's sake. I know you know how to parent, and I know you love these kids more than life itself, but face it—you've barely been present in their lives since they were little. Especially Ethan and Chloe."

I winced.

Her tone softened. "I'm not trying to punish you or condescend to you or act like you're not a good dad. You *are* a good dad. Which is why I think you should be able to see what I'm getting at here." She pushed her shoulders back. "They've been through a lot the last two years. Chloe doesn't even *remember* life before us separating. I'm just trying to make this transition go smoothly for them and for you." She gestured at the nanny. "The fact is, Porter's with them more of the time than even I am. I'm not suggesting you let him tell you how to raise your kids. I'm suggesting that you just tag along with them a few times and watch how he's been doing things, so it'll be easier for you and them when they go home with you."

I met Porter's gaze across the table. His expression was neutral, though he was obviously no more comfortable with this than I was. I really, really wanted to be defensive. I bristled hard at the idea of a nanny—one who'd only been in the picture for a few months—guiding me back into my own children's lives.

But...Tiffany had a point. I'd been gone so much the last few years, I didn't even know what their routines were. When I thought about all the things I'd known about my oldest son at this age—that he'd scream if his sandwiches were cut diagonally, that he *thought* he liked scary movies but would actually have nightmares for days, that he preferred it if I read to him slowly so he could follow along while he was learning to read—I drew a blank with my younger kids.

I released a long breath and leaned back in my chair. "Okay. Okay, fine. If it'll make the transition easier, then..." Porter and I looked at each other. Then didn't. Then did again. Was this as awkward for him as it was for me? Because it was awkward as fuck for me. I fought the urge to drum my fingers. "So, what do you and the kids usually do? I mean, what's a day of Porter and the kids like?"

"Um." He apparently couldn't fight the same urge, and his long fingers tapped rapidly on the table. "Kind of depends on the day. Chloe has preschool three days a week at ten, and the boys have to be at school at nine. She's, um, not exactly a morning child, though." He laughed nervously, meeting my gaze again for a second before dropping his. "If she's got preschool, she sits down with the boys and has breakfast. If not, then she and I will eat after we come back from putting the boys on the bus."

I blinked. It was strange how little of that was familiar, considering we were discussing my own child. If not for the part about her hating mornings—like father, like daughter—I would have been sure we were talking about someone else entirely. "What about days when they don't have school? Weekends and holidays?"

"That depends on..." He gestured at Tiffany. "We kind of play that by ear."

"Okay, but if you have them for an entire day..." I inclined my head.

Porter swallowed. "There are some parks they like to go to. Depends on the weather of course, but I'll take them and let them burn off some energy. If someone has a playdate, I'll drop them off there and take the other two to the playground or something." He glanced at Tiffany. "Sometimes we hit up the zoo or aquarium. The Science Center. Just... you know. Weather. Time. Traffic. Money."

I nodded slowly as he spoke. God, it was like he was living my dream with my own kids—taking them to everything I'd imagined myself taking them to before work had monopolized my life. And he didn't get yanked away for his job because doing all those things with them literally *was* his job.

It was weird to imagine that if I asked him their favorite

parts of the zoo, the aquarium, or the Science Center, he could probably answer without needing to give it much thought. If someone put a gun to my head and asked me the same questions...

Footsteps came up the stairs, and all three of us turned as Noah came across the kitchen toward us. He pointed sharply behind him. "Ethan won't let me take a turn."

I opened my mouth to respond, but Porter caught on to something before I did—Noah was talking to him, not me or Tiffany.

"Did you ask him nicely for a turn once he's done with his game?" Porter asked.

Noah nodded, lower lip jutting out.

"How many games has he played?"

"He's still playing the first. But he's taking a long time and won't let me take a turn!"

Porter smiled, and he came across as gentle, not at all patronizing. "Let him finish his game and give him a chance to give you the controller. You don't like cutting your games short, do you?"

Noah sighed. "No."

"Okay, well, neither does Ethan." He nodded toward the hallway. "Be patient and wait your turn."

Noah huffed, but then he shuffled back down the stairs in that *fine, but you didn't say what I wanted you to say* manner that kids did oh so well.

Porter kept smiling as he watched him go, and once Noah was out of earshot, he chuckled softly. He took a breath like he was about to make a comment but met my gaze and halted. Then he cleared his throat, eyes flicking back and forth between me and Tiffany. "Oh. Shit. I... probably should have let one of you take that, shouldn't I?'

I wanted to be irritated. I really did. Sighing, I shook my head and tapped my fingers nervously. "He came to you."

"Yeah, but still. He's..." Porter shifted uncomfortably.

"It's all right." Tiffany folded her hands on the table and looked at each of us in turn. "So, are we all in agreement about Holden coming along with Porter and the kids?"

Porter and I both nodded, not quite holding each other's gazes.

"Yeah," I said. "We can, uh, coordinate details, but, yeah. Okay."

"Sounds good," Porter said. "Maybe I should...go make sure..." He gestured over his shoulder. "Check on them and their game."

She nodded, and he wisely grabbed the dismissal and ran with it. My ex-wife and I sat in silence until Porter's footsteps had disappeared downstairs. Then I released a breath and raked my fingers through my hair.

She put a hand on my arm. "I promise—this will be good for everyone in the long run."

"Yeah. I know."

But I wouldn't lie—I was reeling. Both from the idea of needing to shadow someone else with my own children, and from that brief interaction between Porter and Noah. It had been one thing to realize that Porter knew the kids and their routines better than I did. That moment with Noah... That took this to a level that was hard to stomach.

Great. My ex-wife had hired a male nanny so my kids could have a male role model. So they'd have the father figure I'd failed to be.

Obviously, he'd done exactly what she paid him to do. He'd filled the shoes I'd left empty. He gave Tiffany a break so she could balance work and life, and he gave my kids the consistent discipline, love, support, and *presence* they needed. I couldn't resent her or be angry at him. He'd only stepped up because I'd left her no other choice but to need him.

But my mind kept circling back to the question that had been battering the inside of my skull since the moment I'd learned about Porter:

Where did *I* fit into this picture?

THE APARTMENT WAS ALMOST UNRECOGNIZABLE FROM earlier today. The empty living room was crammed full of a sectional couch that was probably too big, along with a coffee table and one end table. The rest of the space was stacked high with boxes labeled in black marker—*framed photos, books, misc kitchen crap*. It would probably be months before we were finally free of boxes, packing material, and the just-moved-in ambiance. Still, it was a damn sight better than it had been when I'd left earlier.

Zach was in the kitchen, carefully unwrapping plates and stuffing the bubble wrap into an empty box. "Hey. How did it go?"

"It was, uh, interesting." I pressed my shoulder against the doorway and folded my arms. "Did you know the nanny she hired is a guy?"

"Yeah." He glanced at me before lifting a stack of plates into the open cabinet. "Dude used to be a paramedic or something."

I blinked. "Wait, you knew?"

"Yeah. Didn't you?"

"I..." I sighed, scrubbing a hand over my face. "I guess I missed it."

"Guess so. What's he like?" He reached into a box and

pulled out another stack of bubble-wrapped plates. "How do Chloe and the boys like him?"

"Oh, they love him," I said dryly. I pushed myself off the door frame, picked up a box cutter, and started on the tape of a box marked *glasses*. "The guy definitely earns his keep, that's for sure."

Zach watched me for a moment, an odd expression on his face. "You don't like him, do you?"

"He seems like a nice enough guy." I pulled a glass from the box and cut the tape on the bubble wrap with my thumbnail. "I'm just not thrilled that he's there, if that makes sense."

"He's helping Tiffany out a lot, though."

"I know. But that should…" I pressed my lips together and stared down at the glass I'd forgotten how to unwrap. *Everything he's doing is shit their father and her husband should be doing. He's a full-time reminder of everything I failed to do and everything I failed to be.* I swallowed, then started peeling the bubble wrap off the glass again. "I guess it's just a weird thing to get my head around."

Zach gave a quiet grunt of acknowledgment but let the subject go, and we continued unpacking the kitchen. He'd handled the topic of the divorce with kid gloves ever since the day he'd found out Tiffany was kicking me out. I wasn't sure if it was just too difficult to talk about—he loved his stepmom, and he'd always hated upheaval—or if he was simply giving me a wide berth because it was obviously difficult for me. Either way, I felt both relieved and guilty about it. The divorce and all its resulting upheaval had been my fault, and even at nineteen, it had been tough for Zach, especially since moving to Washington had been on the table. He hadn't wanted to leave Arizona, but he wasn't on his feet financially, and staying with his mother hadn't been an option. He'd really had no choice but to come with me, first to my apartment in Phoenix, and now to Everett.

I set the unwrapped glass on the counter and stole a glance at my oldest son. I owed him bigtime for everything I'd put him through. Hell, was there going to be anything left of my conscience after all this was over? At least I had a solid relationship with Zach. Even if he wasn't thrilled about the move, we were close, we knew we could live together without issue, and I was confident we could weather this.

Because we'd been close since he was little.

Because when he was Chloe's age, Ethan's age, Noah's age—I'd been there. At work during the day, but only a phone call away if he wasn't feeling well, and home at night and on the weekends. At every soccer game and birthday and holiday. By the time my job had started demanding more and more of me, sending me out on the road for weeks at a time with a handful of days in between, we'd had a solid foundation. My absence had caused some friction, but we'd weathered it.

His younger siblings, though...

Something Tiffany had snarled at me during a fight shortly before she'd left echoed in my head: *"At the rate you're going, those kids aren't going to know who you are, and you'll be too focused on your damn job to even notice."*

The words had pissed me off then, but they hit me someplace raw tonight.

Tiffany had seen the writing on the wall back then. And just like she'd predicted, I'd been too focused on my job to notice.

I hadn't noticed just how much the kids and I had become strangers.

I hadn't noticed all the signs that my wife was about to leave me.

And more recently, in all our conversations between her moving to Everett and me following suit, I hadn't paid enough attention to notice that a man named Porter had stepped into my empty shoes and picked up my slack.

Exhaling hard, I scrubbed a hand over my face. I really was starting over, wasn't I? New city. New job. New priorities.

And dear God, please, please *don t let it be too late to be my children's dad.*

CHAPTER 4

PORTER

If there was one area where Tiffany had seriously hit the jackpot, it was with three kids who liked sleeping in. My brother was forever complaining about his girls springing out of bed at five in the morning regardless of what day it was. He was convinced Daylight Savings would be the literal death of him.

Tiff's kids were still early risers—they were kids with way too much energy, after all—but at least they had mercy on us and didn't start bouncing off the walls at sunrise. The boys usually got up around seven, and they'd play quietly in their room until the rest of us started getting up.

Chloe... That child was going to be a night owl someday, I just knew it. She simply did not function early in the morning, and woe be unto anyone who tried to make her. That was why Ashley had ultimately caved and decided she was okay sharing a room with her little sister—they both liked their sleep. If Chloe had a rough night, Ashley would go sleep on the couch or Tiffany would take Chloe into her room. Or, as she'd done more recently, Chloe would crawl into Ashley's bed, and they'd both sleep peacefully until

Ashley's alarm went off. It didn't even surprise me anymore when I'd go in to gently rouse Chloe and find her sleeping in her big sister's bed long after Ashley had left for school.

On the weekends, Tiffany took over the morning routine so I could get some extra sleep. Today, like most Saturdays, I indulged in snoozing until the decadent hour of eight and lounging in bed to screw off on my phone until almost nine. Then I put on my glasses and got up to see if Tiffany needed help. The weekends were kind of negotiable —technically, I wasn't on the clock, but I'd feel like a total dick if I kicked back on the sofa with a bowl of cereal while Tiffany wrangled the kids. So we had this unspoken thing where, if I was home, I helped out. Tiffany reciprocated by never batting an eye if I wanted a day off or just needed some downtime. This was seriously the best job ever.

When I came strolling out this morning, the boys were still in their pajamas, mostly ignoring their breakfast as they tried to do the puzzles on the backs of the cereal boxes. Chloe was a bit more interested in her food than they were, but she had that *one eye kind of open, the other barely focused, zoned out* look I'd expect on a hungover frat boy. With her sleep-flattened blond curls and a smear of jam on her cheek, she was the very picture of *"Do not talk to me until I've had coffee, assholes."*

I fought back a laugh and stepped into the kitchen, where Tiffany was rinsing out some coffee cups. "Hey. You need help with anything?"

"Nope, I've got it for now." She flashed me a tired smile. "Are you still taking them out today?"

As I searched the fridge for something to eat, I said over my shoulder, "I was thinking about it, unless you had other plans."

"Not really, no. In fact..." My stomach somersaulted. I

knew where this was going even before she asked, "Do you mind if Holden comes along with you today?"

"Do I mind?" *Um, yeah, kinda, 'cause he basically intimidates the hell out of me and—* "They're his kids. Why would I mind?"

"I just, you know... Well, like we talked about with him last night, he's not really familiar with their routines now, and I... I feel weird asking either of you to do this, but..." She exhaled. "I'm not kidding—he barely knows them anymore, if he ever did. So it would be good for him to spend time with them and with you. And I think you two should get to know each other anyway, and..." She flailed a hand. "I just want to make sure it's clear between you and me that this is about him, not someone looking over *your* shoulder."

Oh, I was absolutely going to feel like he was looking over my shoulder, and he probably would be, but she didn't need to know how nervous I was about that. So, I just shrugged. "Nah, it's fine." And it really was, but at the same time, it totally wasn't. The dude obviously didn't like me, and he obviously didn't like me being the adult who spent the most time with his kids. Maybe he wouldn't be there for the express purpose of looking over my shoulder, but it would sure as fuck *feel* like he was. I mean, the guy already seemed prickly about the idea that I might be more familiar with his children than he was. So, what? Was he going to be scrutinizing every move I made? Looking for a reason to tell Tiffany, *"See? I told you he was an incompetent jackwagon!"* Ugh. God. He was going to try to get her to fire me, wasn't he? Just to soothe his own ego.

It wasn't like I'd pegged him for a jerk or anything, and Tiffany hadn't talked about him like a lot of people talked about their exes. She'd obviously been frustrated with him a few times, but for a freshly divorced single mom tearing her hair out over having her entire life turned on its head because she'd left him, she really didn't have anything negative to say about him. The man she'd described wasn't someone who'd do something like that.

But guys could be weird. Telling a man in not so many words that he was a bad father was right up there with telling him he had a tiny dick. That kind of thing went right to the tender core of the ego, and hitting that particular button of emasculation could instantly flip even a Super Nice Guy™ into a butthurt Mr. Hyde.

And nothing said *"I have faith in your parenting skills"* like visits supervised by the younger nanny. The younger *male* nanny.

Yeah. No. This wouldn't be stressful or awkward or uncomfortable at *all*. And it was starting today instead of... Well, whenever the hell I'd convinced myself it would start.

"Okay." Tiffany lowered her phone, and I realized that while I'd been paralyzed by my stupid thoughts, she'd been sending a text. Sending *him* a text. "He'll be over in about half an hour."

"Sure. Great." I swallowed. "I'll, um, get everyone ready."

"Perfect." Her smile revealed a hint of apprehension, and that didn't help my nerves in the least. "Just send me a text or something if you need anything. I'll be out shopping with Ashley, but I'll have my phone on."

That was probably supposed to make me feel better, but it didn't. Tiffany always had her phone on in case I needed to reach her about something. Was she expecting there to be a problem today? Was this going to be a disaster?

An all too familiar jittery sensation needled at me. I breathed slowly and willed my pulse to stay down; this was just some moderate uncertainty, not a catastrophic spike in stress, so there was no reason for me to start on a panic spiral. I wasn't going to lose my job. Tiffany wasn't going to send me packing the first time her ex gave me some stink eye.

I rolled my shoulders and pushed out a breath. I was fine. I needed to get a goddamned grip. And maybe, just maybe, take my mom up on that offer to introduce me to her therapist for some anti-anxiety meds. Seriously, I'd been off the ambulance long enough that I shouldn't still be getting those knee-jerk zero-to-sixty *the world is crashing down around me* near-freak-outs anymore, especially not over relatively minor shit like this. It was that inability to cope with heightened stress that had left me with PTSD and driven me out of working as a first responder, and any goddamn day now, I'd remember how normal people processed this kind of—

"Porter?"

I gasped and jumped before I could tell myself not to startle at Tiffany's voice, and I immediately felt like an idiot. Face burning, I laughed and shook my head. "Sorry. Sorry. I'm—"

"Honey, you're really stressing about having Holden along, aren't you?"

Was it the sweat that gave me away? Or the way my hands are shaking? When the fuck did my hands start shaking? Ugh, what is wrong *with me?*

"Um." I cleared my throat. "A bit, yeah."

She put a hand on my shoulder. "Relax. Honestly, if he gives you any issues—which I highly doubt he will—then I'll have him spend time with *me* and the kids. He's not there to evaluate you. He's just there to get back into sync with the kids."

I nodded, pretending my heart wasn't still pounding. "Is it weird that that still makes me nervous?"

"No, and nothing I say will stop you from getting nervous. I just want you to know where I stand."

"Thanks." And I did feel better. A little. But I was still going to be uneasy today, so I might as well make peace with it.

She gestured at the boys. "Shall we get them put together and get them moving so they're ready when he gets here?"

I smiled despite my nerves. "Let's do this."

By the time Holden arrived at the house, Tiff and I had all three kids ready to roll. I'd poured some coffee down my throat and put in my contacts, and I thought I appeared to be a confident adult who totally had this and wasn't a train wreck. As long as I looked the part, I'd be okay. Right?

Holden looked about as uncomfortable as I felt. We exchanged one of those stiff handshakes that screamed uneasiness, but hopefully it convinced his ex and my boss that we could play nice. I knew I'd play nice. The wild card was my ride-along partner. I was kind of surprised he hadn't brought along a clipboard or something, just to make sure I had a heart attack before the end of the day. Yeah, this was gonna be *fun*.

Tiffany was right that nothing she could say would stop me from being nervous about this. We hadn't even left the house yet, he hadn't said a single word or done anything, and it already felt like he was looking for a reason to tell Tiffany to cut me loose, and at every turn, I was sure he'd find something wrong with what I was doing. How much of that was in my head, and how much was in his taut expression and intense blue eyes, I couldn't say. And since I'd been chewed out and lectured more than once over stupid shit by other parents at parks and playgrounds—yeah, nervous.

But Tiffany had promised I wasn't going anywhere, so I clung to that as I led Chloe and the boys out to my car.

At the rear passenger side door, I stopped and took out my phone. "All right. You all know the drill."

In turn, each of the kids stopped beside the car, let me take a picture, and then climbed inside to their respective seat. After everyone was properly strapped into their seats in the back, Holden got in on the passenger side and I slid in behind the wheel.

As he buckled his seat belt, he quietly asked, "Is there a reason you keep pictures of my kids on your phone?" He sounded puzzled, and I couldn't decide if there was a note of accusation, or if I was just that worried about him scrutinizing me. Because Jesus Christ, dude, we hadn't even left yet. Give me some *time* to fuck up.

As I backed out of the driveway, I said, "You know how when kids go missing, they always show a picture of them on the news?"

"Um. Yeah?"

I paused to shift into Drive and glanced at him before I pulled away from the house. "Okay, well, I used to be a first responder, and a lot of the cops we worked with were encouraging parents to take photos of their kids whenever they went out to an amusement park or someplace crowded. Then if something happens, they have a current picture that shows what the child was wearing when they disappeared. Because once people see a picture, they're going to be looking for exactly what they see. This way, the picture is close to what the child actually looks like today, from their clothes to the way their hair is cut." I tapped my nails on the wheel, focusing hard on the road as I drove us out of the neighborhood. "I personally know of at least two cases where that played a big role in the kids being found quickly and safely."

"Oh. That's...wow." If there was any accusation in his tone before, it was gone now. "I never thought of that."

"I didn't either, but in my old line of work..." I swallowed, not sure how far down *that* particular road I wanted to go. "You sort of learn to be vigilant to the point of paranoid."

"If it means keeping my kids safe, don't let me stop you."

Well, that was a relief. First *"What the fuck are you doing?"* of the day, and it ended in my favor. A few more of those—okay, a few dozen—and maybe I'd feel less like I was about to start hyperventilating.

About fifteen minutes down the freeway, as I took the off-ramp that would lead us to the kids' favorite playground, I glanced in the rearview. "Okay, we're going to the park with the green fences. It's wet today, so the metal toys are going to be too slippery. Do you want to play by the soccer fields or at the wooden toys?"

"Wood!" Noah said quickly.

"Ethan? Chloe?"

"Okay," they both said. Neither sounded resigned or unhappy about it, so wooden playground it was.

I parked in the south parking lot, which was the closest to the chosen playground. Holden unbuckled Chloe while the boys unbuckled themselves, and I pulled my backpack out of the trunk. Together, the five of us followed the damp concrete path to the cluster of playground equipment surrounded by sandboxes that were more like mud boxes because this was the Pacific Northwest.

I found an empty graffiti-covered bench near the toys they liked to play on and set the backpack down. Noah,

Chloe, and Ethan were all itching to bolt toward the toys, but they knew the rules, and they waited.

"Okay," I said. "Your dad and I will be over here. How far are you allowed to go?"

Noah pointed toward the row of alder trees a few feet beyond the playground. "As far as the skinny trees."

"Good. And if you find anything you're not supposed to play with?"

"Bring it to you," Ethan said in a *come on, we get it, let's go* tone.

"All right." I waved them away. "Have fun. Keep an eye on your sister."

Ethan took Chloe's hand, and the three trotted off toward a muddy sandbox currently occupied by two other kids around the boys' age. A little girl who looked slightly older than Chloe joined her, and they played with some trucks in the dirt while the boys acted out some characters from one video game or another.

As Holden and I sat and watched them, I struggled to sit still. I was scared shitless that he would find something wrong with what I was doing. I let them roam too far. I stayed over here instead of hovering over them like some of the parents did. I should have been even farther away.

Give me some goddamned feedback so I know what you think I'm doing wrong!

After a painfully long silence, he finally said, "So they like this park?"

"Oh yeah." I tried not to shift nervously and let on that I was still waiting for some biting criticism. "I'd say they like it better in the summer, but I think they really enjoy the mud."

Holden gave a quiet, reserved laugh, which made me

warm all over. "They lived in the desert up until now. Mud is probably still a novelty."

"I grew up here. I can't imagine mud being a novelty."

"Spend some time in the desert, and you'll get it. And hell, I'm just glad these three can finally play outside without someone breathing down their necks." Holden exhaled, absently running a finger along the edge of his goatee. "My older son almost got stung by a bark scorpion when he was a toddler—the bark scorpions are the really dangerous ones—and ever since, I couldn't let any of them outside without worrying myself sick."

"Oh, wow. Tiffany mentioned that, and I just... I can't imagine. I mean, I have some cousins in Eastern Washington, and we had to be careful of rattlesnakes, but we literally *never* saw one. Garter snakes?" I shrugged. "They're harmless."

"That's good."

I nodded toward Chloe and the boys. "Yeah, especially since they were fascinated when we found that snake in the yard a while ago."

"Oh yeah, they told me about that. None of them were afraid of it?"

"Nah. I mean, I held it behind its head and told them not to go near its mouth, and I explained that even though it wasn't poisonous, it could bite and it would hurt. And, you know, told them to be as gentle with it as they are with any other animal." I smiled at the memory. "They were fascinated by it and really gentle. They're great with animals."

That brought a smile out of Holden. "Yeah, they are. If you ever take them to a petting zoo, good luck getting them out."

"Oh, I know." I paused, watching the kids playing happily

in the mud. "You know, maybe next summer, when one of the big fairs comes to town, they might like to go. I could always spend hours wandering through the barns when I was a kid, and they sometimes have baby goats and bunnies and stuff."

"You know we will literally never get them out of there, right?"

"But...then we'd be stuck in a barn with baby goats and bunnies and stuff." I glanced at him. "I'm not really seeing the downside here."

He actually laughed for real, and I almost *died*. I'd been so wound up that it felt amazing to break that tension, but mostly, when he wasn't so fucking serious... Holden was *gorgeous*. He was attractive anyway, but once he let a genuine smile break through? One that crinkled the corners of his eyes and lit up the whole park? Be still, my beating heart.

Across the grass where the kids were playing, Chloe touched something I couldn't see, then jerked her hand back. I straightened, and so did Holden.

A second later, she got up and trotted over to us. She shoved her index finger in my face, revealing a tiny sliver. She wasn't crying—if anything, she was downright indignant at the inconvenience. Her expression was actually really funny, but I forced myself to keep a straight face.

"Uh oh," I said. "Got a sliver, kiddo?"

Her scowl deepened, and she nodded.

"You want me to take it out?"

She nodded, still looking hilariously pissed off at the audacity of that sliver for interrupting her playtime.

"Okay. Hold on." I took out my wallet, and from one of the credit card pockets, a thin plastic pouch containing some tiny stainless tools. I freed one, and Chloe's expression shifted to one of concern, her lower lip trembling like this might make her cry. I showed her the small set of tweezers. "It's okay, kiddo. No needles."

She inspected its ends. Then, evidently convinced I wasn't going to jab her with something sharp, she thrust her hand closer to me. I gently steadied it, holding her tiny finger between my thumb and index finger, and guided the tweezers to the sliver. Fortunately, it wasn't deeply embedded—the end was too small for me to get a grip on with my fingers, but there was just enough for the tweezers to grab.

I paused to glance at the boys—they were still playing with the other kids—and then looked at Chloe. "Hold real still, okay?"

She nodded.

I pinched the end of the sliver, taking extra care so I didn't get any skin with it, and once I had a hold on it, slowly drew it free. I hated doing it slow because it probably stung the poor kid, but this way I could be sure the whole thing came out. If it broke off under her skin, well, that would put a damper on everyone's day.

The sliver came free, and I held it up. "There. All good."

She broke into a big smile. I hadn't noticed it before—probably because I hadn't seen Holden really smile until today—but she definitely looked like her dad right then.

I shook myself. "All right, kiddo. Let me stick a Band-Aid on that, and you're good to go." I leaned down and unzipped the backpack at my feet. "Dinosaurs or kitties?"

"Dinosaurs!" She practically squealed it.

I chuckled, pulled a dinosaur Band-Aid out of the backpack, and put it on her finger. It was probably overkill—the sliver hadn't gone deep enough to draw blood—but if she was going to be playing in the dirt, then I'd rather err on the side of caution and keep it clean. "Okay." I smiled. "Go play."

"Thank you!" She smiled up at me, then turned a somewhat shyer one on her dad, looking like she still wasn't *quite* sure what to make of him. He smiled back and gave her a little wave, and she brightened. She returned his wave, then trotted back to where the other little girl was waiting with the mud and toy trucks.

Holden's face fell a bit, and God knew what was going through his mind after his daughter had looked at him like an almost-stranger. After a moment, though, he shook himself and cleared his throat. "Barely fazes her, does it? Splinters and things like that?"

"Right? I swear, of the three of them? She's gonna be the daredevil."

Holden glanced at me. "How do you figure?"

"Because she has no fear, and she's got a hell of a pain tolerance."

He chuckled. "That's my girl."

"Oh yeah?"

Nodding, he laughed quietly. "I was the same way as a kid. Used to come home from bike rides with blood all over my knees and elbows." He sighed, though he was still smiling. "Guess she's going to be my karma for turning my mom's hair gray before she was fifty."

Oh, so you might get grayer? Because that would be—
Porter. Dude.

I tore my gaze away from him and watched the kids instead. Obviously it was just nerves. Being attracted to someone was a fun kind of nervous, so if I just focused on that—because let's face it, he was hot—then I might forget about the real reasons he had me sweating bullets.

"Por-ter!" Ethan's voice carried over the noise of the

park, snapping me out of my ridiculous thoughts, and Holden and I both straightened. "Noah won't share!"

I started to get up, but Holden's hand on my shoulder stopped me short. "Let me."

I nodded and didn't try to argue. The guy was trying to be a dad to his kids for a change; I was hardly going to stand in his way. So I sat back against the bench and watched him cross the stretch of grass between us and the kids. I held my breath because I had no idea what to expect. Holden barely knew them. They barely knew him. How would this go down?

When he reached the boys, he crouched in front of Ethan, and he nodded along as Ethan spoke. Then he turned to Noah, and he was speaking and gesturing as if he were reasoning with them, rather than chewing them out or berating them.

I released my breath. I supposed it wasn't a surprise. The man had an adult son, for God's sake, and it wasn't like he'd *never* been around his young children. But some part of me had expected him to swoop in, put on the impatient businessman persona, and try to play the authoritarian. Or just that he might be one of those dads who thought he should put the fear of God into his kids. I'd never found the whole authoritarian thing to be effective anyway, and it would probably be a disaster and a half for someone who hadn't been around enough for his kids to even see him as an authority figure.

He didn't do that, though. From where I sat, I couldn't hear what he and his boys were saying, but I could tell from his body language that he was being calm and reasonable. The boys had both lost some steam, and if anything, looked a little disappointed, which meant Dad was going for a compromise. I remembered being a kid—there was something satisfying about smugly watching your sibling take the heat for something, and compromise meant everyone gave and got a little. *So* disappointing when what you wanted was a decisive victory.

I chuckled to myself.

"Oh, hey you." A voice turned my head, and I looked up to see Andre, that super hot construction worker who brought his twins here all the time. He was broad all over, tanned from working out in the sun, and had a grin that never failed to make me shiver. Especially after that night we'd hooked up a few weeks ago.

I rose. "Oh, hey. Long time, no see."

"Yeah, too long." He glanced past me, probably checking on his daughters, who were no doubt playing nearby. Evidently satisfied they were all right, he met my gaze again. "I keep meaning to text you. We *really* need to grab a drink or something one of these days."

Or something. Uh-huh. I knew what that meant.

I grinned. "We do. You still have my number, right?"

"Of course. I made sure I saved it after last time. I'll—"

Holden appeared beside us, and Andre stiffened. Once I saw the hard look on Holden's face, I did too.

"Um." I cleared my throat. "Andre, this is Holden. He's their dad." I nodded toward Chloe and the boys. "Holden, this is Andre. He, uh, brings his daughters here."

They eyed each other as they shook hands, and the gesture was anything but friendly. The air between all three of us was suddenly taut and uncomfortable.

"Well. Um." Andre gestured past me. "I'd better go keep an eye on my girls."

"Okay." I smiled despite my sudden frustration. "Text me?"

Thank God, he grinned. "Will do."

And then he was gone.

Holden eyed me. Glanced at Andre's back. Eyed me again. "Just someone you chat with at the park, huh?"

My face was on fire, so there was really no point in denying anything. "Okay, when I'm at the park with the kids, yes. I just chat with him. When I'm off work and on my own time?" I shrugged as flippantly as I could. "Well, I'm off work and on my own time."

Holden's puzzled look turned to a glare. "So you're out with my kids, and you're picking up—"

"Excuse me?" I snapped. "I don't do anything different than anyone else here." I gestured sharply at all the other parents who were standing around and socializing while they kept an eye on their kids. I glanced at Holden's kids—still playing happily—and turned to him again. "People talk while their kids are playing. *We've* been standing here talking. The fact that he and I talked, took a second to exchange numbers, and then met up later without the kids around, doesn't make me or him negligent, all right?"

He blinked, and I cringed inwardly. Oh, yeah. That would help me stay in Tiffany's good graces—bite her ex's head off when he questions whether I'm taking care of his kids per my contract or adding to my list of booty calls. Especially after I'd all but said out loud, *"You see that guy? I banged him six ways from Sunday, and I have every intention of doing it again."*

I took a deep breath and forced my voice to be calmer. Still pissed off, but a bit less hostile. "Look, I spend the vast majority of my time with your kids. They're my number one priority. Always. But that doesn't mean I don't check my phone now and then, or make conversation with adults standing next to me, or make plans to meet up with people later." I gestured at Chloe and the boys. "I've always got one eye on them. And even if I didn't just then? You were literally with them. Seemed like if there was ever a time I could safely look away, it was when *their own father* had things under control."

Holden stared at me, and then, to my surprise, he deflated. Gaze fixed on his kids, he sighed. "You're right. I'm sorry. I..." He put his hands up and shook his head. "You're right."

I blinked, but didn't let my guard down. "I am?"

"Yeah. Yeah." He lowered his hands. "Sorry. That was... out of line."

"Oh. Um. Okay. Don't worry about it." I had no idea what to say, so I checked my phone and cleared my throat. "It's 11:30. We should think about getting them some lunch." To the kids, I called out, "Hey, Russell kids?"

"Yeah?" they replied without looking up.

"Five minutes, and then we're going."

"Okay." They sounded a little disappointed, but they rarely put up a fuss when it was actually time to go.

Please, please don't make an exception in front of your dad.

"Do you, um..." Holden slid his hands into his pockets. "Should we take them out somewhere? Or home?"

I considered it for a moment. "Probably home. Tiffany said Chloe woke up a bunch of times last night, and the boys are both dragging a bit today, so I suspect they'll all crash after they eat."

Holden blinked. "Oh. They're dragging? What do you mean?"

"Pretty sure they both snuck out of bed to play, and they stayed up too late." I chuckled rolling my eyes. "They do it sometimes. Drives Tiffany up a wall."

"So they're not sick or something. Good."

"What? Oh God no. I think they're just getting their first taste of what happens if they stay up too late and try to function the next day."

Holden actually laughed at that. "I could have sworn my older son just kept going no matter what."

"They will too." I nodded toward them. "To a point. Once they've eaten? Eh, we'll see, but I'd rather be home where they can sleep if they want to than out and about. No point in setting them up to be tired and miserable." I checked my phone again. "Russell kids—three minutes."

"Okay."

And I prayed like hell that this wouldn't be one of those rare days when even my five-, three-, and one-minute warnings weren't enough to stave off a triple meltdown.

I need to look good for your dad. Please, please *do me a solid, kids.*

CHAPTER 5

HOLDEN

I had to give Porter credit—he knew my kids.

At the playground, they still seemed to have plenty of energy, but he didn't change his tune about them running out of steam and they didn't object when he said it was time to go. His five-, three-, and one-minute warnings didn't result in any tears or protests. At the end of that last minute, they said goodbye to the other kids they'd been playing with, dusted off their clothes, and trooped back to the car with Porter and me. He had a towel and what looked like an old horse brush for knocking mud off shoes, and after a quick cleanup, everyone got into their seats without a fuss.

At home, I made sure they'd changed out of any overly dirty clothes and washed their hands, and by the time we came into the kitchen, they were practically bouncing with excitement over lunch. Not fussy or cranky with hunger, but definitely ready to eat.

It turned out that Porter even had lunch prep down to an art form. Ethan was tasked with getting napkins out of the pantry and putting them on the table. Noah filled water cups for everyone. That kept them busy while Porter made sandwiches—ham and cheese, no mustard on Ethan's, no mayo on Noah's. Ethan and Chloe had apple slices and peanut butter with theirs, and Noah had carrot sticks and hummus.

Not twenty minutes after we'd walked through the door, he had all three kids sitting at the table, happily eating their lunch.

And fifteen minutes after they'd eaten and taken their plates and cups back into the kitchen, they were all dead asleep on the couch.

"Wow." I watched them from the doorway between the dining room and living room. "You called that one."

Porter chuckled. "They're pretty predictable."

My heart sank a little. My oldest son had been predictable like that too. And I remembered figuring out the younger boys' patterns when they were infants. That is, once they'd had patterns besides *"wreak as much havoc as possible on Mom and Dad's sleep."* But as my job had picked up speed and I'd spent more and more time away from home... Well, it was hard to notice a pattern without being around enough to see it. As reassuring as it was to know they spent their days in the hands of someone who knew them that well, it was hard to swallow that *I* didn't know them that well.

"I figure we can give them half an hour or so," he said. "Any longer than that, no one will sleep tonight and their mom will have my head."

I laughed, but it took some work. "Sounds like at least two of them are turning into night owls."

"All three, I think." He gestured at Chloe. "Tiffany's caught Ashley reading to her at all hours of the night several times."

"Great. So they're *all* vampires. My oldest is the same way."

"Yeah?" He turned to me. "Like father, like kids?"

"Guilty. Their mom too."

"Awesome. So they were all doomed from the start."

"Don't tell me you're an early riser."

Porter wrinkled his nose. "Ugh. No. But I know how much it sucks to be an adult night owl in a world that expects everyone to function at nine in the morning."

"Oh, yeah. I hadn't thought of that." I watched my snoozing kids. "God help them the first time they experience jetlag."

"Ugh. No kidding. That feeling is the worst."

"Tell me about it. I lived with it pretty much constantly for the last few years."

"No, thank you. I'm a baby about adjusting my sleep by like an hour. Firehouse shifts almost killed me."

I laughed and turned to him, ready to make some comment about how if he thought jetlag was bad, he should try a newborn, but I just...sort of...forgot what I was going to say. Porter's gaze was fixed on Chloe and the boys, a faint little smile on his lips, and the expression was so sweet it reduced my vocabulary to nothing. Part of me wanted to be jealous of a man who thought it was his place to be looking at my kids like that, and part of me was grateful he was clearly as invested in taking care of them as someone in his position should be, but mostly, I was mesmerized.

He turned to me, and I jumped as I realized I'd been staring at him. Porter cocked his head. "What?"

"Nothing. Nothing. I... Nothing."

He eyed me, but thank God, he let it go. Then, he went back into the kitchen and gestured for me to follow him. I gave the kids one last glance, decided they weren't going anywhere any time soon, and went with him.

As I stepped into the kitchen, he leaned against the counter. "Listen, at the park?" He rubbed the back of his neck. "I shouldn't have gotten so defensive. I don't even know why I did."

I shook my head. "No, I get it. I was out of line. I really don't know why I thought someone being paid to watch kids should be glued to them without exception when I know damn well parents aren't."

"Still. I could have been a bit less of an asshole about it." Porter's shoulders sank. "I swear, I don't take my eyes off them as much as it might seem."

"No, I know. I know." I laughed a little. "Take it from someone who's already done one newborn-to-adult pass—if you focus a hundred percent on them a hundred percent of the time, you'll just drive yourself crazy. Everyone talks to other people, checks their phones…"

"Flirts with other parents," he said cautiously.

"Yeah. That too." I paused. "I can't really blame you. To be honest, I probably would have done the same with him."

Porter chuckled. He didn't seem surprised, so either he already knew I was bi, or it was just a non-issue. Either way, he knew now, which meant he wouldn't worry that my response at the park had been homophobic.

Still, the way I'd jumped on him earlier—that really wasn't like me. I was protective of my kids, of course, but I tried hard to be reasonable about it. There was no call for jumping down Porter's throat for talking to that guy or anyone else. He hadn't been ignoring Chloe and the boys. Hell, as he'd pointed out, I'd been focused on them right then, so if there'd been a moment when he'd been well within his rights to relax, that had been it.

I'd just seen Porter talking to that guy, *flirting* with that guy, and I'd—

Holy shit. Had I been jealous?

I replayed that moment when I'd seen him and the guy, and even now, my chest started to tighten and I couldn't help gritting my teeth.

Okay, this was stupid. It made sense to be jealous when my daughter came to him with the sliver in her finger. It was beyond ridiculous to get that way about Porter having a conversation with another man. Even if he was obviously into that man, and—I'd found out later—had hooked up with him.

It's probably a sign that I need to start downloading dating apps if I'm getting jealous of my kids' babysitter, for fuck's sake.

Around half an hour after they'd crashed on the couch, the kids started stirring. Porter had mentioned he wouldn't let them sleep for longer than that, since that would create a bedtime disaster, but they woke up on their own. According to him, they usually did.

Chloe was a little groggy at first, and Noah wanted a snack. Porter gave him some more carrot sticks and hummus, which the other two wanted as well. After they'd had a snack, they returned to the living room with some toys and happily entertained themselves. The boys were making up some elaborate story involving a dozen or so action figures, using the double decker coffee table as the villain's base that needed to be infiltrated. Chloe alternated between watching them and building—and knocking over—small towers with her wooden blocks.

While they played, Porter stayed close, sitting on the couch and reading something on his phone. If the boys started butting heads, he'd shift his attention to them, but they were mostly getting along, so he left them to it.

I took the recliner end of the couch and had my phone out too, but I was mostly watching the scene in front of me. Partly because it was a novelty just to be in the same room as my children again, and partly because I wasn't used to the slow, relaxing pace of a lazy Saturday afternoon. My constant traveling had often been over weekends, and whenever I was home, a day off meant catching up on everything I hadn't done while I'd been gone. Stuff around the house. Laundry. Running errands. There was never time for sitting down and catching my breath. That was what planes and airport lounges were for.

As I sat in Tiffany's living room and watched my kids playing and their nanny reading, renewed guilt swelled behind my ribs. During the last few years of my marriage, I had been home sometimes. Not as often as I would have liked, but there were stretches of a few days or even a couple of weeks sprinkled throughout the year where I'd been home with my family. How much of that time had I wasted getting ready for the next trip when it could have been spent just *being* with them? Had all those other things really been so important that I couldn't do this?

Good God. My entire life had been going on without me while I was flying all over the place to advance my career, and I hadn't even noticed. Sitting here and letting that bitter truth sink in, I was starting to think I should be thanking Tiffany for leaving me when she did. Of course it'd hurt like hell to let her go, but the wakeup call hadn't come a moment too soon.

It had taken her ending our marriage to save our family.

A COUPLE OF HOURS AFTER WE'D COME BACK FROM THE park, a car pulled up outside. A moment later, Ashley and Tiffany came in through the front door.

When she reached the top of the stairs, Tiffany surveyed the scene in the living room. Chloe was in my lap, and we were playing a game on Porter's iPad. The boys were making engine and explosion noises as they pushed cars around on the carpet. Porter was still on the sofa, one leg tucked up under him, his Kindle resting on his arm, and a cup of coffee on his knee.

"I don't see any casts or stitches," Tiffany mused. "So it looks like today went well?"

"Pretty quiet." Porter gestured at Chloe. "Should probably put some lotion on her tattoo before dinner though."

Tiffany clicked her tongue and rolled her eyes. "Don't even joke, you brat. I've already got one minor child who thinks she's getting a tattoo."

"I just need you to sign something when I'm sixteen," Ashley called from the kitchen.

"The day I sign that paper is the day a blizzard hits Phoenix, baby. Keep dreaming."

Ashley huffed with all the indignance a fourteen-year-old could muster, and Tiffany, Porter, and I laughed.

"What's a tattoo?" Chloe asked.

"It's a picture on a person's skin," I said. "A permanent one."

Her eyes lit up. "Can I get one?"

"When you're sixteen," Ashley helpfully supplied.

"*Eighteen*," I corrected.

Chloe just giggled.

"Hey, Chloe?" Porter said. "You know the picture of the mountain lion on my arm?" She nodded, and he tapped his upper right arm, which was covered by his sleeve. "That's a tattoo."

He has a tattoo? Oh dear God.

"And the unicorn on Mom's foot," I said.

Chloe's eyes got even bigger. "I want one!"

"Yeah, maybe someday." I tousled her blonde curls. "But not right now."

She pouted.

"Don't tattoos hurt?" Noah asked without looking up from the red sports car he was scooting along the carpet.

"Yeah, they do." Tiffany grimaced. "A lot."

"They use needles," Ashley said.

Chloe's teeth snapped shut.

"Still want one?" I asked.

She shook her head, curls bouncing with the motion.

"That's what I thought." I pulled her closer and gently kissed her forehead. "Leave the tattoos to crazy people like your mom and Porter."

"Hey!" they both said, but there wasn't any heat behind it.

Tiffany laughed. "Well, as much as I hate to disturb Chloe..." She nodded toward the deck. "Can I borrow you for a minute?"

"Sure. Yeah." I eased Chloe to her feet. She took the iPad across the living room and jumped onto the couch beside Porter. He must have anticipated that, because he'd carefully set his coffee on the end table before she joined him. He put his Kindle aside too, and they resumed the game she and I had been playing.

With my daughter situated and the boys occupied, I followed Tiffany outside. The deck was damp and cool under my bare feet, but the afternoon was comfortable, so I didn't complain.

She glanced back through the sliding glass door as she pulled it closed. Then she faced me, brow furrowed. "So, how did today go?" She sounded like she was expecting the worst.

"It went great. It was..." I glanced back at the house. "You were right—he's really good with the kids."

She didn't even try to hide the sigh of relief. "Oh thank God. I was worried you two wouldn't get along."

I considered mentioning there'd been some moderate head-butting but decided against it. After all, it hadn't been that serious, and I'd come out looking like the asshole, so I'd just keep that to myself. "We did all right. It went better than I thought it would."

"Good. Good. That's really good to hear. And the kids? They had a good time?"

"There was mud. Of course they did."

Tiffany laughed, which made my heart clench. I tried not to think about how long it had been since I'd heard her sound so relaxed and happy. She motioned toward the backyard. "I think that's their favorite part of living here. There's mud everywhere. Especially now that we're getting into the rainy season."

"It's Seattle. Isn't it always the rainy season?"

"You'd be surprised. This past summer had everyone begging for rain."

"Wow. That's, uh, not how I imagined this area."

"Just wait. But at least it doesn't get as hot as Phoenix."

"Ugh." I made a face. "That's one thing I'm not going to miss—Arizona summers."

She opened her mouth like she was about to say something, then hesitated. Our eyes locked. I couldn't read her mind, but I swore I could hear the words that hadn't come to life: *"When was the last time you spent a summer in Arizona?"*

We both looked away.

"Well. Anyway." She cleared her throat and shifted her weight. "I'm really glad things went well today. And that..." She hesitated. When I met her eyes again, she softly added, "I'm glad you're here, Holden."

"Yeah. Me too."

"So, um." Another quiet cough. "Same time tomorrow?" Her brow knitted, and her eyes were full of hope. As if she didn't want to ask out loud if today had been a fluke, or if Porter and I could get along two days in a row.

"I'll check with him. See what he says. But if he's on board, yeah. Definitely."

Tiffany flashed me one of those smiles that had made my heart melt every time over the last ten years. It was hard to swallow that she was only smiling at me like that now because I was getting my shit together and being a better ex-husband than I'd ever been a husband. She was out of my reach now. Our marriage was over. I definitely counted my blessings that she could still smile at me like that at all after everything we'd been through, but I wouldn't lie—it stung sometimes to realize just how much of us was, and always would be, in the past.

"Well. I should talk to him." I motioned toward the house. "Then I'll get out of your hair for the night."

Tiffany nodded. We went back inside, and while she started bustling around the kitchen to figure out dinner for everyone, I went into the living room to talk to Porter.

The boys had left, probably to wash up for dinner, and he was sitting on the couch, carefully reattaching a wheel that had broken off a toy car.

"Hey," I said.

He looked up from putting glue on the broken axle. "Hey." He glanced down and pressed the axle into place, then looked up at me again while he held it to let the adhesive set. "What's up?"

"I, uh..." I glanced over my shoulder. "So, you want to do this again tomorrow? Have me tag along with you and the kids?"

His expression was hard to read. He was obviously uneasy, but I wasn't sure what exactly was making him nervous. Talking to me? The prospect of another outing together? Some angle that hadn't even dawned on me?

God, please tell me this will get easier as we go.

"Um." He cleared his throat. "Do you want to?"

"Yeah. Yeah, I do." I slid my hands into the pockets of my jeans and fought the urge to rock on my feet just to expend some nervous energy. "Do you have any plans with them tomorrow?"

"Not yet, no." He swallowed. "Anything in particular you want to do?"

I shook my head. "You know the area better than I do. And, um, them." Because that didn't hurt to admit out loud. "I can follow your lead."

He nodded, gaze flicking toward the toy he'd been fixing. "Okay. Well. They'll probably be ready to roll by about ten tomorrow. I'll see how they're feeling, what the weather's like..." He trailed off, then cleared his throat and met my eyes, his expression as shy as his voice. "We'll figure it out from there?"

"Sure. Yeah. Sounds like a plan. I'll see you then."

"Great." He smiled, which somehow made him look even less comfortable than he'd been. "See you then."

"All right. Great." We locked eyes for a moment, as if we both expected the other to say something. When neither of us volunteered anything more, he put the repaired car down and mumbled something about needing to check in with the boys about their homework. I grabbed the opportunity and bowed out to head home. He didn't hide his relief at walking away from our conversation, and I supposed I didn't have to ask why he was nervous about me. Apologies or not, I had jumped on him for something stupid, and he'd already been wound tight. Wouldn't I feel the same if my boss's ex was shadowing me like that?

We were on weird ground, but it wasn't as bad as it could've been. Tomorrow was a new day, and we could do this. I could do this. Porter was doing a good job with the kids, and I'd damn sure hold my tongue instead of snapping at him for nothing.

Tonight, though, I'd leave him and Tiffany to their evening routine, and I'd head home to help Zach with our partially assembled apartment.

On the way down the road, though, I glanced in the rearview at my ex-wife's house. A whole lot of weird feelings I couldn't define banged around in my head, but they were mostly good this time. Less doom and gloom, and more like things were actually heading in the right direction.

Yeah. That was it. For the first time since Tiffany had dropped the hammer on our divorce, I was optimistic that things were moving in the direction they needed to be. That while the split had been hard, it was for the best, and its aftermath was better than I could have expected. My priorities had shifted. The kids were still young enough that I had a decent shot at getting back in the saddle before it was too late. And let's face it—Porter had been one of the best things to happen to these kids in a long time. To this family, if I was honest with myself.

Gaze fixed on the road ahead, I released a long breath.

Tomorrow, Porter and I would take the kids on another outing so I could get reacquainted with them.

And for reasons I wasn't quite ready to think too hard about, it wasn't just the kids I was looking forward to seeing again.

CHAPTER 6

PORTER

Over breakfast the next morning, I took a vote, and not surprisingly, the unanimous decision was to go back to the same park today. They knew a lot of the other kids there, especially those who came on the weekends. They'd all slept pretty well last night too, so I didn't see us needing to run back home to let everyone crash. I didn't say it out loud, but assuming all went well at the park, lunch at a fast food restaurant was a possibility. It was an infrequent indulgence, and I didn't dare mention it if there was any chance of revoking it, but I quietly tipped my hand to Tiffany so we could coordinate dinner to balance out whatever they had for lunch.

And at ten o'clock, right on time, that blue Nissan pulled into the driveway.

Nerves tried to get the best of me. I reminded myself we'd already made it through one day together without incident. Or, well, without much incident. An incident followed by repeated and sincere apologies.

However today went, it wouldn't be boring. That much I could probably count on.

We rounded up the kids and headed out to my car. Holden reached for the rear passenger side door, but hesitated. "You, um, want to get pictures of them first, right?"

I was relieved that he'd not only remembered but was cool with it. I wasn't sure why I'd expected him not to be after I'd explained things yesterday, but it was hard to be rational when it came to Holden.

We took quick snaps of the kids, loaded everyone into the car, and headed back to the park we'd visited yesterday. Since it was Sunday, the place was definitely packed. None of the benches were available, so Holden and I found a place on the concrete path where we could stand with a good view of all three kids.

Noah joined a small group who were around his age or slightly older and were playing four-square on the asphalt beside the play area. Ethan watched tentatively from the sidelines; he was kind of intimidated by the game, especially with older kids, but he'd probably join in before long. Chloe found the little girl she'd been playing with yesterday, along with several others, in the muddy sandbox with some toy trucks and dolls.

I scanned the other kids, looking for familiar faces.

"So, um." I leaned in close to Holden and made a subtle gesture to indicate a girl around Ethan's age jumping rope with some other kids. "I try to keep an eye on her. She likes to pick on Ethan if Noah's not around."

Holden bristled. "Seriously?"

"Yeah." I sighed. "And her mom is basically useless about it. So, I just keep an eye on her. As long as she keeps her distance, so do I."

He nodded.

"Ditto with that kid in the red shirt. On the slide." I

nodded in his general direction. "He's pushed Noah off the swings a few times."

"And their parents just let them?"

"Well, his mom is pretty on top of things, but I mean, there's only so much you can do from a distance."

Holden scowled. "Good to know. We actually had a similar problem with Zach when he was in kindergarten."

"Oh yeah?"

"Yeah. He was kind of small for his age, and he was also struggling hard with learning to read because—we found out later—he's dyslexic. So there were a couple of kids in his class who made it their life's mission to make him miserable."

"Ugh." I rolled my eyes. "Poor kid."

"No kidding. At least the parents did something about it after we had a sit-down with them and his teacher." He frowned hard. "Better than the assholes raising the girl who used to bully Ashley."

I blinked. "Oh. Really?"

"Yep. This kid just found every possible way to screw with Ashley. The teacher did what she could, but when we got the parents involved, they didn't give a shit." He huffed out an indignant breath and shook his head. "They honestly thought that instead of telling them how to raise their daughter, we should be teaching ours to stand up for herself."

"What?"

"Right? We finally had to pull her out of that class just to put some space between her and this kid. She couldn't get away from her completely—they saw each other in the halls and at recess—but at least she had some goddamned breathing room."

"Jesus."

Gaze still fixed on his kids as they played in the mud, he asked, "How is Ashley doing, by the way? With the move and a new school?"

"Oh. Um." I fidgeted. "It was a little rough at first. You know—an adjustment. But she's made some friends, and she's really enjoying being on the volleyball team." I smiled. "The coach is encouraging her to stick with it. Says she'll be a solid contender for varsity when she gets to high school."

Holden didn't just smile—he beamed with pride. "That's great. She always did love volleyball."

"Yeah, she does. And she's made friends with most of the team, so she's in heaven right now." I paused. "Some of them are playing basketball next semester. She hasn't decided for sure yet, but I think she wants to try out for the team."

"Basketball? Really?"

I nodded. "She's been playing pickup games with her friends, and since they're all going out for the team..."

"Good. Good for her." That smile—a mixture of pride and relief as he checked in on how his ex-stepdaughter was adjusting to her new life—gave me butterflies. What could I say? There was something endearing about him being that involved and invested in his stepdaughter's well-being. Maybe she wasn't his daughter by blood, but someone screwing with her brought out his protective dad side, and just talking about it now, years later, had his teeth grinding. And then hearing how well she was flourishing with her new friends and sports? He was full of pride I would have expected if we were talking about one of his biological kids. That he had room in his heart for the daughter of the woman he wasn't even married to anymore—that did funny things to my head.

For a while, we watched Chloe and the boys in silence.

Occasionally, I glanced around the park just to see what else was going on.

Nearby, some of the moms were standing around, coffee cups in hand as they chatted and watched their own kids. More than once, I caught them stealing appreciative glances at Holden, and man, I had to fight hard not to chuckle at them openly drooling over him.

I know the feeling, ladies.

As we stood, the shrill sound of a siren came to life in the distance, and my spine straightened.

"What?" Holden asked.

"Nothing." I shook my head and tried like hell to ignore the siren. "Just..." It was coming closer. There was a firehouse not far from here, and that was definitely an engine. One that passed by here frequently enough that I should've been used to it by now. At least I didn't jump out of my skin anymore. Not like I used to. Willing my heartbeat to come down as the siren came closer, I focused on the kids I was here to keep an eye on. In about forty-five seconds, the siren would be at its loudest as it passed the parking lot, and then it would fade into the distance, and I just had to keep my shit together for the next two minutes until I couldn't hear anything anymore.

"Hey." Holden touched my shoulder. "You sure you're okay?"

I exhaled and wiped a hand over my face. "Yeah. Yeah. I'm good. Just, um..." Oh hell. Why lie? Tiffany knew and hadn't fired me for it. I swallowed hard. "Sirens still make me jump. Just a, uh, leftover thing from being a first responder."

"Oh." That explanation must have been enough, because some of the tension in Holden's posture eased. He lifted his hand off my shoulder. "Pavlov's siren?"

I laughed, which didn't make me sound any closer to getting my shit together. "Something like that, yeah." I cleared my throat. "I'm good, though. Just makes me jump."

Holden nodded and didn't press. Thank God. My response went a little deeper than jumping when I heard a siren, but I was already way too wound up today to try explaining the ins and outs of my particular strain of PTSD.

I was just starting to catch my breath and convince my spine to stop tingling when a sharp cry turned every parent's head. Just my luck—Ethan.

He was holding his wrist and crying, glaring at one of the other kids who was making a placating gesture.

I started toward them, but Holden stopped me with a hand on my arm.

"I'll handle it." He smiled tentatively. "Just keep an eye on the other two."

It was weird, letting him step in and do my job, but he was their parent, so I nodded. "Sure. I'll be right here."

I watched him stride across the grass and asphalt to his unhappy son. It was a relief to see Ethan look at him and immediately start telling him what had happened, rather than searching for me. They were all quickly adjusting to the idea that Holden was a grownup they could rely on like their mom or me.

Amy, one of the moms who I saw here a lot, appeared beside me. "Hey, Porter."

I glanced at her and flashed a quick smile. "Hey. How are you?"

"Good." Something about the way she said it told me she hadn't just come over here to make small talk, and my guard immediately went up. Amy was usually pleasant, but she and some of other moms had made it abundantly clear when I'd first started coming to this park that they weren't sure about "a nanny like me." They'd gotten used to the idea after a few weeks, and were friendly to me for the most part, but her tight-lipped smile and uneasy tone reminded me a bit too much of those early days.

"So, what's up?" I asked flatly.

"Well, um." Her voice stayed light, but there was something in her tone that set my teeth on edge. "Do you really think it's appropriate, bringing him along?"

"Appropriate?" I blinked. "Come again?"

"Well. I mean." She folded her arms and shifted her weight, and as she watched Holden with Ethan, her nose wrinkled slightly. "We're all open-minded and all, but there are little children here. So it just seems inappropriate to show up with a boyfriend."

"A boy—' I sputtered. *What?*"

"Like I said, we're all open-minded." She gestured past me and I glanced over my shoulder to see her little clique of mommies, all of whom were watching me with earnest expressions on their faces. Amy touched my arm. "Just, you know, when you're here as a childcare provider, and you're bringing your boyfriend along—especially when everyone's already a little unsure about a man taking care of someone's kids, and we may not have explained, you know, homosexuality to our own kids yet? And then letting him step in and deal with them—it's—"

"What's going on?" Holden materialized beside us, and I'd never been this relieved to see him.

I gritted my teeth and gestured at her. "Amy was just letting me know how inappropriate it is for a male childcare provider to bring his boyfriend along and let him deal with the kids I'm responsible for. Especially since she might not have told *her* kids yet that queer people exist."

Holden's puzzled expression immediately darkened to

one of those looks he must have used on his teenager to indicate that now was a good time to cut the crap. He slid a narrow-eyed gaze toward Amy. "I beg your pardon?"

"Look, look." She put up a hand. "Like I told Porter, we're all open-minded and—"

"Where exactly did you get the idea that I'm his *boyfriend*?" Holden growled, disgust dripping off every word. Especially that last one.

My heart sank. Really? *That* was what was going to piss him off? That someone might have the audacity to accuse him of dating me?

Amy blinked. "Well... I mean, he's..."

Gaze fixed on her, he gritted out, "Porter, would you mind keeping an eye on the kids while I deal with this?"

"Already on it." I watched Chloe and the boys playing with their friends, but I was definitely still tuned into this conversation. And I did steal a glance at Amy to see how confused she was. Yep. Mind blown. Well done, Holden.

Apparently satisfied the kids were duly supervised, Holden went on. "First things first? I'm not his boyfriend." He pointed sharply in the direction of his children. "I'm *their* father."

I wasn't looking at Amy, but I *felt* her breath hitch.

"Oh. Well, I—"

"But even if I wasn't, how is it any of your business if Porter has someone else with him? Do you know the arrangement he has with my ex-wife? Do you know if they have discussed this or not? And for that matter, do you give these little public service announcements to all the straight people who bring partners along? Or do you just single out the gay men because you think it'll break your kids' brains to know that people like us exist?" He tapped his chest.

"Because I *am* queer, so if that's an issue, feel free to get the hell over it."

Amy was silent. Another glance revealed her mouth opening and closing like a fish's.

And Holden wasn't done. "For the record? If Porter *does* show up here with my kids and a boyfriend, then you better believe their mother and I already know about him, and have damn sure approved whether he can be around our kids. This man is *way* too responsible and on top of things to handle it *any* differently, or there's no way in hell their mom would have hired him. So how about you mind your own business, go keep an eye on your own kids, and keep your homophobia away from mine?"

I couldn't resist turning again to see the look on her face.

Her eyes were wide, her jaw slack, and she stared at him like she had no idea how to process everything he'd said. Then her lips came together and her wide-eyed stare turned to a steely glare. With a huff, she spun on her heel, and as she stalked off, muttered "Asshole" over her shoulder.

Holden grumbled something I didn't catch as he shifted his attention from Amy to his kids, who were still happily playing. He blew out a harsh breath and shook his head. "I can't believe she thought you'd be stupid enough to bring some random guy and let him take care of my kids. Idiot."

"Yeah. I... She kind of caught me off guard. I'm glad you showed up when you did." I cleared my throat. "Thanks for sticking up for me."

"Are you kidding?" He turned to me. "I mean, you looked like she'd just insulted your mother, so I figured something was wrong. But then after what you said, I..." He exhaled again, and motioned toward his kids. "If she was nosy enough to think we were dating, could she not have picked up on how much they look like me?" He tsked. "Boyfriend. Pfft."

I blinked. Oh. *Oh. That* was why he'd scoffed at the notion that he was my boyfriend.

He faced me again and cocked his head. "What?"

"Uh..." I broke eye contact and laughed uncomfortably. "Just... when she said she thought you were my boyfriend, you sounded disgusted by it. I thought that meant..." Heat rushed into my face, and I stared at the ground as I shook my head. "I don't know what I thought."

"You thought I was embarrassed that someone thought we were a couple?"

Feeling like an utter tool, I nodded.

"Nah. I just couldn't believe her power of observation stopped at two men talking to each other and not at family resemblance."

I chuckled. "Yeah, they do look like you."

"Poor kids."

We glanced at each other and both laughed, which killed the lingering tension from our encounter with Amy.

As my humor faded, I slid my hands into my pockets and focused on Holden's kids. "Anyway, thanks. For what you said to Amy. Not just telling her off, but..." I swallowed. "All of it. I appreciate it."

"Don't mention it. And I, um, I meant every word." He paused, gaze still fixed on Chloe and the boys. "I'm not going to lie and tell you I was on board with this whole nanny thing from the start. But all it's taken is two days to convince me otherwise. The fact is, you showed up when Tiffany and the kids needed something that I wasn't giving. I can hate myself all I want for not being there like I should've been." He looked right in my eyes. "But I can't hold it against you for picking up the slack."

"That's what I'm here for."

His smile was sad but sincere. "Well, I'm glad someone is."

I had *no* idea what to say to that.

ONCE WE'D FOUND OUR FOOTING, IT WASN'T SO BAD having Holden along on my days out with his kids. In fact—and I wouldn't have said this out loud under torture—I kind of liked having him there. As much as I adored Noah, Ethan, and Chloe, I had to admit that some grownup conversation was nice. The conversations stayed superficial. Who we thought was headed for the Super Bowl. Traffic. The weather. It wasn't anything profound, but it I still appreciated the switch.

Even after what he'd said about being grateful that I was here, it was obvious sometimes that he was struggling with the idea of me being in this role. There were moments when I could see him ready to say something like he had when I'd been chatting with Andre the first day. But then it was like I could watch him talk himself out of it. I couldn't read his mind, so I had no idea if he'd decided he was overreacting or if it just wasn't worth it, only that he'd quite clearly drop it.

God bless him, he was trying. To be their dad. To let me do what his ex-wife paid me to do. To find some balance between the two.

It really was endearing. Without knowing him, I'd wondered to myself if he'd moved to Washington as a power play. Either to win Tiffany back, or to have control that was harder to maintain from a thousand miles away. I'd known asshole parents who weren't above crap like that.

But every time I watched him fight back his own ego

and defer to me even when his pride *obviously* wanted him to take point? It was hard not to believe this was a man who genuinely wanted what was best for his family.

And what could I say? Though I'd never dated a dad before, apparently I was a sucker for a man who so obviously adored his children.

Like, the guy was hot to start with. Silver foxes had never really been my thing, but, apparently, I'd been looking at the wrong silver foxes, because *damn*. It wasn't fair how good-looking this man was.

Sexy or not, every time he interacted with one of his kids, my heart melted a little more. Maybe it was because I'd convinced myself he'd be a distant, domineering dad. I'd had that image in my mind, and suddenly there he was, smiling and laughing with Chloe while he fixed the Velcro on her shoe, or listening intently while Ethan explained at length the intricacies of a video game he and his brother had been playing.

And I was supposed to think and do my job and speak and be a mature, productive adult when I had this man obliviously charming me into a puddle of goo. Right. About that.

I kind of wished he would push back and be a dick. Then we could butt heads. When he'd been giving me shit about Andre, it had been a whole lot easier to dislike him than it was when he was asking about what kind of sandwiches they liked or if Ethan still had an aversion to certain textures of food, and actually making notes in his phone in case he forgot. A good dad gave me butterflies. A dad swallowing his pride and trying *this hard* to be a good dad after he'd made mistakes in the past? Be still, my heart.

I kept all those thoughts to myself, though. I did, after all, want to keep this job, and had a funny feeling Tiffany wouldn't appreciate me ogling her ex-husband while I was on the clock. So... game face on.

After we'd picked up the boys from school, and I was pulling out of the parking lot, I said, "It's Friday and everyone's been awesome this week, so you know what that means." I smiled. "Which do you guys want—ice cream or doughnuts?"

"Ice cream!" came the unanimous response from the backseat.

I laughed. "All right. We'll be there in about twenty minutes."

As the three excited backseat passengers talked about what flavors and toppings they were going to get, Holden faced me. "Friday? Ice cream? Doughnuts?"

I shrugged. "Tiffany and I started it a while back. Everyone was having a rough time adjusting after the move, and after I started, and..." I rolled my hand in the air. "Anyway, once everything started settling, they all had a really good week. No behavior issues. Everyone doing their chores. And Tiffany thought it would be nice to give them a little treat as a reward. So it became a weekly thing."

"And if it isn't a good week?"

"We find something about it that *was* good, and reward them for that." I glanced at him. "Neither of us wanted to get into the whole negative reinforcement thing. Like if two had a good week and one didn't, we're not going to deny them a treat or have them eat it in front of the other. So we always find something positive."

"Oh. And it works? Encouraging good behavior and not...?"

"Totally."

"Huh," he said quietly. "I guess I shouldn't be surprised. Tiffany said she always preferred positive reinforcement over punishment." He paused. "Watching them the last few days, I think she was on to something."

I wasn't sure how to respond. I totally agreed with him—I preferred keeping this positive too—but there was a strong note of guilt in his tone. Tiffany had told me that Holden had always gone for the more authoritarian approach, and that had been part of the reason she'd finally thrown in the towel. He was never abusive or mean, but he'd be gone for long periods, then come home and set back her disciplinary means by incorporating parenting techniques he'd used on his son. The lack of consistency had been frustrating for the kids, driven her up a wall, and ultimately made it impossible to co-parent with him.

So I wasn't sure what to say to him now, when he was seeing her methods in action and trying to get a feel for how his kids had been raised in his absence. He wasn't pushing back, though, so that had to be a good sign.

Since the playground was in Mukilteo, I took everyone to Mukilteo Beach for their treat. While Holden stayed with them at a picnic table outside, I went into a café to get everyone ice cream. A few minutes later, I returned and started handing out cones and bowls. "You're in luck, Noah. They had strawberry banana this time."

His eyes lit up as he took the cone from me. "Cool!"

"Well, yeah." I smirked. "That's the idea—it's ice cream."

Noah groaned.

Beside me, Holden snorted. "Was that... Did you just make a dad joke?"

It was my turn to groan. "Oh God. I did, didn't I?"

He laughed and clapped my shoulder. "Yep. You did."

"I think I just died a little inside."

Holden was vibrating with laughter now.

"What's a dad joke?" Noah asked.

I shot Holden a *"you tell them"* look.

He turned to Noah. "Remember when you'd say 'I'm hungry,' and I'd say, 'Hi hungry, I'm Dad'?"

Noah rolled his eyes. "Yes."

"That's a dad joke."

The kid wrinkled his nose. "Dad jokes are stupid."

"They're funny!" Chloe giggled.

"See?" Holden nudged her shoulder with his elbow. "She gets it."

"Ugh," Noah and I both said.

We continued eating, and as they often did at this place, a seagull landed on the edge of the table, prompting a squeal of delight from Chloe. Noah tossed it a piece of his cone before I could say anything, and I sighed as the big feathered rat with wings grabbed its treat.

"Great," I said. "Now he's going to tell his friends, and they'll all come and ask for pieces."

"They will not," Noah declared.

"Oh yeah?" I dug my spoon into my ice cream. "Give them a minute."

Ethan broke off a piece of his cone and tossed it. "C'mon, seagulls!"

Immediately, two more seagulls came down and started fighting over it. Holden almost choked, he was laughing so hard.

Fortunately, it only took a minute or so before the seagulls lost interest and went searching for something in the garbage cans.

Holden casually spooned some ice cream out of his bowl. "Hey, you guys know why seagulls stay near the sea, right?"

Ethan and Chloe shook their heads. Noah eyed his father suspiciously.

Deadpan as could be, Holden said, "Because if they went to a bay, they'd be bagels."

The two younger kids laughed. Noah buried his face in his hands and made an exasperated noise.

Holden turned a smug look on me. "The dad will always be the king of dad jokes."

I put up my hands in mock surrender. "You win. You win."

"Damn right."

I jabbed the spoon into my ice cream and muttered, "Bagels. Oh my God."

Holden just laughed. "I had to get the title back. Desperate times..."

That almost made me stumble. It was the first time either of us had said anything out loud about competing for the dad role, and it was a joke? A playful comment? Wow. *That* was unexpected.

Or maybe not? I could take some good-natured competition over who had the worst dad jokes if it meant we weren't genuinely clashing and vying for the same place in the kids' lives.

Maybe we really can make this work.

"Can we go play on the beach?" Ethan jostled me out of my thoughts. He pointed at the beach, which was one of their favorites because of all the rocks and shells.

I turned to Holden. He held my gaze and shrugged. *Your call.* I checked the time, and we had an hour or so before traffic would turn into a nightmare.

So, as I rose and started collecting napkins and spoons, I said, "All right. What are the rules?"

"Show you anything we pick up," Noah said.

"Stay out of the water," Ethan said.

"And...?"

Noah sighed. "And don't go too far ahead of you."

"All right. Everyone put your trash in the can, and let's go."

Down at the beach, while the kids picked their way along the rocky shore, Holden and I followed at a distance that meant we could catch up if they needed us, but we could also have some privacy to talk.

We were silent for a little while, though. I wondered if he just needed time to process things, or if his mind was someplace else entirely. I couldn't imagine it was easy for him, being out with me and basically getting a tutorial on his own kids.

I sympathized with him. I really did. It wasn't like he'd bailed on his family and was suddenly trying to come back into their lives after being a deadbeat. For better or worse, he'd been trying to provide for his family. Even Tiffany understood that. She'd just gotten tired of being alone. And after she'd left, he'd apparently figured out that he'd had his priorities out of order. Now he was trying to make up for lost time, and here I was. It was a lot to process.

After a while, he broke the silence.

"So, the way you and Tiffany have been doing things..." Holden kept his gaze fixed on the kids. "The positive reinforcement over punishments. How does... How does that work?"

I wasn't sure what to make of him asking me instead of their mother, but he genuinely sounded like he wanted to know. If I could help him understand, why not?

"Which parts?" I asked.

"Well..." He thought for a moment, watching the kids

following a tiny crab along the rocks. "Say one of them is misbehaving. How do you handle it?"

"Depends on the misbehavior and the kid."

He turned to me, brow furrowed.

"Chloe, for example. She's three, so she's not going to grasp things the same way Noah will. If she's... Okay, let's say she's trying to get into something she shouldn't. There's no point in punishing her or spelling out why she can't have it because that's just going to trigger defiant three-year-old mode, and then we have a battle on our hands that won't do anyone any good. So instead, I'll just redirect her. Get her attention with something else, and basically make her forget about whatever she was trying to get into. As she gets older, I'll explain things more, but for right now, redirection is usually the best approach."

Holden was nodding along but didn't say anything.

I felt weird explaining discipline and parenting to a parent. As if I were waiting for him to poke holes in my methods or something. But he'd asked, so I continued. "Ethan and Noah are both old enough to be reasoned with to an extent. If they're really determined to get to, for example, something fragile, then I'll tell them to let me show it to them. And while they're looking at it, I'll explain that it breaks easily, and that whoever it belongs to would be sad if it broke."

"That works?" He sounded skeptical but interested.

"Usually, yeah. Noah's *really* sensitive, so the idea of accidentally breaking something of someone else's resonates with him. Ethan is very tactile, so if I let him *carefully* touch something, that'll usually satisfy his curiosity. If it's something he really can't or shouldn't touch, then it's a bit more challenging. The part about accidentally breaking someone's things and how that makes people feel usually gets through."

I swore I could see the resistance on his face. It wasn't like I hadn't heard the objections before. My own parents hated the approach Tiffany and I used with her kids.

"You're the adult—you shouldn't have to explain yourself to kids."

"You're going to exhaust yourself."

"Having their hand slapped will keep them from touching things."

I focused on the kids and pushed my hands into my pockets. "They're kids, you know? They're not out to hurt anything. They just don't know all the rules yet."

"They do know how to push boundaries, though."

"Oh, yeah, they do."

"And when they do?"

I shrugged. "I push back."

"Do you?"

I moistened my lips, fighting the urge to shift nervously. "Well, yeah. I'm not a doormat. If they're being defiant or mouthing off, Tiffany and I both let them know in no uncertain terms that it's unacceptable. But most of the time, especially with these three"—I nodded toward them—"there's more to it than just being a pill."

"How so?"

I glanced at him. It felt like he was digging for something, but it didn't raise my hackles. Like he wasn't after some reason to turn around and say *"Ha! You don't know what you're doing!"* I was pretty sure we were past that point anyway, but there was some... I don't know. Some uncertainty? Maybe that was it. As if he wasn't just curious about my experiences with them, but like he really needed someone to fill in some of the gaps between the toddlers he remembered and the little people they were turning into now.

God, that must have been a heartbreaking thing, not knowing your own kids like that. And he must've had to seriously swallow his pride to ask.

He turned to me, chin inclined, and I realized I hadn't answered him yet.

Muffling a cough, I faced the kids again. "Okay. Well. With Ethan, if he doesn't like something, he just whines a little and then chills out. Like if we want to go to a restaurant that's not his first choice. He's pretty easygoing. But if he's hungry?" I whistled. "Nobody gets hangry like that kid."

Holden laughed dryly. "He is his mother's son."

"You said it, not me."

"And you're not going to repeat it, are you?"

The comment was made in good humor, so I cautiously said, "What's it worth to you?"

Holden looked at me again, an eyebrow arched. "You want me to tell Tiffany I got the bagel joke from you?"

I almost choked. "You wouldn't."

"Try me."

"Okay. Okay." I put up my hands. "I won't say a word."

"That's what I thought."

We both chuckled, which eased some of the subtle tension that had been thrumming between us. "Anyway." We continued along the rocky shore behind the kids, and I went on. "So. Ethan's chill unless he's hungry. Noah? He's really mellow and patient, so if he lashes out—like talks back or throws a fit—something's probably bothering him."

Holden stiffened. "Like what?"

"Well, once, the rabbit in his friend's classroom died,

and Noah was really upset about the rabbit being gone and because his friend cried."

"Oh. Really?"

"Yeah. Like I said, he's really sensitive. Stuff like that throws him off, and he gets moody as hell when it does."

"Wow," Holden said softly. "I always knew he was sensitive, but..."

"Yeah. Tiffany's working on getting him to talk about stuff, which helps. And his teacher knows to email us if anything happens that he might be upset about later."

Holden shifted. "I might have to ask Tiffany if she can have the teacher loop me in."

"Sure. Yeah. I... I mean, he's really good about letting us know. I'm sure he wouldn't have any problem adding you."

He nodded, but didn't speak. He watched the kids, who were now using sticks to try to pick up a huge mop of kelp. His lips were tight, brow knitted. What *was* it like to need someone else to fill you in on your own kids?

After a moment, he quietly asked, "What about Chloe?"

"She's as chill as her brothers unless she's tired." I blew out a breath. "God help me if she's tired *and* hungry."

"Oh yeah?"

"Ugh. Yeah. The poor kid had the most epic meltdown at Target a few weeks ago." I cringed. "That was my fault."

Holden eyed me again.

I took a breath. "She was wiped out after a rough night and her preschool class, and I stupidly thought I could squeeze in a few errands before I picked up the boys from school. What I really should have done was take her home, let her grab a nap, and then run the errands after I picked them up."

"So, what happened?"

"*Nuclear* toddler meltdown. Like, 'abandon the cart, go outside, and calm her down while everyone gives me dirty looks' nuclear."

He grimaced. "Her older brother was a champion of those."

"She doesn't have them often. And I mean, like I said, it was my fault. She's three." I shrugged. "She doesn't understand errands and schedules. She just knows when she's hungry, tired, or just plain had enough. I'm the adult—I should be planning better and not pushing her until she snaps. It isn't like she can just go get a coffee and push through until quitting time like we can, you know?"

From Holden's startled expression, he'd never thought of it that way.

"Don't get me wrong," I went on, "it's not like I let them make all the rules or that I don't put my foot down if they're being defiant. Because oh my God, these children can be defiant."

Holden actually laughed, and he nodded as he said, "You don't say."

"Right? They're pretty damn easy most of the time, but they *are* kids. And when things get really bad, I just remind myself over and over that at least I'm not getting puked on by a drunk who's also trying to stab me with a broken bottle."

Holden's breath hitched. "That's happened to you?"

"Happened to me? Pfft. That's a regular Saturday night shift on an ambulance."

"Really?"

I pulled my collar aside, revealing the skin just below my left clavicle. "Really."

His eyes went right to the deep scar I'd bared. "Holy shit. That looks like it hurt."

"Just a bit." I let my shirt go. "These kids can do their worst, and they're not shanking me with a Coors bottle. Perspective."

Holden laughed quietly. "That is definitely a perspective I never thought of before." His humor faded as he watched his kids. "I swear, you'd think I'd have all this down after already raising one kid to adulthood." His lips tightened. "Not that I was necessarily Father of the Year for Zach."

"I don't think there are any perfect parents out there. Or childcare providers. We're all just trying like hell with the knowledge we have."

"True." He took and released a deep breath. "Question is, how do you know when that's enough?"

I sighed. "I wish I knew."

And I wish I knew how to tell you how sweet it is to see you trying this hard.

CHAPTER 7

HOLDEN

I left Tiffany's house that evening while she and Porter were sitting everyone down for dinner. They'd asked me to stay, but I'd bowed out under the pretense of needing to get some unpacking done back at the apartment.

Oh, I had some unpacking to do tonight, but it didn't involve boxes or bubble wrap. I was numb as I left the house. It had been a good day, just like the other days I'd spent out and about with Porter and my kids, but it had been unsettling in ways I didn't know how to process yet.

How did this man have so much insight into my children?

Or rather, how did I have so little?

I mean, I understood the mechanics of how things had ended up this way. I'd been absent. He'd been present. Two plus two equals four.

The part that had my mind whirring was how had I let this happen? All the way home, I alternated between wondering how in the world I'd let things turn out this way, and berating myself for it.

Then I walked into my apartment, and the guilt

burrowed even deeper. One look at Zach, and my foundation shifted. Everything Porter had told me today about Zach's youngest siblings had been unnervingly enlightening. So how clueless had I been with Zach? Of course I knew that every new parent was some degree of clueless, especially since every kid was different enough to throw curveballs for even the most seasoned parents. Still, it seemed like I should have *known* everything Porter had said today. About my youngest three, and in general. I should have been rolling my eyes and saying, *"No shit, dude, I don't need you to nannysplain parenting to me."*

Except I kind of had.

And I felt like shit about that.

At least Chloe and the boys had Tiffany and Porter. Zach, though... For the majority of his formative years, it had been just him and me. I'd had primary custody. His mom... Well if I wasn't winning Parent of the Year, she wasn't even in the running. She had good intentions, but we'd found out the hard way that *"You have no maternal instinct now, but it'll kick in once you have kids of your own"* was a gigantic steaming load of bullshit. Her frustration with trying to be a mom had been a major factor in our breakup, and she'd been largely absent until Zach was in his early teens. They had an okay relationship now, fortunately, which I supposed should have given me hope.

For the first nine years of his life, I had been the biggest parental figure in Zach's world. Had I been enough?

I wanted to believe the proof was in the pudding. Zach was a smart, well-adjusted kid. He'd busted his ass in school, which had been an uphill battle with his dyslexia and some ADD, and he was looking into a community college here in Washington. He was kind, responsible, adored his younger siblings, and as far as I knew, he'd always treated his girlfriends well. He'd done some underage drinking but had taken me and his mom at our word that if he were ever too drunk to drive, he could call us any time. After I'd picked up my sheepish, weaving kid from a party, and after that nasty hangover the next day, he didn't seem all that interested in drinking again. Once or twice I'd seen the telltale signs of weed, but it didn't seem to be anything more worrying than some normal teenage experimentation.

Zach was a good kid, and all signs pointed to him turning into a good adult. For all the mistakes I must have made during his childhood and teenager years, I hadn't screwed him up. That was certainly great, but for God's sake, I wanted more for my kids than just surviving to adulthood and being functional against all odds.

I stepped into the kitchen where Zach was microwaving a couple of Hot Pockets. "Hey, uh, you got a minute?"

"Um. Yeah." He gestured over his shoulder. "I was going to call Mom in a second, though."

"That's fine. Just a minute or two."

"Okay. Sure." The microwave beeped, and he glanced at me as he carefully took out the hot plate. "What's up?"

I swallowed. "Listen, um..." I drummed my fingers on the counter. "You know I tried to be a good dad to you, right?"

Zach's eyebrows shot up. "Huh? Yeah. Of course."

"Okay. Good. I..."

"What's wrong? Tiffany busting your balls or something?"

I laughed. "No, no. Nothing like that. Just, uh..." I released a long breath and leaned against the cabinets. "I swear, watching Porter with the little ones—it's just making me realize how much I was lacking in the parenting department."

"Lacking?" Zach eyed me like I'd lost my mind. "What do you mean?"

"I... I don't even know. Just, he seems so much more competent, I guess. Even with me hovering there watching him, it's like it's second nature for him."

"Isn't it for you?"

"I thought it was. But then he does something different than I would have, and he explains why he did it, and I'm just standing there baffled because I never even thought of it that way." I let my head fall back against the cupboard door. "It's like this guy is taking me to school about parenting my own kids."

"So he does stuff differently? Mom does stuff differently than you do too." He shrugged. "Never seemed weird to me."

"Okay. I guess that's true." I started drumming my fingers on the counter again. "I just hope you know I was doing the best I could with what I knew at the time." *Which was apparently a hell of a lot less than I thought.*

Zach smiled. "I know. I never doubted that." The smile turned to a smirk. "Well, okay, whenever I was really pissed at you, I did, but once I calmed down..." He half-shrugged. "Yeah. I knew. I mean, you were kind of a hardass sometimes, but it's not like I didn't know you were trying to look out for me."

"That's good, I guess."

"It's good. Don't worry about it." He took a soda out of the fridge and popped the tab. "I gotta go call Mom. Good talk."

"Yeah. Good talk." As he headed out of the kitchen, I added, "You know you can tell me if—"

"Quit over-thinking things," he called over his shoulder. "You weren't a shitty dad."

Then his bedroom door closed, and I chuckled to myself. Well, at least one of my kids had turned out all right. I just wasn't sure these days if that was because of my parenting, or in spite of it, but I wouldn't complain about the results.

Fact was, I'd successfully staggered my way through the process of getting one kid from infancy to adulthood. Why wasn't that enough to convince me I could—with both a mom *and* a nanny in the picture this time—do it again?

Okay, this was getting ridiculous. Zach was right. I was clearly over-thinking everything and sending myself into a spiral of self-doubt. I wasn't a brand-new parent. I'd done this before. I didn't need Porter walking me through all of my kids' idiosyncrasies. There was no reason I couldn't jump in and be their dad.

So…what was I waiting for?

Off with the training wheels. Quit the tutorial and play the damn game already. Especially since it was a game I'd already beaten once, even if I probably hadn't gotten the highest score on the board.

Heart thumping, I took out my phone and I wrote out a text to Tiffany: *I think I'd like to try taking the kids for a night.*

Then I stared at the phone, gnawing my lip as I waited for a response. Thank God, she must have had her phone handy, and it only took a minute:

Oh, good! They'd love that.

I exhaled, more relieved than I probably should have been. What had I really expected? That she'd say no and tell me I couldn't take my own kids for the night?

Hell, maybe. She'd wanted me to spend time with them and Porter so I could learn the ropes, so maybe she didn't have much faith in my abilities either.

I could do this, though. And I would.

Would this weekend be good? I wrote back. *So it's not a school night?*

Perfect. Do you have enough bedding for everyone?

I glanced around the apartment. It was only a two-bedroom, and what little furniture Zach and I had barely fit. Still, I replied, *We'll make it work.*

And we would. *I* would. There had been a day when someone had handed twenty-four-year-old me and my twenty-one-year-old girlfriend a newborn, sent us home with a bill and no clue, and wished us the best of luck. It had been terrifying and overwhelming, but we'd made it through, and so had our son. When Noah came along, Tiffany and I had both had years of experience with parenting, and though it had still been exhausting and hard, we hadn't been as clueless and it hadn't been as daunting. Ethan and Chloe? Piece of cake.

So why was I nervous about something as simple as having them overnight in my apartment? My own kids? They were eight, seven, and three, not newborns. All signs said they wanted me in their lives, and that it wasn't too late to get it right.

I'm getting my ex-wife's trust back. I'm getting my kids' affection back.

So when the hell do I get my confidence *back?*

CHAPTER 8

PORTER

Dude I need help.

I sighed as I typed out a response to Holden's text. *What's going on?*

The response was a selfie that said a thousand words. Holden's wide-eyed expression was one of a man who was completely overwhelmed. Chloe was on his hip, her face scrunched up and crying. Behind her, the boys were fighting over a game controller. Zach—I assumed that was Zach—watched them, and if his eyes and body language were anything to go by, he was trying to conjure a teleportation device from thin air.

Texting wasn't going to cut it, and I was in my bedroom, safely away from prying ears. So, I tapped Holden's name and sent the call.

"Hey." One word had never sounded so full of exhaustion and frustration.

"Hey. Do you want me to come over?"

Holden sighed with palpable defeat. "I could really use the extra set of hands."

"All right." I pushed myself up off my bed. "Text me

your address and hang in there. I'll be there as soon as I—" In the background, something crashed, and one of the boys —Ethan, I thought—started screaming at the other.

"Fuck my life," Holden muttered.

"Just hang in there. I'm on my way."

After we'd hung up, I went upstairs to where Tiffany was helping Ashley with her homework in the dining room. Pre-algebra, judging by the way they both looked ready to start doing shots.

"Hey, um." I gestured over my shoulder. "I'm going to run over to Holden's for a bit."

Tiffany straightened. "What for? Is everything all right?"

"Yeah. Just need to go help him wrangle the wild animals."

She grimaced. "They testing him?"

"Mightily."

"Go." She waved me away. "Good luck and Godspeed."

I went back down the stairs and started putting on my shoes. As I was tying one, Tiffany came down.

"Listen," she said quietly. "You are just helping him with the kids, right?"

"Of course." I started tying the other shoe. "Why else would I—" My teeth snapped shut and my hands froze. "What?"

Her expression didn't give anything away except that she had something on her mind. What, I couldn't begin to guess. Folding her arms, she slowly pushed out a breath through her nose, and when she spoke, her voice was gentle, even, and had just enough of an edge to suggest she wasn't fucking around. "Listen, it's none of my business what you do on your own time." She shifted her weight. "But I've seen the way you and Holden look at each other when you think no one's looking."

My heart flipped. She *saw* that? And wait, *he* looked at *me* that way? "You..."

She put up her hand. "You don't have to tell me anything. In fact, I'd rather you didn't. I just need to put my foot down on this one thing."

I gulped.

"I'm glad you and he are getting along," she continued. "But this thing we all have? This arrangement with you and him and me and the kids?" Sighing, she shook her head, and exhaustion radiated off her. "It's taken a lot of time and heartache to get to this, and it still feels delicate and precarious. I don't want to jeopardize what my children have with their father, or what they have with you." She inclined her head and raised her eyebrows. "You feel me?"

She couldn't have been clearer if she'd written *don't you dare fuck my ex-husband* across her forehead in red Sharpie.

I nodded. "Yeah. I feel you."

"Okay." She exhaled, and some of the tension in her posture eased. "Give me a call if you and he need a hand with the little monsters."

I knew a dismissal when I heard it, and my first instinct was to get the hell out of there, but I stayed where I was. "For the record, the kids are my top priority, okay? I'm not going to do anything that's going to screw things up between them and their dad, or them and me, or... anything."

Tiffany nodded. "I trust you."

Aw, crap. She sounded like my own mom just then, and that was the tone my mom used to convey *here's some rope, try not to hang yourself*.

"Anyway." She gestured at the door. "Get over there before they turn the rest of his hair gray."

But more gray would make him look so—

"Okay. On it." I chuckled and took out my car keys. "See you later."

Traffic was light this time of night, so it only took about fifteen minutes to get to Holden's place. As I came up the steps into the hallway outside his apartment, I could hear the sounds of chaos from two doors down. His neighbors must have been thrilled. Judging by the TV volume as I passed one door, they'd found ways to cope.

I knocked sharply on Holden's door.

When he opened it, he released a breath. "Oh thank God." He stepped aside. "Please. Help."

I smiled, trying to look reassuring and not patronizing, and walked into the noisy apartment.

"Hey, guys?" Holden called over Ethan and Noah fighting about something.

Chloe and the boys turned to me, and immediately, the fighting ceased. "Porter!"

"Hey," I said. "What's going on?"

"Check out this game Dad got!" Noah pointed at the screen, the argument evidently forgotten. "It's awesome!"

"Yeah?" I cocked my head. "That why you guys are fighting over the controller?"

They both hung their heads sheepishly.

In a soft, contrite voice, Ethan said, "You want to watch us play?"

"Maybe in a minute. Why don't you guys go ahead and play, though? Nicely?"

They both nodded. Noah handed Ethan the controller, and they sat down on the couch as Ethan started his game.

Beside them, Chloe smiled up at me. She had that faintly blotchy look like she'd been crying, but she was all smiles now. I waved, and she gave me a little wave in return.

Beside me, Holden pinched the bridge of his nose. "I swear, it's like when you take them to the doctor because you think they're on death's door, and the second you walk them into the pediatrician's office..." He flailed his hand toward them. "They're healthier than ever."

"You mean like people who call 911 because Grandpa's having a heart attack, and as soon as the ambulance arrives, he's ready to run a marathon?"

He turned to me, forehead creased. "Yeah?"

I nodded. "Happens all the time."

That got a quiet chuckle out of him, and he sighed as he raked his fingers through his hair. "Great. So when I can't keep a handle on my own kids, call the paramedic, and they magically turn into saints."

I smothered a laugh.

"Oh. By the way." Holden nodded toward the living room. "This is my older son, Zach. Zach, this is Porter." Yeah, I could definitely see the resemblance. Zach was a little heavier than Holden, a little rounder in the face, and his complexion was a few shades lighter, but those eyes and that jaw? Oh yes, this was definitely Holden's child.

Zach got up and shook my hand. "Nice to meet you. They've talked about you like crazy."

Holden winced, though it was subtle.

"Well, they've been excited to spend time with both of you," I said. "Despite some, uh, evidence to the contrary."

"Eh, they're not that bad." Zach shrugged. "They're just little."

"True."

"Anyway." He turned to his dad, and he looked like he was desperate to be anywhere but here. "You still need me?"

"Nah." Holden grimaced. "Thanks for your help. Sorry."

"It's all right." Zach laughed. "Probably karma for all the shit I put you through when I was their age."

"Then you better stay close once they're teenagers," Holden growled, though there wasn't any venom.

Zach chuckled. He left the room, presumably heading for his bedroom, and Holden and I went into the kitchen while the boys continued to peacefully play their game. From the kitchen, we still had a decent view of the living room, so we could keep an eye on all three of them.

He leaned against the counter with a heavy sigh. "I'm sorry to pester you with all this tonight. Now I feel like kind of a jackass."

"No. Don't. I'm happy to help."

"Thanks." He wiped a hand over his face, his palm hissing across his goatee. "I just wish I knew what happened to my confidence."

"Give it time." I gestured at the kids. "I was terrified the first couple of times Tiffany left me alone with them."

He faced me. "Really?"

"Of course! That's a huge responsibility, and I didn't know them."

He started to speak, but then deflated. "God. I want to say 'but I know them.' Except... I'm pretty sure that's exactly it. I feel like I don't know them, and they don't know me."

"Except you do. More than I did when I started out, anyway."

"I don't think you understand how much I was gone."

"Either way, I didn't know them at all, and look at us now." I waved a hand toward them. "It actually didn't take all that long, even if it felt like it in the moment. So there's no reason you can't get that back with them. It's just going to take some time."

He studied me, then smiled a little. "And I guess I have the advantage of you being here to help. You were on your own when Tiffany wasn't around."

"I was, but we got it together."

"But you should have a learning curve. These are my own kids, and it's not like I've never done this before."

I studied him. "Maybe you have the yips."

Holden inclined his head. "This isn't golf."

"No, and... I mean, maybe it's not quite the right description. People with the yips usually lose some physical movement like their putt or their pitch. Or drawing blood, like one of the EMTs I worked with." I shrugged. "But maybe the principle still applies. It's something you've done, a skill you've had down pat, and now there's some block."

His lips quirked, and after a moment, he nodded with a quiet grunt of agreement. "So if that's what's happening here, how the hell do I get past it?"

"Just give yourself time. Cut yourself some slack. Accept that, regardless of why, you and your kids need to get reacquainted, and if you let yourself just ride the learning curve, it'll level out as you go."

He didn't look thrilled at the idea. I supposed I couldn't blame him. Sighing, Holden wiped a hand over his face. "Great. So the only way to not suck at parenting is to *let* myself suck at it until I remember what the hell I'm doing."

"Unless you've got any better ideas." I hooked my thumbs in the pockets of my jeans and leaned against the counter opposite him. "Honestly, from the outside looking in, you're doing better than you think. Just give them time and give yourself time. I mean, it's been months, but they're still in a new environment, which is exciting but also stressful. Tiffany said they drove her insane the first week or two in the new house."

"Really?"

"Oh yeah. They loved the place. The new yard. Everything. But it was new. I think sometimes a lot of us forget how stressful that really is, especially for kids. And they're probably testing you too."

Holden studied me. "Did they test you?"

"Oh my *God*," I groaned. "*So* much."

"Yeah?" He actually grinned a little. "Do tell."

"Ugh. Where to start? Honestly, they just argued with me. About everything. We don't want to leave the playground. We don't want that for lunch. We're hungry. We're not hungry. We're thirsty. We want something different to drink." I made an exasperated noise. "I swear to God, by day three, I was ready to call and schedule a vasectomy. By day five, I was going to steal some supplies from the firehouse and do it myself."

Holden laughed for real. "That bad, huh?"

"Ugh. But then we got used to each other, and things just sort of smoothed themselves out."

"Yeah?"

I nodded. "And can you blame them? They were in a new house in a totally new place. Their parents had just split up. Everything in their lives had changed, and they were trying to get used to all of that. Then in comes this guy they don't know who starts telling them what to do?" I huffed a laugh. "I'm thirty, and *I'd* push back against that shit."

He laughed too, if a little halfheartedly. "But I'm not some new guy. I'm their dad."

"Yeah. But you being here? This apartment? You

spending this much time with them without their mom around?" I shrugged. "That's all new. It's change. There's bound to be some stress there, and when kids get stressed—"

"They act out."

"Sometimes, yeah. So it's not you." I smiled. "Cut yourself some slack. Seriously."

Holden pushed out a long breath, his shoulders sagging. "Thanks. I'm... I keep telling myself that. It's just hard not to doubt myself into the ground after everything."

"Yeah, I know." I smiled. "It shows. But you're doing better than you think."

He searched my eyes. "Then why do I feel like I'm blowing this?"

"Because you're afraid of blowing it." I paused. "Look, it's obvious you've been trying. I can see it. Tiffany can see it." I waved a hand toward the kids. "Tonight, that's a reflection of everyone trying to adjust to new circumstances, not you doing anything wrong."

He gazed silently at the kids, his jaw working even as some of the tension in his face faded away. And fuck me, but my heart melted a little more. It wasn't hard to see why Tiffany felt the need to warn me about Holden. The more I warmed up to him, especially the more I saw him earnestly trying to be a good dad, the more it eroded my professional resolve.

This was so much easier when I thought you were an asshole.

Devoted Dad Holden is too sweet for words.

God help me...

CHAPTER 9

HOLDEN

It was aggravating, the way the kids had suddenly switched to perfect angels once Porter showed up, but it was a relief too. And now that he'd spelled out what they were doing, how they'd put him through the same wringer, and how it was just some growing pains and adjusting to change, I wasn't quite so convinced that a solid relationship with them was out of my reach. Would it happen overnight? No. But now I had hope this evening wasn't as portentous as it had felt in the moment.

While the boys played their game and Chloe played on the floor with her trucks, I reminded myself over and over that this was how parenting worked—lots of long, frustrating periods where I was convinced we'd never get past something, and then we would. It was almost like Sisyphus pushing the boulder up the mountain again and again, except instead of doing it for all eternity, one day the boulder would go over the peak and the work would be done. Of course, there would be another boulder and another mountain, but the sense of futility would be replaced by that euphoric feeling of *we made it*. Sometimes

I was convinced that certain aspects of parenting—like potty training and teaching a kid to drive—were actually hazing and should be outlawed, but "this too shall pass" and all of that.

It wasn't just defiance or behavior problems. When Zach was in grade school, I'd done everything I could to help him with his math and spelling, and for a long time, we both felt like nothing would ever change. The boulder wouldn't move, never mind go far enough up the mountain to roll back down. Then a teacher had recommended we test him for dyslexia, and once that test came back with all the answers to Zach's struggles, there were suddenly solutions and ways to help and accommodate him. It wasn't an overnight miracle cure—he still struggled today, especially if he was tired or stressed—but he'd no longer been beating his head against a wall trying to learn the material, and I'd no longer been beating mine against it trying to help him succeed.

I knew what it was like to struggle as a parent. I knew what it was like to watch my kids struggle and not be able to fix it for them. So while it was frustrating, I should have known that none of this was ever as insurmountable as it seemed in the moment. Zach was living proof that I could parent. Porter going through the same defiance and testing gave me hope that this was just a phase. Parenting yips or no parenting yips, I was not, no matter how much I'd convinced myself I was, doomed to fail at this.

And I had to admit for the millionth time—Porter really was a godsend. He hung around for the evening, mostly letting me handle things with the kids and just being there as a quiet presence to reassure me and to silently remind them that the rules didn't suddenly vanish when they came to Dad's house. We talked a little while the kids played in the living room. Zach joined us for a few minutes when he came out to get a soda, and then it was just us after he went back to his room.

Compared to how the day had started, the evening had turned out pretty damn relaxed.

Right up until, while Porter and I were shooting the shit at the kitchen table while the kids played, the clock hit eight.

Oh no.

Bedtime.

Another area where I'd considered myself competent but now second-guessed myself all to hell, because that was apparently going to be a thing for a while. Memories of the bedtime battles with the boys made my stomach lurch. Combine that with them testing me and lashing out against all the stress and change in their worlds?

"Oh God." I turned a plaintive look on Porter. "They're going to test me with the bedtime routine, aren't they?"

He offered a sweet but knowing smile. "Depends. You can get ahead of them, though."

"How's that?"

"Tiffany and I both swear by those five-, three-, and one-minute warnings for this." He nodded toward them. "Tell them that in five minutes they have to put on their pajamas and brush their teeth."

I eyed him dubiously.

He gave another nod in their direction as if to say, *"Go on, trust me."*

Okay. Well. He was here to help me deal with the aftermath if he was wrong, so...

I cleared my throat. "Hey guys? Five minutes, and then it's pajamas and teeth."

There were some disappointed sighs, but then, "Okay," from both boys.

Porter craned his neck. "I think Chloe's already asleep."

"Is she?"

"Yeah. You want me to get her ready for bed while you wrangle the boys?"

"You don't mind?"

"Nah. I've got this." He flashed me a quick smile, then got up.

I watched as he leaned over the couch, gently scooped my daughter up off the cushion, and eased her onto his shoulder. Oh my God, that was adorable. She wasn't going to be small enough to carry like that for much longer, and I was yet again thankful for something else I hadn't been too late for.

And the way he carefully held her, letting her head rest on his shoulder with her blond curls going everywhere, his hand flat on her back—yeah. Seriously adorable. I stared at them as he took her down the hall to my bedroom, where she'd be sleeping.

I was worried about this guy with my kids?

I shook myself and looked at my phone. I gave the boys another minute, hesitated because I was still second-guessing myself, and said, "Three minutes. Then pajamas and teeth."

More sighs, but they nodded. Noah started wrapping up his game. Ethan started putting his Matchbox cars into their crate. By the time I reached the one-minute warning, they were reluctantly putting things away and shutting things off. I tried not to think about how this would have gone down if I hadn't sent out the mayday text to Porter. I still felt like an utter failure for reaching out to the nanny to help me with my own kids, but... I mean, what could I say?

He was good at what he did, and everything had been peaceful since he'd arrived.

The boys changed into their pajamas, and I supervised while they brushed their teeth. Then they helped me put some sheets and pillows on the couch.

As we were settling onto the couch with a book, one of them on either side of me, Porter came out of the bedroom with Chloe on his hip. She was in her pajamas—bright green with red and blue trucks all over them, kind of like the ones Ethan was wearing—and though she was bleary-eyed, she was awake.

Oh no. Is she going to be up all night now?

But Porter smiled. "She wanted a story." He set her on the couch, and without hesitation, Chloe climbed into my lap. The boys shifted to accommodate her, and then everyone settled.

Porter took a seat on the end cushion. Admittedly, I was glad he was sticking around for this part. God knew he'd been here longer than I had any right to ask him to stay, but having him bolt in the middle of the bedtime routine might cause some setbacks. So, I was grateful he stayed.

After a story—okay, two, because I was a sucker—the boys were nodding off and Chloe had fallen asleep against my chest.

Putting them to bed after that was easy. The boys just had to shift onto their respective sides of the couch, and I carried Chloe into my bedroom and tucked her into the small bed I'd wedged in beside mine.

Just like that—bedtime was done. Everyone was down for the count, and the apartment was silent except for the muffled sounds of a TV show coming from Zach's bedroom.

I stepped out into the hall with Porter and shut my

bedroom door. Then I released a breath. "That was, um, a lot easier than I thought it would be."

He laughed softly. "I think you're underestimating yourself. And them. They're trying. You're trying." He shrugged. "Just be patient."

"Yeah, I know. But I'm pretty sure it wouldn't have been as peaceful without your help."

"Well, glad I could help, then." Our eyes met, but then he cleared his throat and dropped his gaze. "I, uh, should probably get out of here, though."

"Right. Right. It's... God, I can't believe how long I've kept you."

"It's okay. I'm happy to help."

We quietly walked up the hall and through the living room where the boys had already fallen asleep, and I stepped out the front door with him.

"Listen," I said. "Thanks again. I know I killed your entire evening, but... I appreciate it."

Porter's smile made something flutter in my chest. "It's all right. I'm, uh..." He actually blushed as he glanced past me. "The house was kind of quiet without them. I don't mind."

Oh. Dear. God. Was my heart melting? Because I was pretty sure my heart was melting.

I laughed to get some breath moving. "Yeah, it is kind of jarring when they're not there, isn't it?"

"A bit. Yeah. Anyway. I'll..." He gestured over his shoulder with this thumb toward the parking lot. "I'll get out of your hair."

"Thanks again, though. I mean it."

"I know you do. Just text me again if you need help."

"I will." Funny how quickly I'd gone from bristling at the idea of needing this young stranger's help with my own kids to being grateful for the lifeline. My confidence could seriously come back any goddamned day now.

We exchanged smiles and murmured goodnights, and he headed down to his car.

I watched him go, not quite sure how I felt about... well, anything. My confidence as a parent was both trashed and boosted. I was mortified that I'd had to reach out to Porter for help, but at the same time glad I'd spent the evening with him, and not just because he'd helped me get a handle on things with the kids. We'd spent most of the time talking. Not about anything in particular, just conversation to pass the time while we kept an eye on Chloe and the boys, but it had been relaxed and comfortable, and...nice.

Well, he was gone now. The kids were in bed, and I wasn't going to be far behind them.

And for some reason, I was pretty sure I'd be thinking about Porter all night.

THE NEXT MORNING WAS A BIT TOO CLOSE TO LAST night for my comfort. Noah was spoiling for a fight against any of his siblings, including Zach. Chloe responded to every request with "I want *Mom*."

At least they were willing to eat breakfast, though. Ethan was hungry but refused to eat anything I had in the house, so he was in the downward hangry spiral where the longer he went without eating, the more upset he became about being hungry, but he still wouldn't eat. About the time I'd reached the end of my tether and was ready to snap at him, I paused as something Porter had said last night echoed in my mind:

"They're stressed even if they don't realize it because

their whole world is in flux and they have no control over it. They don't know how to express that."

I crouched in front of the sofa where Ethan was pouting after his last outburst. "Hey, buddy. Look at me."

He sniffled, then finally cut his eyes toward me.

"What *do* you want for breakfast?"

He thought for a second. "Cheese and berries."

I furrowed my brow. "Cheese and berries?"

"Cottage cheese and frozen blueberries," Noah said from the kitchen table, in a *"duh, Dad"* tone. "That's what Porter makes for breakfast sometimes."

"Oh." I thought fast, then met Ethan's gaze and put my hand on his arm. "Okay. I don't have those, but I'll make sure to have them next time you stay over, okay?"

He nodded, but his chin was quivering, and his eyes were welling up. Ethan wasn't really prone to crying, but he didn't do well with being hungry.

"Could you do me a solid today and just have cereal?" I asked. "And then you can pick where we go to lunch before I take you to Mom's?"

That...actually seemed to work, and he brightened a little. "I can?"

"Yeah."

He wiped his nose with the back of his sleeve. "And you'll get cheese and berries next time?"

"Definitely. I'll even check with Porter, so I get the right ones."

He smiled faintly, then nodded. "Okay."

I stood, and Ethan got up and headed for the kitchen. I closed my eyes and exhaled. It worked. I could have kissed Porter for that.

Okay, where did that come from?

I shook the thought away and got up to get Ethan some cereal.

He was still less than thrilled, but he ate his cereal, and after breakfast, he wasn't quite so cranky. When lunchtime rolled around, he wanted to go to some sandwich shop I'd never heard of. Noah said he liked the place and was on board with going. Chloe's eyes lit up when I mentioned the name. Okay, winner for all three kids. That was promising. I checked the menu on my phone, and it looked like they had some reasonably healthy food, not to mention small enough portions for kids, and it was only about ten minutes out of the way. I texted Tiffany to let her know I was taking them to lunch and might be a little bit later than we'd agreed on, which was fine by her.

Lunch was peaceful and uneventful, and dear Lord did I bask in peaceful and uneventful after last night. I wasn't going to rest on my laurels and assume that last night was the end of it, but I felt better about things now.

With everyone happily fed and playing with the toys from their kids' meals, I drove them back to their mom's house.

Porter came out to give me a hand with their bags—not that they had much—and in a matter of minutes, the boys had taken off to play outside and Chloe was pushing some trucks around on the living room floor. Tiffany was out on the back deck talking to her sister on the phone and occasionally glancing down at the boys. Just a quiet afternoon at home.

"Well, I guess that's everything." I turned to Porter in the kitchen. "Guess it's my turn to get out of your hair."

He smiled, which shouldn't have made my stomach all fluttery like that. "That's up to you and Tiffany. I'm not throwing you out."

"Still." I paused. "Before I go, though—what's this cheese and berries they like for breakfast?"

"Oh. That." He waved a hand. "Just some thawed out frozen berries with some cottage cheese on top. They saw me eating it once, asked to try it, and they've all been hooked on it ever since."

"So I'm gathering. Any particular kind?"

"Nah. Noah's not a big fan of frozen raspberries, but otherwise..." He shrugged. "Berries. Cottage cheese. Done."

I chuckled. "Good to know. Guess I'll be stopping for groceries on the way home. Anything else I should know?"

"Not off the top of my head. I mean, you know about Ethan being picky about food textures."

"Right. Right. He's always been that way. Nothing soggy or slimy."

"Exactly. Which—now that I think about it, he's got a huge aversion to any kind of fried fish now. Fish and chips, fish sticks, that kind of thing."

"Yeah?"

"Yep." He sighed. "He ordered fish and chips at a restaurant a while ago, and they were so undercooked..." He wrinkled his nose and shuddered. "We sent them back, let's put it that way. He took one bite, flipped out, and he gags if anyone even suggests them to him now."

I laughed dryly. "Just like his older brother."

"Really?"

"Oh yeah. Zach's not quite as touchy about texture, but if he gets a bad order of something *one time*, he'll never touch it again."

"Can you blame him?" Porter made a face. "One of the firefighters at my firehouse made these enchiladas that gave the entire house food poisoning. It was two years before I could even stand the smell of Mexican food, and I still can't eat enchiladas."

"That's a damn shame."

"I know, right?" he grumbled. "But once bitten..."

"Yeah. I get that."

We both laughed, and I realized we'd held eye contact longer than we probably needed to. And that some heat was rising in my cheeks at the same time some color was blooming in his.

"Anyway. Um." I cleared my throat and motioned toward the door. "I should get—"

"Oh hey, Holden?" Tiffany came back in. "Before you take off, can I borrow you for a second?" She tilted her head toward the deck.

"Um. Sure. Yeah." I exchanged smiles with Porter again, then followed her outside. "What's up?"

She chewed her lip and crossed her arms, and, for a painfully long moment, seemed like she wasn't sure what to say. Finally, she took a deep breath. "Listen, I want you and Porter to get along, but..." Her eyes flicked toward the house —probably toward him—and then narrowed as they shifted back to me. "Maybe not *that* well?"

"What do you mean?"

She cocked her head in true *don't play stupid with me* fashion. "Do you think I was born yesterday?"

I blinked. "Tiff, I have no idea what you're talking about."

"So I was hallucinating when I just watched you two chatting? You weren't flirting with him?"

I barely kept myself from rolling my eyes. "We were talking about food for the kids. I was not flirting with him."

"But you do think he's attractive."

"Yes, because he *is* attractive, but that doesn't mean—"

"Holden." She pinched the bridge of her nose, then dropped her hand and met my gaze again. "Please tell me you're not—"

"I'm not doing anything. Yes, Porter is attractive." I paused. "He's hot, okay? But that doesn't mean I'm trying to hook up with him or anything."

She didn't look convinced.

"For God's sake, I'm—"

"I'm serious. Maybe I'm being paranoid and jumping the gun, but the bottom line is I *need* him. Everything has been like night and day since I hired him. After all the horror stories I've heard about awful nannies, there's no way I'm taking for granted that anyone I hire *after* him will be half as good."

"And you're worried that if something happens between him and me, that he'll leave."

"Yes!" Tiffany threw up her hands. "Either he'll quit to get away from you, or things will be unbearably awkward between..." She exhaled hard and shook her head. "Please, Holden. You know I would never tell you who you can and can't date, and I really, really do wish you the best in finding someone new, but..." Her brow pinched and her voice was plaintive as she whispered, "Not him."

I showed my palms. "Not an issue. He's cute, but not an issue."

She searched my eyes, and slowly started to relax. "Okay. I just wanted to make sure we're on the same page."

"We are. I promise."

"All right." She exhaled. "Well, um. How did last night go? Sounds like he helped you?"

I hated admitting that I'd needed his help, but yeah, I had, and yeah, he had. I filled her in, She didn't seem to think that raised any giant red flags about me needing supervision with the kids, though, so that was reassuring. Maybe I was, as usual, overthinking things.

Once we'd finished talking, I headed out, and as I passed through the living room, I glanced at him. He was sitting cross-legged on the floor, helping Chloe set up some blocks for her trucks to knock down.

And fuck me, but my heart fluttered.

Especially when he looked up at me and smiled one of those smiles again, and she did too, and suddenly there was nothing in the world more adorable than my baby girl and Porter playing together on the floor. If not for Tiffany standing behind me, and the conversation we'd just had outside, I'd have snapped a picture on my phone.

The image was committed to memory, though, so I said goodbye to Chloe and Porter, put on my shoes, and left.

As I drove away, my pulse was all over the place. Had Tiffany picked up on something I hadn't from Porter? Or was it just true that being told you couldn't have someone made that someone even more desirable? Yeah, I'd had some impure thoughts about Porter from the start—especially once my ego stopped trying to find something wrong with him—but now that he was off limits, he was made of pure temptation.

"Oh fuck. I'm losing my mind," I muttered to the steering wheel. I understood where Tiffany was coming from. I sure as hell wouldn't screw around with him just to spite her. That wasn't who I was, and it wasn't who we were as ex-spouses. And for all I struggled to know my kids, I knew Tiffany. She wouldn't have said anything unless she thought there was actually some potential for something to happen between me and Porter. And for that something to happen, this attraction couldn't be one-sided.

Had she seen something I hadn't? Noticed a look in his eye when I wasn't looking?

Not that it mattered. She'd made it clear that he was off limits, and I didn't blame her for laying down this boundary.

But the line she'd drawn in the sand may as well have been an arrow pointing straight to the man who'd already occupied way too many of my thoughts.

CHAPTER 10

PORTER

How weird was it that after a handful of outings, it already felt weird when it was just me and the kids? Or maybe it wasn't weird. It just wasn't as fun. I really, really missed having Holden along for the ride.

Except I was being ridiculous. My mom had warned me that spending most of my time around young children would make me crave adult interaction, so that must have been what was happening now. Tiffany and I had quickly become close friends, and we stole every opportunity we could for some grownup conversation (booze optional, depending on if either of us had to play responsible adult any time soon). She'd even mentioned more than once that one of her favorite things about her new job was the constant adult interaction.

And I'd caught myself grabbing on to adult interaction whenever I could find it—parents at the park or school pickup, conversations with random strangers on errands, being chattier than I'd ever been with cashiers and servers. I mean don't get me wrong, I'd always been chatty and polite, but the last few months? Yeah, there'd been a bit of an uptick in that department. After years of being around other adults all day long—sometimes even getting ribbed for being the youngest on shift—I was suddenly spending the majority of my time with kids.

Then along came Holden, and...adult interaction.

Now that the weekend was over, the kids were back at their mom's, and Holden had gone back to work, I missed him because I missed having someone to talk to.

Clearly this was a sign that I needed to spend some time with my friends before I went out of my mind. I adored Chloe, Ethan, and Noah, and would step in front of a bus to save any of them without hesitation, but obviously I was overdue for some time with people my own age, ideally while drinking and cursing at referees of some sport or another on TV.

So, on Thursday night, I went out with some friends I hadn't seen since before I'd started working for Tiffany—Cora, a former EMT I'd worked with for a few years before she'd transferred to another house, and Alex, an emergency department nurse whose snark had often been the highlight of my shifts. Cora was working in admin at the hospital now, so she had blessedly regular nine-to-five hours, which meant we only had to work around Alex's wildly unpredictable schedule these days.

When I walked into the tavern where a lot of the firefighters and medics liked to hang out, they'd already grabbed a booth. I stopped at the bar to get a beer, then joined them.

"Hey, honey!" Cora stood up and hugged me. "Long time, no see!"

"Not my fault anymore." I let her go and hugged Alex. "My schedule's as easy to work around as yours these days."

"Ugh." Alex let me go and glared at me. "You people and your...schedules."

"Hey, don't be a hater." I sat down beside Cora. "Just because we got smart and moved to jobs that don't require unholy hours."

"Pfft. You both miss getting bled on, puked on, and shit on. Don't lie."

Cora and I glanced at each other, then shook our heads and said in unison, "Nope."

"So transparent." Alex eyed me. "How is your new gig working out anyway?" He wrinkled his nose. "Are you really doing the nanny thing?"

"Yeah, and it's going pretty good. My boss is awesome, and so are her kids."

"Not little hellspawn?" Cora asked. "I swear I had visions of someone dropping their problem children on you."

"Oh God, no. They're great, especially once you get a feel for their routines and—" I stopped myself before I bored my friends into comas with a long, rambling monologue about the kids I spent the majority of my time with. "It really is a good job. They're easy, and I mean, having a place to live is a hell of a bonus."

Alex clicked his tongue. "Man, for room and board on top of a salary, I'd play nanny and wear a French maid costume."

I snorted. "You say that like you wouldn't wear a French maid costume anyway."

He tsked and rolled his eyes. "Bitch."

"He's got a point, hon," Cora said. "You totally would."

"You know what? Fuck you both."

Cora and I laughed.

The conversation drifted to each of our various jobs,

how some mutual friends were doing, and of course—as was tradition when a bunch of medical professionals were in the same room—reminiscing over war stories. There was an unspoken agreement to steer away from the horrific calls and stick to the ones we could laugh about, like the cat that hitched a ride on Cora's ambulance and stole her partner's sandwich, or the pregnant woman who'd puked all over my back while I'd been stabilizing her son's broken ankle.

It was nice to be around other grownups and talk about things besides that asshole gym teacher, sneaky ways of getting kids to do chores without them realizing they were doing chores, and how much we all quietly hated the latest cartoon character whose grating voice we had to listen to ad nauseum. I could curse. I could make crude jokes. I had a cold beer in my hand and a couple of longtime friends with me who enjoyed the exact opposite of family-friendly conversation.

And I...still felt off.

Yeah, it was a relief to have some adult time, but that nagging feeling I'd had all week? Where I'd been hyperaware of the empty passenger seat? Where I'd caught myself wishing my boss's ex-husband would suddenly text and say he was taking the day off and would be joining me for the day after all? That hadn't budged.

Maybe it wasn't adult time I needed.

Maybe it was Holden.

And that didn't make any sense at all, and someone needed to get me a few more beers, because alcohol seemed like the only solvent that might get through this weird funk.

Or maybe I just want Holden, damn it.

I shoved that thought away. Or at least I tried to. Wanting Holden? My boss's ex-husband? The father of the kids I was employed to watch? Talk about the last man on earth I should have been getting starry-eyed over, even if my boss *hadn't* explicitly warned me off him. What was wrong with me?

I took a deep pull from my beer. Okay, I was definitely losing my mind. Constant exposure to cartoons had broken my brain. That was the only possible explanation. I had to write to the FDA and the FTC and let them know that certain kids' shows needed serving sizes or maximum exposure level warnings because too much of that shrill, brightly colored shit could damage a man's brain to the point that he thought he wanted a piece of his boss's temperamental ex-husband. Like, *really* wanted a—

"Hey, Supernanny." Alex bumped my shoulder with his. "Why so quiet?"

I cleared my throat. "Just, uh..." *Because my psyche is irreparably broken by family-friendly programming.*

Cora smirked. "Come on. What's his name?"

I damn near snapped my neck turning to her. "Huh?"

She rolled her eyes. "Dude. I rode on an ambulance with you for four years. I know you. Don't even try to tell me you aren't all stupid over a man."

"I..." Well hell. Tiffany had caught on. My friends apparently had too. Did that mean I had it bad? Crap.

"C'mon." Alex gave me another nudge with his shoulder. "Deets, bro. Tell us all about him so we can live vicariously through your dick."

"Pfft, speak for yourself," Cora muttered. "I'm getting plenty of dude, thank you."

Alex rolled his eyes. "Slut."

She kicked him under the table and turned to me. "Anyway. Dude? Deets? Dick?" She thumped the table with her knuckle. "Out with it."

"Um. Well." I cleared my throat. "So, the kids I'm taking care of? Their dad is in town now."

My friends' eyes widened.

"Ooh," Alex said. "Awkward?"

"Kind of, yeah."

Cora's eyes got huge. "Baby, please tell me you do not have a crush on your boss's ex-husband."

"Uh..." Well, shit. If I did, could I blame it on the mind-altering effects of overexposure to cartoons? Probably not, but that wouldn't stop me from trying.

"FYI," Alex said in a stage whisper, "you're blushing."

"Shut up," I muttered.

"Ooh, he's right." Cora grinned, eyes gleaming with curiosity. "C'mon. What does he look like?"

"Well..." I pulled out my phone. I hadn't expected a picture I'd snapped of Holden and the boys the other day at the playground to come in handy like this, but I wasn't going to argue. I flipped to the photo, then turned my phone so my friends could see it.

As soon as he saw the picture, Alex put a hand to his chest and turned wide eyes on me. "Oh my *Lord*. You need to get that man into bed at *once*."

"Alex!" Cora rolled her eyes and grabbed my phone away. "Bruh. That's his boss's ex."

"Yeah? And?" Alex flailed a hand toward the phone. "Ex means he's single. Unless someone else has come along and beaten Porter to the punch." He eyed me expectantly.

I shifted in my seat. "I, um, I'm pretty sure he's single, yeah."

"Uh-huh. And there is no way in hell that man"—he pointed emphatically at my phone—"is going to stay single for long. Quit waffling and get his pants down."

I burst out laughing. "Yeah. Okay. And find another job while I'm at it, right?"

He tsked. "I didn't say do it in front of the ex. A little discretion, sweetie. Duh." He paused. "Except he's probably straight, isn't he?"

"Actually..." I cleared my throat as renewed heat bloomed in my cheeks. "I have it on pretty good authority that he's not."

Alex sucked in a breath and grabbed my forearm. "What are you *waiting* for, then? He's queer, hot, and single. *Bang. Him.*"

"He's also my boss's ex-husband."

"And?" Alex shrugged. "Ex. Ex-husband. Ex-her-problem."

"It's really not that simple. I wish it was."

He groaned theatrically. "You're killing me, Porter."

I laughed but didn't really feel it. "Yeah? And have you ever done that cardiologist you were always swooning over?"

I fully expected a sheepish "No," but to my surprise, Alex beamed. He fucking *preened*. "Now that you mention it? Yes. Yes, I have."

"What?" Cora and I both scoffed.

"Since when?" I asked.

Alex grinned. "Well, it turns out the good doc likes the same bathhouse I do in Seattle, so..."

AT THE END OF THE NIGHT, I SAID GOODBYE TO ALEX and Cora, then headed to my car to go home. I didn't start the engine yet, though. Instead, I took out my phone and thumbed to the photo I'd shown my friends of Holden and his boys.

One look at his smile, and my heart skipped.

My brain went back to that night he'd asked for help with his kids. He could have easily lost his temper and made the night worse, but no, he'd done what he'd been doing since he'd arrived here—swallowed his pride and let someone else help. And once things had calmed down, we'd just hung out until it was time to put the kids to bed, and watching him cuddle on the couch and read a couple of stories to his kids? Oh my God, my heart. If he'd had any doubts left that his kids wanted a relationship with him, I hoped like hell that night—that moment on the couch—had erased all those doubts. They wanted him in their lives.

And God help me, so did I.

When it came to dating, my M.O. was usually to sleep with a guy a few times, and if the conversations between orgasms were interesting enough, things might progress to a relationship. My last two boyfriends had been booty calls first, and our relationships had started in bed. I was all about getting any question of sexual incompatibility out of the way before deciding if this was someone I wanted to actually *know*.

Then along came Holden, and my usual M.O. was turned on its ass. Oh yeah, I wanted to do all kinds of things with him in the bedroom, but I was as drawn to *him* as I was to his body. Here was this guy who'd owned his mistakes, swallowed his pride, and was trying his damnedest to do right by his family. He was sweet and funny. He could turn me to goo just by smiling at one of his babies.

I was intrigued by him in ways I'd never been. If he gave me a choice between sex and just sitting down for a drink and talking, I would legitimately have to think it over.

Alex and Cora were right—I had it bad for him.

I shook myself, turned off the screen, shoved my phone back into my pocket, and started the car. It didn't matter how bad I had it for Holden. I had it even worse for a steady paycheck and a job that didn't leave me with nightmares and flashbacks.

I could fantasize about Holden all I wanted. I wasn't risking my new, stable life for him or anyone else.

No matter how tempting he was.

CHAPTER 11

HOLDEN

The first domino just fell.

I groaned as I read the text from Tiffany on my way into the office from my car. It had only been a matter of time, so it was no surprise, but fuuuck.

So, my first time around as a dad, I was a little slow on the uptake when it came to a lot of things. I was twenty-four, had grown up as the youngest of three (not to mention the youngest of eight grandkids), and had precisely no experience with children. Not surprisingly, it took me a while to get the hang of... well, basically everything.

I had no doubt I'd forgotten a few things in the years between my oldest and the younger three, but there were definitely lessons I learned raising Zach that were burned into my being and would be until the day I died. Things like not keeping the house completely silent when the baby was sleeping unless we wanted to walk on eggshells for the rest of our lives. Or that, before introducing a child to a TV show, movie, or song, it was wise to decide if you could handle watching or hearing it four hundred times a day.

Or, more to the point, from the time Zach had started

preschool, I had understood all the way to my core that once the school year started, it was only a matter of time before someone brought home a microbe, and when they did, everyone in the house was getting it. *Everyone.*

Today, per my ex-wife's text, the first domino had fallen.

I quickly wrote back, *Who and how bad?*

I was just sitting down at my desk when she replied, *Chloe. Up all night w/fever.*

I winced. *Poor baby. Doctor?*

Nah, her fever broke. She's just unhappy.

Do you need anything? I was edgy about leaving work early—I really liked this place so far, and didn't want to fuck that up—but if my kids needed me, my kids needed me.

Tiffany wrote back: *Ok for now; might need help once the boys go down.*

Keep me posted.

And the boys didn't take long to go down. By the time I came back from lunch, Tiffany was on her way home early to pick up Ethan from school, and Noah had called to say he wasn't feeling good either.

You sure you don't need an extra pair of hands?

As soon as I sent it, I winced. Of course she didn't—she *had* an extra pair of hands. Which was good. Hell, someone like Porter would've been a godsend even when Tiffany and I were still married. And having him there meant I didn't need to bail on work and put my new job at risk when I'd barely started here. So I pushed my ego aside and didn't take it personally when she said she had things under control. I just sent, *Ok. Let me know if you need anything.*

Throughout the rest of the day, I checked in. Chloe was miserable, and it sounded like the boys were crashing hard too. Tiffany and Porter had both been in touch with the pediatrician, who didn't think any of them needed to be seen, and there wasn't much to be done except mitigate the misery and ride it out. From Tiffany's texts, she was exhausted already, trying to keep up with three very unhappy kids.

On my way out of the office, I called her. "Hey, do you need me to pick anything up for the kids? I'm heading home, so I could be there in forty-five minutes or so."

"Actually..." She exhaled. "I was going to stop when I picked up Noah, but as soon as I saw him, I needed to get him home."

Alarm raised the hairs on my neck. "How bad is he?"

"Just miserable." She laughed softly. "Might be a bad cold, might be the man flu. Hard to tell."

I laughed. If she could joke about it, then that was enough to ease my nerves. "Okay, well, what do you need me to get?"

"How about I text you a list?"

"Perfect. I'm leaving the office now."

"Okay. And you really don't mind?"

"Of course not." I pulled open the driver's side door and slid into the seat. "They're my kids too."

"I... I know. That's not what I meant. I mean, we—"

"I know. But it's no problem, okay? Just tell me what you need, and I'll be there as soon as I can."

"You do realize if you show up here, you're going to catch whatever bug this is too, right?"

"You're not talking me out of this, Tiff."

"All right, all right. Just full disclosure, that's all."

"Uh-huh. See you soon."

I left the office and headed for the grocery store near both our places. I barely even needed to glance at the list she'd texted. I knew the annual microbe battle supplies by heart:

chicken soup, Sprite, cough drops, Vicks, and several crates of tissues. I went ahead and got some to keep at my place too; Tiffany wasn't kidding that it was only a matter of time before I got sick if I didn't stay away, so I might as well be prepared.

During our texts, she'd mentioned that the front door would be unlocked, so I let myself in. "Hey, it's just me."

"We're all up here," Tiffany called down from the kitchen.

I took off my shoes, then went upstairs. "Here's everything." I held out the bag. "I couldn't remember what kind of cough drops they'll eat, so I got the honey lemon and eucalyptus."

"Perfect. They like the eucalyptus, but I'll keep the honey lemon for myself." She grimaced. "God knows this thing won't pass me by."

I laughed. "Nope. Never does."

"Can't wait." She started unloading the bag's contents onto the counter. "Oh, you're a lifesaver. Thanks for stopping."

"Tiff, you don't have to thank me for helping to take care of my own kids."

"I know, but..." She bit her lip, her forehead creasing as if she had no idea how to say what she was thinking.

"The fact that I've done such a piss poor job of it the last few years means I damn well better step up now." I gave her shoulder a gentle squeeze. "I'm trying to be their dad again, and not just when it's fun, you know?"

She nodded and finally smiled. "I'd say you're off to a good start."

"Let's hope. So how are they doing now?"

"The boys are both racked out. Chloe's in the living room with Porter." She frowned. "Poor baby's had a fever off and on all day." She handed me one of the packs of tissues I'd bought. "Could you take these to Porter?"

"Yeah. Will do."

In the living room, I immediately zeroed in on Chloe and Porter. He was sitting on the couch with his feet on a toy chest, and Chloe was in his lap, buried in blankets and snuggled against his chest. Only her face was visible, her skin flushed with fever and eyes red with tears.

The weirdest mix of emotions hit me all at once. Mostly it was that heartbreaking, helpless feeling of seeing my baby girl so obviously miserable, but in the background, there was this odd combination of jealousy and an almost overwhelming desire to break out a camera and snap a picture of them. Here was this man taking over where I was supposed to be, cuddling with Chloe while she weathered her fever, and I wanted to gnash my teeth and demand to know who the fuck he thought he was. But I also kind of wanted to stare at him, and how gently and sweetly he soothed my sick, unhappy daughter. I really wanted to say, "Okay, I'll take it from here," and move her onto my lap, but she looked perfectly comfortable with him. As comfortable as she could be when she was sick, anyway. Why jostle her just to assert my position in the pecking order?

So I sat on the couch beside them and set the tissues where he could reach them. "How's she doing?"

"Not real happy."

I touched her flushed cheek, and it was hot. "I thought her fever broke."

"It did." Porter gently smoothed her unruly blond curls. "She's been up and down all day, though. And since last night."

"Poor kid." And now that he mentioned it, I felt for him too—he had dark circles under his bloodshot eyes, and there were three open cans of Red Bull on the end table beside him. Probably all that was keeping him upright.

He touched her forehead and frowned, then sighed and rested his hand on her back. "I'm keeping an eye on her temperature. In case it gets too high or stays up for too long."

I nodded and was about to say I'd have been doing the same when Chloe interrupted with a deep, painful-sounding cough, and she immediately crumpled into tears. I instinctively wanted to reach for her, but held back because Porter was carefully holding her and easing her upright.

"Hey, hey." His voice was soft, and he steadied her when a cough jolted her tiny body. She burrowed against him, alternately crying and coughing, and he just kept murmuring to her and rubbing her back. As her coughing fit quieted, the crying faded too, and she settled on his chest with her thumb in her mouth. Porter kept a hand on her back, and he shifted his hips a little, a hint of a wince flickering across his lips.

"You want me to take her for a minute?"

Porter glanced down at her, absently stroking her back through the blanket. I thought he'd insist it was fine, but to my surprise, he met my gaze and grimaced. "Actually I could stand to get up for a minute or two. My foot's asleep." He gingerly flexed his left foot as if for emphasis.

"Okay. Let's trade."

Porter gently lifted her up to transfer her to me, and... damn. If ever there was a moment to make me realize I needed to fix things with my kids, it was when Chloe regarded me uncertainly before looking up at Porter. He must have read her unspoken *"Should I?"*, because he smiled and gave her a nod.

Apparently trusting his judgment, she let herself be moved from his lap onto mine, and she curled against me.

Porter stood, and he tugged at his T-shirt, which I realized was damp with sweat. Not surprising, given the heat radiating off Chloe. Guilt prodded me from all directions. I should have been the one sitting here, shirt soaked with sweat and feet falling asleep while I took care of my own daughter. She should have been asking me for reassurance before I handed her off to the guy she wasn't sure she was supposed to trust, not the other way around.

I held her a little closer and kissed the top of her head, and I vowed to myself that by the time the next school year's microbe came along, she'd see me as the dad I should have been all along. God knew I'd already made more headway than I'd expected.

Movement caught my eye, and I looked up to see Ethan trudging in, face flushed and hair sticking up. He seemed a little surprised to see me, but then crawled up onto the couch and huddled against my side.

I wrapped an arm around him. "How are you feeling, buddy?"

Ethan winced. "My throat hurts." God, I believed it—poor kid sounded like he'd been gargling broken glass.

"He's still warm," Tiffany said as she and Porter came back into the living room, "but I wouldn't call it a fever yet." She turned to Porter. "Do you think his glands are swollen, though? They felt swollen to me earlier."

Porter frowned. He came closer and crouched in front of Ethan. "Is it okay if I check something on your neck?"

Ethan nodded and sat up a little. He swallowed and winced again.

Porter brought his hands up. His brow furrowed as he carefully felt around the sides of Ethan's throat. Then he let go, and as Ethan returned to leaning against me, Porter rose. "His lymph nodes are a *little* swollen, so maybe it wouldn't hurt to take him to the doctor tomorrow."

She pursed her lips. "You think it can wait that long?"

He shrugged. "Yeah. They're not all that big, and they don't seem to be tender. I'll check them again before he goes to bed."

"Okay. I'll go ahead and call. It's too late to get him in tonight, but I can at least make an appointment for tomorrow." She glanced at Chloe, who was still curled in my lap, then turned to Porter again. "Do you think we should take the other two in while we're at it?"

Porter's lips quirked. He watched Chloe, and after a moment, he nodded. "Just to be on the safe side."

Tiffany turned to me. "What do you think?"

"Um." I glanced back and forth between them. "I think he knows what he's talking about. Do you need me to take time off to take them in?"

"No, I think we can handle it." She took out her phone. "I better call before they close."

"While you do that," Porter said, "I'll put some more soup on. That seemed to help with their throats."

They both left the living room, and I gazed down at Chloe. As much as it was still hard to swallow that Porter was the best choice to take care of the kids, I had to admit there was something comforting about having a paramedic staying with them night and day. No, he couldn't diagnose or treat everything in the world, but he was trained to know when something was an emergency and when it could wait. Whenever I made the call to hold off on medical attention for one of the kids, I'd lose sleep for days wondering if I should have handled it differently. If they were going to get worse, or if I'd overlooked something vital.

When Porter said they should see a doctor, but it could wait until tomorrow... What could I say? I believed him.

I refused to let myself go down that mental road of feeling threatened by Porter. I'd done that enough when I'd first met him. He wasn't a threat. I was still their dad. He was someone who was here to fill in where Tiffany needed help, and she definitely needed all the help she could get with three sick kids in the house. The fact that he had medical training? *Bonus*.

I'd just try to ignore the fact that I'd been the one to leave some of those gaps so she needed help in the first place. Or that he came with bonus skills I couldn't have provided if I'd wanted to, like paramedic training. Or that after just a few months, he was already closer to all three of my youngest kids than I'd ever been.

Every time I looked at Porter with one of my kids, I swore I could hear the universe telling me, *"Guess you should've stepped up while the game was still set to 'easy', idiot."*

But, I thought as I looked down at my daughter curled in my lap, it wasn't too late.

I kissed the top of her head, and she wriggled closer to me.

It's definitely not too late.

CHAPTER 12

PORTER

We were finally in the homestretch. The boys were still coughing and sniffling a little bit, but they felt a million times better. Enough they could play outside and go back to school. Chloe was basically back to normal, which meant she couldn't understand why Tiffany and I were moving so slowly. At three, she was a little young to grasp the idea that whatever she'd brought home from preschool would eventually drop Mom and the nanny too.

The first day all three kids went back to school, Tiffany woke up with a vicious sore throat and some hardcore congestion. I had about three hours to smugly think I might've dodged the bullet before that gross scratchy feeling started in the back of my throat, signaling that I would be wishing for sweet death by dinnertime. Sure enough, not long after I'd picked up everyone from school, I couldn't breathe, couldn't swallow, and could barely talk.

"Ugh." I dropped onto the couch beside Tiffany. "Kill me."

She sniffled. "Come on. It's not that bad."

"It is," I whined. "It so is."

She laughed, which made her cough. "Don't tell me you get the man flu."

"Hey." I tried to scowl, but it just made my sinuses hurt. "Don't judge me."

"Oh, I'm judging you."

I glared at her as best I could without actually using any of the tender muscles in my face. So, probably not much of a glare, and more of a pathetic narrow-eyed stare.

Eh. She wasn't the first to give me hell for getting the man flu, and she probably wouldn't be the last. I didn't care. I'd once tried to walk off a fractured foot, and after that drunk had shanked me with a broken bottle, I'd insisted I was fine right up until I'd passed out from blood loss. But the minute I started sniffling or my stomach hurt? I was down for the count. I reserved my manly manliness for injuries. I was the biggest baby in the world when I was sick, and I made no apologies for it.

"So what do we do tomorrow?" Tiffany croaked. "We're both going to be on our asses, and they've got school, homework, playdates..." She groaned. "Shit."

Just the thought of getting up off this couch made me tired. Waking up, getting everyone ready for school, ferrying them to all their destinations, feeding them again, and helping with homework? Fuuuck.

About the time I was wondering how much NyQuil it would take to put me in a coma, Tiffany said, "I should call Holden."

Holden. Oh. Right. There were more people in this picture than just the two of us.

"You think he can get the time off work?"

"Only one way to find out." She was thumbing something into her phone. A text, I figured. She seemed to go back and forth with someone—probably Holden—though I was off in please-kill-me-land and wasn't noticing much besides how much my throat and sinuses hurt. Finally, she put her phone aside and started to get up. "He's on his way."

"Huh?"

"Holden. He's going to take everyone for the night so we can be miserable in peace."

"Oh my *God*, he's a saint." I paused. "How the hell is he not sick? Does he have some magic pill that he's holding out on us?"

She laughed dryly. "Probably."

"What a jerk."

"I know, right?"

We both laughed—then coughed—and went to get everyone ready for a surprise night at their dad's place.

When Holden arrived, he looked at each of us in turn, eyes wide. "Holy shit. You two *do* look like you could use a break."

Tiffany made a gravelly, miserable noise, and handed him Chloe's backpack. "You're sure this isn't going to—" She paused to cough a few times. "You're sure this won't be an issue with work?"

"It's fine." He took the backpack. "My boss understands. I've got this, Tiff. I promise."

She frowned but then nodded. "Okay. Thanks, Holden."

"Any time. You two take it easy." He met my gaze. "You sure you don't need me to stop and get anything?"

"We'll be fine." Tiffany glanced at me, a smirk playing at her lips. "I will, anyway. Don't know about this one."

"Hey," I protested weakly. "Shut up." They both laughed, and I rolled my eyes, which hurt. "You guys suck."

Holden chuckled. "Anyway. I'll get them out of your hair. Take care tonight, all right?"

"Thanks," we both said.

In a matter of minutes, he had everyone out the door and off to his place for another evening of camping at Dad's house. As soon as they'd left, Tiffany and I breathed sighs of relief. I felt kind of guilty, being relieved that the kids were gone, but at least this meant we could be sick and oblivious without accidentally neglecting someone. I was too sick for responsibility, dammit. At least Ashley could fend for herself for a few hours, and she usually wasn't all that social with us in the evenings anyway. Especially when she had homework.

Ashley made herself some grilled cheese and disappeared into her bedroom. Tiffany and I spent the evening indulging in stupid TV and the remaining chicken soup and Sprite. Then, after a shot apiece of NyQuil, we both crashed early.

The next morning, I slept in for almost an hour but didn't dare push it beyond that. It was way too easy to screw up my sleep pattern, and I didn't want to be jetlagged on top of being sick. As much as it sucked, dragging myself upright and pouring some coffee down my throat would be the best thing in the long run.

The stairs up from the bottom floor—where my bedroom was—to the second level seemed bigger than they usually were. They took a hell of a lot more work to climb, anyway. By the time I was at the top and trudging into the kitchen, my muscles ached and my head spun, and damn if I wasn't a little bit winded too.

Tiffany was already there, making herself some foul-smelling tea. Ashley's jacket and backpack were gone, so she must have left for school. Which made sense, given the time. What about the boys? And Chloe? Didn't they... Shouldn't we...

Oh. Right.

It took a minute for my brain to catch up that Holden had taken them to his place last night. And had Tiffany explained how long that arrangement was for? Was it just for tonight, or did I need to go pick up Chloe?

"So what's the deal for today?" I asked groggily. "Am I picking up—"

"You're doing the same thing I am." She sipped her tea and swallowed with a wince. "Absolutely nothing."

"But...the kids?"

"Holden dropped the boys off at school on his way to work, and Zach is watching Chloe until it's time to take her to preschool. Zach will pick them up again this afternoon, and Holden and I will figure it out from there depending on how you and I are feeling."

"Oh. Okay." Glad she had that figured out, because God knew my brain wasn't functioning well enough to arrange something that complicated. Had I been this stupid last night? I didn't think so, but at this point, what the hell did I know?

"Porter?" Tiffany studied me. "You all right?"

"Yeah." I leaned against the counter, more grateful than I should've been for the support. My whole body wanted to collapse on the floor. "Just feel like shit."

"I can see that." She touched my forehead and grimaced. "Okay, man flu or not, you do have a fever."

"Awesome."

"Why don't you go back to bed? The kids are taken care of for today, and I'm just going to stay home and veg. You look like you could use some more sleep."

"I'm going to fuck up my sleep schedule."

"Uh-huh. Welcome to being sick."

"But if I—"

"Porter." She looked right in my eyes, her expression far too intense for someone as sick as she was. "I'm way too tired to be anyone's mom right now, but I will one hundred percent turn into *your* mom if you don't go back to bed and get some rest."

I didn't have it in me to argue. Somehow, I was pretty sure she did.

So I put up my hands. "Okay. I'll go get some sleep."

Then I went back downstairs, took off my glasses, and faceplanted into bed.

By the time I woke up again, it was dark out. That didn't necessarily mean much—it was fall in the Pacific Northwest, which meant the sun went down at like four—but still. It hadn't even been ten in the morning when I'd gone back to bed. Right?

I fumbled around until I found my glasses, and once those were finally on my face, blinked a few times before squinting at my phone. 7:22 pm.

Whoa. Okay, apparently Tiffany had been right—I did need rest. And while I still felt like I'd been flattened by a freight train, I felt less like a halfheartedly reanimated corpse. I'd take any improvement I could get.

A quick shower gave me hope that I would one day feel fully human again. Amazing how much difference something like that could make. Then I got dressed, didn't bother with my contacts, and shuffled out of the room to rejoin society.

There were voices upstairs, so the kids had apparently

come back from their dad's. The faucet was running and dishes were clanking, so Tiffany must have been cleaning the kitchen. I figured I should see if she needed help.

As I came up the stairs, I glanced into the living room. Ashley was curled on one end of the sofa under a quilt, clutching a box of tissues and staring miserably at the TV. The boys and Chloe were coloring at the coffee table, all looking a hell of a lot more bright-eyed and bushy-tailed than they'd been recently.

I stepped into the kitchen to hunt down something to eat but halted in the doorway.

Holden looked up from scrubbing out a frying pan, and he smiled. "Hey. You look a few degrees closer to human than you were last night."

"That has to be promising, right?" I coughed into my elbow and shuffled toward the fridge. "What are you doing here?"

"Tiffany went down a couple of hours ago." He nodded toward the hallway. "She's still asleep."

"Ha. And she said I had the man flu."

Holden chuckled. "That's typical Tiff—keep going until she's absolutely sure everything's under control, and the minute it is?" He made a gesture like a tree falling. "Timber."

"Ugh. Poor girl."

"Yeah. She should be okay, though. I'll check on her before I leave to be sure, but she seemed miserable in that 'this sucks but it'll pass' kind of way."

I blinked. It was still kind of strange to me how friendly they were. For a freshly divorced couple, they were doing all right.

Holden turned to me, features taut. "She was actually

pretty concerned about you. She was worried you were *really* sick."

"Nah, I'm good." I shuffled toward the fridge to get some Sprite for my tender throat. "Just an admittedly big baby when I feel like crap." I narrowed my eyes at him. "Speaking of which, why aren't *you* sick?"

Holden laughed dryly. "Oh, I'm sure I'm getting there."

"Really?"

"Uh-huh. Nobody escapes the annual respiratory massacre unscathed."

I tsked as I started pouring myself some soda. "This was *not* mentioned in my packet from HR."

"Well, no. She didn't want to ruin the surprise."

"Hmph." I took a drink, pausing to let the fizz soothe my throat before I swallowed it. "You were a lifesaver last night, by the way." I capped the Sprite bottle. "I don't think either of us was in any frame of mind to take care of them."

"Don't mention it." He paused to rinse off the pan he'd been scrubbing. "They're my kids, remember?"

"I know. I know. I didn't mean to imply..." I chewed my lip and turned to put the Sprite back in the fridge. "Just...it was helpful. Is all I'm saying."

"With everything you've been doing for this family, I'm pretty sure Tiffany and I owed you one." When I faced him, his expression was full of sincerity. "Giving you a night off so you could get better seems like the least we could do."

"Well. Still. I appreciate it. I'm sure she does too."

He smiled, then cleared his throat and turned back to the dishes he'd been washing. "Listen, since you and Tiffany both still feel like crap, why don't I take them over to my place again?"

I chewed my lip. It really seemed like I should get Tiffany's input on this. It wasn't my decision to make, after all. But Tiffany was sick enough I shouldn't wake her up, I was too sick to be useful, and Holden was healthy, coherent, *and* their father. Plus Ashley was sick now. So I supposed it was kind of a no-brainer.

"Sure," I croaked.

"I'd take Ashley too, but that apartment is so tiny..." He grimaced.

"I'll be okay." Ashley appeared in the doorway and coughed into her elbow. "Thanks, though."

"You sure?" Holden asked. "We can make space."

"It's fine." She smiled as brightly as anyone could be when they were sick and miserable. "I'm just going to watch TV and eat cough drops."

Holden nodded. "Okay. Well. If either of you need anything, you know how to reach me. We're only fifteen minutes away, so I can swing by Walgreens or whatever. Or Zach can when he gets off work."

"I'll keep that in mind," I said. "Thanks."

Another nod.

After he'd finished cleaning the kitchen, Holden checked on Tiffany. She was still asleep but didn't have much of a fever anymore, so that was encouraging. While she slept, I helped him get everything together for Chloe and the boys. By that point, Chloe had dozed off on the couch, so he carefully picked her up, and... Damn. There was something jaw-droppingly adorable about watching him walking out to the car with Chloe sound asleep on his hip with her head on his shoulder, and Ethan's hand in his free hand.

And you're worried it's too late for you to be their dad?

It was still pretty obvious at times that he was second-guessing himself left and right, feeling like he wasn't sure where he fit in the picture these days with his own family.

Like when he questioned if he'd packed everything each kid needed, or when he'd pause and silently have some internal debate. I couldn't tell what he was mentally flailing about, only that the uncertainty was definitely there.

He had this down more than he realized. Maybe he wasn't Tiffany's husband anymore, but he was stepping up and being Dad, and he was doing a damn good job of it.

And maybe I'd just had way too much cold medicine in the last twenty-four hours, but watching him play the uncertain-but-determined dad did seriously crazy things to my heart.

Do you have any idea how sweet you are with your kids? Or what that's doing to me?

TURNED OUT HOLDEN WAS RIGHT—THE MICROBE spared no one. He took the kids for the weekend so Tiffany and I could recover, and when I went to pick them up on Sunday, he had that telltale scratchiness in his voice. By Monday afternoon, he'd texted Tiffany and said he and Zach were both sick as dogs. Holden had even called in sick to work, which actually alarmed Tiffany because apparently he *never* called in sick.

"This is the guy who wouldn't call in sick when he had a damn kidney stone," she said that morning. "And he sure as hell isn't going to take a day off from a brand new job unless he's dying. I should make sure he doesn't need medical attention."

She'd called, but Zach answered, since apparently his dad was out cold thanks to the bug and several gallons of NyQuil.

"He'll be fine," Zach had apparently insisted. "He just doesn't want to get the rest of his office sick."

"Well, that explains it," she'd said after she'd hung up. "Kidney stones aren't contagious."

"So he'll take care of his coworkers, but not himself?"

"Holden in a nutshell, honey. Holden in a nutshell."

"And now I feel like a wuss for getting the man flu while Mr. Kidney Stone still goes to work."

Tiffany laughed, which didn't make her cough for once. "The gods favor no one. Some of those war wounds you've told me about?" She grimaced, shaking her head. "Holden may be able to knuckle through an illness or even a kidney stone, but make him bleed? Oh Lord."

I snorted. "Oh, he's one of *those*."

"Uh-huh. The sight of blood doesn't bother him. The sight of his own blood?" Another grimace.

"I had a few patients like that." I chuckled, leaning against the counter. "One probably just needed some super glue or a few Band-Aids, but the sight of blood made him pass out. Hit his head hard enough we had to take him in for a CT scan."

Tiffany smirked. "That would be Holden."

"God. Now I don't feel so bad about being a baby when I get sick."

She just rolled her eyes and laughed.

Finally, a week and a half or so after Chloe had woken up with a fever, everyone was well and truly on the mend. Zach and Holden still sounded vaguely scratchy, but everyone was back to work or school and running on all eight cylinders. None of us were getting the side-eye from the cashiers at Walgreens because we needed industrial-sized boxes of decongestant, though that one place would probably always regard Zach with some suspicion. He hadn't even realized why they were looking at him funny until he was halfway home and figured out that buying a huge stack of cold meds while wearing a Breaking Bad T-shirt didn't exactly convey *"nope, not cooking meth over here."*

Otherwise, things were mercifully back to normal in the Russell households.

With October here in full force, we were well into the Pacific Northwest's gray season. Days were wetter and cloudier, and I watched my weather apps like a hawk for windows where I could take the kids outside. Might as well enjoy it while we could. They were always happier when they got some time outside. I wasn't opposed to taking them out when it was wet or chilly—Tiffany and I had already talked about taking them into the mountains to go inner tubing this winter—but the nicer days were more enjoyable for everyone.

Today, the kids were off school for Columbus Day, and the weather was holding but could get sketchy in a hurry. If I piled them all in the car right now and took them to a park, by the time we got there, it could be wet and nasty.

Instead, I got everyone into their jackets and took them into the backyard to burn off some energy. Chloe and Noah wanted to play on the swings while Ethan was content to move mud around with a yellow Tonka bulldozer.

The swings were wet, so I wiped down the seats and chains with a towel. Once they were dry, I stepped aside. "All right. Have at it."

I helped Chloe onto one swing while Noah got on the other. I pushed her gently—as much as she could be a fearless daredevil, she didn't enjoy swinging high or fast like her brothers did. Given the nightmares I had of her falling off the swing like I'd seen a boy her age do at the playground?

That was fine by me, and I never encouraged her to do more than she was comfortable with.

Noah, however, was all for swinging as high and fast as he could.

"Stay in the swing," I warned as he pumped his legs to go higher. "No bailing out, okay?"

"I know." He sounded put out, just like always. He and Ethan loved bailing out of the swings here and at the park, and I was *more* than happy to enforce their mom's rule against it. I'd responded to too many calls for injuries that had started after some kid had swung high and flown out, thinking they'd be able to land without incident. They probably could most of the time, but the only times I ever saw them? Not so much.

Noah turned to me. "Hey, can you take a video for my dad?"

"Sure." I came around so Chloe could see me. "I'm gonna step away for a minute, okay? I'll be right over there." I pointed to a spot about eight feet away where I planned to stand.

She nodded and smiled. "'kay."

I smiled back. God, that kid was cute.

Then I took my place and pulled out my phone. "Ready?"

Noah nodded. I pressed Record and gave him a thumbs up.

He waved at the camera. "Hi, Dad!"

I grinned, watching him swing and make faces. Holden was going to love this. I was about to stop the video when Noah said, "Dad, watch this!"

And a second too late, I realized what he was about to do.

"Noah, don't."

But as the swing came forward, he did—he bailed out.

Before I could even move, he landed on the hard, slippery ground.

Toppled over.

Grabbed his foot.

And cried.

CHAPTER 13

HOLDEN

During meetings, I always kept my phone on silent but face up on the table beside me in case something urgent came through. If a notification lit up the screen, I'd steal a glance, but otherwise leave it until after the meeting.

Today, as I sat with my boss and a couple of colleagues discussing sales strategies for wooing a potential new client, the notification that popped up on my phone stopped me mid-sentence.

Porter: FYI, not serious but taking Noah to Urgent Care. Injured foot.

"Holden?" David, one of my colleagues, prodded.

"Um." I cleared my throat. "I'm sorry. I just got an emergency message from home. One of my kids—"

"Go, go." My boss, Sarah, all but shoved me out of my chair. "We'll fill you in on everything via email."

"Thank you." I grabbed my phone and laptop and hurried out of the conference room. This had actually been one of the big selling points of this job—the company understood that people had lives outside of work, and that family emergencies really were emergencies. I cringed at the thought of taking off like this just days after I'd been out sick—way to make an impression at a new job—but there wasn't much to be done about it.

On the way to the car, I fought the urge to call Porter and get a rundown of the situation. He needed to focus on my son, not on conveying everything to me. Instead, I texted to ask which Urgent Care location he'd be using, and then hurried down to my car. By the time I reached the parking lot, he'd responded with an address, which I put into my GPS.

Thank God, it was only twenty-five minutes away. Well, fifteen when the driver was a worried father.

I parked, hurried inside, and went up to the receptionist. "My son is here. Noah Russell?"

She peered up at me. "Can I see some ID, sir?"

There was a part of me that wanted to get frustrated, but I reminded myself that this policy was in place to protect patients. If some strange asshole showed up asking to see my kid, they better show some goddamned ID, so I wasn't about to complain about being asked to do the same.

After she'd looked at my driver's license, the receptionist summoned a nurse. The nurse came out through the door beside the desk and motioned for me to follow her. "Right this way, Mr. Russell." She led me down a short hallway, knocked quietly on a closed door, and then pushed it open. "Noah, honey? Someone's here to see you."

I stepped into the room. From the gurney, Noah took one look at me and crumpled into tears.

"Hey, hey." I sat beside him and wrapped my arms around him. "It's okay, buddy. I'm here." He leaned into me and cried as I stroked his hair. "What happened?"

"I hurt my foot," he said through his tears.

Porter sat in a chair opposite me, grimacing as he watched us silently.

Still holding onto Noah, I asked him the same question: "What happened?"

Porter frowned. "They were playing on the swings in the backyard. He bailed out and landed on some uneven ground." He gestured at Noah's left foot, which was wrapped in icepacks and ACE bandages, and propped up on a couple of pillows. "It was swelling up and bruising, and he couldn't put weight on it, so I didn't want to take any chances. Brought him here."

I nodded, still stroking Noah's hair. "Where are Chloe and Ethan?"

"At a neighbor's house." He must have seen the renewed concern in my eyes, because he added, "She babysits them all the time when Tiffany and I can't be there."

"Okay. Okay, good." I didn't know the neighbor, but if Tiffany trusted her, that was good enough for me.

Noah was starting to calm down, and he pulled back, wiping his eyes on his sleeve.

"You okay, buddy?" I asked.

He nodded. "It hurts."

"I know." I squeezed his shoulder. "Is the ice helping?"

He looked down at his foot, then nodded again. "A little."

I turned to Porter. "Has the doctor said anything?"

"Not yet. They did an X-ray when we first got here." He shrugged tightly. "Just waiting to hear back."

"Any idea how long it'll be?"

Porter exhaled, glancing at the door, and shrugged. "In a place like this? Anybody's guess. Just depends on how many people are ahead of us and if anything is more urgent."

I sat on the edge of the gurney and patted my son's leg. "Guess it's just as well we're here and not at the ER, then."

Porter shuddered but said nothing. Then he tugged his phone out of his pocket, opened up a game, and handed it to Noah, which kept him entertained while we waited for the doctor to come back with his X-ray results. He and I didn't say much. I was wound too tight, worried sick about what those X-rays might show, and Porter seemed... Hell, I couldn't put my finger on it. He was quiet, but twitchy—knee bouncing with the rapid tapping of his heel, his whole body shifting constantly as if he couldn't get comfortable. It was hard to tell under the fluorescent lights, but I swore there was a hint of sweat at his hairline.

What was I supposed to be reading into that? A paramedic this nervous over the results of my son's X-rays? How bad *was* Noah's foot?

Half an hour after I arrived, there was another knock at the door, and this time, it was Tiffany.

Noah teared up again, which made me think maybe he wasn't in horrific pain. Not after he'd sobbed to me, calmed down enough to play a game, and was now sobbing on his mom. That was encouraging, actually—chances were he'd scared himself more than anything, and while his foot certainly hurt, it most likely wasn't a catastrophic fracture. I hated seeing him upset and in pain, but it was a relief that the injury was probably more bark than bite.

Except...Porter. He was still tense and fidgety. And yeah, there was definitely some sweat gleaming on his forehead. His inability to relax was doing nothing for mine. Noah wasn't in as much pain as he'd initially seemed, but Porter wasn't drawing an easy breath. What the hell?

Finally, a woman who seemed way too young to be a doctor—Christ, I was getting old—came into the room. She introduced herself to all of us, then tapped a flat screen on the wall. Some X-rays appeared. "Well, the X-ray didn't show any fractures."

Tiffany, Porter, and I immediately released our breaths.

The doctor gave us a sympathetic smile before she went on. My mind was going in too many directions to hold on to everything she said, but the gist was that Noah had a moderate sprain. Ice, elevation, ibuprofen. Crutches for a couple of days until he could comfortably put weight on it. No running or strenuous activity, including soccer, which apparently they were playing in P.E. at school.

Noah was mildly disappointed he wouldn't get a cool cast for all his friends to sign, but the soccer ban brought fresh tears to his eyes. "I can't play?"

"Sorry, honey." Tiffany leaned over the gurney and kissed his forehead. "Not until your foot feels better."

Beside her, Porter exhaled. He wiped a hand over his face and rolled his shoulders. Then he rose. "Listen, um, since everything's under control in here, I'm going to step out for a second."

"Sure." Tiffany flashed a quick smile at him. "Thanks for everything."

His smile was tight, and he quietly said, "Don't mention it."

Then he slipped out.

I glanced at Noah, then at the door Porter had gone through. What the hell had he been so twitchy about? He was a medical professional himself, for God's sake. That had been a hiring point. But he freaked out over what turned out to be a sprain? What if this had been something serious? I was supposed to trust him with my kids when he couldn't keep it together in the face of an emergency? One that had happened on *his* watch?

Anger had my feet moving before I could think twice, and I followed him down the hallway. "Hey. Porter."

He turned around, his jaw tight and his face faintly flushed. "Hey. I just need—"

"It's just a sprain," I hissed, gesturing back at the room. "So why were you freaking out in there? And why the hell is he even here if we could have just handled this at home?"

Porter blinked, but then his features hardened. "I told you. It was bruising quickly and he can't walk on it. That could mean a fracture, so I—"

"You couldn't have run it by Tiffany or me before you made that decision? Do you know how expensive this kind of thing is?"

He narrowed his eyes. "Do you want me to wait when your son might have a broken foot?"

"Did you really think it was broken? Or did you just panic?"

Porter's eyes widened but only for a second. Glaring right back at me, he ground out, "I thought that if I were an EMT responding to a call, and I saw that much bruising on a foot a kid couldn't put weight on, that I'd damn sure tell his parents to take him in and get it X-rayed." He stepped closer and lowered his voice slightly. "I know how much this kind of thing costs, okay? I saw, every single day, the effects of healthcare being so expensive, to the point people didn't get help until long after they needed to. Believe me, I am the last person you need to be lecturing about how much this costs."

I narrowed my eyes. "How the fuck did he even *get* hurt like that? Were you watching him, or—"

"*Hey.*" Porter stepped right up into my face. "I get that you're freaked out that your son got hurt. I fucking get it, and I would be too." He stabbed a finger at me. "But don't take it out on me. You wouldn't have been able to stop him from getting hurt any more than I did, and you'd have done the same damn thing I did by bringing him in here. And you'd have been rattled too, all right? Paramedic or not, I'm human, and yeah, seeing your son get hurt like that shook me up. So *back off*."

He didn't wait for a response before he turned on his heel and stalked down the hallway.

I stared at his back. As he disappeared around the corner, I leaned against the wall and sighed. Christ, I suddenly felt like a dick. Porter had me dead to rights. Hell, I'd literally watched in helpless horror as Zach had fallen off his bike and broken his arm in two places. There'd been nothing I could do then, and there'd probably been nothing Porter could have done today.

And truth be told, I'd have brought Noah in for an X-ray even if his foot hadn't been that bruised. I'd have handled the situation exactly the same way Porter had, twitchiness and all, and I had no right to be lashing out at him because I felt guilty that I hadn't been there. Or because I'd misread signals Porter might not have even known he was sending.

I poked my head in to make sure Tiffany and Noah were still doing all right. Then I followed Porter.

He wasn't in the waiting room, so I stepped out onto the sidewalk.

I found him leaning against the brick wall, bent over with his eyes closed and his hands on his thighs. He didn't look up or say anything. He was probably hoping I wouldn't say anything either.

As I came closer, though, I realized his knees were shaking. He was breathing slowly and deeply, the way people did when they were trying to pull themselves together. The way he swallowed made me think he was trying like hell not to throw up, and I couldn't be sure he was winning that particular battle.

I approached cautiously. "Porter?"

He tensed but didn't open his eyes. He swallowed again, harder this time.

"Hey, are you all right?"

He nodded and put up a shaky finger as if to say *give me a second*.

My stomach clenched. What the hell?

After a moment, he rolled his shoulders. Slowly, he straightened up and leaned fully against the wall. He breathed deeply for a moment, then ran an unsteady hand through his sweat-dampened hair. "Sorry. I..." He moistened his lips. "I'm good."

"You sure?"

Porter nodded again, looking anything but good.

"Okay. Well. Listen, I came out here to apologize for coming at you sideways in there. And I will definitely get to that, but... Seriously, are you all right?"

Jaw working, he nodded, and he finally croaked, "Just, um... Didn't want Tiffany or Noah to see..." He exhaled and wiped his hand over his face.

"See what, exactly?" I took a cautious step closer. "What's going on?"

Porter's shoulders sank. Eyes closed, he pressed back against the brick wall. "This is why I quit being a paramedic," he whispered shakily, as if the admission physically hurt to say out loud. "Couldn't..." He swallowed hard again, like he was *really* struggling not to throw up. "Every time I finished a call, I'd lose it."

"Lose it?" I furrowed my brow. "How do you mean?"

Porter moistened his lips. "The stress. It got to me. A lot

of EMTs get burned out, and I kept pushing through even after I burned out." He laughed bitterly. "Maybe if I'd given up sooner I wouldn't have fucking PTSD from it. Not as bad, at least."

I blinked. "Holy shit. So this..." I gestured at the clinic. "Is this a trigger for you?"

Cheeks darkening, Porter lowered his gaze and nodded. "I can keep it together in the moment. While I've got something to focus on and someone's depending on me, I can handle it. The minute it's over and I'm by myself and I can actually think?" He shook his head. "It all comes crashing in." He rubbed his eyes and dropped his hand. "Then it's just a question of how bad the flashbacks and panic attack will be, and whether I can talk myself through it."

"So you..." I stared at him. "You brought Noah in and took care of him, knowing this was going to trigger a panic attack?"

Porter lifted his head and met my eyes. "What was I supposed to do? He was my responsibility, and he was hurt."

And I thought I'd felt like an asshole on my way out here.

"I knew I could hold it together until the situation was over," he went on. "I'd just need a few minutes afterward for..." He gestured at himself.

"What if Tiffany or I hadn't been here?" I tried to keep my voice gentle so he didn't think I was accusing him.

"Worst case scenario?" He swallowed. "Tell Noah I needed to use the restroom, ask a nurse to keep an eye on him, and step out for a few minutes." He searched my eyes. "I can still do my job and take care of them. I'm not—"

"No, I get that. I do. But I'm thinking you could stand to take the rest of the night off."

Porter straightened up so suddenly, I was surprised he didn't crack his head against the bricks. "What? Look, I'm serious. I can still do my job. I—"

"Relax." I patted the air. "I'm not questioning whether you can do your job. But I was an asshole to you in there, and I feel like I owe you a break. And quite possibly a drink."

He stared at me uneasily.

I sighed. "You did everything you should have done for my son. I was completely out of line. Let me at least try to make up for some of that."

Porter chewed his lip, glancing at the clinic. "What about the kids? I'm still on for a few more hours."

"I'll work it out with Tiffany."

He studied me uncertainly. Then he deflated as if all the fight had gone out of him, and he gave a subtle nod. "Okay. Thanks."

"Wait right here."

CHAPTER 14

PORTER

THE AFTERNOON HAD BEEN A ROLLER COASTER, THAT was for sure.

Now I was standing outside the Urgent Care clinic, hating the way my T-shirt stuck to my sweaty skin and hating even more that Holden had seen me like that. I'd hoped like hell I could keep myself together until I was home with the kids. Maybe disappear to the bathroom for a two-minute freak-out and hope no one noticed.

But I'd known without a doubt it would happen sooner or later, regardless of whether anyone saw it, which was why I'd texted Tiffany and Holden. Even though I'd had everything under control, and there was no reason for them to leave work and run code to the clinic, I'd quietly hoped they would get here and take over, if only so I could step away and have my breakdown in peace.

I sure as hell hadn't expected Holden to tear into me just before I fell apart, never mind come out and try to both help and apologize. It couldn't have been that long between when he'd bitten my head off and when he'd come outside. It *felt* like ages for me because time went all wonky when this happened, but I knew it had been a few minutes at most.

And now he wanted to take me out and make up for being an asshole and talk to me about everything, and with the way the afternoon had been going, I couldn't begin to guess how *that* would go.

While he was inside the clinic, though, presumably working out logistics with Tiffany, I stole the opportunity to calm myself down a bit more. I'd known the instant I'd made the decision to take Noah to the clinic that this was coming. Just taking my mom's dog to the vet last fall for a couple of stitches had kicked off a spiral like this. Handling first aid stuff at home? No sweat. Splinters, cuts, bruises, scrapes, burns—got it. The minute there was transport to a medical facility, even if the "patient" was a foul-tempered toy poodle in a carrier on the passenger seat of my car, my brain went into ambulance mode. Then we'd get there, and the familiarity—the smell of disinfectant, the dingy white linoleum, the florescent lights, the lab coats—would send me back, and all those synapses that couldn't cope with being an EMT anymore kicked into gear.

As soon as I'd come home from the vet and handed off the freshly cone-of-shamed dog to my mom, I'd gone into the bathroom and puked. Everyone had teased me about not being able to handle blood or stitches, and I'd let them because it was easier than telling them my mind had turned into a horror show of mangled limbs, torn flesh, arterial spray, and futile chest compressions. They wouldn't have understood the feeling of *"the patient lived this time, but it's only a matter of time before you can't save one,"* and how real and present that felt even months after I'd resigned.

This afternoon, my gut had told me Noah's ankle was sprained, and that ice, elevation, and a tight bandage would do the trick. But the bruising and his inability to put any weight on it at all—I just couldn't take the chance. So I'd brought him in, and I'd prayed like hell the entire time that I could rein in the panic and flashbacks until I could hand off Noah to his parents. He needed an adult who was focused and calm, and he definitely didn't need to see me in the throes of a full-on flashback. If only for Noah's sake, I'd had to keep it together, and by some miracle, I had.

Holden chewing me out had probably helped, actually—the anger had tamped everything else down until I could get outside and out of sight. I hadn't banked on him coming after me. And apologizing. And being concerned. And now...this? Taking me out for a drink? Calling today a roller coaster was no exaggeration.

He came out of the clinic, keys in hand. "You ready?"

I glanced at his keys. "What about my car?"

"We'll come get it later." He gestured toward his. "I'll drive for now."

I didn't argue. As much as it killed me to admit it, I wasn't in any shape to drive right then. Fortunately, he didn't make me admit it. We just got into his car, left the clinic, and went looking for a place to grab a drink and maybe some food.

That didn't take long. There was a bar and grill type restaurant not far from the clinic, and we snagged a booth in the bar. It was quieter in here, especially this time of day, and God knew I needed that.

My stomach was still too queasy to think about eating, but an ice-cold beer sounded good.

I cautiously met Holden's gaze across the table. "Would you, um, think less of me if I ordered a beer?"

He shook his head. "No. I did say I was buying you a drink."

"I know, but I..."

"Don't sweat it. I might get one myself."

"Really?"

He nodded and didn't elaborate. Fine by me. Because I really did need that fucking drink.

We ordered, and after our beers had come, we both drank in silence for a moment. And oh, yeah, this was exactly what I needed. I didn't drink to self-medicate as a general rule, but I figured a beer after one of these episodes was acceptable. It didn't happen very often, after all, and the beer soothed the remaining anxiety skittering along my nerves. I wasn't looking any gift horses in the mouth tonight.

After we'd each finished about half our beers, Holden pushed his aside and folded his hands on the table. "So what happened outside the clinic—that's from being a paramedic?"

I nodded, staring into my beer. "A lot of us—first responders, I mean—wind up with PTSD, and it plays out differently from one to the next. For me, it's jumping out of my skin at alarms and sirens, and crashing after a medical situation."

"Crashing?" He tilted his head. "Like a panic attack?"

"Kind of. Sometimes." I sighed and leaned back against the bench. "Sometimes I just feel kind of shaky and break a sweat. Sometimes... Yeah, sometimes it can be a full-blown panic attack."

"Jesus." He was quiet for a moment, and though I could see wheels turning in his head, I had no idea where his mind was going. If he was going to grill me about my triggers and panic attacks or what. Finally, he took a sip of his beer and quietly asked, "How long were you a paramedic?"

Okay, that was an easy enough line of questioning. I wrapped my hands around my beer bottle, letting the condensation on the bottle be the reason for my clammy hands instead of having sweaty palms. "I lasted eight years. Most of the EMTs I worked with made it to five before they started itching to get out of the ambulance. Some people look for promotions or admin type jobs so they're still in the department, just not on the ambulance anymore. Others..." I shook my head. "When it's time to get off the bus, it's time to get off the bus, and if that means quitting, so be it."

"I never realized it was that bad."

"I didn't either. And I didn't believe everyone who told me. When you first start, it's not so bad. It's an exciting job, and you feel like you're actually helping people." I exhaled, my shoulders sinking under an invisible weight that had been there for so fucking long. "But then you realize it's nonstop. One minute, you're helping a twelve-year-old who's in diabetic shock. Then you're getting called out to a horrific car accident. Then it's some freak accident on a construction site. After that, if you're lucky, it's lunch."

"Whoa. So you're seeing all of that in one shift."

I nodded. "One thing after another. The first time you have your hands on someone when they die, it changes you. And you kind of expect it to get easier over time. Like you might get numb to it? But then you *do* start getting numb to it, and that fucks with your head because you literally felt someone's heart stop beating, and it affects you, but not as much as you feel like it should. Except at the same time, you can feel that person's death on top of all the other deaths you've witnessed, and it's just so fucking much to—"

Holden's hand on my arm startled me. So did the realization that his touch had stilled the shaking I hadn't noticed. Not even when the bottle had started rattling against the table, a sound I only noticed when it stopped.

I took a slow, deep breath and nudged the beer bottle

away before I sent it flying off the table. "Sorry. I'll be okay. Just gonna be shaky for a few hours, probably."

"Has it been better since you quit?"

"Better, yeah. I still jump out of my skin if an alarm goes off, even if I know it's just the smoke detector telling us all that Ashley's trying to cook. But sirens... medical emergencies..." I shivered. "Alarms and sirens make me jump. Minor things, like putting a Band-Aid on a cut or icing a bump or bruise? That's easy. Once it becomes a situation where there are hospitals and clinics involved? That trips the switch in my head."

"So it's not the emergency itself. It's the venue."

"Kind of. Minor injuries still give me a jittery feeling, but it's not a big deal. Actually transporting someone to a medical facility kicks my inner first responder into gear. Something about, well, ambulating someone—it takes me back to being on the ambulance."

"And that's...common?"

"PTSD is, yeah." I rolled my shoulders to try to get ahead of the stiffness creeping up my back and into my neck. "It's affected everyone I know differently. I used to ride with one EMT who gets a jolt of adrenaline every time she hears sirens, and it takes her a while to come back down after. A guy from another shift can barely function because he has so many nightmares, he can't sleep. And then there are others who just got burned out and had to move on to another career, and for the most part, they're fine now." I wrung my hands under the table to channel some nervous energy. "It could've been a lot worse, though. One of my mentors is on full disability now because the job destroyed his spine."

Holden's eyes widened. "Whoa. Seriously?"

I nodded. "Oh yeah. Nobody makes it through a career

as an EMT without some back problems. You're contorting into weird positions, lifting people onto stretchers, getting thrown around in the back of an ambulance, sometimes getting attacked by patients. Knee and back problems are pretty much a given."

"So you have problems too?"

"Not as bad as my mentor, but my knees are about a decade and a half older than the rest of me, and my neck and back get sore faster than they should." I picked up my beer and took a deep pull. "I'm lucky—I didn't get any serious injuries, and the PTSD doesn't run my life. I've known combat vets and EMTs who have it a lot worse than I do. I can function normally ninety-nine percent of the time, but sirens, any kind of medical emergency—it all trips the synapses that don't know I'm not a paramedic anymore."

"Like what happened today," he said softly, a hint of a grimace on is face.

I nodded. "That's the worst of it for me. That, and nightmares sometimes."

"But it only happens *after* an emergency." He took a sip from his own beer. "You seemed pretty calm and cool during."

"Yeah, definitely. The trigger isn't the emergency itself. It's when it's over. Once it is, then my brain shifts into..." I chewed my lip. "It's hard to explain. The emergency gives me a jolt of adrenaline, but when it's over, once the situation is under control, I'm expecting the next call to come from dispatch. It's like the worst part isn't the situation I'm dealing with now. It's what might be coming *next*. Because on a really busy shift, it could be one horrific thing after another, and that was always what got to me the most—no matter what we saw or dealt with on a call, it could *always* be worse, and I never knew what we'd have to deal with next."

"Wow. I... I'll be honest. I never even thought about how that job must affect people who do it."

"Neither did I," I said dryly. "Not until I was studying to become one."

"But you did it anyway?"

"Well yeah. I mean, someone has to. And don't get me wrong—I don't regret becoming a paramedic. I'm glad I have the education I have from being one. But go back to it?" I shook my head. "Not a chance. I literally have nightmares about being on the ambulance again."

"I bet." Holden tapped his thumb on the table as he studied me. I cringed inwardly, expecting him to come at me with some comment to downplay what I was dealing with, or maybe suggest I wasn't fit to take care of his kids if I couldn't take care of myself. I definitely didn't expect him to ask, "Is there any way Tiffany or I can help?"

I blinked. "What?"

"Well, I mean, if something like today happens again..." He laughed softly. "And knowing my kids, it will." Sobering, he met my gaze. "Is there anything we can do for you?"

I stared at him, literally speechless.

He must have taken my silence for not understanding, because he went on. "Obviously in a situation like today, one of us will be there as soon as we can. We're at the mercy of jobs and traffic, but..."

"No, I get that," I whispered. "And I can handle the situation. Even if you're both hung up somewhere." I swallowed. "I'm not going to freak out on your kids."

"I don't imagine you will. It looked to me like you held it together until Noah was in someone else's hands and you were on your own."

Cheeks burning, I nodded. "I'm always good until the situation is completely over. Then, well..."

"Right. So that's why I'm asking. What can we do?"

"There isn't really much anyone can do. I just have to sort of ride it out and let it run its course."

He furrowed his brow. "Have you tried therapy? Anxiety meds? Something?"

The heat in my face intensified, and shame twisted in my stomach as I shook my head. "No. Not yet. I guess I thought it would get better with time."

"It hasn't?"

"It's..." I hesitated, not sure how far to tip my hand to the man trusting me with his kids. Then again, since he *was* trusting me with his kids, he deserved the truth. "It's gotten better, but it's going to be a long road." I watched him uneasily. "If you're worried I'm not safe for the kids to be around, then I—"

"No, no." He dismissed that idea with a sharp shake of his head. "Honestly after today, that's definitely not an issue."

"It isn't?"

"No." Holden sighed, shoulders sinking, and he stared down at his hands. "You said yourself the trigger is taking someone to a medical facility. And even though you knew what you were setting yourself up for, you erred on the side of caution for my son and took him in." He met my eyes, his expression more intense than I'd ever seen it. "If I didn't have faith in you before, I do now."

I gulped. "I had to. His ankle, it was—"

"It was a judgment call. You could have easily iced it, elevated it, and hoped for the best, and we both know *now* that he probably would have been fine."

"I didn't know that in the moment."

"How likely did you think it was he'd broken something?"

I squirmed under his scrutiny. "Not very. Just that... That if he did, it was better to treat it sooner than later."

Holden was nodding before I'd even finished speaking. "Even if it meant triggering your PTSD."

"Yeah."

"You prioritized my son's health and well-being. There's really not much more a parent could ask for." He sat up, folding his arms on the edge of the table. "But I also don't want you *de*-prioritizing yourself. No one's in this to compromise *your* health and well-being. So if there's anything we can do, just say so."

I nodded, my throat suddenly tight, and my voice was thick as I said, "I'll keep that in mind. Thanks."

"Don't mention it." Some of the intensity in his expression eased. "So, out of curiosity, how did you get from working as a paramedic to taking care of kids? I get why you left that job, but why childcare?"

I laughed self-consciously. "Desperation, I guess?"

Holden cocked his head.

I cleared my throat and sat up a little, dropping my gaze from his intense eyes to my own fingers absently rubbing at a crack in the hardwood table. "To tell you the truth, I started perusing ads for anything I could possibly qualify for. A friend told me about a website where people hire for handyman type stuff and domestic help, and I thought, well, it would at least keep the cash flowing until I found something more permanent. That's where I found Tiffany's ad."

"And you like it?"

"Oh hell yeah. Especially since there's so much less pressure than my last job."

Holden chuckled. "And here I am struggling to remember how to parent, but it's an easy job for you."

"I didn't say it was easy. It's just less pressure. The pressure in that field is *wild*. There were so many ways I could mess up and kill or cripple someone. This parenting thing? It's easy. Well, I mean, not *easy*. But it's not hard in the sense that if I don't make the right split-second decision, I could miss an internal decapitation or arterial bleed. With the kids, if I accidentally teach them a swear word or they eat a bug, it's not the end of the world."

Holden furrowed his brow, then laughed. "I never thought of that, but I guess you're right. Kind of puts things in perspective, doesn't it?" He sighed, shaking his head. "I'm not gonna lie. When all this started, I thought it was a little weird, a guy taking care of my kids. Not because I thought you might be less qualified, or that you might not be safe. Just that you're the male figure in their lives these days. More than me."

"You're still their dad, though," I said softly. "Nothing I do is ever going to change that."

"Nothing *you* do, no." He swallowed. "It's on me, not you. And I guess when I first moved here, I thought you were... you know, competition."

"I don't want to be, if that makes a difference. I'm just here to make sure they're taken care of during the day and Tiffany isn't overloaded. There's nothing that says we can't all work together, you know?"

Holden nodded, and a faint smile finally broke through. "Yeah. I think it's become pretty clear that we can."

As I held his gaze across the table, I had to admit that despite the head-butting earlier, I felt better than I had since I'd first met Holden. I'd always believed we could work together. Tonight, more than ever, I believed he *wanted* to work with me.

Our server appeared beside us, making us both jump, and the moment was broken.

"Can I get you anything to eat?" he asked.

Holden looked at me again. "You hungry?"

When we'd first arrived, I'd been too queasy to even think about food, but now? Yeah, I was feeling a lot better. And hell yeah, I was hungry. "Uh, I could eat." I picked up the menu that had been lying neglected on the table this entire time. "Might need a minute or two, though."

"No problem." The server smiled. "I'll be right back."

CHAPTER 15

HOLDEN

With the air cleared between us, Porter and I perused the menu and ordered dinner. By the time it arrived, we'd shifted gears completely from our fraught conversation to something blessedly lighter.

Namely, our exes.

"So this one guy I dated?" Porter tsked. "He was a total badge bunny. He *loved* cops."

"But he was dating a paramedic?"

"Well, yeah," he said dryly. "Because I was gone for three days at a stretch for my shifts, so he could happily spend that time blowing his way through every police department within two hundred miles."

"You're shitting me."

"Nope." He stabbed a piece of steak with his fork as if for emphasis. "I probably wouldn't have found out when I did, except he and Officer Common Sense were screwing around in the squad car when he had to respond to a call."

I grimaced. "Don't tell me—you responded to the same call."

"Bingo. The officer pulls up, and there's my boyfriend,

sitting in the front seat looking like the dog that shit on the living room carpet."

"Holy crap." I laughed. "I suppose it was good that there were cops *and* medics there?"

Porter chuckled, shaking his head. "Eh, it wasn't that bad. Couple of the firefighters loudly asked if they should turn the hose on him, and the look on his face was pretty priceless when he thought I was going to take them up on it."

"Yeah, I can imagine. I assume that was the end of things with him?"

"Oh yeah. By the time my shift was over the next day, he'd moved his shit out of my apartment and basically ghosted me. Which..." He smirked. "Don't let the door hit you, jackass."

"Good for you. Life's too short for that shit."

"Seriously." He sipped his water, and his eyes sparkled with mischief as he met mine. "So tell me about some of your exes. I can't be the only one at this table with some '*I can't believe I ever dated that idiot*' stories."

"No, you're not." I thought for a moment. "Okay, before Tiffany and I started dating, I had this boyfriend..." I sighed and rolled my eyes. "Brett. Fucking *Brett*."

Porter laughed so hard he almost choked. "Oh my God. That's literally *exactly* how Tiffany described him."

"What? She mentioned him?"

"Uh-huh." He cleared his throat and took a quick sip from his water. "She used those exact words. Complete with the sigh. No joke."

"Oh. Really?"

"Uh-huh. Sounds like he was a, uh, popular dude."

"Oh my *God*." I rolled my eyes again. "And Tiffany

knew him longer than I did. I swear she and I bonded over commiserating about the guy."

"Wow." Porter laughed. "That bad?"

"He's... I mean, he's not a *bad* guy. He's actually pretty sweet, and we're still in contact." I took a breath. "But no one—not even my oldest son's mother—has ever been as high maintenance as fucking *Brett*."

"Do tell."

"Ugh. Where do I start?" I cut off a piece of chicken and dragged it through some barbecue sauce. "For one thing, I should have known when he was hesitant about dating a single dad. But I figured, hey, everyone's going to think twice about that, right? Then he decided he was okay with it...for a while."

Porter cocked his head. "What changed?"

"He realized that primary custody meant I had my son more often than not, and that no, we really couldn't pawn him off on his mother or a babysitter every damn night so we could go out."

"For fuck's sake. How old was Zach during all this?"

"He was about Ethan's age. And I mean, he's always been a pretty low-key kid."

"Yeah, but come on. It isn't like you can just leave him at home with the remote and a can of Chef Boyardee at that age."

"Right? I think I knew it was time to bail when I realized dating him basically made me a single father of two, and..." I shook my head. "No, thanks."

"Oh God." Porter wrinkled his nose. "That would've sent me out the door too. Like I don't mind dating someone with kids, but I don't want to be my partner's parent."

"Yes! Exactly." I ate a piece of chicken, and after I'd

swallowed that, said, "He also had this weird hang up about dating a bi guy."

Porter's eyebrows quirked. "Seriously?"

"Yep. Some guys do. Hell, some women do. But I swear, every time an attractive woman so much as walked through my peripheral vision, he'd start accusing me of checking her out and wanting to bang her instead of being with him."

"If he was that focused on women, maybe he was bi too."

I snorted. "I actually suggested that once. He was *not* amused."

"Imagine that." Porter laughed wickedly, unaware of what that was doing to my pulse. "It must be exhausting to be that insecure."

"Ha! You want to talk about insecurity?" I picked up my drink. "Let me tell you about when we went to my sister's wedding…"

As we compared notes on exes and laughed about past relationships, it was hard to picture the two of us facing off in the clinic's hallway. It was surreal to imagine that happening within the past hour or so.

About the time we'd finished eating and had gotten refills on our water, Porter glanced at his phone, and straightened. "Oh crap. It's almost six." He met my eyes. "We should check in with Tiffany. Make sure Noah's doing all right."

"He's probably fine if she hasn't called, but…" I took out my phone. "It wouldn't hurt to check in." I pulled up her contact and sent the call.

"Hey," she said.

"Hey. How's Noah doing?"

"He's good. The doctor just said to keep it wrapped, iced, and elevated, so he has an excuse to sit back and play video games." She laughed. "His foot hurts, but he doesn't complain very loudly with a controller in his hands."

I chuckled. "That sounds like a good sign. Is he going to be okay to go to school tomorrow?"

Porter's eyebrows shot up.

"I'll see how he feels in the morning. It's just a sprain, but he's still having a tough time walking on it, so it might not be a bad idea to keep him home for a day. Just to rest it."

"Okay. Text me and let me know what you decide, okay?"

"Of course. Is Porter still with you?"

I met his gaze again across the table. "Yeah, we're getting some dinner."

"Some—oh." The silence on the other end needled at me, as did her flat tone when she said, "How is that going?"

"Fine." I schooled all the defensiveness out of my tone. Porter didn't need to know that Tiffany suspected—correctly—that I'd been looking at him "like that" recently. "He just needed to decompress after everything today. It kind of rattled him."

Porter dropped his gaze as he blushed.

More silence on the line, followed by a guarded, "Okay. Just dinner?"

"Yes."

"Okay." She sounded dubious, but she didn't push. "Okay, well, I'll let you go, and I'll keep you updated about Noah."

"Perfect. Thanks." I hung up and quickly filled Porter in.

He grimaced. "I feel bad leaving her to it, and for him getting hurt at—"

"Porter." I shook my head. "It wasn't your fault. And she's got everything under control."

"I know. I just..." He sighed, pressing an elbow onto the table and rubbing the back of his neck. "I just feel really bad. Both about what happened, and about keeping you away from him right now. Your son's hurt, and you're here dealing with my bullshit."

"It's not bullshit. Noah's in good hands. I, um, wanted to make sure you were, too."

He stared at me as if he wasn't sure he'd heard me right.

"Look, no one's an island in all of this," I went on. "That's literally one of the reasons Tiffany and I fell apart— she was doing all the work, being the single parent, and I wasn't taking care of her or the kids. Sure, I was paying the bills, but..." I hesitated, shame pressing down hard on my shoulders. "The night she told me she wanted a divorce, she asked me to think back to the last time I'd so much as asked how she was holding up. Even if my job demanded I travel most of the time, was it really too much to ask to check in and make sure she was doing all right? And the thing was, I couldn't—and still can't—remember the last time I asked her that. So, that's part of me trying to do things differently now. And since you're the one doing a lot of the legwork where the kids are concerned, it only makes sense for me to make sure you're all right too. And when you're not..." I spread my hands. "I should do something about that."

Porter blinked. "I... Wow. I really appreciate that. I mean, I'm the hired help, so I—"

"You're still a human and you're still doing a ton of work for the benefit of my kids." I paused. "And the part about feeling bad over what happened to Noah? If it's any consolation, Tiffany and I do the same thing."

He met my eyes, forehead creased. "What do you mean?"

"Any time one of the kids gets hurt, even if it wasn't

humanly possible for us to do a damn thing about it, we beat ourselves up for it. It's kind of par for the course."

Some of the tension melted out of his face, and he lowered his hand to the table. "Really?"

"Oh yeah. When Zach was five, he fell off his bike while I was watching him and broke his arm in two places." I winced, shaking my head. "It's been years, and just thinking about it still makes me cringe. I know up here"—I tapped my temple—"that there was nothing I could do. And ultimately, his arm healed, and he doesn't seem to have any lasting damage from it. But I didn't sleep for days after it happened just because I felt so damn guilty."

"Oh."

"I think that's why I came at you sideways earlier. I still feel guilty that my kids even *need* a nanny, because let's be real, I'm the one who fucked up my marriage, and that's why we're all living here now. So then when one of them got hurt, it was like this reminder that I should have been there. That it's..." I sighed. "That it's my fault neither of his parents were there when he got hurt."

"But you're not going to be there 24/7 for any of your kids. It's not possible."

"Not 24/7, no." I absently chased a green bean around my plate with my fork. "But with as often as I was gone over the last few years? I'm not gonna lie—it stings when something reminds me how much I haven't been there."

"You're obviously making up for lost time now." Porter smiled. "They haven't stopped raving about how much they love having you around these days."

Talk about a bittersweet reality. "That shouldn't be a novelty, you know?"

"But it's better than continuing the pattern you had before, right?"

"Okay, true." I exhaled. "I just, you know, hope that offers some perspective so you don't beat yourself up over what happened to Noah, and that I was an asshole for suggesting it was your fault. It could've just as easily happened on my watch, and I'd have taken him to the emergency room without a second thought. Not Urgent Care—the emergency room."

He held my gaze, then nodded, and a lopsided smile formed as he said, "So we'll just agree that no one's to blame for kids inevitably putting gravity to the test?"

I laughed. "Yeah. Yeah, we can agree to that." I paused, then sheepishly added, "Isn't like I didn't do the same shit when I was a kid."

"You and me both." He held up his right arm and pushed his sleeve back, revealing some barely visible scars under his wrist. "Got the pins and screws to prove it."

"Oh yeah? How'd you get those?"

Chuckling, he rolled his eyes and tugged his sleeve back into place. "So, there was this tree in my neighbor's backyard..."

As we shifted the conversation away from our guilt to the hijinks of our youth, the tension eased in my neck and shoulders. It seemed to leave his too—his features softened, and he was quicker to smile than he'd been all evening. I especially liked that part. Porter had a gorgeous smile, and I happily shared even the most embarrassing stories from childhood just so I could see him laugh. No, I still couldn't tell the story about the badly judged homemade bike jump when I was twelve without blushing, but it was worth it for the way his face lit up with a genuine, carefree laugh.

Part of it was sheer relief that he was on an even keel after things had been rough earlier today. Looking at him now, it was hard to fathom that he'd been talking himself down from a panic attack just a little while ago, or that he'd been beating himself up over being unable to stop my son from hurting his foot.

And part of it... Holy shit. Regardless of the circumstances that had led to us sitting here in this restaurant tonight, I had to admit I was completely mesmerized by him. With the tension gone and the head-butting forgotten, we were just two guys having a conversation over dinner, laughing at our own ridiculous histories, and God help me, but every time he smiled, my heart skipped.

Porter had been attractive since the day I'd met him, but tonight, he was...*attractive*. He was the first person to turn my head since my divorce, and as I spent time with him and actually talked to him, he was doing more than turn my head. He was smart, and he was level-headed even during a crisis. He could take control of a situation and keep everyone around him calm simply by being calm himself. When I'd stupidly lashed out at him, he'd stood his ground and hadn't taken shit from me.

It was like everything that had made him a good paramedic also made him someone I wanted in ways I probably shouldn't. He had a brain, he had a backbone, and he had a heart. Wrap that up with a pretty face and gorgeous body, and exactly *how* was I supposed to string together a coherent sentence around him? Every time I opened my mouth, I was sure something like "do you want to have a drink sometime when I'm *not* apologizing?" would tumble out.

Was I out of my mind, even fantasizing that there was a snowball's chance in hell that the attraction might be mutual? Or was it just wishful thinking fueled by glowing smiles and a few exchanged looks that lasted longer than they probably should have?

And, for that matter, some wishful thinking because connecting with Porter that way would mean skipping some of the bullshit that came with dating as a single parent. I remembered from the period after Zach's mom and before Tiffany how daunting it was returning to the dating pool. From the sound of it, it was ten times worse for moms than dads—there was a bigger stigma against single moms than single dads—but it was still more challenging for a parent than for someone who wasn't. Did I tell someone upfront that I had kids? Did I wait until we'd broken the ice a little? How soon did I introduce them? Would my kids like them?

If by some chance the planets aligned in my favor and I had even a glimmer of hope that Porter might be interested in me, all of those issues were moot. He already knew my kids. They adored him. He was well aware that I had an adult son as well as the three little ones. He even knew my ex-wife, and she and I both trusted him alone with our kids.

Christ, wouldn't that be a stroke of much-needed good luck? A smart, articulate, attractive man who knew I was a dad, loved my kids, and got along with my ex-wife? Which god did I need to sacrifice something to in order to get on *his* radar?

Assuming of course he had any interest at all in the forty-four-year-old single dad who was buying him dinner as a feeble attempt to make up for being a dick to him while he was right in the middle of fending off a goddamn panic attack. Because that kind of shit would sure endear someone to me. And assuming there was a chance in hell that anything could happen between us without Tiffany choking us both.

But a man could dream, right?

CHAPTER 16

PORTER

By the time we'd finished eating, I definitely felt better about things with Holden. I was exhausted, too. Everything with Noah had left me wrung out, and the conversation with Holden had been such a relief on so many levels, it had taken what energy remained. Tiffany had already known about the lingering issues from my old job, but Holden hadn't, and I was beyond relieved by the way things had gone after I'd told him.

It wasn't just that he understood my anxiety now. Something about the conversation had made things between us feel less...adversarial? Was that the word? Less tense, anyway. It hadn't even been that bad—so much less than I'd envisioned on day one—and tonight felt better. In fact, once we'd cleared the air tonight, things had actually been friendly. Maybe even—if I squinted hard enough—flirty.

Which clearly meant that one beer had been more than enough, and I needed to go home and sleep off the rest of my anxiety, because I was losing my mind. Flirty? Holden?

I wished. Except, no. No! That would be bad. Bad Porter! Bad!

After our friendly-and-not-at-all-flirty dinner, Holden drove us to where I'd left my car. We'd ended up staying later than I'd expected at the restaurant, so it was almost eight when we made it back. No surprise—the parking lot outside the Urgent Care clinic was dark and deserted.

He pulled in alongside my car and shifted into Park but left the engine idling.

I unbuckled my seat belt. "So, um. Thanks. I think I really needed this tonight. Talking to someone about it and..." I trailed off, not sure how to finish the thought.

"Don't mention it." He faced me, his features illuminated in the headlight beams ricocheting off the clinic's windows. "And listen, I meant what I said earlier—I really am sorry for the way I came at you earlier." Holden sighed. "Honestly, you're doing a great job with the kids. Tiffany raves about you all the time, and I can see why. I'm just running myself ragged trying to figure out how to be their dad again, which is no excuse to lash out at you. So...I'm sorry." He shook his head. "I was completely out of line. So we're clear, I really, *really* appreciate everything you've been doing for my kids, and I know they're in good hands when they're with you."

I smiled but wasn't sure what to say. Especially not when I was holding his gaze across the console. Somehow, I found my voice again, though. "I accept the apology. But I get it, okay? You're their dad, and I'm this guy who's come along and taken over a lot of the things dads do."

Holden winced.

I searched his eyes, then softly added, "If you're afraid I'm replacing you in their minds, I really don't think you have anything to worry about."

Holden studied me skeptically.

I chewed my lip. "When Noah got hurt today, he actually had me filming him on the swings. For you."

"Really?"

"Yeah." I pulled out my phone and queued up the video. Pressing my elbow onto the console, I held up the phone so he could see it and hit play.

On the screen, Noah was swinging on the swing set, and waved at the camera. "Hi, Dad!"

Holden laughed, and it was only then that I realized he'd leaned in close to see it. Fortunately I wasn't too distracted, and remembered to pause the video before Noah's ill-fated bailout.

"I'm glad they haven't forgotten about me," he said softly.

"No, they definitely—" I turned to him, and oh, yeah, we were sitting really close now. Like, *really* close. My pulse went into overdrive, and when his eyes flicked from mine to my lips... Oh my God. Now that our earlier clash was a distant memory, and I wasn't pissed at him and he wasn't snarling at me, and we'd had a heart-to-heart, and now that my post-call crash was over...

Holy shit. This man was the father of the kids I was paid to take care of. He was supposed to be, for all intents and purposes, my employer.

But I'd never caught myself staring into a boss's eyes like this. Had I ever worked for someone with eyes that intense or lips that perfect?

No, but I wasn't working for him. I was working for his ex-wife. Which meant it was a supremely bad idea to keep staring at him like this, regardless of the fact that he was staring back at me the same way. Or maybe because of that. One of us had to be the smart one and...do...something.

"I should go," I whispered, but I didn't move.

"Yeah. Probably." He didn't look away.

I did move this time, but not toward the door. He did the same, both of us gravitating toward each other. There was absolutely no misinterpreting the shrinking distance between us, and no pretending it was one of us moving in for the kill while the other passively waited for something to happen. No, he was leaning, and I was leaning, and my heart went wild as we narrowed the space enough to let me catch a hint of his aftershave. The way his eyes darted from mine to my lips? The way my whole body reacted when he subtly but noticeably moistened his own lips? Oh, fuck yeah, we both knew damn well where this was going.

We paused when we were so close that if I turned my head just a little, my nose would brush his. I could feel his breath, warm and ragged on my face, and I had no doubt he'd have been able to feel mine if I'd been able to breathe at all. We were right there. So close. One lifted chin away from crossing more lines than we already had. In my mind, we'd already crossed them, and I could already feel the softness of his lips against mine. I suddenly needed to know if his goatee would be soft or coarse against my chin, and—

And just like that, Holden jerked back. "God, what are we doing?"

I bit down on a defeated sigh as I returned to the passenger seat. "I have no idea."

We glanced at each other, then quickly broke eye contact, both fidgeting and clearing our throats.

"I'll um…" I fumbled with the door handle. It finally came open. "See you later, I guess."

"Yeah. Uh. See you later." He paused. "Thanks again for taking care of Noah today. And all the kids. Every—you know what I mean."

"I do, yeah. Thanks for dinner. And the beer."

"Don't mention it."

Our eyes locked again, and something about his expression told me I hadn't hallucinated that moment over the console, and that he was quietly freaking out over it too. It really happened. So now what?

Now it was definitely time to get out of his car.

I mumbled another thanks, then got out and hurried to my own car. He pulled away, and admittedly, I breathed a relieved sigh when his engine faded into the night. I paused before putting my key in the ignition, and I looked back at the empty space where his car had just been.

What in the holy fucking fuck had just happened?

And more to the point—what was going to happen now? Because there was no way either of us could pretend we hadn't almost kissed in his car, or that anything about the look in his eyes (and probably mine) meant that we would have stopped at just kissing.

Tiffany had made it clear she wasn't okay with this particular line being crossed, and I was bound and determined to respect that, but *damn*. Now I knew Holden really had been looking at me like that. Whatever had been going on in my head, he reciprocated, and there was something crackling between us, and in the name of staying employed and respecting Tiffany's boundaries, I *had* to ignore it.

I swore under my breath and turned on the engine. I needed to get back to the house. I needed to check on Noah, check in with Tiffany, pretend I hadn't absolutely come within microseconds of having Holden's tongue in my mouth, and maybe sleep.

This entire day had been one hell of a roller coaster.

And I definitely hadn't imagined it ending like this.

CHAPTER 17

HOLDEN

As soon as I was a few blocks away from the Urgent Care clinic, I pulled into the parking lot of another business park and went around behind the building so I wouldn't be visible from the road. There, alone in the shadows, I stopped, put my car in Park, and groaned aloud as I covered my face with both hands.

What. The hell. Was *happening?*

Every time I replayed that exchange before Porter got out of the car, it seemed more surreal. Had we... Did we almost... What would we be doing now if I hadn't pulled back? Because we'd been on a collision course with each other, and I'd been absolutely caught up in the idea of kissing Porter, and we'd both been moving in like we were on board with it happening right then and there. If I hadn't backed off, or if the opportunity presented itself again and I went for it, there was no doubt in my mind that Tiffany would kill me. Sitting here now, though, recalling the way he'd looked at my lips and then my eyes, I had to wonder if it would've been worth my ex-wife's wrath.

It had been a long, long time since I'd been so ridiculously into someone that I turned stupid and reckless, but that was me to the letter when it came to Porter. Just because I'd had the presence of mind to put on the brakes tonight didn't mean I would next time, and if the heat between us had been any indication, there *would* be a next time.

I rubbed my eyes with the heels of my hands. I had no idea if I wanted to stay away from Porter or find every excuse imaginable to be near him.

Okay, that wasn't true. I knew which of those options I *wanted*. What would I actually do?

Guess that depends on how stupid and reckless I get next time I see him.

I dropped my hands into my lap and sighed as I stared out the windshield. This had to be a result of my libido coming back to life. After eighteen-plus months of not caring about sex—and I couldn't even remember the last time I'd had sex with Tiffany before we'd separated—I was bound to feel like an insatiably horny teenager the first time someone pinged my radar.

Yeah. That made sense. This was no more "him and only him" than those crushes I'd had in high school where I hadn't been able to imagine being drawn to anyone except that out-of-my-league basketball player or that singer whose concert tickets I couldn't afford. I'd moved on from them, and I'd move on from Porter to someone more attainable.

Except he is attainable. That look in his eyes... Oh God...

I sucked in a breath as a shiver shook goose bumps to life all over my body. I couldn't have Porter, but for reasons even more frustrating than the basketball player who'd never have given me the time of day or the musician who didn't know I was alive. Porter was *right there*. He'd looked at me like that. He'd moved in when I had, leaving absolutely no room for misinterpreting what he'd wanted out of that moment. If I hadn't backed off, we'd probably still be in that Urgent Care parking lot, and I'd know what Porter's mouth tasted like and what he sounded like when he was—

I exhaled hard and shifted in the driver's seat. All right, this was out of control. I needed to get my ass home, download Tinder or whatever else everyone was using these days, and start directing my newly-awakened libido toward people I could touch without causing strife.

First things first—get out of this parking lot before some cop happened along and asked what the hell I was doing.

When I walked into the apartment, Zach was on the couch, a bowl of cereal on his chest, and he surreptitiously took his feet off the coffee table as I came in. "Hey."

"Hey." I hung my jacket by the door. "Cereal for dinner?"

He shrugged. "Eh."

I chuckled. Better than some of the frozen crap he liked or the diner food he got from work, so I didn't push. I opened my mouth to ask what he'd been up to this evening, but he spoke first.

"You have a date tonight or something?"

I froze. "Uh. What?"

"I don't know." He spooned out some cereal. "You just look kinda..." He waved a hand on front of his face.

"I do?"

"Yeah. It's kinda how you looked after you went out with Tiffany the first time."

I blinked. Whoa. Shit. So much for being subtle. I cleared my throat and busied myself putting my wallet and keys in their places on the counter. "No, just taking care of some stuff with Noah. He hurt his foot today and—"

"What?" Zach sat up so suddenly he nearly dumped his cereal on the table. "Is he okay?"

"Yeah, yeah." I smoothed the air. "Just a sprain."

"What'd he do? Soccer injury?"

"Bailed out on the swings."

Zach laughed and rolled his eyes. Sitting back on the couch, he shifted his attention back to his cereal. "I told him he was gonna get hurt doing that."

"We all did," I muttered, opening the fridge to hunt down a beer. "He's fine, though. Sore, but nothing serious."

"That's good."

As Zach ate on the couch and I popped open my second beer of the night, my mind went back to his question when I'd walked in through the door. He thought I'd been out on a date? Because I had some look I'd also had when I'd first started dating Tiffany?

He didn't seem bothered by the idea, which I supposed wasn't a surprise. He didn't even remember his mom and me being together, and I'd dated off and on throughout his younger years until I'd married Tiffany. Now that I thought about it, he'd been Chloe's, Ethan's, and Noah's ages when I'd dated, so maybe he'd have some insight about what it was like to be in their shoes.

I went into the living room and sat on the couch with my beer. "So, I have a question."

"What's up?"

I took a pull from my beer. "When I was dating before Tiffany—and when I was dating Tiffany—what was that like for you?"

Zach scooped some more cereal out of the bowl. "What do you mean?"

"I mean, did it bother you? Your dad dating someone?"

He shrugged. "I don't know. It was kind of weird, I guess? I didn't really know what dating was, though. And I liked Tiffany better than Brett, so..."

"Ugh." I scowled as I brought my beer bottle up for a sip. "I can't think of many people who aren't better than Brett."

"No kidding. What the hell did you see in him, anyway?"

I grunted and waved a hand. "Hell if I know."

Zach chuckled. "Glad I'm not the only one."

I wasn't sure if he meant he echoed the sentiment about my ex-boyfriend, or if he was glad he wasn't the only one who'd dated a lemon, but either way.

"Why do you ask?" He tilted his head. "You thinking about dating again?"

"I don't know." I shrugged, wondering if I looked or sounded more convincing than I felt. "Maybe. It's been almost two years since Tiffany and I separated." *And there's someone I can't have who I also can't get off my mind.* "So why not?"

His lips quirked, and there was something unspoken lurking in his expression.

"What?" I asked.

"Just..." He paused, then cleared his throat. "Are you going to go, like, meet people? Or..." He held up his phone.

"I don't know yet, to be honest. I was thinking of downloading some apps tonight and seeing how that works."

The vague discomfort in his face intensified a little. "Oh."

"Why?"

"I, um... Well, I just think it might get weird if we're

both using the same apps." He wrinkled his nose. "I mean, what if we both swipe right on the same woman?"

I barked a laugh, relieved *that* was the only angle that bothered him. "Damn it, Zach. Way to make it weird."

"Hey, I'm just saying. We're both getting into dating in the same area, and I do not want to go out with some girl who ends up recognizing you."

I laughed. "You want me to stick to men until you lock someone down?"

He met my gaze. "Could you?"

I rolled my eyes. "Shut up."

Chuckling, he put his phone on the coffee table. "Have you even used one of those apps before?"

"Nope. I think there were some websites or apps or whatever back then, but I never used them, so…"

"I figured. Just, um, you know, look around and see what everyone else is looking for. Some of the apps are for people who want to date. Some are people looking for things I really don't want to think about my dad looking for."

I snorted. "So you won't look over my profile if—"

"*Dad.*"

I just laughed, but it faded. Tapping my fingers on my beer bottle, I said, "I don't even know what I want, honestly. Maybe I'm not even ready for this. Maybe I should just be focusing on your brothers and sister."

"Who says you can't do both? Tiffany is."

I raised an eyebrow. "Is she?"

"Yeah. Didn't she tell you?"

"It, uh, hasn't really come up. I mean, I'm glad to hear she's putting herself out there, but we hadn't talked about it."

"So put yourself out there too." Zach half-shrugged. "What do you have to lose?"

I stared into my beer bottle, wondering if that question had a simple answer, or if putting myself out there would make things complicated. And for that matter, what was the point when I knew I'd be comparing each and every profile to the person I was trying not to think about. I couldn't imagine an electronic profile and some text messages stacking up to Porter throwing a football for my boys or carrying my sleeping daughter to bed. Just thinking about that made my heart do things I'd never felt it do before.

No, I wasn't ready to put myself out there. Even if I didn't have other priorities in my life right now, Porter existed. He'd slipped into my world while I wasn't looking, and he'd embedded himself under my skin while I wasn't paying attention, and there was nothing on Tinder that would get him off my mind.

Finally, I sighed and shook my head. "I don't know. Maybe I'll set up a profile eventually. We'll see."

Zach's brow furrowed. "Why do you keep second-guessing yourself so much?"

"Huh?"

"Ever since we moved up here, you're always asking how I felt about this or that thing you did as a dad. Now you're freaking out about even thinking about dating again."

"Well, yeah. Because I'm trying to focus on being the parent I should've been when—"

"Dad. Dude." He rolled his eyes. "You were a good dad. I turned out okay. Why are you so freaked out?"

"I..." I pressed back into the couch cushion. "I guess being a parent the second time around is harder than I thought. The first time should make me feel like I know what I'm doing, but everything's changed since then, and it's making me question every decision I made the first time." I laughed dryly and shook my head. "That probably doesn't make any sense."

"Eh." He shrugged again. "The way my friends and I all bitched about our parents when we were younger, every parent fucks up. And even when they don't, we're going to bitch about them anyway. At the end of the day, we all turned out all right, and we know our parents were doing the best they could. That's about all you can do, right? Just live your life, Dad. Yeah, it's weird when your parents start dating other people, but it's weird when they start new jobs too. I got used to it. They will too. It's all good."

I blinked, startled by my son's casual but profound wisdom. "Good point. I'll... I'll keep it in mind."

He nodded, evidently satisfied that I'd gotten the message.

I had, but I still didn't see myself downloading any of those apps. Some part of me really didn't want to think about the possibility of my son and me moving in the same dating pool, but I was starting to think that was kind of a moot point. Unless he'd suddenly discovered he was bisexual and developed a thing for his half-siblings' nanny, we probably wouldn't have an issue.

Because God help me, there was only one person on this planet who had my attention.

CHAPTER 18

PORTER

The next couple of days were mostly occupied with keeping up with Noah's pain, bandages, and ice. His foot was really sore the day after the injury, so Tiffany kept him home from school. He made it halfway through the next day before he called me in tears because his foot hurt. I had Chloe with me, so she and I brought him some ibuprofen. After the nurse put some icepacks on his ankle and the ibuprofen had a chance to kick in, he felt good enough to stay at school. By the time I left, Chloe was bored and tired, which made for a fussy afternoon, and of course once Ethan got home, he wanted to play harder than either of his siblings—or his nanny—could handle.

By the end of the week, though, things had mostly returned to normal. Noah still used his crutches at school, but he'd carefully walk without them at home. He wasn't in nearly as much pain now and felt up to doing more than just sitting back with his foot covered in icepacks. Which was good—one of his friends was having a slumber party for his birthday on Saturday, and Noah would've been devastated if he hadn't been able to go.

In fact, Tiffany and I would both have some much-needed downtime this weekend because Noah would be gone most of Saturday and into Sunday, and Holden was taking Chloe and Ethan until Sunday night.

And damn, I'd been so caught up in keeping plates spinning this week that it didn't even register that Holden was coming over until his car pulled in the driveway on Saturday morning.

That wasn't to say I hadn't thought about everything that had happened in his car or the conversation we'd had at the restaurant. I had. Constantly. I'd just been so scattered that it hadn't really sunk in that he was coming here. That we'd be breathing the same air in T-minus not very fucking long.

I'd heard his car pull up, heard his footsteps on the stairs outside, heard the door open, and still wasn't even a little bit prepared when he walked into Tiffany's living room.

Our eyes locked.

And the subtle hitch of his breath did *nothing* to help me pull myself together.

If I'd had any illusions that he might've forgotten about the other night, or that he'd brushed it off as nothing, those illusions dissolved in the heat in those smoldering blue eyes. Oh my God. I hadn't thought it was possible, but if I was reading him right, he was even more off-balance over the near-kiss than I was, and that said a lot.

Holden broke eye contact, and the sudden snap in tension made me sway on my feet. Good thing Tiffany wasn't in the room—this little exchange would've been impossible to explain away.

"So. Um." He cleared his throat. "Are they ready?"

As if on cue, Ethan and Chloe came thundering down the hall, calling out, "Daddy!"

"Hey guys!" He turned around, a smile lighting up his face and not helping me regain my composure at all. Ethan and Chloe hugged their dad, and a moment later, their mom appeared behind them.

"Porter, is their stuff together?" she asked.

"Yeah. Yeah." I motioned toward the bedrooms. "Let me grab it and I'll take it out to the car." I didn't wait for a dismissal, and hurried down the hall to get their things, relieved for a moment to catch my breath.

In Ethan and Noah's room, I paused to do exactly that. Okay. Okay. I'd be fine. The other night had happened, and fortunately Holden had been smart enough to keep a hell of a lot more from happening. Things would be a little awkward but not as awkward as they could have been, so I'd ride this out until I could be in the same room as Holden without getting tachycardic. Between now and then, well, I'd have to hope for the best.

I shook myself, picked up Ethan's bag, and swung into Chloe's to get hers. Then I put on a pair of flip flops and went out to Holden's car with the luggage.

Apparently my brain was an absolute train wreck today, because I made it all the way to the back of the car before I realized the trunk was shut. Crap. Now I'd need to—

The lid popped, startling me.

I glanced toward the house, and Holden smiled from the porch. He gestured with the remote, then turned to supervise Ethan and Chloe putting on their shoes.

Why did that moment make my brain go blank? What in God's name was wrong with me?

Oh.

Right.

Holden was what was wrong with me.

C'mon, dude. Get a grip.

I put the bags in the trunk and shut the lid. As I started up the walk, Holden and his kids were on their way down.

"Bye, Porter." Chloe gave me one of those cute little waves.

"Bye, kiddo. Have fun."

She smiled and continued down the walk. I said goodbye to Ethan, too, and—

Suddenly found myself face to face with Holden.

I didn't let the eye contact linger this time. Instead, I gestured back toward the car and watched Ethan and Chloe getting into their respective seats. "So, um. I packed everything. The usual. You should be, uh, good to go."

"Great. Thanks." He started past me, but hesitated. "Listen, um, I was going to take them out today. Hadn't really settled on where or what or...' He hesitated again, then blurted out, "Do you want to come with us?"

I straightened. "Really?"

"Yeah." He smiled, a hint of shyness and uncertainty in those hypnotic eyes. "They like having you along and—" He stopped abruptly, and I swore I heard an unspoken *"So do I."* Blushing, he cleared his throat. "You still know their habits and everything better than I do."

I was admittedly speechless for a beat or two, but finally found my voice. "Sure. Yeah. Just, um, let me put my shoes on and grab my jacket."

That smile. Oh, God. That smile.

"Okay." He nodded toward the car. "I'll get them buckled in."

"Good. Right. I'll..." I motioned toward the house. "Be right back."

We held each other's gazes for one two, three conspicuous seconds, and then broke away at the same time to continue in opposite directions.

In the house, my heart thumping, I took off my flip-flops, then went up the stairs to find Tiffany. She was in the kitchen, pouring herself another cup of coffee.

Over her shoulder, she said. "They ready to go?"

"Yeah, they're... Actually, Holden wanted me to come with him."

She turned around, eyebrows up. "Say what?"

"He, um..." I shifted my weight. "I think he's still a little uncertain about everything."

Skepticism radiated off her, especially as she narrowed her eyes. "Porter, is—"

"We're just taking Ethan and Chloe out." I smirked and hoped it hid the *oh shit, she's on to me* pounding in my chest. "If we were going to do something we shouldn't, do you really think we'd do it with the kids around?"

That apparently got through. Her features relaxed, and after a second, her shoulders did too. "Okay. Okay." She put up her hands and laughed. "I'm sorry. I don't know why I'm so paranoid about this. I guess I just really, really want things to stay smooth with all of us and the kids."

And now I felt like an even bigger asshole.

"I get it. I really do. But we're just taking Ethan and Chloe out for the day."

She nodded, and a soft smile formed on her lips. "You know, I'm glad you two are getting along. And that he's willing to ask you for help. He's never been one of those guys who gets led around by his ego, but... Well, you know what I mean."

"Yeah, I do."

"Anyway." She shook herself and shooed me toward the door. "Go. Have fun."

"Will do."

Pretending my conscience wasn't already having words

with me, I headed downstairs to put on my shoes. And as I put them on, I reminded myself that we really were taking Ethan and Chloe out. This wasn't a clandestine date. It wasn't an excuse to hook up. An excuse to spend time with the man I was drooling over? Totally. But we wouldn't exactly have much opportunity to do anything. So was there really any reason to beat myself up over it?

I told myself no, but as I walked down the steps toward the car, and Holden looked at me from the driver's seat, my reflection in his dark sunglasses—oh yeah, there were reasons to beat myself up over this. His kids would be our top priority today, but would I be stealing glances at him? Hell yeah. Maybe test the water and subtly flirt with him? Well, what could I say? Part of what had drawn me to being a first responder was being a thrill junkie. Surreptitiously flirting with a man I wasn't allowed to date? That was irresistible for this thrill junkie.

I ignored my inner responsible adult, took my usual backpack of supplies from my trunk, and got into his car on the passenger side. He glanced at me, and we both smiled, and I wondered if he was struggling as hard as I was to make it look like he wasn't out of breath.

As he drove us out of the neighborhood, I cleared my throat. "So, did you have any plans for the day? Anywhere in particular you wanted to take them?"

"Well." He tapped his thumbs on the wheel and craned his neck to look at the sky. "The weather is supposed to stay nice today. There's always the—" He flicked his eyes to the rearview, then back to the road. Dropping his voice, he said, "There's always Woodland Park."

The zoo? He wanted to take his kids—and me—to the zoo? Oh, Lord help me...

"That's an option. Just, um, fair warning?"

He glanced at me. "Hmm?"

I drummed my fingers on the armrest. "Look, you know what's there, right?"

"Uh. Animals?"

"Uh-huh. And I'm kind of a sucker for them. *All* of them. So if I basically turn into a squealing fanboy over a squirrel or something..."

To my surprise, Holden grinned, which almost brought that squealing fanboy out of me right then and there. "Okay, sold."

"Really?"

"Yeah. Because this I gotta see."

The Woodland Park Zoo was easily one of my favorite places to take Chloe and the boys. They loved it, and I hadn't been kidding when I'd warned Holden that animals scrambled my brain. What could I say? I adored critters.

So did Chloe and Ethan. Once we'd told them where we were going, they'd been so excited they could barely sit still. By the time we'd gotten out of the car to unbuckle them, they'd already unfastened their own restraints and were ready to bolt for the gate. They didn't—they knew better—but they were sure ready to.

The line at the entrance wasn't too long, fortunately, and they only had to be patient for a few minutes before their dad finished dealing with the annual pass. Then we were inside the park and ready to explore.

Not far from the entrance was an enormous colorful map, and bless them, they used pictures of animals so even the little ones who couldn't read yet could make sense of it.

"All right, let's make a plan." I hoisted Chloe up onto my shoulders so she could see the map. "Do you guys want to go to the savannah first? Or the rainforest?"

"Goats!" Chloe said.

"They're across the park, sweetie," I said. "We'll get there, but which way do you want to go?" I showed them a few different routes that would eventually lead us toward the farm animals that Chloe so loved and also made a note of what time the raptor shows were so Ethan would get to see one.

I put Chloe down and turned to Holden, hoping he read the *any thoughts?* in my expression.

He shrugged. "I'll follow you."

"Okay. Well." I motioned toward the left. "Let's head toward the—"

"Porter! Look!" Chloe tugged my hand and pointed, and as if on cue, a gigantic gray squirrel came out of the bushes, two huge peanuts stuffed into its mouth.

"Oh my God." I crouched beside Chloe, grinning. "Isn't he cute?"

"He's fat!"

Laughing, I nodded. "Probably from all those peanuts he's—oh, look at him!" The squirrel darted across the path and partway up a tree. A second later, another chased him, and Chloe and Ethan weren't the only ones enjoying the hell out of watching the fat squirrels chase each other around a trash can.

I glanced up, and the amusement on Holden's face brought a rush of heat to my own cheeks. We hadn't been here two minutes, hadn't seen a single exhibit yet, and my inner dork was on full display. Over a *squirrel*. Technically two squirrels, but still.

I cleared my throat as I rose. "I'm not joking. It's going to be like that *all* day."

"Well then, we'd better get walking." His smile did things to my pulse and my knees that it had absolutely no right to do. "Because I'm looking forward to it."

CHAPTER 19

HOLDEN

It was cute as hell to watch Porter and the kids at the zoo. Unbeknownst to him, I'd decided to follow his lead on everything and not just the direction we took. I let him set the pace for wandering around the sprawling wildlife park.

That was, to say the least, educational.

I learned that Ethan was utterly fascinated by big cats, especially the snow leopards. For that matter, I'd never realized how interested he was in birds, or how much he knew about them. He could identify all kinds of birds at a glance without even looking at the placards, and he was mesmerized by the raptor show.

Chloe loved everything. If it was a critter, she adored it, and I was pretty sure her favorite thing was the petting zoo in the farm animal exhibit. Watching giraffes, zebras, and hippos was fine and good, but she could actually *touch* the sheep and goats, so that was a winner for her. And for Porter. Long after Ethan started getting restless and wanted to move on, Porter and Chloe were still enthralled with the petting zoo. Fortunately, there were some squirrels nearby that kept Ethan entertained, so no one had any complaints.

Then, once Chloe had had enough of petting the sheep and goats, she took Porter's hand and led him out of the exhibit.

"Okay." He'd unfolded the map and held it where they could all see it. "Where to next?"

And then we'd continued through the zoo.

The whole time we were there, Porter never made any attempt to drag them away from an exhibit. If they wanted to watch the otters play for half an hour, then we watched the otters play for half an hour. He made sure we had plenty of time to get to the raptor show not only before it started, but before the close-up seats were full, so Ethan was able to snag a spot in the front and see without anyone blocking him. When Ethan wanted to ask the raptor handler detailed questions about the hawks and eagles, Porter occupied Chloe by pointing out some sparrows nearby or quietly going over the map and figuring out what she wanted to go see next.

At first, I'd been kind of impatient, thinking we should get moving if they wanted to see everything. But after the first hour or so of leisurely strolling between exhibits, I started to see what was going on.

He wasn't rushing them. He didn't need to.

Our tickets were for the entire day, as was our parking space. There was no need to sprint through everything, and that would just leave everyone tired and cranky anyway. Aside from getting us to the raptor show on time, he only made a serious attempt to steer the group in a certain direction once, and that turned out to be a subtle means of herding us all toward the food court. By the time Ethan and Chloe started showing the first hints that there might be *I'm hungry* tears on the horizon, Porter had them seated at a table and was distributing burgers and chips. The zoo didn't allow lids or straws, so Porter filled all the fountain drinks about three-quarters full to make them easier to handle without spilling.

The guy seriously thought of everything.

After lunch, Porter and I were both feeling a bit lazy, but the kids—being kids—had found their second wind. Fortunately, Woodland Park Zoo had an enormous lawn where people could have picnics and kids could play. In the interest of letting them both burn off some energy, we sat at a picnic table and sent them off to join some other kids who were playing some sort of game.

"Ethan, stay with your sister, okay?" I said.

"I will." Ethan took Chloe's hand, and they headed toward the other kids.

As soon as they were out of earshot, Porter exhaled hard. "And now? A break."

I laughed. "You didn't seem like you were running out of steam."

"I wasn't. But then I ate." He groaned. "Now I just want a nap."

"Yeah, good luck with that." I paused. "I get the feeling you've done this before. Wrangled them at the zoo."

"A few times, yeah." He flashed a toothy grin. "I mean, how many jobs let you kill an entire day at the zoo with people who are totally down with spending hours on end looking at animals?" He nodded toward the kids. "Tiffany encourages me to take them to places like this as often as possible, so why not?"

"Getting paid to go to the zoo." I chuckled. "Doesn't sound like a bad gig."

"Nope." He rolled his shoulders and tilted his head to

one side, then the other, as if relieving some fatigue. "And don't let today fool you—it hasn't been perfect sunshine and roses every time."

"No?"

"Ugh. No. I made the mistake of coming here in the dead of August. The day ended up being super hot by the standards of everyone around here—including the animals—but not your Arizona sun-worshipping children." He tsked and rolled his eyes. "The whole city is basically dying. All the animals are hiding, sleeping, or both. And I've got three kids on my hands who don't get why they can't see any animals at the zoo. It did not go well."

"No, I don't imagine it did."

"Fortunately, the day wasn't a total loss. They were more than happy to go to the aquarium instead, so at least they got to see some animals."

"Good save."

He laughed dryly. "Thank God I thought of it before traffic kicked up, or..." He grimaced.

"Yeah. Good thing."

He turned to me, inhaling like he was poised to say something, but then our eyes met. I thought I felt his mind go blank, but after a second, realized that was my own mind. One look at him and...nothing. Nothing except how much I'd been thinking about him for the past few days, and how being with him today wasn't helping at all.

Porter swallowed. So did I.

We both glanced toward the kids—they were still happily playing—then met each other's gazes again, and I *swore* I could feel the, *"So about the other night..."* thrumming in the air. For the life of me, I couldn't tell from his eyes how he felt about it. If we should have stopped. If we never should have started at all. If we needed to find some way to be alone as soon as possible so we could see where the other night had almost gone.

Porter broke away this time, and cleared his throat. "We should, um, get them moving. If we want to see the rest of the park before it closes."

I released a breath, not sure if I was relieved or frustrated. "Sure. Okay. Let's..."

He turned to me again, and for the second time in as many minutes, that eye contact made me lose my train of thought. One look, and I had nothing.

What the hell? I hadn't been this tongue-tied and stupid over someone since I was a damn teenager.

I dropped my gaze, shook myself, and got up.

Ethan and Chloe didn't need five-, three-, and one-minute warnings today. Though they were obviously enjoying the game with the other kids, Porter just casually mentioned that if we left now, we could watch the penguins get fed, and both kids were immediately running toward us.

We left the picnic area, pausing at the edge to check the map and make sure we were heading in the right direction, and continued toward the penguin exhibit. As we walked, my son and daughter bouncing with energy and excitement, Porter and I exchanged looks. And smiles. And...fuck. Fuck. *Want.*

All the way through the rest of the afternoon at the zoo, I'd expected the kids would provide a welcome distraction, but they really didn't. It was hard to pretend I wasn't feeling anything for Porter when I was constantly noticing Porter with the kids.

I'd admittedly brought him along just because I'd wanted to jump at an opportunity to be with him. What I'd do once we were out and about, I'd figure out as we went—I hadn't thought that far ahead when I'd extended the invitation.

Now, aside from the loaded glances we exchanged at every possible opportunity, we were both almost completely focused on Ethan and Chloe, which didn't really surprise me. What did surprise me was how much I loved that. How easy it was. Exchanging looks and almost kissing in the car had been enough to distract me all week, but watching this man with my kids never ceased to turn me into a tongue-tied wreck. Good Lord, my pulse raced every time he held Chloe up so she could see over a barrier or helped Ethan with some of the unfamiliar words on placards outside exhibits. Stopping to tie a shoe, taking someone to a bathroom, answering endless questions—he just rolled with it, never once sighing with annoyance or in any way giving them the impression they might be an inconvenience.

He wasn't a doormat for them, of course. He never was. If one of the kids tried to ask a zookeeper a question while they were talking to someone else, he'd gently but firmly remind them to wait their turn. After Ethan accidentally elbowed a little girl by the orangutan exhibit, Porter quietly asked him to apologize. No tearing into him. No belittling or berating. Just "Ethan, could you apologize for bumping into her, please?" To which my son responded, softly and sincerely, "I'm sorry. I didn't mean to." And that was the end of it. Later, when Chloe got excited about seeing some monkeys, she got in front of a boy about her size, blocking his view.

"Chloe," Porter said. "Let him see too." She'd looked over her shoulder, realized the boy was standing there, and moved so they could both see.

And I was hardly leaving all the parenting to him. I was doing the same things he was. It just made my heart flutter every time he did. Yeah, he was getting paid for this, but it was a Saturday, and he'd have been well within his rights to stay home and take a well-deserved day off.

But no. He was here. With me. And that moment we'd shared in my car the other night couldn't begin to compete with every single moment he spent being relentlessly amazing for my kids.

That other night had been all physical. In the car, he'd brought the embers of my libido back to life. I'd hardly thought about sex at all since Tiffany and I had separated, and I'd been so stressed and depressed I hadn't really cared about how little I'd wanted sex.

This, though? Seeing Porter with my kids? This was the kind of thing that made my attraction run so much deeper than sex. It was what had tipped the scales with Tiffany—that first time she and I had taken Zach with us to a movie. Watching the two of them chat excitedly about the characters over dinner afterward, I'd known I was going to marry her.

I was getting way, way ahead of myself, comparing my early days with Tiffany to whatever the hell was happening (or I was imagining) with Porter. This was physical attraction. Plain and simple. Okay, physical attraction nudged along by him unknowingly hitting all the right notes to win over this lonely single dad's heart.

One thing at a time, though, and if I was a smarter man, that one thing would be finding another outlet for all this hunger. Except I didn't want another outlet. I wanted Porter. I wanted to take him to bed and see how hot this chemistry really was. I wanted to talk with him—openly and without any guard up—and see if these long looks came from someplace more than physical. I wanted to be with him and my kids at the zoo, the beach, or hanging out on the couch. I just wanted him.

How would I explain this to my ex-wife? No idea.

The only thing I was sure of was that this was a train I couldn't have stopped if I wanted to.

And I didn't want to.

Traffic in this area apparently didn't need a reason. It was a Saturday evening with no sports events or major concerts happening in Seattle, but the freeway was still stacked up for miles because why the fuck not? The reader boards overhead indicated that the drive from Seattle to Lynnwood was almost fifty-five minutes instead of the usual twenty, and Everett was past Lynnwood.

"What the hell?" I muttered.

Porter thumbed through something on his phone. "Looks like there's some weekend construction in Northgate, and there's a wreck in Mountlake Terrace." He sighed and lowered his phone. "I know some back roads that'll get us there... Well, we might not save much time, but we'll be moving."

"Sounds good to me. Which way?"

He craned his neck and looked up ahead, then pointed in the same direction. "Take the ramp coming up."

He was right. Getting off the freeway and onto Highway 99—a four-lane road that ran parallel to I-5—was much less frustrating. The speed limit was only fifty-five, and there were traffic lights, but at least it wasn't stop-and-go.

"This was a good idea," I said as we sailed through another green light. "I'm still not used to the traffic here."

"Phoenix doesn't have traffic?"

"Oh, it does, but I had a fairly short commute that didn't hit the really nasty spots."

"Lucky you."

"Says the guy who commutes up the stairs in the morning."

"Hey." He wagged a finger at me. "I still have to ferry some of the troops around and sometimes end up in Boeing traffic because of it."

I laughed. "Okay, okay. I take it back. Your commute is…half-terrible."

He huffed, and I glanced at him just in time to see him roll his eyes. "Behave, or I'll teach your kids songs from Barney."

"You wouldn't."

"Try me."

"You know, I can still tell Tiffany I got that bagel joke from you."

"Hand to God, Holden. I will have them singing the 'I love you' song by bedtime."

I laughed putting up my hand. "Okay! Okay! You win. Anything but that."

"That's what I thought."

I huffed dramatically. "You know, it's dirty pool to play Barney against a father who raised a kid through that era."

"Desperate times, desperate measures."

"Jackass," I said just loud enough for him to hear.

"Daddy, what's Barney?" Chloe asked.

"Nothing, sweetie." I looked in the rearview. "Just a bad creature from a scary movie."

Her eyes widened, and she didn't press.

"That's messed up," Porter said under his breath, but he was obviously trying not to laugh.

"Tell me it's not true. Tell me Barney isn't a bad creature from a scary movie. Or TV show, I guess."

He laughed, shaking his head. "I'm not gonna argue."

"No, you're just gonna use it to keep me in line."

"It works, doesn't it?"

I shot him a good-natured glare, and he laughed again. He started to say something but froze, pulling in a sharp breath and stiffening.

I glanced at him. "What?"

But then I heard it—sirens.

They'd vaguely registered, enough that I'd subconsciously looked around to make sure I didn't need to move over, but I wasn't really aware of them until Porter reacted.

I checked the rearview again, and this time saw flashing red lights coming up on my left. I eased into the right lane, and a second later, a fire truck went screaming past with an ambulance not far behind. In no time, they were both disappearing down the highway, sound fading into the distance.

Beside me, Porter released his breath so subtly, I doubt I'd have noticed if he hadn't told me everything the other night.

"You okay?" I asked.

He nodded. "Yeah, yeah." He laughed and ran a slightly unsteady hand through his hair. "I really can't wait until the day I stop jumping out of my skin at the sound of an emergency vehicle."

"Does that ever happen?"

"God, I hope so." He rolled his shoulders. "Sorry. I... What were we talking about?"

"I think you were threatening to weaponize Barney songs to keep me in line."

That brought the smile back to life. "Oh yeah. And don't you forget it, because I will so do it."

I chuckled and just kept driving.

By the time we were getting into Everett, it was almost time for dinner. Porter glanced back at Chloe and Ethan, who'd been happily playing with the stuffed animals I'd bought them on the way out of the zoo—a snow leopard for Ethan, a penguin for Chloe, plus the enormous hippo I'd picked up for Noah.

Voice soft, he said to me, "We should probably think about getting them some food."

"Good idea." Tapping my thumbs on the wheel, I pursed my lips. "I should drop you off at home at some point, though."

"I'm fine with stopping to feed them first."

"You don't mind?"

"Of course not. I'm not going to make them go another half hour without food on my account. And..." He hesitated. When I glanced at him, our eyes locked for a fleeting second, but it was enough time for me to read—even if I was imagining it—that even if the kids weren't hungry, he wasn't in a hurry to leave. My heart sped up for the millionth time today. What a coincidence—I wasn't in a hurry for him to leave either.

"Um. Well." I focused on the road and cleared my throat. "If you're not in a big rush, why don't I take them back to my place, get them going with something to eat, and then I'll have Zach watch them while I take you home?"

"Okay. Sure. That works. Thanks."

I didn't turn to him, so I didn't see him smile, but I heard it in his voice. I *felt* it.

Do I have to take you home?

My oldest son was totally amenable to keeping an eye on his siblings while I drove Porter home. He'd started working recently, but he didn't have to work until later tonight, and anyway, he adored Ethan and Chloe. In fact he seemed kind of disappointed that Noah wouldn't be there this evening.

On our way out, I clapped his shoulder. "I owe you."

"It's all good, Dad. *Go*."

Porter and I left the apartment, and I tried not to notice that while we'd been together all day, this was the first time we'd really been alone. No kids to see or hear something inappropriate. No prying eyes to notice two men who were way more into each other than society liked to think about.

Just Porter. Just me. Just fifteen minutes in the car between my house and my ex-wife's.

This is going to be the longest fifteen minutes of my life, isn't it?

It definitely would be if we rode in silence, so I flailed for something to say, and finally settled, on, "By the way, I was really impressed today."

"What do you mean?" He smiled cautiously. "By how fast a squirrel or a bunny can reduce me to a complete dork?"

I laughed. "Okay, there was that. But..." Sobering a bit, I glanced at him. "The way you handled the kids. Everything. It was... I mean, I'd have been trying to move them along so they could see everything. You didn't rush them at all."

"I wanted them to enjoy themselves." He paused. "For the record, I do enforce that the world doesn't revolve around them, and that they can't keep everyone waiting." He shifted in his seat. "But sometimes I let them call the shots. It makes them feel important, and like it's important to me that they're enjoying themselves and seeing what they want to see."

"So, a balance between the two."

"Exactly."

"Yeah, I noticed that. It's, um, really good to see." I stole a glance at him. "I definitely know they're in good hands."

Porter smiled, but he said nothing. Or hell, maybe he did. That smile had short-circuited my brain, just like it had been doing all day. God, I could barely focus around him. I hadn't felt like this in years—driven to distraction by another person

We drove in silence for a moment, and then he quietly said, "By the way, thanks for bringing me along today. It was a lot of fun."

"It was." I paused, gnawing my lip. "Can I, uh... Can I confess something?"

"Uh." He shifted subtly. "Is this something I'll have to take to the FBI?"

A laugh burst out of me. "I mean, you can if you want, but..."

He chuckled, but quickly sobered. "Okay. Shoot."

I swallowed. "Today wasn't just because I like how you interact with my kids. I asked you to come along because..." I stared hard at the road ahead. "Because I wanted you there."

"Really?"

"Yeah."

"Oh."

We exchanged a fleeting look, and I had no idea what to say. The other night was still hanging between us, and today had all kinds of new implications. So what now? What did we do with any of that?

I eased to a stop at a stop sign. The intersection was deserted, so I could've just slowed down and rolled through, but no, I stopped. And I stayed stopped. And blood pounded in my ears as I debated which way to go. Oh, I knew which way to drive—a right turn would take us to Tiffany's neighborhood—but right here, right now, which way did I *go*?

"Holden?" Porter's voice was soft, but the sound of him saying my name made my pulse pound even harder.

Why was I just sitting here? Why were we just idling instead of doing...*something*? How long were we going to play the game of trying to parse mixed signals before someone finally acted?

Well, Holden? How long?

Gripping the wheel for dear life, I pushed out a breath. "Fuck it. I can't lie, Porter. I really, really want to kiss you right now."

My heart was pounding so hard, I almost missed his answer: "So what are you waiting for?"

I turned to him. Across the console, he was barely visible in the pale glow from the dashboard and headlights, but I could feel him looking right in my eyes. "You serious?"

"Are you?"

We held each other's gazes, a volley of silent dares zinging back and forth in the electrified air between us.

Then, heart racing, I shifted into Park, reached for his face, and—

Oh God.

Finally.

Porter's lips were against mine.

We both froze for a few seconds—no one moving, no one breathing—before his lower lip nudged mine. With a long, slow sigh, I let him deepen the kiss, and...holy fuck.

Everything—the softness of his lips, the heat of his skin under my hand, the rush of his breath past my cheek—drove me wild. As much as this kiss brought my world to a halt, it might as well have been the first time I'd ever kissed anyone at all.

Porter slid his hand up into my hair, and I wished like hell I'd done this somewhere other than the front seat of my car. Maybe somewhere we could have pulled each other all the way together, and I could actually feel him.

He broke the kiss with a gasp, touching his forehead to mine and breathing hard against my tingling lips. "God. I...I want you so fucking bad."

"Me too. Been...thinking about you like crazy. Since the other night."

"Same. Should've..." He brushed another kiss across my mouth, and the soft whimper that escaped his lips nearly did me in. "Should've dragged you into the backseat when I had the chance."

Oh. Sweet. Jesus.

Abruptly, he broke the kiss, though he didn't pull away. "Shit. We can't...like this..." He moistened his lips and met my eyes in the low light. "Tiffany's going to get suspicious if I come stumbling in late after being out with you."

I smoothed his hair. "And I promised Zach I'd be home in time for him to go to work."

Porter made a frustrated sound even as he came in for another kiss. "How do we do this?"

"Don't know." I kissed him again, lightly this time. "We'll think of something."

"Yeah, well, can we think of something soon?" He squirmed, biting his lip. "Because now that I've had a taste..."

A low growl escaped my throat as I claimed a deep, hard

kiss. Oh, we'd be doing something about this soon. We had to. Now that we'd crossed this line? Admitted we wanted each other? Kissed the way I'd been dying to kiss him since the other night? Dancing around each other much longer would either result in public indecency or someone needing a fire extinguisher.

I drew back and held his gaze. Breathing hard, I said, "Let me get you home for now. Then we'll... We'll just have to find an opportunity."

"Find it and take it," he said. "I can't wait, Holden."

"Neither can I. Let's—"

A car horn startled us all the way apart. Shit—we'd apparently been stopped long enough for someone to pull up behind us, and now they were honking and flailing for us to get out of the way.

I quickly pulled into the intersection and went right. With another honk, the driver flipped me the bird, squealed his tires, and took off in the other direction.

Porter and I glanced at each other. His face was flushed, his eyes wide and his lips just slightly swollen. Thank God for the shadows keeping us mostly hidden below the belt. There was undoubtedly a bulge beneath his just like there was beneath mine, and if I indulged in a look, I'd start hunting down a motel, consequences be damned.

I stopped in the driveway behind Tiffany's car, and we turned to each other. We didn't dare share another kiss out here in front of Tiffany's house, but we stole a long look, and Porter slid his hand over my thigh just before he unbuckled his seat belt.

"See you soon?" he asked in a hoarse whisper.

"As soon as possible."

We held each other's gazes, and I was two seconds away

from saying to hell with it and taking him someplace else when he wisely opened the door and got out.

As he walked up to the house, I drove off in a daze. I swore I could still feel and taste his kiss, but it was almost impossible to believe it had really happened. I'd fantasized about him enough times, how was I supposed to comprehend actually kissing him?

Lord help me when we found the time and privacy for more than a kiss.

That might just kill me.

HOT GUY OR NO, I HAD TO FOCUS ON MY NEW JOB so I didn't get fired. I needed this job so I could stay close to my kids. Especially since this company was one of those rare gems that understood that families were important. I could *not* afford to lose this gig.

That didn't stop me from texting with Porter whenever I was alone in my office or an elevator, though. And I could tell when he was alone, too. When he was in nanny mode, the messages were usually pictures of the kids or otherwise benign.

When he was off the clock, though? Or all three kids were at school? Holy shit. He was a *relentless* tease.

You're going to give me tennis elbow, you know.

Never gonna look at that stop sign the same again.

Literally put salt in my coffee this morning & its your fault.

But nothing scrambled my brain more than the message he sent on Wednesday afternoon as I was coming back from lunch: *T's taking the kids to her sister's place tonight. ;)*

Emojis didn't usually get a response out of me, but that

winky-face at the end of his text was too suggestive to ignore.

Does this mean you have the night off?

Damn right it does. You have any plans?

No. I hesitated, then decided to get brave and add, *Pretty sure I have lube, though.*

As soon as the text was gone, I was a mortified, jittery wreck. Seriously? *Seriously?* Why not just send him a dick pic while I was at it and make sure I'd fully blown my chances with him?

My text tone pinged, and I cringed as I picked up the phone.

Well, there goes my concentration for the next few hours.

I laughed, and I was even more out of breath than I'd thought. My hands were shaky as I tapped out, *See you tonight?*

Almost immediately, he said, *Your place or... uh... your ex-wife's?*

Oh fuck yes. I was pretty sure we both knew the answer, but I wrote back, *Good thing my son works nights, isn't it?*

That an invitation?

Don't make me beg.

OMG.

I laughed, imagining him squirming in his seat and biting his lip. Blushing, too. He had to be blushing.

And now I was the one squirming in my chair and biting my lip. Christ. I hadn't been with a man since before Tiffany and I had started dating. I could have sworn none of the men I'd ever slept with had been anywhere near as attractive as Porter, but it was possible I wasn't being objective. Right now, no one was more attractive than the man who was coming to my apartment later this evening.

I'll text you when Tiffany leaves, he wrote back. *Be there as soon as I can.*

Looking forward to it.

I put my phone down and shifted my attention to the presentation I'd been working on.

What do I do for a living again?

CHAPTER 20

PORTER

"So, any big plans for the night since you have the house to yourself?" Tiffany pulled her purse up on her shoulder. "Or you just going to take it easy?"

"Eh." I shrugged. "Some friends want to go out and grab a bite, so I'll probably hang out with them for a while."

"Sounds like fun. Well, we'll be back..." She waved a hand. "Whenever we get back."

"I won't wait up."

"Good idea. I'll see you sometime tomorrow, probably."

"Sounds good."

I helped her get everyone out to the car, seated, and strapped in. Then I waved as Tiffany backed out of the driveway, and the second her car had disappeared around the corner, I got in my car and got the hell out of there. I very carefully didn't burn rubber in the neighborhood—God knew someone would be on the phone with Tiffany if *her nanny* was driving like Andretti—but the minute I got on the freeway? Pedal to the floor.

At least, that was the plan. But this was Snohomish County, and much like Seattle to the south, Snohomish

County was plagued by traffic. So much traffic. *So* much. I tapped my fingers on the wheel and muttered "C'mon, c'mon," at the car in front of me, as if the driver might magically cut a path through the long line of bumpers and windows stretching out as far as the eye could see. More than once, I slid my gaze toward the shoulder and wondered if—just this one time—I should risk driving on it.

The incredibly horny side of me thought it was a damn good idea.

The first responder side... not so much.

But there was no way in hell I was wading through this nonsense all the way to Holden's exit. He was only three ramps up the freeway, but it could easily take me twenty minutes to get from one to the next. And fortunately, I knew this area like the back of my hand. Maybe I'd been too distracted to check the traffic report like any self-respecting Northwesterner, but I damn sure knew some alternate routes.

When I was finally close enough to the first off-ramp, I sped down it, then wound through some back roads until— yes, yes, *yes*—Holden's complex came into view. Naturally, I had to wait for a light to change, and it was the longest red light on the fucking planet and *dude what the fuck just turn green already!*

After a few hundred years, it changed, and I pulled into the parking lot. I parked in a guest spot, got out, and took the stairs two at a time to his second-floor apartment.

I hadn't even made it to the door before Holden opened it. One look at him, and I just about tripped over my own feet, but I recovered and made it inside.

"Hey, sorry I'm—" The word "late" didn't make it off my tongue before Holden kissed me, his goatee brushing my chin. He pushed me back a step, and the click of the door shutting behind me sent a delicious shiver through me. So did being pinned like this, held in place by the body of the man I'd been fantasizing about nonstop.

Whatever restraint there'd been when we'd kissed in his car, it was gone now. We were alone. Behind closed doors. There was no one around to catch us, and no doubt about what we both wanted.

"I just got home from work," he said between kisses. "Haven't...even had a chance to change clothes."

"Don't need to change them." I tugged at his belt. "Just take them off."

"Mmm, that's one option." He slid his hands down over my ass and growled, "That said, I don't know about you, but I could go for a shower."

"Ooh, now you're speaking my language."

His lips curved against mine, and then he started kissing down my neck. "Figured you'd like that."

"Uh-huh. Long as your evil plan includes fucking me while we're in there."

"If it didn't before," he growled, "it does now."

The moan that escaped my throat didn't even sound like me, but who cared? As long as it encouraged him to—

Abruptly, Holden tensed. "*Fuck*. I don't have any condoms." He drew back and met my gaze, eyes full of hope. "I don't suppose you stopped on the way here."

"No, but... Um." I swallowed. "Look, I'm on PrEP, I've been tested millions of times, and I've used condoms with every guy I've been with."

"And I haven't touched anyone since the divorce."

Our eyes locked.

Speak now or forever—

Holden kissed me again, pressing me back against the door. Nothing about his kiss or his touch said *"okay, time out, let's run up to Walgreens,"* and I was damn near shaking with excitement now. I wanted him, and I'd been going out of my mind with need ever since that first kiss, and every time some obstacle came down between us and the sex I'd been fantasizing about, my need for him got even stronger. Much more of this and we were going to wind up fucking right here against his living room wall.

"S-so, about that shower…"

Holden groaned softly, paused for one more kiss, and then led me down the hall.

Neither of us said anything. Our hands were shaking. We were both out of breath. There really wasn't much to be said that we hadn't covered in the living room or in days' worth of texts we'd used to wind each other up.

He turned on the shower, and we both took off our clothes without any fanfare. Stripteases or undressing each other could be fun, but I was way too wound up for that. Just give me that gorgeous man without any barriers.

As he reached in to check the water temperature, I took full advantage of the chance to look him up and down. Whoa. He was even hotter naked. Shoulders I could grab onto. Hips I could do the same with. Dark hair sprinkled across his chest. The treasure trail leading from his navel downward.

And when he looked right in my eyes and grinned as he gave his erection a slow stroke, my mouth watered. Like mine, Holden's cock was pretty average, and as far as I was concerned, that was the perfect size for anal. Not so big I'd need poppers just to take him, big enough for some definite stretching, and just the right size for him to fuck me deep and hard without hurting me.

He nodded toward the shower, and we both got in. It was no surprise that we weren't focused on getting clean.

Clearly this had just been an excuse to expedite the nakedness and start pawing at each other, and I wasn't about to complain. Standing in the middle of the bathtub, hot water pouring over and between us, we made out and touched and... Holy shit, I loved how he kissed. I loved how sure his mouth was without being too aggressive. His hands were the same way—sliding all over my wet skin with certainty and hunger, and I had no idea if he was pulling me to him or if I was just leaning into him because I could. Whatever. The end result was my body pressed up against Holden's. Worked for me.

He slid a hand between us and started stroking both of us, and I was supposed to stay standing? How?

Though if he pinned me to something, that would probably keep me upright. And that could definitely be arranged...

"You have any preference?" I was breathless already. "Top or bottom?"

His other arm tightened around my waist as his hand tightened around our cocks, and he murmured, "My only preference is whatever makes you come the hardest." He licked his lips. "Didn't you say something about fucking you?"

I nodded. "Uh-huh. I did."

His grin made me tingle like every single dirty text he'd sent me in the past week—*combined*.

He brushed his lips across mine. "Fair warning—I haven't been with a man in years," he whispered, almost groaning as he stroked us between our bodies. "Might... Might be a bit rusty."

I rocked my hips, fucking into his fist and against his cock. "N-no complaints so far."

Another grin, one I felt rather than saw, and then he

kissed me. His free hand groped my ass, and his nails dug in and burned as they dragged across my skin, the cool-hot pain driving a delirious moan from my lips. I gripped his shoulders just to stay up, and when my own nails bit in, he moaned too. Oh Lord. If we got into the *you claw my back, I'll claw yours* feedback loop, we'd both lose our minds.

Holden broke the kiss and drew back a little. Eyes locked on mine, he sucked his middle and index fingers into his mouth, then let them slide free in a gesture so pornographic it made my knees weak. "Turn around."

Yeah, didn't have to tell me twice. As soon I was facing the wall, he put a hand on my hip and pushed my thighs apart with his knee. I flattened my palms on the wall as he worked his spit-slicked fingers into me. He was rough about it, but seemed to intuit exactly how rough I could handle before it would go from *hot* to *no*. The invasion wasn't gentle or polite, and dear God, I hoped that was a preview of what was to come. Especially with as rough as he'd been since we'd started fooling around. I was hardly a virgin, but it had been a long time since someone had manhandled me the way he did, and I was putty in his hands.

And desperately needed his dick in my ass.

My vocabulary had diminished to "ungh," so I did the next best thing: fumbled for the lube, got a good enough grip on it to pop the top, and handed it to him over my shoulder.

A breath of laughter cooled my wet skin. "That a hint?"

"Maybe."

He took the lube bottle. A second later, he put it back on the soap tray, and he steadied my hip with one hand. I closed my eyes, toes curling with anticipation, and the instant he nudged at my ass with his cock, I moaned.

He laughed softly. "I'm not even in yet."

"Yeah. Well." I leaned back against him. "Could you maybe do something about that?"

"Hell yeah I can." He pressed harder, and we both swore as the head of his cock slid into me. "Oh God..." he moaned in my ear as he pushed deeper. "This is...probably going to be a quickie, so I hope you can handle two rounds tonight."

The sound that escaped my throat was close enough to "yes please." I clawed at the wall, as turned on by the thought of a second round as I was by his cock moving inside me. More of this? Hell, yeah.

"Jesus, Porter," he breathed. "Fuck..." After a few easy, careful strokes, he was moving smoothly in and out, still whispering curses and my name as he started to pick up speed. "Oh fuck, baby..."

I kept my palms against the shower wall for leverage, and rocked my hips as much as I could without losing my footing.

Holden stopped suddenly. He twisted a little, and I was about to ask why, but then the shower shut off. The bathroom was instantly silent except for our harsh, panting breaths and—when he picked up riding me again—the slap of his hips against my ass.

"Like that?" he asked through his teeth.

I responded with a ragged groan.

Holden buried his face in my neck, his wet goatee cool against my skin, and groaned as he thrust hard enough to knock the breath out of me. "Ungh, God..." He huffed a breath across my skin. He kissed my shoulder, and then I felt teeth. He gasped. "I'm—*fuck*." He dug his teeth into my shoulder, driving a cry out of me that fell to a whimper as he forced his cock as deep as I could take it. He shuddered, hips jerking against my ass, and then he sagged against me with a sigh of "Jesus…"

I hadn't come yet, but I was panting and trembling as if I had. I'd hoped like hell that sex with Holden would be as good as the flirting leading up to it, and I was not disappointed. Holy fuck.

Holden nuzzled my neck. He reached around, and when his fingertips brushed my hard cock, his lips curved into a grin against my neck. "Good. You haven't come." He withdrew slowly. "Means I get to suck you off."

"Fuck. Yes, please."

He didn't tell me to turn around this time—he *turned* me around. My shoulders met the cool wall, and I had just enough time to gasp before Holden went to his knees, and my gasp turned into a moan as he sucked my dick between his lips. His fingers pushed roughly into my ass, and my palms hit the wall as my back arched and my knees wobbled. His hand picked up right where his cock had left off, fucking me fast and hard, and that along with his mouth… oh God.

There were so many reasons I shouldn't have been hooking up with Holden, but staring down at him now as he blew me and fingered my ass… seeing him wet and disheveled and flushed from fucking me…

To hell with what I should or shouldn't have been doing. I couldn't get enough of this man.

"Jesus, Holden," I breathed. "Don't stop. Don't—oh fuck!" He crooked his fingers, and my knees almost dropped out from under me. I had to grab his shoulder to stay upright, and even that almost wasn't enough as I came hard in his eager, talented mouth.

A second before it would've been too much, Holden sat back on his heels and looked up at me, a grin on his full lips.

I sagged against the wall, breathless and trembling, and I was no closer to pulling myself together when—eyes still locked on mine—he rose. He cupped my jaw, leaned in, and kissed me hard and deep, and...*fuck*. A rough, hungry kiss that tasted like my own cum? Sign me the hell up.

"I wasn't kidding about that second round," he growled, lips barely leaving mine. "And I fully intend to last longer this time."

I didn't say a word. I couldn't remember how.

So I just kissed him again and hoped he heard my *"Oh, fuck, yes"* loud and clear.

CHAPTER 21

HOLDEN

OH MY GOD, THIS MAN WAS HOT.

Stretched out on my bed, totally naked with tousled wet hair and a satisfied grin on his lips? That was an image I'd be dreaming about for days to come.

"You just gonna look?" He ran his palm down his smooth abs. "Or join me?"

"That's a no-brainer. I like the view, but..." I lay down beside him on the bed. Immediately, he slid right up next to me, and I loved the way his body felt against mine. Even more than that, the way his mouth tasted as he claimed a long, gentle kiss.

In the almost two years since my ex-wife left, sex hadn't really crossed my radar, but now that I was having it again, I was hungry for it. I physically ached for it. And now that I had someone to kiss? Especially someone who was this enthusiastic about it? How the fuck had I gone this long without kissing?

Well, I was making up for lost time now. Whether we were just kissing for the hell of it or to turn each other on, I was perfectly happy.

After a while, he drew back, and we settled onto the pillows, hands still drifting over each other's skin, but neither of us trying to start anything. He had something on his mind, though. I could tell by the crevices between his eyebrows and the way his eyes kept losing focus.

"Hey." I smoothed his still damp hair. "You still with me?"

"Yeah. Yeah." He shook himself, then met my gaze. "Just thinking. I mean—how the hell do we do this?"

"What do you mean?" But then the piece clicked into place. "Tiffany."

Porter grimaced. "Yeah."

Tiffany's warnings about flirting with Porter echoed through my mind, and I sighed as I stroked his damp hair. "I don't know. She won't be happy if she finds out."

He tensed.

"That doesn't mean we shouldn't do it," I said quickly. "Just...let's keep it to ourselves for now."

"For now?" He seemed dubious.

"Until we figure out if it's something we need to tell her about. If we're just going to fool around for a while, then there's really no point, right?" I brushed a few damp strands off his forehead. "If we decide we want to..."

"If things get serious?"

"Something like that. If we're doing more than sleeping together."

He pursed his lips. "I don't like going behind her back, but you're probably right. As long as it stays out of her sight and the kids' sight, there's really no reason to say anything."

"Exactly. You don't mind keeping it on the down-low, do you?"

Porter shook his head. "No. It's fine. As much as I don't

like lying to her"—he grimaced—"it's probably for the best in this case.'

"Yeah. If it does start bothering you, or you think we should tell her, just talk to me, okay?"

He nodded, and some of the apprehension in his expression eased. "I will." Then he grinned, and he leaned in for a kiss. "In the meantime..."

I definitely didn't protest as we sank into each other's arms and got lost in another kiss. I'd always loved kissing, but Porter's kiss was straight up addictive. When we were winding each other up, he was aggressive and needy, taking what he wanted and making no apologies for it. But now, when he was sated and relaxed, his kisses were softer. Lazier.

Except that didn't last long. Not that I was surprised. I'd been going out of my mind wanting him, so of course I was going to get turned on all over again.

Porter pressed his hips against me, and yep—he was getting aroused again too. As his cock brushed my thigh, he sucked in a breath.

"Somebody's horny tonight," I teased.

"Uh-huh." He closed his fingers around my cock, and it was my turn to gasp. "Not the only one, am I?"

"God, no. Not with you in my bed."

He pushed out a ragged breath and stroked me slowly. "So if I said I wanted you to fuck me again...?"

"Oh, Jesus." I was out of breath as I whispered, "Can you take me again?"

"Mmm..." He shivered, pushing his cock into my fist. "Yeah. Just...slower."

"I can do that." I brushed my lips across his and whispered, "I want to come in you again."

Porter whimpered. "You...talk so dirty..."

I grinned and kissed him again. "That a good thing?"

"*Oh* yeah."

"Good to know." I nipped his lower lip. "Now how about you turn over so I can do more than talk?"

He shivered hard, and as I reached for the lube, he rolled onto his stomach. Fuck, wasn't that a sight. He'd been hot as hell up against the wall in the shower. Spread out like this, kneading the edge of the mattress and squirming just a little as if he were rubbing his dick against the sheet? He was like a damn gift. A horny, hungry gift just begging to be ridden.

I stroked on some lube, then settled over the top of him. I slid the head of my cock along his crack a couple of times before I pressed against his hole, and he moaned into the pillow as I sank into him. Jesus, it was like I'd never done this at all. Like it was the first time we'd ever touched, that I'd ever been inside him, even though it had been less than half an hour since I'd fucked him up against the bathroom wall.

He grunted softly as I bottomed out.

"This okay?" I panted in his ear.

He nodded, chin scraping across the pillowcase. "Fuck, yeah."

"Yeah?" I started to withdraw again. "Not too—"

"It's good." He gripped the edge of the mattress and arched against me. "God..."

I buried my face against his neck and breathed him in, and I rocked my hips, moving in and out of him so slowly I thought I might come unglued. Not sure if I needed more leverage or just more of him, I slid my arms under him and hooked them over his shoulders, my thumb pressing in just above his mountain lion tattoo.

"Jesus, Holden," he moaned, arching against my chest. "You feel so... Oh fuck..."

"So do you. And FYI," I breathed in his ear, "this is how I like being topped too."

"Good to know." He tilted his head, offering up the side of his neck. "'Cause this is how I like topping."

I swore, let my lips skate across his neck, and then sank my teeth into his shoulder. He gasped, his entire body tensing, and his ass clenched hard around my cock. I was careful not to ride him too hard and make him sore, but he felt so good, and I was so close, and I couldn't resist trying to push deeper inside him as I neared the edge.

"You gonna come?" he asked.

Hell, I was. There was no holding back, not even after I'd already come once tonight. Dry spell, be gone.

"I am," I murmured. "And then I'm going to blow you again, so you better not come."

That got a whimper out of him, which did nothing to help me hold back. I was so close, right there, right there, and then Porter whispered, "Oh God, baby," and I thrust deep as I came inside him. Holy fuck. Holy. Fuck. So that was what it felt like to come so hard I almost cried. Whoa.

My orgasm had barely started to taper before I was overcome with this irresistible need to make him feel the same way, so I slurred, "Turn over on your back."

I pulled out, and as soon as he'd rolled over, I nudged his legs apart. He didn't resist, letting his thighs fall open as I settled between them, and when I slipped a couple of fingers into his ass, he groaned. Again when I took his cock deep in my mouth.

"Oh Jesus..." His voice had that delicious shaky quality of a man getting close, and I was determined to keep him there and then send him higher. Licking, sucking, fingering—whatever it took, I wanted him in the stratosphere again.

His hands raked through my hair, and his hips rose enough to push him deeper into my throat. It was just the right amount of forceful—enough to let me know exactly what he wanted without making me worry he'd choke me or that he wouldn't let go if I wanted him to. And I didn't want him to. I wanted him to hold onto my hair and fuck my mouth until he came. It had been so long since I'd sucked cock, I literally couldn't figure out *how* long, and it had taken until tonight for me to realize how much I'd missed it. Oral had always been one of my favorite things in the world anyway, regardless of what equipment my partner had or who was giving or receiving, and I loved the way a thick, hard cock felt between my lips and on my tongue.

"God, Holden..." He moaned, gripping my hair so tight my scalp stung. "I'm gonna come. Keep... oh God, yeah..."

I was the one to moan this time. I wasn't just turned on by the idea of him coming in my mouth. I was greedy for it. It had been *years*, and this was just the man to break that long, long dry spell, and dear God, I wanted him to unload on my tongue again right fucking now.

And in the next instant, with a cry that gave me goose bumps, he did exactly that. I swallowed everything he gave me, and when he sagged back onto the bed, I carefully withdrew my fingers and sat up.

Now *that* was a sexy view—Porter, sprawled on my bed, sweaty and disheveled with a shaking hand over his eyes, his cock still hard, looking like he'd been thoroughly fucked.

"So." I gave his inner thigh a stroke, grinning when he gasped and arched. "Another shower?"

Hand still over his eyes, he slurred, "Hope water's included in your rent, or your bill is going to suck."

"It'll be worth it. Come on."

"Just... just gimme a sec."

He only needed a minute before he apparently decided he could stand up, though he did sling an arm around my waist and lean on me on the way into the bathroom.

In the shower, he turned to me and lazily rested his forearms on my shoulders. "If you're this insatiable now, I feel like twenty-something you would have killed me."

I laughed. "I wasn't as good at sucking dick in my twenties, though. Stamina only goes so far if you don't have the skill to back it up."

Porter quirked his swollen lips like he was really giving it some thought. "Okay. I can't argue with that." He dragged his hands up my back and lifted his head for a kiss. "You're not lacking in skill or stamina, so you won't hear me complaining."

"I don't want to hear you complain." I nipped his lower lip. "I want to hear you beg and moan."

His soft whimper made my whole body tingle. What I wouldn't have given for the opportunity to spend an entire day in bed with him, just finding every way imaginable to make his breath hitch and his toes curl. He was so deliciously responsive, and exactly what I needed to leave my long dry spell in the dust. It was entirely possible *he'd* kill *me*, but what a way to go.

"I don't know exactly how we're going to do this," I murmured. "How we're going to fly under Tiffany's radar." I paused for a long kiss. "I just know I don't want to stop."

"Neither do I." He carded his fingers through my hair, making me shiver. "We'll figure it out."

"We will." I kissed him again, and I fully intended to say something else, but I got lost in the softness of his lips against mine, and the way his fingertips trailed down my back. Surprise, surprise—it didn't take long for the kiss to deepen and our breaths to start getting harsher and faster. He held on tighter, and when his hardening cock grazed my thigh, he moaned.

I doubted I had a third orgasm in me tonight, but I was pretty sure Porter did.

I was right.

CHAPTER 22

PORTER

NOT SURPRISINGLY, THAT NIGHT WAS ONLY THE beginning of Holden and me being inseparable. Well, as inseparable as schedules and secrecy allowed, but every chance we had, we were in his bed. Or his shower. Or that one time over his kitchen counter because we'd both spun each other up too much to even make it to the bedroom. In between, there were texts. Endless, flirty, dirty texts. When we were feeling really brave—or were just too horny to care—there were even some hushed Facetime conversations that always left me gasping.

We were careful to keep this on the down-low. Neither of us felt particularly great about lying to her about this, but I was on board with Holden's approach—see how things went between us, and if it looked like we had some staying power, then sit down and fess up to Tiffany. She was a reasonable person, and while I didn't imagine she'd be happy to find out we were seeing each other despite her warnings to both of us, I held out hope that we could all be adults about this.

Because nothing said adulthood like sneaking around

with the guy you've been expressly forbidden from dating. Fuck.

And we weren't only sneaking around. Holden still went with me sometimes when I took Chloe and the boys out. With three high energy kids, two adults were better than one, and for the most part, we focused our attention on them rather than each other. Yeah, there were plenty of stolen glances and suggestive grins—even some discreet texts now and then—but we had an unspoken agreement that when we were out and about with his kids, they were priority one.

Today, Holden had been able to cut out of work early since he'd stayed late a couple nights in a row, so he'd joined us at a playground near Ethan and Noah's school. There wasn't much daylight left, being early November, but there were streetlights, and all three kids were bundled up and had more than enough energy. Might as well let them burn it off before the boys had to sit down with their homework (such bullshit for a first and second grader).

When it was finally getting cold enough that Holden and I were losing feeling in our ears and noses, we called the kids and headed for the car.

We didn't get far, though—someone had a schnauzer wearing a blue knitted sweater, and Chloe immediately started toward it.

"Chloe," I said, keeping my voice firm but not harsh.

She halted and looked back at me.

I gestured at the dog. "Remember what we say?"

Chloe bit her lip, glancing back and forth from me to the owner. Finally, in a tiny, shy voice, she said, "Can I pet your dog?"

The woman holding the leash smiled. "Of course,

honey." She crouched and scratched behind the dog's ears. "Just let him sniff your hand first."

Chloe hesitated, then cautiously held out her hand. The dog sniffed it, and when he licked her fingers, she giggled and carefully petted his fuzzy head while he wagged his tail. The boys joined in, and they went through the same motions—let him sniff their hands, and then gently pet him.

"You've got them well-trained," Holden said quietly. Had this been back in the very beginning, I was pretty sure that would have been snide, or at least had an edge to it, but it didn't now. Especially not with that fond smile while he watched his kids petting a dog.

I shrugged. "I treated a lot of dog bites when I was on the ambulance. Since they're all suckers for animals just like I am, I wanted to make sure they learned to be careful."

"Smart." We both watched for a moment as the kids—beaming the entire time—petted the happy schnauzer.

"Chloe still forgets sometimes," I said. "But she's getting it, just like the boys have."

Holden nodded, and when I stole a glance at him, he was still smiling, gaze fixed on his daughter.

Oh God. Chloe and I may have been suckers for animals, but I was undeniably a sucker for this man. I'd never dated anyone with kids before, and I'd never really thought about it, but holy crap, I was thinking about it now.

Okay, so I was starting to get why my sister insisted her husband had become a hundred times more attractive the first time she'd seen him holding a baby. On his own, Holden was mind-blowingly sexy. In dad mode? He was attractive in a whole different way. Not in a sexual way—it was more like I was getting a look at his soft, sweet side. It was like that firefighter I'd had a crush on during my last two years at the station. He'd been gorgeous and—look, he was a firefighter, and there was a reason they always asked him to pose for the annual calendar. Enough said. Then we'd all been at his house for a barbecue, and he and his wife had recently adopted a couple of kittens. I swear, the moment I saw him with those kittens, I fell ass over teakettle in love with that man.

That was the kind of oh-my-God knee-melting that happened when I saw Holden with his kids. The snug jeans, rolled up sleeves, and hints of gray in his hair and goatee? Those all piqued my libido's interest. Stealing a kiss in his car when we both knew damn well we shouldn't? Same deal. *This*, though? Seeing him doting on his babies or just smiling like the proud dad he was? Oh hell, that hit me right in the feels.

Tiffany, please forgive me, but how the hell am I supposed to say no to this?

WHEN HOLDEN AND I HERDED THE KIDS INTO THE house after stopping at the grocery store, Ashley and Tiffany were getting ready to head out.

"Oh good, there you are," Tiffany said. "I was just about to call and ask when you were getting back. Do you have dinner covered for tonight?"

I held up the reusable shopping bag. "Give me about twenty minutes."

"Perfect. Listen, Ashley has a volleyball game tonight out in Oak Harbor, and it doesn't even start until eight. So, we'll probably be back late." She turned to Holden as she put her phone into her purse. "You staying for dinner?"

"Um." He glanced at me. "You don't mind?"

Tiffany laughed and rolled her eyes. "Yes, Holden. I

mind you spending more time with your kids." She tsked. "Of course it's fine."

"Yeah, but it's your house, and—"

"And your kids are here. Unless Porter has some objection?"

They both turned to me.

"No, no." I shook my head. "No objection."

"Well, then." She smiled and pulled her purse strap onto her shoulder. "Have fun." And with that, she left the kitchen, calling down the hall, "Ash? You ready to roll?"

Holden and I waited in uncomfortable silence until Ashley and Tiffany had gone out the front door.

"She doesn't suspect a thing, does she?" I asked under my breath.

Gaze still fixed on the empty doorway, he said, "Nope."

We exchanged uneasy glances. I suspected he felt as guilty as I did. Tiffany trusted us not to be sleeping together, took us at our word that we *weren't* sleeping together and *wouldn't* sleep together, and what were we doing at every opportunity? Basically anything two dudes could do in bed without someone needing medical attention.

"So." I cleared my throat. "You're staying?"

He pressed his shoulder against the door frame. "Well, I'm already here. And Tiffany knows I'm here."

"True. The kids will probably be thrilled to have you stay." I tried and failed to suppress a smile. "I'm pretty sure I can live with it too."

Holden laughed. "You flatterer."

I just chuckled, but sobered. "You sure, though? I mean..."

He turned serious too and glanced over his shoulder as if he thought his ex might suddenly materialize on the stairs. Then he came a little closer. Not enough to touch me, but enough he could lower his voice to something more discreet. "I feel weird about it too. Doing this without her knowing. But let's play it by ear for a little while longer, see how things go, and then..."

"Then we'll talk to her."

"If we think this is something worth bringing up, yeah."

I mulled it over, then nodded. "Okay. I can live with that." It was still going to make me feel guilty as hell every time I looked at Tiffany and every time she trusted us alone, but I'd go with it for now. Maybe that made me stupid or an asshole, but the choice was between probably losing my job and giving up the man in front of me. And, God, I just couldn't let this thing with Holden go.

I shifted my weight. "So. Um. If you're staying, do you mind getting hands washed while I get food going?"

The tension in his features eased into one of those disarming smiles, and he nodded. "All right. Will do."

Just like we had all day, and every time we were out with his kids, we kept our focus on them. I made dinner while Holden had them wash their hands and set the table. When dinner was over and everyone had taken their dishes into the kitchen, he took over cleaning while I set the boys up with their homework on the kitchen table. Then, while Chloe played quietly in the living room, I helped Noah with his schoolwork and Holden focused on Ethan's. This was kind of odd when I considered the clandestine thing we had going on, but in the moment, it worked. It felt so normal and domestic.

Tiffany, if you saw us like this, would you understand why I want him like that?

But I tried not to think about that.

Once homework was done, the boys joined their sister in the living room, and Holden and I hung back in the kitchen where we could see them but talk without really being heard. As I poured us each some coffee, I realized he had a weird look on his face. Like he was deep in thought, and not about anything good.

I handed him a mug. "What's on your mind?"

Holden took the mug with a murmured thanks, and fixed his gaze on his kids again. "I think... I think Ethan might be having some of the same problems Zach did."

"Oh." I glanced at Ethan, then turned back to Holden. "What kind of problems?"

He sipped his coffee and set it on the counter beside him. "When we were looking over his spelling, he was flipping letters the same way Zach does It might just be that he's still learning to read and write, but that was the kind of problem Zach had early on."

"Is he dyslexic?"

Holden nodded. "I'm wondering if Tiffany and I should get him tested. If he's got the same thing his brother has, then the earlier he can learn to work around it, the better."

"Good idea." I watched Ethan for a moment. "Now that you mention it, he has struggled since school started. He has a hard time reading out loud too, but if you read something to him, he's like a steel trap."

"That sounds like Zach." Holden picked up his coffee again. "I'll definitely talk to Tiffany."

I made a mental note to keep an eye on Ethan's progress with reading and spelling, and then Holden and I shifted to lighter topics. We finished our coffee and moved to the living room, and while the kids played, we continued talking about whatever. Before I knew it, it was bedtime.

Disappointment pushed down on my shoulders. It had been such a chill evening with Holden. I wasn't ready for it to be over yet, but I was sure he'd head for the door once the kids started getting ready for bed.

Except...he didn't.

He stuck around while they put on their pajamas and brushed their teeth, and when everyone piled onto Noah's bed for their story, he sat on the foot of the bed and watched while I read to them. A few weeks ago, that would have been way too much pressure for me. I'd have been sure he was looking for any reason to tell me I was doing something —everything—wrong. But tonight, everyone was as relaxed as we'd all been when the roles had been reversed and I'd been the one sitting back while Holden read to his kids. In fact, it was even more relaxed than that. If anything, all I could think was, *How have we not been doing this all along?* And I didn't care how crazy that was.

When story time was over, I took Chloe into her room. With everyone happily tucked in, Holden gently pulled the boys' bedroom door shut, and we went into the living room. As we sank onto the couch, he released a relieved sigh. "Lord, I am so glad those kids go down easy now."

"Haven't they always?" *And do you know how much I love the fact that you haven't left yet?* "I mean, I know you were kind of worried that first night at your place, but..."

Holden barked a laugh. "Oh, my sweet summer child." He shook his head and whistled. "Noah was basically the easiest newborn ever, so we thought we'd lucked out. The minute he turned one? Oh my *God*."

"That bad, huh?"

"Ugh." Holden wiped a hand over his face. "I shit you not, it makes me tired just thinking about trying to put that child to bed from the time he was one until... Well, it's kind of a blur at that point because Ethan came along, and he just..." He rolled his eyes. "His sleep chip didn't come preinstalled, let's put it that way. So then we had two toddlers who refused to be on the same schedule, wouldn't fall asleep for anything, and we pretty much resigned ourselves to never knowing what it was like to feel rested again. You want to know why there's such a big gap between Ethan and Chloe?" He gestured emphatically down the hall. "That's why."

I snorted. "Too tired to go through the motions?"

"I think we spent a solid year glaring at each other like '*I swear if you touch me, I will end you.*' And then once we did get back into that groove, suddenly Tiffany's pregnant with Chloe, and we're both terrified because we just got our life back." He grimaced. "Plus Chloe was so active while Tiffany was pregnant, we were both convinced she was going to be born with an actual allergy to sleep."

I cringed. "Oh no."

Holden smiled. "Turned out she was the easiest out of all three. Seriously, the only easier sleeper I ever had was Zach." He waved a hand. "You'd have to ask Tiffany about Ashley's early years."

"I'm kind of afraid to ask."

"You and me both." He paused. "This doesn't bother you, does it? Me talking about my life with Tiffany? Including... You know..."

"Insomniac children sabotaging your sex life?"

"Yes. That."

I shrugged. "Not really. I feel like it should, but it doesn't." I put my hand on his knee. "Because I want you to tell me about yourself, and she was a big part of your life. So no, it doesn't bother me."

"It's not weird?"

"Holden." I chuckled. "We're sitting in your ex-wife's living room while she's not here and your kids—who I'm paid to take care of—are asleep down the hall. Yes, everything about this is weird." *Except it feels the opposite of weird.* "But I'm not complaining if you're not."

He seemed to consider that for a moment. "Okay. When you put it like that..."

Our eyes met, and we both laughed.

He checked the time on his phone. "How late do you think Tiffany will be?"

"Don't know." I checked my own cell. "It's only eight forty-five, and she said the game didn't start till eight. Plus they're in Oak Harbor, which is a solid hour from here."

"So, you're saying we've got some time." There was a feisty note in his voice that gave me pause.

"We do, yeah." I inclined my head. "What did you have in mind?"

"Well." He glanced down the hall, and when he met my gaze again, he had a wicked glint in his eye that made my pulse jump. "They're probably out cold by now."

I swallowed. "You think?"

"Uh-huh." He slid his hand over my thigh, the gesture a *lot* more suggestive than when I'd put my hand on his knee. "And we've got time before Tiffany and Ashley get home."

"So you...want to..." I closed my eyes and shivered as his hand drifted higher. "Oh God..."

"Think we have enough time?"

"Keep touching me like that and you won't *need* much time." I bit my lip. "You really think we should sneak off and fool around, though?"

"We're not leaving." He grinned. "And it's not like I've never snuck off and fooled around while the kids were asleep."

"Yeah?"

"Uh. Yeah." He winked. "Notice how I have more than one kid?"

I snorted and wrapped my arms around his neck. "I hadn't thought about it like that. Pretty sure we don't have to worry about you knocking me up, though."

He huffed a laugh as he drew me in closer. "Well that's a load off my mind."

I chuckled, but then his lips met mine, and the humor vanished in favor of melting into his kiss and his embrace. Holden was such an...artful kisser. It was the only way I could describe it. Everything he did seemed so calculated and methodical, designed with the laser-focused purpose of turning me to putty in his hands, and at the same time it felt so languid, almost lazy, like it was as easy and natural as breathing. No calculations necessary.

Whatever. My brain was offline, so nothing I thought of made sense. I hadn't made out like this since I was a teenager—fully-clothed, kissing and groping on the sofa while we listened in case a door opened—and I'd forgotten how hot it was. The way his hand slid up my thigh to my hip and onto my ass. How his goatee brushed my chin every time he moved his jaw. The softness of his lips against mine. I was utterly hooked on him. No two ways about it.

And I wanted him right the hell now.

I pulled back and met his gaze. "You know, I do have a bedroom nearby."

"You do, don't you?" He licked his lips. "Maybe we should..."

I nodded.

We got up, and we took a moment to quietly double-check that everyone was asleep. They were—wearing them out at the playground, for the win—so we hurried downstairs as quickly and quietly as possible, slipped into my bedroom, and left the door open just enough we could hear if anyone needed us.

And then? It was on.

Holden wrapped his arms around me and kissed me the way I'd been dying for him to kiss me all evening—deep and messy, punctuated by little moans and sharp inhalations.

"We have to stay quiet," I whispered between kisses.

"We will." Then he kissed me harder. He pushed me up against the wall, pinning me there with his hips and his kiss and his hands for good measure. Staying quiet was definitely easier said than done, especially when he started on my neck. Having his lips skating along the side of my throat at the same time he was rutting against me, his thick hard-on rubbing mine through our jeans—I was ready to lose my mind.

"Get that shirt off," he murmured against my jaw, "before I come all over it."

I shuddered hard, grateful for the wall and his body pinning me to it, or I'd have melted to his feet. Between us, hell if I knew how, we pushed my shirt up and off, and his came off too, and then we were kissing with skin right on skin.

I wanted more, though. Fuck, I wanted him naked. Or at least less dressed than this. I slid a hand between us and fumbled. Zipper? How the fuck did a zipper work? Why couldn't I remember? I could usually think pretty clearly even when I was turned on, but Holden was like a magnet to a hard drive. One hot, eager touch, and everything went blank.

Fortunately, he still had his wits about him, and somehow—magic, probably—he got my pants unzipped, and then my cock was in his hand, and he was stroking me while I was stroking him, and…yep. Magnet. Hard drive. Blank.

"Jesus, Porter," he whispered between breathless kisses. "I want you...so fucking bad. So..." He trailed off into a moan, then claimed a deeper, harder kiss than before. Kissing was the only way to keep each other absolutely silent, and I loved kissing, so we made out hungrily, muffling soft moans as we jerked each other off.

He broke away first and whispered, "You getting close? Getting there?"

"Uh-huh. Getting... Oh God..."

Abruptly, he was on his knees, and I gasped as the fist around my cock was suddenly replaced by the wet heat of his mouth. He held my hips still with strong, unrelenting hands, pinning me in place so there was nothing I could do but stand there and enjoy his lips and tongue sliding up and down my cock. Which... okay, yeah, twist my arm. Stand here and lose myself in an enthusiastic blowjob from a man with a relentless and talented mouth? Bring it. Fucking bring it. Because oh *God*.

I wanted to fuck into his mouth, but with my hips in his iron grip, I couldn't move, and the restraint made me excruciatingly restless. It was like my inability to move kept me from doing anything with all this building energy, so it rolled over into my impending orgasm, and...fuck...

"Christ, Holden... How the hell do you... What is..." My back arched off the wall, and I had just enough presence of mind left to remember that we couldn't make much noise, so I pressed my teeth into my lip just to keep myself quiet. Even that wasn't helping, though, so I clapped my hand over my mouth, and not a moment too soon—I had no idea what he did with his tongue, but out of nowhere, I was coming, trying like hell to fuck into his mouth, except damn if he'd let go of my hips.

With a shudder, I sagged against the wall, and suddenly

the hands on my hips were the only thing keeping me from sliding down to the carpet. Then he was against me again, using his body to keep me up, and the touch of his lips made me shiver again. The way he'd kissed me upstairs had melted my brain, but now? With my cum on his tongue and his bare chest pressed to mine while my head still spun from that orgasm? Holy shit.

"God, you turn me on so much," he said, lips barely leaving mine. "I want...ungh..." His hard-on rubbed my hip, and we kissed again, *just* muffling both our moans.

I needed to do something about how hard and aroused this man was, so I pushed him back a step and dropped to my knees, pulled him in by his unzipped pants, and went down on him like my life depended on it.

"Oh, yeah." His voice was a ragged whisper as he dragged his fingers through my hair. "That's it, baby. Oh... *Jesus...*"

I didn't hold back at all. After he'd made me come that hard, I was bound and determined to return the favor in full. I didn't hold his hips still, though, and he started rocking them, sliding his cock in and out of my mouth. When I didn't stop him, he thrust a little harder, as if experimenting, and I hummed to encourage him.

A hand slid into my hair. He wasn't forcing me, just steadying me, and oh yeah, that was hot. The way he grunted and gasped, fucked into my mouth, held me still as if he thought I might pull away—I wanted him in pieces, and he was definitely getting there.

"I'm gonna come," he slurred. "Gonna... You ready for me?"

I made a soft sound that hopefully translated to "hell yes." It must have, because he gasped, shuddered, and shot cum across my tongue.

Holden slumped forward, resting a hand on the wall to keep himself upright. I wiped my hand across my mouth, then stood, and his other arm encircled my waist and pulled me in for a lazy, breathless kiss.

"In case it wasn't obvious," he said, still trembling. "That was fucking amazing."

I grinned and kissed him again. "Well, you're the one who raised the bar."

He laughed, sounding vaguely drunk, and wrapped his arms around me. Together, we leaned against my bedroom wall and just let the afterglow wash over both of us.

"We really need some time alone again," he whispered after a while. "Where we have all the time in the world and we don't have to be quiet."

"Yeah?" I licked my lips. "Why's that?"

He grinned, making my knees wobble. "So I can spend a whole damn night making you scream."

I couldn't speak. I just shivered.

And oh yeah, we needed to do that.

Like...*stat.*

CHAPTER 23

HOLDEN

Zach and I were finally settled into the apartment enough that I could regularly have Chloe, Ethan, and Noah for entire weekends. It would still be a little tight, though maybe less cramped now that I'd be sleeping on the couch while Chloe took the loveseat and the boys took my bed, but until I could get a bigger place, we'd make do. They called the arrangement "camping at Dad's house," and, eh, it wasn't that far from the truth, so why not?

So, on Friday afternoon, while Zach got to work making a meal his younger siblings loved—I owed him big time—I drove over to Tiffany's place to pick them up. She must have been working from home, because she came to the door when I arrived.

"The kids are in the backyard with Porter." She gestured over her shoulder. "He's trying to wear them out a little so they'll sleep tonight."

I laughed. "Much appreciated. Man, if we could bottle that energy and sell it..."

"Right." She sighed. "Oh, and by the way, I'm taking the kids to my mom's in Salem next weekend."

"Got it. How long is that drive, anyway?"

"About four hours, give or take."

I whistled. "Good thing you'll have Porter along."

"Actually, I won't."

"Really?"

Tiffany shook her head. "There's just not enough room at Mom's place. That, and my brother is going to be there, and he's still kind of weirded out by the idea of a male nanny." Rolling her eyes, she muttered, "Whatever."

"Oh. Uh. Good luck on the drive, then?"

"Eh, I'll have my sister with me."

"Okay, so you'll be all set, then."

"Definitely. I just wanted to give you a heads up, though. In case you were making plans."

"Didn't have any so far, so thanks for letting me know."

"Don't mention it." She shot me a look with an undercurrent that was subtle, but unmistakable: *I'm not kidding, Holden. Keep your hands off the nanny while we're out of town.*

Or maybe that was my conscience superimposing my own guilt into her expression. She'd taken me at my word that nothing was going on between me and Porter. She trusted us. I hadn't been close to a perfect husband, but I *had* been an honest one. Lying to her didn't feel any better now that we were divorced. When I figured out how to tell her the truth...

Yeah. Not looking forward to that day.

While Tiffany returned to folding some laundry in the living room, I went out onto the deck. Porter glanced up at me and grinned but quickly schooled his expression.

"We're playing a game, Dad," Noah announced. "Can we finish?"

"Sure. I'll watch."

I couldn't begin to make heads or tails of the rules—some hybrid of baseball, soccer, and God knew what else—but they were having fun, and that was the important part.

I let my gaze slide to Porter, and the conversation with Tiffany echoed through my mind. So, he'd be home for the weekend? No one around? Despite the unspoken and quite possibly imagined warning from my ex-wife, I was seriously intrigued by what kind of trouble he and I could get up to with a couple days of total freedom.

The sliding glass door opened behind me, jarring me out of my thoughts. I figured it was Tiffany, and heat rushed into my face because I was sure she'd just busted me thinking about a sordid weekend with the nanny.

But then Ashley said, "Holden?"

I looked over my shoulder. "Oh. Hey, kiddo."

In the open doorway, she glanced over her shoulder. Then she stepped all the way out onto the deck and eased the slider shut behind her. As she came across the deck, her eyes down and her hands in the pockets of her jeans, she seemed uncharacteristically shy and small. Like she was hunched in on herself.

Concern straightened my spine. I was half tempted to call down to Porter or lean inside and grab Tiffany because this was definitely uncharted territory. My stepdaughter and I had mostly gotten along, but we'd never been what I'd call close.

But I stayed put, and I turned to face her fully. "What's up?"

Gnawing her lip, she rested an elbow on the railing and stared down at her half-siblings and Porter in the backyard. "I, um, heard you and Mom arguing a few weeks ago. About her thinking you had a thing for Porter."

My tongue tried to stick to the roof of my mouth. "Um. Okay?"

"And a while ago, I heard her say something on the phone to Aunt Carly about your ex-boyfriend."

"Did she?"

"Yeah." She searched my eyes. "So, you *had* a boyfriend?"

"I did, yes." *I kind of do now, but you don't need to know about that and neither does your mom.*

She took a deep breath and finally met my gaze. "So are you gay?"

"I'm bisexual."

"Oh. And Mom knows?"

I nodded.

Ashley shifted her weight. "Did she know when you were married?"

"Yeah. I've been out since college. That ex she was talking about? If he's the one I'm thinking of, he introduced me to your mom."

"Oh." Ashley fell silent, and once again watched her younger siblings playing with Porter.

I pressed my elbow onto the railing and studied her. "Why do you ask?"

Ashley seemed to shrink a little more. She folded her arms, cradled her elbow, and started chewing her thumbnail.

Okay, *those* were some lines I could definitely read between.

"Is it okay?" I asked softly. "That I'm bi?"

She nodded. "Yeah. It's..." She pulled in a deep breath, looked me in the eye, and blurted out, "If I wanted to come out to my mom, would you be there with me?"

"Sure."

"Really?"

"Of course."

She exhaled hard, as if she'd genuinely worked herself up and convinced herself I'd either say no, or I'd out her to her mom and get her in trouble. It didn't have to be rational. God knew my mind had gone down similar roads when I'd come out to my folks, and I'd been five years older than Ashley was now.

"Whenever you want to talk to her," I said. "Just say the—"

"Can we, um, do it now?" She pointed over her shoulder with her thumb. "I kind of want to get it over with."

"Oh. Uh, yeah. All right." I made an *after you* gesture at the sliding glass door. "Whenever you're ready."

She nodded. "Okay." Another deep breath, and then she pushed her shoulders back and headed for the door.

I started to follow, but paused to turn back. "Hey, Porter?"

He looked up. "Yeah?"

"I'll be inside with Tiffany whenever they're ready to go."

He gave me a thumbs up, then returned his attention to the game, and I caught up with Ashley as she stepped into the living room.

Tiffany was still folding laundry, arranging everything in stacks on the couch and baskets at her feet. She had her back to us, and Ashley glanced at me. I nodded.

Ashley took a deep breath. "Hey, Mom?"

"Hmm?" Tiffany turned around. Immediately, her eyes darted toward me, and as they flicked back to her daughter, they widened with alarm. "Yeah, honey?"

"Um." Eyes down, Ashley wrung her hands in front of her. "Can I tell you something?"

More alarm registered on Tiffany's face. She put down the shirt she'd been folding and faced her daughter fully. "What's on your mind?"

"I, um." Ashley swallowed. "I started going out with someone. At school."

"Oh." Tiffany glanced at me again, and I was pretty sure I heard the piece click into place. To Ashley, she said, "Um, what's their name?"

Ashley lifted her chin. I couldn't see her face, but I suspected she was searching her mom's expression as she'd done mine. Then, so softly I barely heard her, she said, "Sara."

"Sara." Tiffany furrowed her brow. "Sara with the glasses?" She gestured at her hair. "Or the redhead?"

"The glasses." Ashley giggled a little as she said it, and I could practically feel the relief rolling off her. "We started going out a couple of weeks ago."

"Oh." Tiffany broke into a smile. "I wondered about that, to be honest."

Ashley blinked. "You did?"

"Honey." Tiffany picked up the shirt she'd been folding and started folding it again. "I was born at night, but I wasn't born last night."

"Huh?"

"I've seen how much you smile when she's around compared to your other friends." Tiffany put the folded shirt on top of the stack and picked up another from the pile. "So I kind of had a hunch."

"So you're not mad?"

"Of course not! I love Sara." She paused, the shirt half-folded in her hands, and cocked her head. "Is that why you stopped having her come over as much? Because you thought we might figure something out?"

Ashley's face turned bright red and she stared at the floor.

I put a hand on her shoulder and gave it a gentle squeeze, but didn't say anything.

She looked up at me, her expression filled with renewed trepidation. "Can you be there when I tell my dad too?"

I pretended not to notice the way Tiffany tensed. "Of course. Just give me some warning, but I'll make it happen."

She smiled at me, and it was probably a brighter smile than any she'd directed at me in all the years I'd known her. "Thanks."

"Don't mention it."

To her mom, she said, "Well, I have homework. I just, um, wanted you to know."

"Thanks for telling me, sweetheart," Tiffany said.

Ashley nodded, and she left the living room for her bedroom.

Tiffany watched her go, then turned to me. "How long have you known about this?"

"She told me just now. She, um, asked if I'd come with her to come out to you."

"Oh." Tiffany's brow furrowed. "Did she think I'd freak out?"

"She didn't say. But I can tell you from experience, any kid is going to be nervous about telling their parents. She's probably got more friends who've been accepted by their families than not, but there are probably at least a few who *weren't* accepted." I grimaced. "Even in this day and age, I doubt there are a lot of kids who take for granted that they can come out to their parents without some kind of backlash."

My ex-wife frowned. "Okay, I get that. I just hope I didn't raise her to think I'd have a problem with her being gay."

I shook my head. "Nah. I don't think so. But any time a kid is bringing up something that has even a minute chance of getting them disowned, even if they're ninety-nine percent sure their parents would happily wave a rainbow flag at a Price parade, they're going to be scared."

"Okay, I guess that makes sense." She sighed. "Well, I'm glad she had support. So, thank you for being there for her."

"Of course." There was still some uncertainty in her eyes, so I went on. "She's not my biological daughter, but that doesn't mean I stopped caring about her the day you and I signed our divorce papers." I exhaled. "I'm just glad she felt safe enough to come to me."

At that, Tiffany smiled. "I'm not surprised about that part."

"Really?"

"Sure. She's never thought of you as being her father, but you've been there in ways her father never has. That didn't go away with the divorce either."

I wasn't sure how to respond to that. "How, um, how do you think Jay will take it? Finding out she's gay?"

Tiffany huffed out a breath, scowling as she always did when someone mentioned her jackass first husband. "Well, I think it'll be good for her to have you as backup, let's put it that way."

"Great." As it was, there wasn't a lot of love lost between me and Jay. For Ashley's sake, we'd done our level best to get along while Tiffany and I were married, but things had never been particularly warm between us. I couldn't imagine this would help.

But if Ashley wanted me there when she came out to

her dad, I'd be there in a heartbeat. No hesitation. He didn't have to like me. He'd damn sure respect his daughter.

Downstairs, a door opened, and thundering footsteps told me the kids had come in.

"Sounds like the wild beasts are done playing," Tiffany mused.

"Yeah, they sure sound worn out."

She laughed. "Uh-huh. Good luck tonight."

"Thanks." I sobered. "I better go help him round them up. And, um, keep me posted about Ashley and talking to her dad. I mean it—if she wants me there, I'll be there."

"I will. And I'm serious—I really appreciate you being there for her tonight." She stepped closer and hugged me tight. "Thank you, Holden."

Closing my eyes, I returned the hug. "Any time."

After she'd let me go, I headed downstairs to give Porter a hand with Chloe and the boys. He was supervising while they took off their muddy shoes and coats, and they fell all over themselves trying to give me the highlights of their game.

"Hey, hey, slow down," I said with a laugh. "You can tell me all about it in the car, all right? How about going and getting your things so we can go?"

Didn't have to tell them twice. All three thundered up the stairs, sounding like they were wearing combat boots even though they were in socks.

I chuckled as I turned to Porter. "Wore them out for me, eh?"

"I tried." He smirked. "Good luck."

"Yeah, their mom said the same thing." I glanced back at the door to be absolutely sure we were alone, then stole a quick kiss. "So you're going to be off work and unsupervised next weekend?"

The gleam in his eyes told me he was very much on the same page. "Sounds like it." He winked and started toward the stairs, throwing over his shoulder, "Might have to make some trouble."

Hell yeah, we'd make some trouble.

We could plan that later, though. For the next couple of days, it was me and the kids, and from the sound of it, they were ready to go.

After they'd said goodbye to Porter and their mom, they carried their backpacks out to my car and climbed into their respective seats.

I hadn't even put the key in the ignition when Noah said, "Dad, can we get McDonald's?"

Immediately, Ethan and Chloe chimed in with their approval of this idea.

"I don't know, guys," I said like I was really torn. "If we get McDonald's, then who's going to eat the spaghetti Zach is cooking?"

The collective gasp in the backseat made me chuckle. Whenever Zach had babysat his younger siblings when Tiffany and I had a rare date night, he'd made spaghetti for them, and that kid made some dynamite sauce.

"Spaghetti!" Ethan said.

"So, no McDonald's?"

"Spaghetti!" they all said in unison.

"All right, all right." I started the engine and backed out of Tiffany's driveway. "Let's go get some spaghetti."

While I drove, they amused themselves with a couple of toys, and my mind wandered back to the whole exchange with Ashley and Tiffany. Her mom's comments about me stepping up to fill in where her own father had failed were difficult to swallow. Wasn't that what I'd been afraid of with Porter? That he'd usurped my role and claimed pieces of my relationships with my kids that I could never get back? Had I done exactly that with Jay's daughter?

Except he'd had ample opportunity to step up and be a decent dad. There was a reason Tiffany had left him when their daughter was only six months old, and from what I'd heard, he hadn't even been all that upset when Tiffany had moved Ashley up to Washington several months ago. I'd been beside myself, but Jay hadn't seemed to care. He was probably relieved he'd only have to take his kid during the summer now instead of every other weekend. Ashley was probably relieved too, and I suspected she was dreading coming out to him. It wouldn't have surprised me in the least if he'd snarled some comments about Tiffany's "queer husband" over the years within earshot of her. God knew he'd done it within earshot of me enough times.

Christ, no wonder she'd been nervous going to her mom. She probably knew for a fact that at least one of her parents would be an asshole about it. Who was to say the other—the one who'd been married to that asshole for a while—would be any better?

I sent up another *thank you* that she'd felt safe enough to come to me. And I didn't feel the least bit apologetic about filling someone else's dad shoes. Quite frankly, if one of the places I'd failed was in making my children feel safe enough to say something like "I'm gay," then I deserved to have someone else grab that role. They damn sure deserved to have someone in their lives they could approach with something difficult like that.

And for all I'd screwed up as a parent, I had hope that I'd gotten this part right. If Ashley felt safe with me, then the little ones hopefully would too. If they didn't, at least I knew they had Tiffany and Porter. Maybe it would be a bitter pill to swallow that they felt better approaching their mom or nanny than me, but I could swallow that pill if it meant my kids had *someone*.

Except did I really have to worry that they wouldn't come to me? After all, I'd come into Ashley's life when she was a little older than Chloe was now. Now, though her mom and I were divorced, there was still enough trust and safety for her to come to me for help coming out to her parents.

If I could pull that off with my stepdaughter, then maybe I was overthinking how much damage I'd done to my relationships with Chloe and the boys. I couldn't get back the lost time with them, but maybe I could salvage more than I'd realized.

I released a long breath and adjusted my grip on the steering wheel. Maybe I was getting over my parenting yips after all. If nothing else, I'd count tonight as a few points for the *"stuff I got right"* side of the scoreboard.

I glanced in the rearview at Noah, Chloe, and Ethan, all strapped into their car seats, ready for a weekend of "camping at Dad's house" and chowing down on their brother's famous spaghetti.

Maybe this would be a chance to add a few more points to that side of the scoreboard.

CHAPTER 24

PORTER

Zach's job at an all-night diner had turned out to be a godsend for Holden and me. Since Zach worked a lot of late nights, that gave us the perfect time to snag a few hours of privacy. A couple of times, he'd come home early, and I'd had to hide in Holden's bedroom until Zach had either gone to take a shower or gone to bed, at which point I'd slip out and head home. For the most part, though, it worked out nicely for us. On Zach's off nights, he and Holden would sometimes spend time together. When he was at work, though? Game on.

Tonight was one of his work nights, and Holden and I were lounging lazily in bed like we often did. This was quickly becoming one of my favorite parts of our secret evenings together. The sex was great and all, but cuddling in bed with Holden was second to nothing.

Except tonight, Holden seemed kind of quiet. In fact, he was distant. He wasn't pushing me away—he'd been absently running the backs of his fingers up and down my arm for a few minutes—but he wasn't quite...here.

"Hey. What's wrong?" I lifted myself up on my elbow and held his gaze. "You're somewhere else tonight."

"Sorry. Sorry." He trailed his fingers along my forearm. "Just thinking."

"About?"

"Just...how things..." He waved a hand and sighed as if he couldn't find the words. "How we got here, I guess."

"What do you mean?"

"You working for Tiffany. How that ended up happening, and how that led to this, and... I mean, I'm thrilled it led to this, but..."

I studied him. "You're still telling yourself at every turn that you've failed them, haven't you?"

Holden blinked. "What?"

I held his gaze, keeping both my voice and expression soft. "I can see it in your eyes." I laced our fingers together. "For what it's worth, every day since you moved back to town, they've asked if they're going to see you that day."

His breath hitched. "They have?"

"Without fail."

Holden swallowed. "What do they say on days when they won't see me?"

"They usually ask when they *will* see you. And I won't blow smoke up your ass and tell you they're not disappointed, but they seem to understand. They know you have to work just like their mom does." I smiled and rubbed my thumb alongside his. "Before you pick them up to take them to your place, the boys tell me nonstop everything they want to do once they're with you. And as soon as they come back, they fill me in on everything." I held his gaze. "I know you're worried the ship has sailed and you won't ever be their dad they way you want to be, but I promise you—they are *so* happy to have you back in their world."

Holden released a breath and dropped his gaze to our hands. "Wow. Thank you. For telling me all that."

"You're welcome." I lifted my chin and pressed a soft kiss to his lips. "And the roads that got both of us here weren't exactly fun, but it's hard for me not to be thankful for them now. For mine, at least."

"Yeah. Me too." He shook himself. "Sorry. I didn't mean to be a downer tonight."

"It's okay." I smiled. "I get it."

"And my confidence *is* getting better. You've helped a lot, and... Anyway. It's better. The doubts just like to creep in sometimes."

"Don't worry. I totally understand." I paused. "And hey, we still need to figure out what we're doing next weekend while Tiffany and the kids are in Oregon."

A playful grin curved his lips, his expression brightening. "We do, yeah." He slid his hands up my back. "Hmm. A while weekend. No supervision or anything."

"Right?" I lifted my chin and kissed him lightly. "So what do we do with it?"

He held my gaze, and I fully expected something to the effect of *"fuck until we knock the plaster off the walls,"* but instead, Holden said, "Let's get out of town."

I blinked. "What?"

"Just take off somewhere for the weekend where no one knows us, and we can go out like a normal couple for a change."

My heart fluttered. *We're a normal couple?* "And fuck a lot, right?"

Holden grinned. "Well, obviously."

"So, where should we go?"

"Don't know. You've lived here longer than I have. What's interesting and within reasonable driving distance?"

I quirked my lips. There were some places out on the Olympic Peninsula, or we could dash up to Canada and spend the weekend in Victoria or Vancouver. There was Ocean Shores, except... No, that was a long ass drive, and the weather would probably suck this time of year. The mountains, though—I hadn't been up in the mountains in a long time. "We could go to Leavenworth."

Holden looked at me like I'd lost my damned mind. "An Army prison?"

I laughed. "This is a different Leavenworth. It's... I don't know, I guess this town decided to give everything a Bavarian theme. You kind of have to see it to get it." I let my fingertips drift over his hip. "But it's up in the mountains, feels like it's a million miles from anything, and it has hotels."

"*Sold.*" He grabbed his phone off the nightstand and opened a travel app. He typed in "Leavenworth," then scrolled a couple of times and stopped. "Okay, here's a place with a suite that's available, has a huge bed and a Jacuzzi tub, and doesn't cost a fortune." He tapped the screen and muttered, "Twist my arm."

I could barely sit still. Holy shit. We were actually doing this!

"And...booked." He put his phone aside and faced me again, a wicked grin on his lips. "This is going to be awesome."

"Yeah, it is."

"I'll see if I can cut out of work a couple of hours early that day. Then just text me as soon as Tiffany and the kids are on the road, and we'll take off."

"I will. Oh my God, I am *so* looking forward to this."

He drew me in close, and just before he claimed a long kiss, he murmured, "So am I."

"Okay." I surveyed the bags staged by the top of the stairs. "Looks like you all have everything."

Tiffany nodded, giving the neat piles of luggage a once-over. "I think we do. I swear I'm forgetting something, though."

Carly, Tiffany's sister, shook her head. "Honey, we're going to Mom's house, not the moon. If you forgot something and Mom doesn't have one, we can find it in Oregon."

"I guess." Tiffany scanned the bags again, then shrugged. "Okay. Let's rally the troops, then."

Between Carly, Tiffany, Ashley, and me, we rounded up the younger kids and had everyone—even Chloe—carry something out to the car. Tiffany's car was big enough to seat all six of them, but I was admittedly dubious about fitting everything into the trunk.

To my surprise, though, with a little Tetris-style creativity, it fit.

"So what are you going to do with the weekend?" Tiffany asked.

"I don't know yet." I slid Chloe and Ethan's tiny suitcases into the carefully packed trunk. "I might drop in and stay with my parents for the weekend."

"Smart man." Tiffany winked. "Let someone wait on you for a change."

"Pfft. That'll be the day. I guarantee my mom has a mile-long list of things she needs done around the house."

"Have fun with that."

"Gee. Thanks."

After Tiffany and I had buckled Chloe and the boys into their seats, Ashley wedged herself into the middle seat in front, and Tiffany got behind the wheel.

Carly paused and turned to me. "By the way, thank you again for everything you do. You've been a godsend for my sister."

I smiled. "That's what I'm here for." *And you can all hit the road any time now.* I felt like a bit of an ass for mentally shooing them out the door, but I was itching for my weekend with Holden to get started, and I didn't want to waste a minute of it.

She looked like she might say something more, but Ashley huffed. "Can we *go?*"

That snapped Carly out of her chattiness. She gave me one last smile, then got into the passenger seat. Thank God.

I waved at them as Tiffany backed the fully-loaded car out of the driveway. The second she started pulling away, I texted Holden: *They're gone.*

Then I went back inside to grab my own bag, which was fully packed on my bed downstairs.

I didn't dare have Holden come by the house. All it would take was one nosy neighbor commenting to Tiffany that her ex-husband had been over while she was out of town, and I'd be... maybe not out of a job, but probably wishing I was.

Instead, I left my car in a friend's garage while he was on his rotation at the firehouse, paid him twenty bucks for his silence, and was waiting on the curb when Holden pulled up. Elaborate and paranoid, maybe, but a little overkill on this end would mean I didn't spend our entire getaway worried that Tiffany might come home early or Zach might make an offhand comment that would tell her something was up.

So far, so good.

"Ready for this?" Holden asked with a wicked grin as I buckled my seat belt.

"Are you kidding?" I leaned across the console to steal a quick kiss. "I've been counting down the minutes."

"You and me both. Let's get the hell out of here."

I had visions of us flying up the freeway all the way to Leavenworth, but of course, that wasn't going to happen. This was the more-or-less Seattle area, and a lot of people were on their way home from work. Not surprisingly, I-5 coming out of Everett was always a bitch this time of day. Highway 2 wasn't much better, especially through Snohomish and Monroe during the afternoon commute. Judging by all the black and red on my traffic app, our two-hour drive to Leavenworth would probably be more like three once all was said and done. I was okay with that, though. Riding shotgun with Holden, a couple of overnight bags behind us and a whole weekend ahead of us, I was absolutely chill. He seemed to be too.

"Want some music?" I asked as we crawled up the highway.

"Sure. What do you have?"

"A lot of country. Is that cool?"

"Hell yeah. Put it on."

I connected my phone to his car stereo, set iTunes to shuffle, and adjusted the volume so we could hear the music but still talk. Immediately, a Ty Herndon ballad came to life, and Holden subtly tapped his finger on the wheel in time to the music.

For a long time, traffic crawled, music played, we chatted, and little by little, we inched toward our destination in the mountains. I was glad I'd taken the paranoid approach to stashing my car and taking off; I was still nervous about Tiffany finding out about this, but I wasn't really worried. There was no way in hell she'd come back into town early and stumble across my car in Holden's parking lot or something. We had a cover, we had alibis, and now we had nothing to do but enjoy the weekend and each other.

The song changed again, and Holden side-eyed my phone. "Is it just me, or do you have a *lot* of Ty Herndon on here?"

"Oh, I have a lot." I studied him. "Why? Do you want me to put on something else?"

"Didn't say I didn't like him. Just noticed you apparently like him a lot."

"Guilty. And I mean, why wouldn't I? I loved him when I was younger, and then when he made his comeback and came out?" I put my hand to my chest. "Be still my heart."

"Oh yeah, he's gay, isn't he?"

"Yep. He's smoking hot, he's talented as fuck, and he's gay." I clicked my tongue and shook my head. "His man is one lucky dude."

"Uh-huh. So that's who you're thinking of whenever we—"

I burst out laughing. "Shut up. As if I can concentrate on anything—never mind fantasizing about someone else—while your dick is in my ass."

Holden squirmed in the driver's seat.

"Don't tell me you're getting antsy already," I teased.

"Don't tell me you're not."

"Touché. Well, if you get too frisky, I'm pretty sure there are some camp areas and trailheads off some of the side roads." I flashed him a toothy grin. "You ever banged someone over a picnic table?"

"Not when it's forty-two degrees out."

"That's not quite a no."

Holden laughed. "For the record, no, I haven't, and no, I *won't* when it's forty-two degrees out."

I huffed with exaggerated annoyance. "You're no fun."

"Are you telling me you've done it?"

"No, but I'm open to new experiences. Especially when I've got a hot man and a bottle of lube within reach, and I don't want to wait another hour and a half to do something with him."

I *loved* the way he squirmed. Holy shit. Naturally, I couldn't resist teasing him. "So if it wasn't forty-two out, would you be game?"

"I'd...consider it."

"Ooh, that's promising."

He chuckled and took his eyes off the road just long enough to glance at me. "What about you?"

"It wouldn't be my first outdoor, public, or cold-as-balls fuck, so..."

"Is that right?" His fingers tapped rapidly on the wheel, no longer keeping time with the song playing in the background, but drumming like he needed to get rid of some nervous energy. "You sound like you've had some adventures with guys in the past."

"I've, uh, done a few things it's probably just as well my mom doesn't know about, let's put it that way."

Holden laughed. "Yeah? Like what?" He glanced at me, a wicked sparkle in his eyes. "What's the wildest thing you've ever done with a man?"

"Wildest thing I ever did...hmm." I quirked my lips. "Well, a firefighter once blew me in the back of an ambulance."

Holden glanced at me again, eyes wide. "No way."

"Mmhmm. It was a really, really slow night, and we'd kind of been circling each other for a while, and, well..." I shrugged. "One thing led to another, and suddenly we're in the back of the bus with my dick down his throat."

I swear to God, Holden actually shivered.

"Yeah?" He sounded kind of breathless. "How was it?"

"Considering how fast he had to work in case a call came in, and how much trouble we would have been in if someone had caught us?" I whistled. "It was fucking *hot*."

"I believe it," he said in a hoarse whisper.

"And actually, he *wanted* to reenact that scene from *Backdraft*. You know, where they fuck on top of the hoses on the fire truck?"

"He wanted to? Are you saying you didn't?"

I snorted. "Fuck no. Not when I've seen the whole movie and I remember the scene where the truck pulled out of the station while they were still on top of it."

Holden huffed. "And here I thought you were the adventurous type."

"Hey now. There are lines." I shot him a look. "What about you? Any wild adventures from your past?"

"Well, this one time—" His teeth snapped together. "I, uh, probably shouldn't be regaling you with things I've done with your boss."

I laughed and squeezed his knee. "Honey, please. Whenever Grandma takes the kids, your ex breaks out the merlot with either me, her sister, or both, and let's just say I probably know more about your sex life with her than you think."

"Is that right?"

"Uh-huh."

"What has she told you?"

"Hmm." I thought about it for a moment. "Apparently there was an incident where you two almost got arrested."

Holden barked a laugh. "Oh Jesus. She told you about that?"

"Well, yeah." I nudged his thigh. "So now *you* tell me about it."

"But you already know the story."

"I know her version."

"I don't imagine mine's much different than hers."

"Only one way to find out."

He rolled his eyes and chuckled. "Perv."

"Uh, yeah? Isn't that why you're whisking me off to a cabin in the mountains for the weekend?"

"Okay, you've got me there." He pulled in a deep breath, his gaze fixed on the long line of traffic in front of us while his fingers tapped even faster on the wheel. "Okay, well, after Noah and Ethan were old enough we felt comfortable leaving them with a sitter, and I was actually home for a decent stretch, we finally had a long overdue date night. We went to see a movie, and I guess we both really wanted to get to the 'date' portion of the night." He shifted in his seat. "First time I ever got someone off in a movie theater."

"Ooh." I'd heard that much from Tiffany, but the confirmation from Holden made it infinitely hotter. "So when can *we* go see a movie?"

Holden laughed again, and he was definitely breathless this time. He paused to change lanes and get around a slow-moving van. Once he'd squeaked in ahead of that guy, he went on, "Anyway, we didn't quite make it to the credits, and, uh, didn't quite make it out of the parking lot."

I clicked my tongue. "You dirty dog."

"Yeah, that's pretty much what the cop said."

"He was really going to arrest you?"

Holden rolled his eyes. "I don't know if he would've actually booked us, but he made a lot of noise about it. Then Tiffany faked a call from the babysitter, and played it up that one of the boys was sick and we needed to get home *right now.* The cop took pity on us, warned us he'd arrest us for real if he caught us again, and sent us on our way."

"Wait, she faked a call? How?"

"While the cop wasn't looking, she set an alarm on her phone that sounded just like her ringtone. When it went off, she pretended to answer it, and…" He rolled his hand in the air.

"Holy shit." I put a hand to my heart. "I had no idea she was devious when it came to eluding the cops."

Holden laughed. "She usually isn't, but she was feeling no pain that night, so…"

"Yeah, apparently. Wow."

He chuckled and stole another glance at me. "Are you sure it's not weird?" He arched an eyebrow. "Talking about me and Tiffany like this?"

"Pfft. It would be weird if I was picturing Tiffany, but quite honestly, my mental porno camera is pretty fixated on you."

I seriously loved the way he squirmed when I said shit like that. Flustered Holden was the hottest thing ever.

Are you sure *you're not game for that picnic table thing?*

CHAPTER 25

HOLDEN

Almost three and a half hours after we'd left Everett, Porter and I checked into the immense chalet tucked into the forest outside of Leavenworth. Not a moment too soon, either. After hours of swapping tales of past sexual exploits, I was ready to come unglued if we didn't start making some dirty memories of our own. Seriously, if I didn't get this man into bed in the next five minutes, that whole screwing over a picnic table suggestion was going to happen for real, and it was *thirty*-two degrees out now.

Finally, though, I keyed us into our room.

And we both stopped.

And stared.

When I'd booked the place, I hadn't paid much attention to the details. The thought of taking off somewhere with Porter for the weekend had been distracting as all hell, and the only things that had registered were "California king bed" and "Jacuzzi tub." If we were going to steal away for a couple of days, we might as well do it in style.

In my eagerness to book it, I'd apparently missed a couple of key words in the listing:

Honeymoon suite.

Because if this *wasn't* a honeymoon suit, then I was the Queen of England.

I mean, it was tasteful. I guess. But dear Lord, there were hearts and roses *everywhere*. The deep red comforter on the giant four poster bed was piled high with pillows that had to have been designed with Valentine's Day in mind, and beside the bed was a champagne bucket and a pair of flutes on the nightstand. Paintings on the walls that were subtly erotic and just pushed the envelope of what a hotel could put up without making someone faint. Yeah, this room was something else.

The suite had, without a doubt, been designed for guests who wanted to spend their stay having as much sex as humanly possible. I'd have bet money the red sofa and matching armchair were—and not by accident—sturdy enough to withstand the weight of two or more adults, and stable enough to stay upright during all kinds of acrobatics.

In stunned silence, we took in our accommodations.

"Is this..." Porter cleared his throat. "Are we..."

"Hand to God, I didn't realize it was..." I gestured at our surroundings. "I just saw California king and Jacuzzi tub and clicked *book*."

He turned to me, eyebrows up. "Jacuzzi tub?"

I could feel myself blushing, and shrugged as I grinned sheepishly. "Yeah, remember? It... sounded like it could be fun."

He pressed his lips together, fighting a losing battle against a laugh.

"What? You don't think we could use a tub like that to our advantage?"

"Oh, I think we can. We absolutely can." He pointed emphatically at the door that must have led to the bathroom. "But I swear to God, if that tub is heart-shaped, I will die. Straight up *die*."

I laughed. "Well, now I'm curious. We should go look."

On our way across the wide suite, we left our bags by the bed and continued into the bathroom.

And yep: heart-shaped tub. Complete with rose petals and candles.

"Oh my God." Porter doubled over laughing. "Oh my God, I can't. I just can't."

"I swear... I swear I didn't see this on the..." But I was laughing too hard to speak, so I gave up and leaned against the doorframe just to stay upright.

"This room..." He was practically wheezing. "Oh Christ. Everything about it...is hilarious."

"It's not supposed to be hilarious." Jesus, I had to wipe away tears. "It's supposed to be hot so we can fuck."

"Oh, baby." He turned to me, still laughing, though his eyes were gleaming with more than just amusement. "That won't be an issue." Grinning, he slid his hands into my back pockets and pulled me closer to him. In a sultry voice, he purred, "And hey, since we have this place for the whole weekend, you know what we should absolutely do?"

I wrapped my arms around him and pulled him closer. "Do tell."

The grin turned wicked and his eyes narrowed just a little. "After we've fucked each other senseless, we should absolutely order wings and pizza, and binge watch the last two seasons of *Gotham* while we drink champagne straight from the bottle."

A laugh burst out of me. "No, no, we can't do that."

"What? Why not?"

"You don't drink champagne from the bottle." Tsking, I rolled my eyes. "That's what Solo cups are for." I nodded back toward the room. "They even go with the décor."

His eyes lit up. "Oh my God, I *love* the way you think."

"I figured you'd like that. Now c'mere." I cupped the back of his neck and kissed him, and it only took a couple of seconds for his grin to soften against my lips. He moaned and pulled our hips together. Yeah, this room may have been ridiculous, but it could have been a clown theme and I still would have fucked him on every surface. Okay, maybe not a clown theme, but I could work with this.

"For the record," I murmured against his neck, "I'm seriously on board with ordering delivery." I paused to nibble his earlobe. "Because then we don't have a reason to leave the room, and *you* don't have any reason to be dressed."

Porter shivered, whispering a barely audible, "Oh God..."

"I wonder how many times I can make you say that tonight."

"Ungh." He shuddered hard. "But are we gonna do this in the bathroom doorway? Or find someplace horizontal?"

"I just can't decide if I want you on the bed or in that ridiculous tub."

"We've got the whole weekend. Pretty sure we can use both a few times."

I laughed and raised my head. Letting my lips brush his, I growled, "But where to start?"

"Well, we've been in the car for a few hours," he panted. "We could...we could probably use a shower?"

I met his gaze and grinned. "You really like showering together, don't you?"

Smiling innocently, he shrugged. "And you don't?"

"I didn't say that." I gestured over my shoulder at the

other side of the suite. "Maybe grab the lube in case we need it?"

The way he bit his lip made my whole body tingle. God, yes. This weekend would be amazing.

Over-the-top Valentine's Day décor or not—in this case, floor-to-ceiling Pepto Bismol pink tiles—the shower was spectacular. Tons of room for both of us. Some serious water pressure. Water that got *hot*.

The minute we were under the spray, we picked up where we'd left off in the doorway, but with hot water rushing over us and no clothes between us, there was a whole new level of hunger in the way we kissed and touched. After hours in the car, spinning each other up with stories about past sexcapades, I finally had him like this, and I wasn't stopping until Porter came so hard he couldn't stand up.

I pushed him up against the too-pink tiles. This was easily my favorite way to make out with Porter—his body pressed up against a wall and trembling as he panted and moaned between kisses. He gasped, arching his back, and I bent to kiss his neck as he kneaded my hips. I traced every hot inch of his throat, then worked my way back to his mouth, and when I claimed it again, I was rewarded with a muffled whimper.

Porter dug his nails into my hips and broke the kiss enough to whisper, "You...gonna fuck me or not?"

I laughed against his lips. "What's your hurry?"

"My hurry," he growled, "is that your dick isn't in my ass."

I shivered. Well, okay then. As much as I loved bottoming, I could not get enough of topping this man, and obviously he wanted it too.

I was about to turn him around and ride him against the

wall like I had the very first time, but no—I wanted to see his face. If he was going to come unraveled after I'd spent hours getting him spun up in the car, then I wanted a front row seat.

"Let's do this out there." I shut off the water. "In front of the mirror."

Porter blinked, but he didn't protest. We got out of the shower and dried off enough that we wouldn't slide on the slick floor, and for good measure, I dropped a towel in front of the counter so neither of us would slip. Then I bent him over the sink and pushed his thighs apart with my knee.

"Mmm, yeah," he moaned. "C'mon."

"In a minute." I poured some lube on my fingers. "Gotta make sure you're ready for me."

"I've *been* ready for you."

"Uh-huh." I pushed my fingers into his hole just the way he liked—rough enough to make him grunt, not so rough that he'd be in pain. "But once I'm in you," I purred as I slowly fingered him, "I want to fuck you. So I need to make sure you're ready for me."

Porter moaned again. I couldn't tell if it was frustration, anticipation, or a mix of the two. I just knew I was enjoying the hell out of it. As much as I wanted to be buried to the hilt in him, I loved driving him insane.

"*Holden*." His back arched and he met my eyes in the mirror with an expression that was somehow half-glare, half-pleading. "Just. *Fuck me.*"

I debated teasing him just because it was fun. But damn it, he wasn't the only one who'd been spun up and climbing the walls in the car.

So, I slipped my fingers free and stroked some lube onto my cock. Then, steadying both of us with a hand on his hip, I guided myself in. I'd barely touched the head to his well-prepped ass when he swore under his breath and rocked back against me.

Forget teasing him. I wanted him, and I wanted him now.

"Let me see your face," I breathed.

He lifted his head, meeting my gaze again in the mirror, and I pushed into him, and God, yeah—the look on his face as he took me. Fuck. Water droplets ran like sweat down his face, and he bit his lip and squeezed his eyes shut as I picked up speed.

"Jesus Christ, Holden..." He sounded close to tears, and he let his head fall forward, but I wasn't having it. I had him in front of a mirror so I could see his face, damn it, so I slid my hand into his wet hair and pulled it back, and he clenched around me as he moaned, "Oh fuck."

"You getting close?"

"I've been...been close since we...oh God..."

I gripped his hips tighter and rode him harder. "Come, baby."

Porter bit his lip as he reached down and started jerking himself off.

"That's it," I said, gritting my teeth as I tried to keep up this delicious rhythm. "That's it, let me see your face when you get there. Oh yeah, that's it, baby..."

His whole body tensed, and his lips parted as his as clenched hard around my dick, and the bathroom's acoustics made his helpless cries echo as he came.

The instant he sighed and slumped over the counter, I pulled out, pumped myself a couple of times, and gasped as I shot cum all over his ass and lower back. Then I sagged over him, an arm around his waist and my other palm against the counter to keep us both upright.

"That..." he said, touching his forehead to the counter as

if he needed something to cool him off, "is exactly what I needed."

"Me too. Want to go see how comfortable that bed is?"

"Oh my God, yes."

We cleaned ourselves off, then headed into the bedroom. It took a moment to knock all the goddamned pillows on the floor, but once they were out of the way, we climbed onto the bed without even bothering to pull the covers back.

We'd barely hit the mattress when Porter suddenly laughed and clapped a hand over his mouth.

I eyed him. "What?"

Still giggling, he pointed upward, and I looked.

"You can't be serious." I rolled onto my back. "A mirrored ceiling? Really?"

And he was right: above the bed was an enormous mirror.

We both burst out laughing. Oh, we'd have some fun with that mirror, but right now it was reflecting the two of us, bare-ass naked and sprawled on the bed, cracking up over the fact that our "honeymoon suite" included, well, that.

As he pulled himself together, Porter eyed the mirror. "Is a mirrored ceiling safe even around here? I mean... Hello, earthquakes? Multiple active volcanoes in the region?"

I shrugged. "With the building codes in this state, I would imagine it's made out of some kind of tempered, shatterproof glass, and anchored to the ceiling so tight that God Himself couldn't knock it down."

"Well, let's not tempt Him..."

Chuckling, I wrapped my arms around Porter and kissed his cheek. "I don't think you have to worry. You just..." I nuzzled his neck. "Have to worry about being distracted by our own personal porno while I'm blowing you or something."

He swallowed hard. "Oh God, when you put it like that..."

I laughed against his throat. "Figured you'd be on board."

"Uh-huh." We faced each other on our sides, and Porter ran his fingers through my hair. "I'm really glad we did this. Coming here, I mean."

"Me too." I kissed him softly. "We're not going to be able to move on Sunday night, though."

"Probably not. But it'll be worth it."

"Damn right it will."

CHAPTER 26
PORTER

Ever since I became a first responder, there were things I'd learned not to take for granted in relationships. Time together, mostly. Especially uninterrupted time. Having enough downtime to spend together, those rare moments when my shift schedule lined up with a boyfriend's nine-to-five, and actually making it through a meal, a movie, or sex without my phone going off.

Dating Holden had given me a renewed appreciation for those things. I was no longer on call or spending seventy-two hour stretches at the firehouse, but a lot of stars had to align if we wanted to share an evening.

And we had never, not once, spent an entire night together.

So as my eyes fluttered open to the morning sun gently flooding our gaudy red honeymoon suite, and Holden's breath whispered past my neck as he dozed against my back with his arm draped over me, I was in heaven. I'd always loved waking up with someone beside me, and I intended to savor every second of this rare indulgence with Holden.

What would it take to have this every single morning?

I closed my eyes and wriggled back against him. He murmured softly, then kissed the side of my neck, and the softness of his goatee and scratchiness of the stubble around it gave me goose bumps. Maybe I was getting ahead of myself, thinking about this being an all-the-time thing, but right now, it sounded good, and I wasn't awake enough to think very deeply about it.

"We don't have to get up yet, do we?" he grumbled.

I suppressed a smile. What could I say? His *don't make me get out of bed* grumpiness was cute as hell. "We don't have to go anywhere, baby."

"Good." He tightened his arm around me and buried his face against my neck. "Too comfortable."

"Mmm, me too." I laced our fingers together. "The hotel does have a pretty promising breakfast menu, though."

"Yeah?"

"Mmhmm. I looked at it last night. Bunch of shit I can't pronounce, but it says they have the biggest pancakes on this side of the Cascades."

He was nuzzled close enough I felt his brow furrow. "But which side of the mountains is this?" he asked in a sleep-slurred voice. "Are we in Eastern Washington or Western Washington?"

"I don't know. Does it matter?"

"If they're claiming to have the biggest pancakes on one side, I need to know *which* side we're talking about."

I burst out laughing and felt a breath of laughter against my neck. "If this is what you think about when you're half-awake, we have got to smoke weed together."

That got a stronger laugh out of him, and he kissed behind my ear. "Too bad my company's got a zero tolerance policy."

"What? That's not fair."

"I know, right?" He nipped my ear this time, making my toes curl and my breath catch. He gently freed his hand and started sliding it down my waist toward my hip. Then, his voice clearer now, he growled, "Guess you'll just have to deal with me sober."

I didn't have a witty response.

But it turned out I *really* liked sober Holden first thing in the morning.

DESPITE JOKING ABOUT SPENDING ALL WEEKEND IN BED or binge watching, we did leave the hotel that day. After all, I'd brought Holden to Leavenworth, so I might as well show him the town.

I'd never been to Bavaria, so I couldn't say if any of the town's architecture was accurate or not, but it was certainly charming, especially up against the backdrop of thick forests and snow-dusted mountains. The buildings along the main street had the painted stucco and exposed timber look that I'd always thought was Tudor style (hey, I never claimed to know architecture). They had peaked roofs and balconies with elaborately decorated railings, along with bright designs painted all over balconies, doors, and stucco.

I could smell soft pretzels coming from somewhere, and so help me, I was having one before this day was over. Assuming I found the source of that mouthwatering smell, which I was bound and determined to do.

We had apparently missed Oktoberfest by a couple of weeks, and that was fine with me. I liked beer as much as the next person, but my previous line of work had left me with a bit of an aversion to booze-themed festivals. Yay for another casualty of my last career.

There wasn't a whole lot to do in town, but there were some cool shops selling everything from tourist tchotchkes matching the Bavarian theme to bookstores to specialty candy makers. I wasn't sure that would be Holden's thing, and maybe it wasn't. Still, he seemed perfectly happy wandering from shop to shop, laughing over ridiculously tacky tourist souvenirs and picking up a few things for his kids. There was a teddy bear wearing lederhosen that we both agreed Chloe would love, and a toy shop sold wooden trucks that all three kids would lose their minds over.

"Look at you, getting a head start on your Christmas shopping," I teased as we waited in line at the toy shop.

Holden chuckled. "Yeah, just wait until December—I'll realize this is *all* I've bought and have to do some panic shopping online."

"You know, there's a mall around that does some big event every year where husbands and dads who've put off shopping get turned loose and have to do all their shopping on Christmas Eve."

He quirked an eyebrow. "Seriously?"

"Yep. I mean, obviously they've never encountered my sister who has never even started shopping outside of twenty-four hours before anything, but yeah."

"Oh hell, they could put me and Tiffany in that box."

"Really?"

"Uh-huh. I can remember at least three Christmases where we both realized on like the twentieth that we hadn't done *any* shopping." He grimaced. "When you procrastinate that hard, you have to get really creative, believe me."

"I bet. Meanwhile I'm always done with mine before Black Friday." I buffed my nails on my shirt. "We can't all be superstars."

Holden laughed and rolled his eyes. "Shut up."

I just chuckled, and we kept wandering through the shops. No destination. No rush. We found the place making soft pretzels, and Holden made a throaty little noise that sounded like *oh my God yes give me now*. Obviously we stopped for pretzels, which turned out to be amazeballs dipped in awesomesauce. We nibbled on those while we checked out windows full of nutcrackers and intricately decorated beer steins.

I loved how everything about this weekend was unhurried and decadent. Since we had such a finite amount of time to slip off together, I'd expected it to feel rushed and frantic—like we had to get in as much sex and togetherness as we could while we had the chance.

It was the opposite, though. Like time had slowed down and pushed Sunday night far enough into the future that it barely crossed my mind.

That in and of itself was a little unnerving, though. If I'd had any illusions before this weekend that what I had with Holden was just fun because of the thrill of sneaking around, those illusions were long gone. There was no lingering rush from secretly taking off together. Nothing about this felt forbidden or dangerous.

It just felt...right. It felt like I was exactly where I needed to be, with the person I needed to be with, when I needed to be there, and being anywhere else with any*one* else would've been wrong.

The only time it crossed my mind that there were reasons we shouldn't be doing this was when I thought I saw someone we knew. A glimpse of a blonde ponytail that (phew) wasn't Tiffany's. A bright pink parka that was (fortunately) being worn by a girl who wasn't Chloe. A little boy calling out to his mom, but turned out (thank God) not to be Ethan or Noah.

There were moments of panic where I thought we might get busted, but then I'd realize we were fine. Then I'd take one look at Holden and forget there'd ever been anything to worry about.

As we wandered out of a bookshop, Holden paused to look at a table of self-help books. I wondered for a second if he was looking for something to help his progress with his family, but he gestured at the display as if it had jogged his memory about something.

"Oh, hey, I meant to tell you..." He turned to me. "One of my co-workers is married to a retired firefighter. And I guess he's had some trouble adjusting."

I straightened. That wasn't what I'd expected. "Yeah, it's, uh, that's not all that uncommon."

"No, but he found a therapist who I guess specializes in anxiety and PTSD in first responders."

My ears perked up. "Really?"

"Yeah. I, um, I didn't tell her who it was for, just said I knew someone who might be interested, but..." He took out his wallet and fished out a card. "I got the therapist's number."

Speechless, I took the card. It was one of Holden's business cards, and on the back, he'd neatly written *Dr. Emily Martin*, followed by a phone number, an email address, and her website.

"I didn't want to be presumptuous," he said softly, almost shyly. "But when she mentioned this lady had made such a difference for her husband, my first thought was that maybe she can help you too. With the... you know, the stress."

"Yeah, maybe." I tucked the card into my wallet. "I'll give her a call when we're back in town." As we started walking again, I turned to him and smiled. "Thanks. That's really sweet. That you thought of me. I mean."

He smiled back. "Of course I did."

"Still. Thanks."

We continued into the next shop, but my mind was stuck on that conversation. Aside from other first responders, only a handful of people in my life knew the details of my PTSD and anxiety. It was a tough thing to admit, especially since not everyone had been as understanding.

"Dude, it's not like you were in a warzone. Get a grip."

"My brother-in-law has been an EMT for years and says that's nonsense."

"If you can't handle stress, how are you going to function in the real world?"

That's the kind of reaction I was used to from people. But today, out of the blue, Holden had given me contact information for someone who might actually be able to *help* me do something about this jittery shit.

As we wandered out of that shop and on to the next one, I whispered, "By the way, I really mean it—thank you. For the card. That's seriously sweet and it means a lot. More than you know."

Holden smiled again, and he let his elbow brush mine. It was a shame we weren't back in our room. Now was one of those times I could have absolutely gone for a long, tender kiss —partly to let him know how grateful I was for him, and partly because I just wanted to. But out in the open like this? Maybe not. Once we got back to the room, I'd make it up to him.

For now, we kept walking, and my mind kept right on whirring because seriously, none of the guys I'd dated had taken this all that seriously. They all knew a neighbor or an uncle or whatever who was a retired firefighter and did just fine, and paramedics on TV were well-adjusted, so I was just being dramatic.

And then along came Holden.

How do I deserve you?

Right then, a lady walked out of a store in front of us with two bright orange Pomeranians in her arms, and I almost tripped over my own feet.

I gasped. "Your dogs are so *cute*."

She beamed, turning so the pair of fluffy Poms were looking up at me with their stupidly adorable little smiling fox faces. "Thank you. You can pet them if you'd like?"

"Yes, yes, please, yes." I held out my hand, and both dogs craned their necks to sniff and lick my fingers. The way she was holding them, I couldn't see their tails, but the dogs were wiggling like they were trying to wag them anyway. "Oh my *God*."

Holden chuckled. "I think you just made his whole day."

"Uh-huh." I tousled the fuzzy head of one of the dogs, and the other slurped my hand. I wasn't going to lie—they really had made my whole day. As if the man standing beside me hadn't already.

I said goodbye to the dogs, thanked the lady for letting me have a moment with them, and we continued in separate directions.

Holden nudged me with his elbow. "I gotta say, you're really cute when you see something four-legged and fluffy."

"So you don't mind me stopping every two feet to pet them?"

"Of course not." His expression made my knees go all rubbery. "You get to pet a dog, and I get to watch you smile like that."

I really did stumble that time.

Laughing, Holden caught my arm, and he held on until I had my feet under me. "You okay?"

"Yeah. Yeah, I'm good. Just, uh... this super sweet romantic side of you is kind of hazardous."

And then he actually *blushed*, and I almost died. Oh God, he was so fucking cute like this.

We continued walking, but then Holden sobered. In a quiet, resigned tone, he said, "You realize that if we keep doing this, sooner or later, we're going to *have* to tell Tiffany."

"Do you..." I hesitated. "I mean, do you think we're..."

"Serious enough?"

My heart skipped for some reason, and I nodded mutely.

"Don't you?" he asked.

"I... Yeah. I do." I wrinkled my nose. "Just... Ugh. That's going to be an awkward conversation."

"I know. And she won't like it. I think we should tell her, though. Maybe not right away, but...sooner than later."

My heart sped up. The thought of telling her scared the hell out of me, but the fact that he wanted to—that he thought this had enough legs that it was worth laying out on the table—was mind-blowing.

Holden went on. "She's a reasonable person. And things are amicable between us. I'd like them to stay that way." He stopped and turned to me. "Which means I want to be honest with her."

"I get that."

Holden tilted his head. "You're okay with it, right?"

"Of course! Yeah. But I guess..." I slid my hands into my jacket pockets and avoided his gaze. "And maybe this is the worst possible time, and way too late in the game to even bring this up, especially when you're talking about telling her about us..."

"Am I over Tiffany?" The question was gentle. He didn't sound defensive or even surprised.

Silently, I nodded.

Holden didn't speak for a moment, which didn't do much to unwind that uncomfortable something in my gut. Finally, he took a deep breath. "Yeah. I am. There's still a lot there that'll take time to sort out, but I've made my peace with our marriage being over."

I lifted my gaze and searched his eyes.

Apparently he saw something in mine, because he stepped closer and, even though we were in public, he touched my cheek. "If you're worried I'm still carrying a torch for her, don't be. I won't tell you I'm miraculously cured of any feelings I had for her or for our marriage, but I will say those feelings have been getting a lot less noticeable since a certain nanny came into the picture."

My heart skipped. "Really?"

He laughed softly, brushing his thumb across my cheekbone. "Porter, if you hadn't noticed, you're the one I'm texting nonstop and sneaking off with at every opportunity. And you're the one I took off into the mountains with and am seriously considering telling my ex-wife about even though it'll make some waves." He moved in closer. "You're not a Band-Aid for what she left behind. You're something I never knew I was missing."

And then, right here on the sidewalk in front of God and everyone, Holden pressed his lips to mine.

All my sudden irrational apprehension about him and Tiffany melted away.

Tell Tiffany about us? Hell yeah, tell Tiffany about us. Maybe not immediately. Maybe not until we'd really sat down and figured out how to approach this. But tell her? Yes. God, yes. Tell everyone. Change Facebook statuses, go out in public, share a chaste kiss in broad daylight in the middle of Leavenworth—the whole nine yards.

Though it had been a gentle kiss—we didn't dare go for more out in the open like this—I was out of breath when Holden broke away. So was he.

"So," he panted. "Do you want to stay out or head back to the room?"

I bit my lip. "If we go back, can we crack open that bottle of champagne and see how comfortable that heart-shaped tub is?"

'Damn right we can. Let's go."

CHAPTER 27

HOLDEN

As much as I'd laughed about the honeymoon suite's ridiculous heart-shaped tub—and I still maintained that it was ridiculous and hilarious—I had to admit, it was pretty nice. There was plenty of room for us to sit opposite each other and still stretch our legs out comfortably.

"It's really nice of them to provide plastic champagne flutes." Porter handed me one of the two he'd just filled, then sat back with his own. "Because otherwise there's no way in hell we'd be drinking in this tub."

"Of course we would. We'd just go get some of those plastic Solo cups, remember?"

"Oh yeah." Porter nudged the bottle away from the edge so it was within reach, but in no danger of tumbling into the tub. "Either way, I'm not drinking out of a glass flute in here. I'm enjoying myself way too much to have this all wrecked by some submerged broken glass."

I grimaced. "I hadn't thought about that."

"Only because you haven't been trained to see the entire world as a giant minefield of catastrophic injuries waiting to happen."

I shot him a look over the rim of my glass. "Dude, I've been through the toddler stages and taught one teenager how to drive. I am well aware that all the world is a minefield, thank you very much."

It was his turn to grimace. "Oh God. And you'll still bring glass into a tub?"

"I told you—I've been through the toddler stages and taught one teenager how to drive." I held up my drink. "I don't care about the container—just give me booze."

He laughed. "Okay, okay, that's fair." Beneath the water, he slid his free hand between my shins and rested it there, gently grasping my calf. I loved how much this man loved touching. "Ahh, someday I really need to get a place with a tub like this."

"What? Heart-shaped?"

Porter clicked his tongue and rolled his eyes. "Yes, Holden. I want a heart-shaped tub in my house. No, I mean one that fits two people this comfortably."

"I get that." I sipped my drink. "I mean, I'll be lucky if I can afford a place here that doesn't require me to shower in the backyard with the garden hose."

He barked a laugh. "It's cute how you think you'll find a place with a backyard, let alone a garden hose."

"Eh, yeah. There is that." I groaned as I brought the champagne up to my lips again. "Fuck Seattle and its real estate market."

"Tell me about it," he muttered. "I swear half the reason I took the nanny job was the free room and board. I mean, there really aren't many jobs I *wouldn't* do if it came with a place to live."

"Now that I've seen the rent around here?" I whistled, shaking my head. "Hell, I'd take a job with free room and board."

"We could always start our own whorehouse."

"What?" I sputtered.

"I'm just saying." He shrugged innocently and started ticking points off on his fingers. "High demand. Work is fun. You're not on your feet all day. Everyone gets their own room. Lube and sex toys are a frigging tax write off."

I eyed him over my glass. "I feel like you've given this a lot of thought."

"Hey." He shrugged again as he reached for the champagne bottle. "Unemployed times call for desperate measures."

"Can't argue with that."

He topped us both off, and we settled back into place. "You have to admit, a whorehouse would be a lot more fun than some other jobs out there."

"Ugh. Like my last one."

"Yeah?" He cocked his head. "You know, I just realized I don't even know—what *do* you do? Tiffany said it's some kind of sales, but not, like, what you sell or who you're selling it to."

"Sales, yeah. I basically convince other companies to buy what my company produces."

"Which is...?"

"At the current place, software that tracks production, inventory—things like that. The place before that, it was equipment that made emission ventilation cleaner and more efficient."

Porter blinked. "Those sound like totally different things."

"They are." I took a swallow of champagne, hoping it might rinse away some of the sudden bitterness in my mouth. "I spent sixteen years internalizing every single goddamned thing there was to know about that product line, and in a matter of months, none of it matters anymore. The only thing I took away from that job is the generic ability to sell a product." So much for rinsing out the bitterness. "I mean, I worked myself into the ground and killed my marriage for that company. Now no one cares about anything I did there. Nothing I did matters except that it gave me enough sales skills to land the job I have now. Which, that part's great, but it just makes me wonder what the point was of everything I did, you know?"

"Wow. That sounds rough."

"It really is. If it had just been nine-to-five, I could live with it. But the higher I moved up the food chain, the more they demanded of me, to the point I was on the road a hell of a lot more than I was home. They made a killing off me. I got a divorce."

Porter exhaled, shaking his head. "That was the kind of thing I was afraid of in college, to be honest."

"Yeah?"

"Yeah." He absently ran his fingertip along the surface of the water, creating little swirls and ripples. "That I'd get some job that didn't matter. I wanted to do something where I felt like I was, you know, *doing* something."

"That's why you became a paramedic?"

He nodded. "I just underestimated how much it would take out of me."

"I get that. I guess the gods favor no one."

"Right?" he muttered and took a sip of his champagne.

The conversation was threatening to take an incredibly depressing turn, so I said, "That whorehouse is sounding better and better."

Porter laughed. "Right? But I like what I'm doing now." He met my eyes, and a gentle smile formed on his lips. "It's had some unexpected perks."

"You're telling me." I gave his leg a little squeeze under the water and was rewarded with a subtle shiver. "And mine is one I can clock out of at five so I can spend some time with my family and still have plenty of time and energy for..." I winked.

"Time management for the win, eh?"

"Something like that."

We both chuckled.

I moved my foot slightly, and as I did, bumped Porter's elbow. "Shit. Sorry."

"It's all right." He drained his glass, put it on the tube's edge, and slid his hand under my ankle. Then he drew my foot into his lap. Just having it resting on his thigh was nice, but then—

"Whoa." I almost dropped my own champagne.

Porter grinned, and he gave the sole of my foot another firm stroke with his thumb. "You like foot massages?"

"I've, uh..." I closed my eyes and shivered. Opening them again, I said, "I've never had one."

His eyebrows shot up. "Never?"

"Never."

"Hmm." Beneath the water, both hands went to work on my foot. "We should change that."

I definitely didn't protest. I'd loved Porter's strong, talented hands from the start, but the things he did now were pure magic. Sometimes a touch so light it bordered on ticklish. Sometimes one so firm it bordered on painful. My feet hadn't been particularly sore from wandering around Leavenworth earlier, but now that he was massaging one, I was suddenly aware of the vague ache in the other.

As if he'd read my mind, Porter let my foot rest in his lap and reached or the other. Oh, *hell* yeah.

"Where did you learn that?" I groaned. "Hogwarts for paramedics?"

Porter chuckled. "Dated a guy who worked retail. We both had sore feet all the time, so we learned on each other. And it turns out..." He did something to my arch that made my spine tingle. "It's kind of hot too."

"You don't say," I breathed. "Good God. You keep doing that, you won't need to touch anything else."

"Oh yeah?"

"Uh-huh."

"But what if I *want* to touch 'anything else'?" His wry grin made me squirm.

"Well." I grinned. "Don't let me stop you."

Porter licked his lips. He eased one foot down, then the other. Then he got up onto his knees and came closer. He straddled me, and before our lips even met, he closed his fingers around my cock. I had just enough time to gasp, and then he kissed me. I slid my hands over his hips and his gorgeous ass. He groaned softly into my kiss, and again when I kneaded his powerful muscles. The alcohol and whatever magic he'd worked on my feet had nothing on what he was doing with his mouth, not to mention the sheer presence of him on top of me in the hot water.

I slid a hand up into his hair, pulled his head back, and had my lips on his neck just in time to catch the vibration from his low groan. He rocked his hips against me, exhaling hard as I kissed up and down his skin. The closer I came to his mouth, the faster and shallower his breathing became, and by the time my lips found his again, he was trembling and panting.

His slow, easy strokes were mind-blowing. Not like he was trying to jerk me off—just teasing and touching while he kept right on kissing me. I did the best I could to return the favor, but it was almost impossible to concentrate on what I was doing with my hand. This was the slowest, most languid hand job I'd ever experienced or given. Between the hot water, the alcohol, and our lazy strokes, I wasn't even sure either of us *could* come, but I didn't care. I was enjoying this way too much to want an orgasm if an orgasm meant this being over.

"We stay in here much longer," I murmured between kisses, " the water's going to get cold."

Porter lifted his head. A hint of disappointment appeared in his eyes, but before that disappointment had a chance to fully set in, I added, "So let's take this to bed, because I really—" I tightened my grasp on his cock, and practically groaned, "—want to ride you."

A whimper slipped past his lips, and I grinned as I lifted my chin to kiss him again.

"Bed?" he asked.

"Bed."

CHAPTER 28

PORTER

I was pretty sure we dried ourselves off faster than anyone in history had ever dried off. It seemed like mere seconds passed between Holden pulling the plug on the tub and me pulling him down on the bed.

Everything in the tub had been so languid and sensual. Now we were hungry and greedy, kissing hard and groping with bruising fingers. Thank God for the alcohol and the lingering heat from the tub, or we both would've gone off in no time.

Holden broke the kiss and looked at me, eyes on fire with need. "Didn't you say something about fucking me?"

"Think...you said something about riding me, yeah."

"Uh-huh." He arched a brow.

I nodded sharply toward the nightstand. "Get the lube."

I prepped him with a couple of well-lubed fingers, but Holden was even less patient than I was. As soon as he'd relaxed enough to easily take my fingers, he said, "Get on your back. Now."

Like I'd say no to that.

The second my shoulders hit the sheets, Holden straddled me, and my pulse went wild. I steadied my cock with one hand, his hip with the other, and guided him down until the head of my cock pressed against his ass. I held my breath as anticipation curled my toes. Above me, Holden closed his eyes, his expression an odd mix of relaxed and focused, and he exhaled slowly through his parted lips as he eased himself down. He was seriously tight, so I stayed perfectly still and let him take control. I just lay there and enjoyed the hot, delicious slide of my cock easing bareback into his tight hole.

He groaned softly, and I grinned up at him. "Like that?"

"You kidding?" He bit his lip, rose, then started down again. "Feels... Jesus..." A few more strokes, and he had me buried all the way inside him. He leaned back, resting a hand on my thigh, and—

Oh. Fuck. That mirrored ceiling.

I'd watched myself in mirrors before, but never like this. This wasn't bent over a counter or stealing a glance in a closet door or a mirror above a dresser. This was... God, this was a mirror that existed solely to capture the most pornographic possible view of two people fucking, and it served its purpose well. The motions of our bodies left nothing to the imagination, and the sight of him, muscles tense and quivering with exertion, his back and ass and shoulders on full display as he moved fluidly on top of me... Holy hell, I was pretty sure I could get off from nothing more than what I saw.

"That view is... amazing."

Holden looked up, and he breathed a quiet laugh. Returning his gaze to me, he said, "Like watching yourself?"

"Oh, yeah." I slid my hands up his thighs. "Especially love watching you like this."

He grinned. Then he leaned down and buried his face

against my neck, and just as I was shivering from the new view, he bit my shoulder, and I moaned. And yeah, the view was *hot*. In fact, the mirror must have been curved or tilted slightly, because with him leaning down like this, I could just see my cock sliding in and out of him. I kneaded his perfect round ass, partly because I wanted to, and partly to spread his cheeks so I had an even better view of myself fucking him.

"This is so hot," I whispered. "Jesus..."

He moaned against my neck.

"I can... God, I can see..." I forgot how to speak, so I thrust up into him, hoping that conveyed the message. Even if it didn't, who cared? We were fucking, and the mirror saw everything, and so did I, and this was easily the hottest thing I'd ever experienced.

"That's it, baby," he murmured. "Best porno you've ever seen, isn't it?"

I bit my lip and arched, digging my nails into his powerful quads. "God, yeah."

He pushed himself up again, and as he leaned back on his hand, I couldn't figure out where to look. I didn't want to take my eyes off Holden, but the view of us in the mirror was just too hot to ignore.

"Keep watching," he breathed as he started stroking himself. "Keep watching, baby."

Oh, I did. Him. The mirror. Him again. His hand furiously pumping his cock. His face. Our reflection. As if I wasn't already losing my mind over fucking him.

I bit my lip and thrust up into him.

"Oh God..." His whispered words were barely more than a ragged breath. "God, Porter..."

He gasped, and he clenched so hard around me that I gasped too, and in the reflection I watched his cum streak across my stomach, and I didn't see a damned thing after that because I was coming too, eyes squeezed shut as I released inside Holden.

We both shuddered a few times, and struggled to catch our breath. Then he lifted himself off my cock and dropped onto the bed beside me. As we curled close to each other, the mirror above us ceased to exist. I couldn't look anywhere but into those heavy-lidded blue eyes.

"Think we should take a shower?" he murmured.

I glanced down at the cum still on both our stomachs. "Yeah. Probably." I met his gaze again. "In a minute."

For the time being, we wiped away the cum with some tissues from the nightstand, then lounged together, taking up only a fraction of the enormous bed.

I loved this. The sex was great, but lying together, enjoying this luxurious, decadent laziness? Perfect. Just perfect. Especially with nowhere else in the world we needed to be. Well, nowhere else we needed to be right now. Tomorrow, though...

My heart sank. I trailed my fingertips up Holden's arm. "Do we really have to go back?"

Holden smiled sleepily. "Yeah. We have to go back." He lifted his head and brushed a kiss across my lips. "Not right this minute, though."

"Good." I slid my hand up his side. "I don't want to move."

"You don't have to. We have time."

"Awesome. I don't even want to get up and take a shower yet."

He hummed softly, kissed my temple, and made no effort to change my mind.

After a while, I whispered, "We should do this again."

Holden's tongue ran across the inside of his lip. "With or without the honeymoon suite?"

I looked around the room, and when I met his gaze again, I grinned. "I don't know. The décor's a bit much, but the mirror and the tub kind of make up for it."

"Yeah, they do." He kissed me softly. "Say the word, and I'll book it again."

"I'm gonna hold you to that." I ran the pad of my thumb along the edge of his goatee. "But how do we do this? When we get home, I mean? Like, *when* do we tell her?"

Holden sighed, sliding his hand along my forearm. "I don't know. I really don't." He looked at me through his long lashes. "I just know I want to."

My heart fluttered. "Me too. But.."

"We'll find a way," he whispered and drew me in closer. "It might take a little time for things to shake out, and Tiffany might need some time to warm up to the idea, but we'll find a way to do this."

I wanted to ask how he could be so sure, but I was afraid that instead of reassurance, he'd let the cracks show. Admit he was as worried as I was that there was no way we could be together without screwing up my job or his relationships with his ex-wife and kids. Maybe that made me a coward, but right now lying in bed with Holden looking at me like that, I couldn't handle any doubts. I needed to believe, if only for tonight, that there really was a way for us to make this work.

So instead of asking, I lifted my head, cupped his cheek, and pressed a kiss to his lips. Slowly, he wrapped his arms around me, and I did the same, and we tangled up in a long, lazy kiss. God, I loved how it felt to be in his arms. I was pretty sure I'd always liked being held by other people, but I'd never noticed it the way I did with him. I hadn't paid enough attention to how guys before him had held me to know what it was he did differently, just that it was different somehow, and I loved it.

His embrace was solid and strong, as if he was afraid I might slip away, but at the same time, he'd run his hands all over me, his touch soft and light. A caress of my arm gave me goose bumps. Another of my face damn near melted my heart. A long slide of his palm up my back made me want to fuck him all over again. And then there'd be another soft little caress, and I'd melt again.

Where have you and your magic hands been all my life?

Well, wherever they'd been, they were here now, and neither of us was in any hurry to be anywhere else. The longer this went on, the more obvious it became that it wasn't stopping at a kiss. I started getting hard again. Before long, so did Holden. The kiss was still gentle and lazy, but there was heat behind it now. The hunger growing between us wasn't like it had been in the tub, though. This wasn't the need that had driven us into bed so we could drive each other wild. It was no less intense, just…different. Less *"I need to make us both come"* and more *"I need you."*

"Fuck me again," he breathed. He brushed his lips across mine. "Just go slow. I… God, Porter, I just need you again. Right now."

I shuddered, and I was out of breath when I whispered, "Let me get the lube."

As I lubed myself up, Holden rolled onto his side. I molded myself to him and carefully slid inside. Since I'd already fucked him once, he took me easily this time. When I was all the way in, our bodies were locked together from our shoulders all the way to our feet.

I didn't look at the mirror above us. Not even once. My entire focus was on the man in my arms. The man whose skin was hot against mine, who moaned as I slowly and gently rocked my hips to move inside him. I didn't care what we looked like—just what we felt like. And right now, I felt like I could as easily break down crying as I could come in him again. I'd had him all to myself since we'd left Everett, and now I didn't want to let him go. Not to go back to our normal lives, not even to slip out of him and get out of this bed. There was nothing in the world I needed or wanted except for this, and I couldn't get enough of how he overwhelmed me.

Why can't we do this all the time?
Why can't we do this forever?

This wasn't like any sex we'd had before tonight, but it made perfect sense. Like now that we'd gotten the single-minded horniness out of the way, we could actually focus on each other, on really being together. And now, my God. How were we going to do this when we got home? Because sneaking off for a quickie whenever we could grab it—that wasn't going to cut it anymore. I needed more of this. The long nights. The lazy mornings. The soft, chaste kisses in broad daylight on sidewalks.

It wasn't just the sex that had my heart galloping right then. It was him. It was Holden. It was this man who I wasn't supposed to be with, and who I suddenly couldn't see myself being without.

I held him tighter, savoring every stroke and every second of this hot, sensual closeness.

"Oh God..." Holden's hips jerked under mine, and I held my breath as I thrust a *little* harder, and just like that, we both groaned as his orgasm set mine off, and we came together.

Sinking down on top of him, not giving a damn about all the cum and sweat and lube, I let my head fall beside his.

He sighed happily underneath me, and even after I'd pulled out and gone soft, we just held each other for a moment while we caught our breath.

When I finally made myself sit up, my skin was cool and tingly with the absence of his against mine. I'd have bet money that once we'd cleaned ourselves off, we'd be right back in this bed, tangled up and holding each other.

And I didn't see myself wanting to let him go any time soon.

What happens if I fall for you?

Our eyes met, and my pulse jumped again.

What if I already have?

CHAPTER 29
HOLDEN

After the long bath, the champagne, two orgasms apiece, and a shower, it was a miracle either of us was still conscious. From the way Porter was swaying a little as he took out his contacts and brushed his teeth, he probably wasn't staying conscious much longer. I was no better.

The bed really was obscenely huge, and the first night, we'd settled on one side so we could at least reach one of the nightstands. Tonight, with both our phones charging next to his glasses and our wallets, I settled on my back and he cuddled up against me with his head on my shoulder.

"Oh my God," he murmured. "I'm gonna fall asleep."

"It's okay." I stroked his hair. "I won't be far behind you."

He murmured something I didn't catch. A moment later—yep, he was asleep.

As he dozed peacefully, I pulled my gaze from him and looked up at the ceiling instead. We'd both enjoyed the hell out of that mirror while we'd been fooling around. I could only imagine the acrobatic positions that would look seriously hot as we watched our own personal porno play out live, but right now... Right now that mirror served a very different purpose. The view did things to my heart I didn't think I'd ever felt before. Like I was getting a bird's eye view of myself with a man I'd thought I only wanted for sex, but now I wasn't so sure.

Our surroundings may have been over-the-top and cliched, but the two of us like this? Lying together on this absurdly huge bed where we'd been having amazing sex earlier? Relaxing with Porter's head on my chest and my arm around his shoulders? That was just perfect. Who was I kidding? We could be in a craphole motel with a hard bed and neighbors screaming at each other next door, and I'd still feel like this. Of course I would—I was with Porter.

It wasn't just that every time I looked at him, my heart sped up and I started thinking about all the ways we could fool around. He turned me on and drove me wild in bed, and I couldn't remember ever being as satisfied as I was with him.

But now that the orgasms were over and the cum was wiped up and the dust had settled, here we were—tangled up together, occupying so little space that this California king looked ridiculously oversized. We didn't need a bed this big. The only way to make use of it was to pull apart, and just thinking about that made me draw him in. Porter cuddled closer, the arm across my stomach tightening just as mine had around his shoulders.

I wanted this—what we were doing right now—and I wanted it all the time. As much as I'd resisted having him in the picture at all at first, now I couldn't imagine him *not* being in it. In the picture, in my bed, in my life—I just wanted him here. Full stop.

Which was ironic, when I thought about it. I'd been convinced at the beginning that he'd get in the way of me being close to my kids again. Instead, the kids had brought me closer to him. And I wanted him to stay there. I wanted to have him, my kids, and a friendship with my ex-wife, and there had to be *some way* to make all of that work.

Closing my eyes, I kissed the top of his head. He murmured in his sleep and nuzzled my shoulder, sending warmth all the way down to my toes. I was too exhausted to act on it, but every time he touched me, I wanted him more. Had since day one. It had actually been a little startling when my libido had suddenly woken up from its post-divorce hibernation. I'd wondered a few times if I'd ever want to have sex again, and if I even cared that I didn't. Then Porter had come into my life, and oh, yes, I absolutely did want sex again. As often as possible, please.

Still, I hadn't seen myself developing feelings for anyone. Not in the near future, anyway. I needed to focus on my kids, my job, and getting my life back on the rails. Those feelings were just going to have to wait a little while.

I stroked Porter's hair as I gazed up at our reflection.

Those feelings were *supposed* to wait a little while.

But then you showed up.

I pressed a kiss to the top of his head.

And here they are.

CHAPTER 30

PORTER

It was fitting that we'd chosen to spend our weekend in a town that looked like a Bavarian village, because coming back to Everett was like coming back from someplace a lot farther away. It felt like I'd been gone for months, not a long weekend, and that we'd been on the other side of the world instead of a hundred miles up the interstate.

Holden dropped me at my friend's house, and we stole a long kiss in the driveway before I got out and let myself into the garage where I'd left my car. Just being alone after he'd left felt strange—we'd been joined at the hip almost the entire time we'd been away, and his absence rang in my ears.

We definitely needed to take another trip like that. Five minutes back in the real world, and I was already itching for more of this weekend.

For the time being, though, the real world wouldn't wait, so I backed out of my friend's garage and headed back to Tiffany's house.

When I got there, her car was in the driveway, but when

I let myself into the house, everything was eerily silent. As I took off my shoes, I could see Tiffany upstairs in the kitchen, pouring herself some coffee, but otherwise? Still and silent.

"Hey, hon." Tiffany smiled. "How was your weekend?"

"Good. Good." I forced myself to return the smile despite the knot of guilt in my chest and started up the stairs. I'd done the Walk of Shame a time or two, but this was definitely my first time doing it after I'd spent the weekend plowing and being plowed by my boss's ex-husband. Especially when I lived with said boss.

Well, Mom. You were right. This job is definitely *full of new experiences.*

"So. Um." I slid my hands into my pockets. "How was everything at your mom's?"

Tiffany groaned. "Chaotic. I think all the cousins wore each other out."

"Yeah?"

She nodded sharply toward the living room.

I peeked around the corner as I cleared the top step, and okay, now I understood why the house was so quiet. Ethan and Chloe had both racked out on the sofa. Noah looked like he'd been playing with his action figures on the floor, and just face-planted, one toy still in his outstretched hand.

"Wow," I said. "Think this will bode well for bedtime?"

"God, I hope so." She laughed, shaking her head. "I couldn't have kept them awake if I wanted to, though, so tonight... Well, we'll have to see how it goes."

"Yeah. I guess we will."

"Fingers crossed." She held up her crossed fingers, then gestured for me to follow her into the kitchen. "So what did you end up doing for the weekend?"

Your ex-husband. Repeatedly.

I cleared my throat and slid my hands into my pockets. "Just my mom's usual to-do list."

She laughed. "Everyone keeps you busy, don't they?"

"Well, you know what they say about idle hands."

Tiffany chuckled as she picked up her coffee. My guilty conscience needled at me, but I tried my level best to ignore it. I didn't need my boss catching on that maybe I'd been doing something other than helping my mom trim back her rosebushes for the winter.

While we caught up about the weekend and checked in about schedules for the upcoming week, I couldn't get Holden out of my head. The entire trip kept replaying, everything from talking in the car to lounging with champagne in that heart-shaped tub to cuddling in that ridiculous bed.

I was in so far over my head, and maybe I could figure out what to do about that if I could stop swooning over Holden for a few minutes. Who knew that my boss's ex-husband would go from not liking me to taking me to bed and making me feel like the only man in the world?

And Holden wanted to tell her. Maybe not quite yet, not until we'd had a chance to figure out when, how, and exactly what to tell her, but he wanted to be honest with her. And so did I. He was right that she was a reasonable person, and if we played this carefully, it might not blow up in our—

"Porter?"

I shook myself. "Hmm? What?"

She laughed. "You spaced out on me."

"I, uh…" I cleared my throat, sure my cheeks were glowing. "Yeah. I did."

"Uh-huh. Okay, well, I was asking what you thought we should do for dinner tonight?"

"Oh. Well." I glanced around the corner at the three racked-out kids. "We could just order out."

"Sounds good to me. Any preference?"

"Whatever's easiest."

She ended up ordering from one of the pizza places down the road. She and I really liked their pizza, but the boys preferred their pasta dishes, so they each got a takeout container of spaghetti while Tiffany, Ashley, Chloe, and I split a couple of large pizzas. Tiffany and Chloe went with pepperoni, but Ashley—a girl after my own heart—shared my love of Hawaiian, especially with extra pineapple. There'd be a ton of leftovers, which everyone would be thrilled about. Cold pizza for breakfast? Hell yeah.

As we all dug in, Ethan looked across the table at me, a few garlic bread crumbs stuck in the smears of spaghetti sauce at the corners of his mouth. "Are you and my dad boyfriends now?"

Good thing I hadn't been trying to take a drink right then, or everyone at the table would've been wearing it.

Beside me, Tiffany stiffened. I didn't look, but I could feel her eyes on me.

As casually as Ethan had asked, I responded, "Why would you think that?"

"Because Danny said his mom told his dad you have a boyfriend. Like how Isaiah's dad has one. And she thinks it's Dad."

"Oh. Um " I was seriously waiting for Tiffany's eyes to literally burn holes into my skull. "No, we're not boyfriends. He just comes with me sometimes because he's learning his way around town and he's learning everyone's new routines. We're both there because of you three, not because we're dating."

"Oh." Ethan went back to eating as if nothing were

amiss. Noah glanced at me uncertainly but then continued eating as well. Ashley seemed about as interested in the conversation as Chloe, which is to say...not at all.

Couldn't quite say the same about their mom, though. From across the table, Tiffany shot me one of those looks that said we'd be having a *conversation* once everyone else was out of earshot. *Crap.*

Sure enough, after dinner was cleared away and the kids had scattered to play or do homework, Tiffany turned to me in the kitchen. "Porter."

"Yeah?"

"I need you to tell me straight." She looked right in my eyes. "*Is* there something going in between you and my ex-husband?"

Fuck my life. I already felt like shit for panicking and lying to Ethan. He'd caught me off guard, and I'd had no idea how to respond, and...fuck. Not how I'd intended to handle this when it finally came up. So what was I supposed to say now? "No." I shook my head. "No, there's nothing."

Her eyebrow arched with unmistakable skepticism, which did nothing to quell the panic *or* the rush of guilt.

"I'm not going to tell you he's unattractive." I shrugged. "I'm a gay man with eyes. But that doesn't mean there's anything going on. And besides, you know how people are. I'm not exactly subtle about being gay, so of course all the parents are going to assume that any man I'm chatting with is my boyfriend. I mean, the second time Holden and I went to the park? One of the moms accused me of bringing a boyfriend with me because they didn't realize he was their dad."

Tiffany studied me, then deflated, releasing a long breath. "Okay. Okay, those are all good points."

"You wanted us to get along, right?" I laughed cautiously. "We must be, if people think we're seeing each other." Oh fuck, I felt like crap now.

The attempt at humor paid off—she chuckled, and some more tension eased from her posture. "All right, that's true. Okay." She waved a hand. "Sorry I asked."

"It's fine. No harm, no foul."

We exchanged smiles, and part of me died inside. I hated how easy it was to look her in the eye and lie through my teeth. Must've been all the years of *"You'll have to ask the police"* or *"I couldn't tell you—that'll be the officer's decision"* when I knew damn well the cops would be waiting to arrest the patient as soon as they were discharged. Sometimes after I'd called them in myself. I didn't technically lie to them, but I absolutely deflected and avoided telling them the God's honest truth. And maybe that was why I could tell Tiffany to her face that no, I wasn't seeing Holden, despite my body still aching from just how much seeing him I'd done over the past seventy-two hours.

I wasn't sure exactly when my feelings for Holden had become, well, feelings. All I knew was that sometime between when we hooked up and when we'd fallen asleep together last night in Leavenworth, things had gotten... complicated. Really, really complicated. And now, in a moment of panic, I'd lied to the kids.

What the hell were we supposed to do now?

CHAPTER 31

HOLDEN

"Can we talk before you and the kids take off?"

Something about the way Tiffany said it made my gut twist. Part of me thought I was just irrationally paranoid that she might have caught on to where Porter and I had been over the weekend and why. Except, no—I knew her tells, and there was no doubt in my mind this was going to be an uncomfortable conversation. I just didn't know what it would be about.

"Um. Yeah." I cleared my throat. "Sure. What's up?"

She motioned for me to follow her. The evening was chilly, so I was glad she didn't pick the deck. Instead, we went downstairs to the rec room down the short hall from Porter's bedroom. Guilt prodded at me as I remembered the quiet quickie we'd had in there while the kids slept upstairs; Tiffany would've had my head if she knew about that.

In the rec room, she shut the door and faced me. "Listen." She wrung her hands like she always did when she was nervous. "I still absolutely want you spending time with the kids. As much as possible, actually."

Okay, *this* was taking an interesting turn.

I inclined my head. "But...?"

Tiffany chewed her lip. "But I think it needs to be... separately. From me, and from Porter."

I blinked. "Uh, why?"

She hesitated, and finally pushed out a breath. "Honestly? Because the kids are getting confused. You've been spending a lot of time at the house, and with them and Porter, and they're starting to think..."

My stomach somersaulted. Oh, shit.

She took a deep breath, squared her shoulders, and looked in my eyes. "They're starting to think we're going to get back together."

"We're—" I shook myself. "Wait, what?"

"They're confused. To them, it looks like you're easing back into their lives, and by extension, *our* lives." She swallowed. "*My* life."

I furrowed my brow. She was lying. The quick way she spoke, the way she conspicuously held eye contact—I'd learned long ago those were tells. But which part was a lie? And why? What was she hiding?

But I was hiding something too, so even if I wasn't sure it was the most rational response, I didn't push. Somehow, I was sure that if I did, she'd see the cards I was trying to keep close to the vest, and this could get ugly in a hurry.

Damn it. As much as I wanted to tell her about me and Porter, and had wanted to since we'd gone to Leavenworth, this was probably not the best time. Things suddenly felt too "off" between us. Too volatile. Too tense in ways I didn't entirely understand.

Christ. What do I do now?

"Look," she went on, "I want them to know that we get along and that we're friendly. We're doing a good thing by modeling amicable exes for them. But maybe we've done that too well." She met my gaze. "They've been through enough. I don't want to get their hopes up."

"Neither do I," I said quietly. "So, what do you suggest?"

"I think..." She chewed her lip and finally took a deep breath. "I think the best thing is to just have you come pick them up whenever they're going to stay with you, and not linger around the house too long."

"Define 'too long'."

Her jaw tightened. "Come on, Holden."

"I'm serious." I showed my palms. "Because I don't want to confuse them either, but I didn't even realize what we were doing *was* confusing them." Especially since I hadn't spent that much time at the house. Where in the world was this coming from?

She flicked her eyes away from mine.

What aren't you telling me, Tiff?

"We'll just have to play it by ear." She finally looked at me again. "All I'm asking is to make it as clear as possible to them that we get along, but we're not getting back together."

"Have you tried talking to them about it?"

Another flick of her eyes. "Yeah. I have. And they say they understand, but if we keep giving them mixed messages..."

I chewed the inside of my cheek. I really wanted to dig at this and figure out what was actually going on. Tiffany wasn't prone to lying to me, especially since she kind of sucked at it. If anything, the woman was usually honest to a fault. So I had no idea what to make of this.

For now, though, I nodded. "All right. Well, let me get them in the car and get out of here, then. I'll make it quick when I drop them off too."

She exhaled. "Okay. Thanks." She smiled thinly. "I really appreciate it."

"Yeah. Don't mention it."

What the hell is going on?

And if I got to the root of why *she* was lying, would I need to tell her why *I* was lying? Because I didn't want to hide my relationship with Porter anymore. I wanted us to be open and honest with her, even if the initial adjustment was a bit bumpy. But this? This was a wild card. I had no idea what to think or do.

I wanted to do right by my kids. I wanted to be honest with my ex-wife.

But I also wanted Porter so bad it hurt.

What the hell do I do now?

OKAY, THIS WAS A WEIRD COMBINATION OF FEELINGS. Physically, I felt amazing. Dropping onto the bed beside Porter, relaxed as hell after a feverish round of sex and a long, lazy shower, I was pretty sure I could have drifted off to blissful sleep if not for the other side of that feelings coin —everything in my head.

Even as Porter and I had been driving each other wild, there'd been a nagging twinge of guilt in the back of my mind. The same one that had been bugging me for the past few days, ever since I'd talked to Tiffany before taking the kids for an evening. With no pursuit of orgasms to hold my attention now, that twinge swelled and became something I couldn't ignore anymore.

And the source of that guilt was lying beside me, head resting on my chest and an arm draped across my stomach. I wrapped my arm around his shoulders and kissed the top of his head, which didn't help my conscience at all.

After a moment, Porter looked up at me. "What's wrong?"

"Hmm?"

"I don't know. You've just been a little...not here."

"I'm sorry." I smoothed his wet hair. "Distracted, I guess."

"I can see that." He slid his hand up the middle of my chest. "What's on your mind?"

I sighed. Was there any point in hiding it from him? After all, it did involve him. "I, um, I had an interesting conversation with Tiffany the other night."

Beside me, Porter tensed. "Yeah?"

"Yeah." I rubbed a hand over my face. "She's worried I'm spending too much time at her place. Giving the kids the wrong idea."

"What?" He turned onto his side, pushed himself up on his elbow, and eyed me. "You aren't at the house that much. What does that even mean?"

Exhaling, I slid my hand down his hip and onto his thigh. "I guess the kids are getting the wrong idea about me and her."

"About—" He blinked. "About you and her? Not about you and me?"

"Like they're getting their hopes up that we'll get back together."

"Oh." He looked as confused as I felt. After a moment, though, he pushed out a long breath and rolled onto his back. Staring up at the ceiling, he rubbed the back of his neck. "I don't think it's because the kids are asking if you and Tiffany will get together. It's because they think *we're* together."

My breath hitched. "They do?"

"Yeah. They do."

"Do they even... I mean, at their age, do they get..." I gestured at myself, then him.

"What? Two guys being together?"

I nodded.

"Oh yeah." Porter waved a hand. "One of the teachers at Noah's school is a lesbian, and there's a boy Ethan plays with at one of the parks who has two dads. They don't think anything of it."

"Oh. Well, that's good. I mean, in general. In this situation..." I cleared my throat and shook myself. "So they think we're dating?"

"I guess one of the moms from the park was telling her husband they thought you were my boyfriend, and it got back to the kids." Porter sighed again. "Ethan asked me about it at dinner the other night. Right after we got back from Leavenworth."

I shifted a little. "Did he seem upset by it?"

"No. And I think that's kind of what bothered Tiffany. That the kids might like the idea. Or at least get used to it."

"Yeah, that... That sounds about right." And it explained what Tiffany had been holding back. I wasn't sure why she'd balked at actually asking me if I was dating Porter. Or accusing me of it. Maybe she didn't want to know, and she'd fallen back on a flimsy excuse about not wanting the kids to think she and I were reconciling.

Porter sighed. "The worst part is I lied to her and the kids. I... Ethan's question caught me off guard, and I panicked, and I—"

"Hey." I squeezed his hand. "I get it. I do. No, it's not ideal, but in the moment... I get it."

Porter rubbed his forehead, then dropped his hand and met my eyes. "So what do we do now?"

I exhaled. "I'm not really sure."

He studied me, and I could see his thoughts as if they were written across his forehead. The solution to our situation, even if it wasn't palatable for either of us.

No way was I ready for that, though. There had to be a way, and damn if I wasn't going to try like hell to find it. I took his hand in both of mine and pressed a kiss to his knuckles. "I know I want this. I want *you*. That's really all I know right now."

"Me too," Porter whispered. "We'll find a way."

"Yeah, we will."

Neither of us sounded as convincing—or convinced—as we probably wanted to. Gazing into Porter's beautiful brown eyes, I definitely *wanted* to find a way to keep this thing going.

But deep down, I was scared to death there *wasn't* a way.

CHAPTER 32
PORTER

On Tiffany's front porch with my hand on the doorknob, I paused. Could I really face her right now? Or the kids? Because good God, this guilt was going to drive me insane. Flying below her radar had been one thing. Still enough to make me feel guilty, but bearable.

But I'd lied to her face about it. I'd lied to the kids about it. Holden and I had reassured each other a dozen times this evening that we'd find a way to make this right, and when I'd been lying in bed with him, nothing had seemed more important.

Coming home to Tiffany and the kids, though, I felt like a husband coming home from his mistress's place. My obligations to them were professional, not romantic, but they were depending on me. All of them. And they *trusted* me to be on the up and up.

I closed my eyes and exhaled. We'd find a way. We had to. Otherwise I was pretty sure I'd never sleep again.

Schooling all the guilt out of my face, I keyed myself inside. I toed off my shoes and headed upstairs. As soon as I cleared the top of the steps, Tiffany turned to me. "Oh my God, I am so glad you're here."

"Yeah? What's up?"

She scowled. "It's Noah. I've..." Tiffany threw up her hands. "I've tried to talk to him, but he's just been a holy terror today."

"That not like him. What's he been doing?"

"Fighting with his brother and sisters over everything. Talking back to me. Throwing the mother of all tantrums when I asked him to fill water for dinner." Her tone and expression turned plaintive. "I've done everything I can think of. Any chance you can talk to him?"

"Sure. Of course. Where is he?"

She gestured down the hall. "He's been in his room for the last hour or so. Got into it with Ethan, stormed off, slammed the door, and hasn't been out since."

Wow. Yeah. That was definitely not like Noah unless there was something really bothering him. And after my conversation with Holden... Oh no. Could that be it? "I'll, um, go talk to him."

"Great. Thanks."

With my heart in my throat, I went down the hall to the boys' bedroom and tapped gently on the closed door. "Noah? Can I come in?"

From the other side came a flat, "Yeah."

I pushed open the door.

Noah was sitting cross-legged on the floor beside his bed, a small pile of Legos beside him and something half-built in his hand. He didn't look up.

"Hey." I shut the door behind me. "What are you building?"

"Spaceship." The answer was as terse as it was quiet.

I sat on the carpet across from him. "Listen, your mom says you've had a tough day. What's going on?"

Noah shrugged. He pawed through the pile of Legos, probably searching for a piece.

"There something you want to talk about?" I pressed.

"No."

"Okay, well, is there something that's making you upset? Your mom and I are concerned about—"

"Are you really going out with my dad?"

My heart sank. I hated being right sometimes. But I didn't let it show that I'd been thinking along those lines before coming in here. "Um. What?"

Noah still focused intently on searching for a piece, his motions sharper, sending pieces tumbling out of the pile.

"Hey. Look at me."

He huffed, then sat back and met my eyes.

"Is that what's bugging you? You think something's going on with me and your dad?"

Dropping his gaze to the partially built spaceship in his lap, he nodded.

"Can you tell me why?" I hoped my nerves weren't coming through in my words.

"That kid who told Ethan he thinks you and Dad are going out—he keeps saying it, and he says his mom is sure."

God grant me the serenity not to have words with gossipy parents...

I schooled my irritation out of my tone. "If your dad and I *were* going out, would that bother you?"

Noah nodded again.

My stomach tightened. I felt oddly like I was in a minefield now, and tried not to notice how that feeling was reminiscent of my days on the ambulance. How I was all too familiar with cautiously walking into a situation where there was no telling what I'd find, only that I'd have to think fast and hope like hell I made the right decision so it didn't turn into a disaster.

This isn't a medical emergency, I reminded myself. *This is a kid who's upset about something, and I just need to find out why.*

My voice came out as barely a whisper as I asked, "Why does that bother you? Because we're guys? Or...?"

"No, it's not that." Noah sniffled, and I almost jumped. I'd been caught off guard by his answer about what was bothering him, and I was startled all over again by the way his chin quivered when he asked, "What if you and Dad break up like Mom and Dad did?"

I swallowed. "Is that what you're afraid of?"

He nodded, focusing hard on the pieces in his shaky hands. "If you and Dad break up, then you'll go away." His voice was barely audible as he added, "Or Dad will again."

My heart may as well have snapped in two right then and there. Oh God. What were we putting this kid through? If a hypothetical relationship between me and Holden stressed him out this much, then what would the real thing do to him?

I took a breath and forced my voice not to betray anything except pure calm and optimism. "Noah. Look at me."

He sniffed, then he finally did, and it took a lot of work not to react to that shine of tears on his lower lashes.

I held his gaze despite the guilt knotting my stomach. "I'm not going anywhere. And neither is your dad."

"But Dad said that too." Noah wiped his eyes on his sleeve. "And then he was gone for a long time."

I had no idea if he meant Holden's extensive travel for work or him no longer living with Tiffany and the kids. It was kind of heartbreaking to realize these kids probably didn't understand the intricacies of their parents' relationship—only that Dad hadn't been there.

"Your dad's back now, though."

"I know. But if you and Dad break up..."

My heart sank. "You're afraid he'll go away again or—"

"Or *you'll* go away forever." The waver in his voice was excruciating. No wonder he'd been acting out all day —the poor kid had abandonment issues already, and now he was just waiting for either me or his dad to up and vanish.

I touched his arm. "Hey. Listen up, okay? I'm here to take care of you and your brother and sister. The three of you are my priority. I'm not going anywhere."

He searched my eyes, and I prayed to God the kid saw nothing there but sincerity. I wasn't lying about any of that. At least, I hoped I wasn't. If Tiffany got pissed at me for dating her ex, well...there wasn't much I could do about that.

"*Are* you and my dad going out?"

I'd take it up with my battered conscience later, but I didn't know what else to do, so I looked him right in the eyes and said, "Your dad and I are friends. He's been working hard to be your dad again, and I've been helping him with that."

Noah released a long breath, his thin shoulders dropping, and the relief painted all over his expression said that, yeah, my conscience would have a few choice words for me later on.

"How do you feel about your parents dating people?" I asked. "Now that they're divorced?"

Noah's jaw worked. Then he shrugged. "I don't know." He looked up at me. "But some of the kids in my class—

their parents have boyfriends and girlfriends and stuff. And then they break up."

"And the boyfriend or girlfriend goes away?"

He nodded. "I think I'd be sad if my mom or dad broke up with someone. If I liked them."

"Yeah, that would be hard." I chewed my lip, not sure what to say.

"There's a girl in my class, and her dad went out with her karate teacher. And when they broke up, she had to start going to a different karate place."

"That made her sad?"

"Yeah. 'Cause she liked the teacher." Noah met my eyes. "If you and Dad went out, and then you broke up and went away, then Mom would get somebody else. And I don't want anybody else."

Oh God. My heart.

"I'm not going anywhere." My voice sounded hollow to my ear.

"Promise?"

Oh hell. What was I supposed to say?

But I meant it. I absolutely did. I had no control over whether Tiffany sent me packing, but yeah, I meant what I said, so I nodded. "Promise."

As soon as I said it, my stomach lurched. There was no way I could be sure I was keeping that promise. I fully intended to, but if Tiffany fired me for fucking Holden, the only thing that would register to the kids would be me leaving. It wouldn't matter why. And now, on top of that, I'd have broken a promise I'd made to Noah.

I'm sorry, kid.

I swallowed hard.

And I'm sorry, Holden. I think we're about to have a conversation neither of us wants to have.

The promise that had me ready to implode with guilt seemed to shake the remaining worry out of Noah. He picked up his spaceship again, though he didn't resume looking for pieces. "I'm glad you're staying."

"Yeah. Me too." I forced back the acid in my throat. "You want to stay in here and play? Or come out in the living room with Ethan?"

Noah quirked his lips, then shrugged and pulled the Lego instructions closer. "I want to finish this."

"All right." I started to get up. "I'm going to go have a chat with your mom. If you want to talk some more, just come find me, okay?"

He nodded, and for the first time since I'd come in here, he smiled for real. "Okay."

I returned the smile, then left his room.

I closed the door behind me, and paused to whisper, "Fuck," into the empty hallway. I hated myself for lying to Noah, but what the hell was I supposed to do? Tell him the truth? The kid had been through enough the last couple of years, and the last thing he or his siblings needed was more uncertainty. Tiffany had told me from day one that she wanted to give them some long overdue stability and adults in their lives they could depend on.

There was no way to frame this thing with Holden and make it compatible with what I'd been hired on to provide for his and Tiffany's kids. I didn't even know how to explain the conversation I'd just had with Noah to his mom. I couldn't lie to her. Lying to the kids—whether in a moment of panic or because I couldn't bring myself to hurt them—had been bad enough. My conscience was already at critical mass.

Well, I made this bed. Might as well lie in it.

Pretending I didn't feel like I was about to throw up, I

headed down the hall to the living room where I'd left Tiffany.

She rose from where she'd been sitting on the couch, her brow was creased with worry. "Did you get anywhere with him?"

"Yeah, he's..." I glanced over my shoulder, stomach knotted and heart thudding. Then I turned to the living room, where Chloe was playing with some stuffed animals and Ethan was coloring. Ashley was on the couch, phone propped on her knee as she divided her attention between that screen and the TV. To Tiffany, I said, "Maybe we should talk on the deck."

Alarm made her eyebrows jump. "Um. Okay. Hey, Ash? Can you watch them for a few?"

"'kay."

Tiffany and I stepped out onto the back deck, and the hiss-click of the sliding glass door sent my pulse skyrocketing.

I put my hands on the railing and stared out at the backyard.

Tiffany stopped beside me, arms folded loosely, and her hip pressed against the railing. "So, what did he say?"

I swallowed. "He was upset because of what Ethan said at dinner the other night. About me dating Holden."

"Oh." A few beats of silence went by. "He... What bothered him about that?"

Steeling myself, I moistened my lips, then faced her. "Someone at school brought it up to Ethan again. The rumor about Holden and me. So Noah was afraid if there was something going on between us, that we'd eventually break up, and one of us would disappear."

Tiffany's expression was more unreadable than it had been in all the months I'd known her. She was staring at me, scrutinizing me, but what was going on behind her eyes? No clue.

"So what did you tell him?" Her tone was flat, as unreadable as her face.

I fought the urge to shift my weight nervously. "I told him the truth—that I'm here to take care of him and his siblings, and that I'm not going anywhere. And that his dad moved here to be close to them too, so he's not going anywhere either."

Tiffany's features subtly hardened. "Did you tell him you're seeing his father or not?"

"I told him I'm not."

"Was that a lie?"

Fuck. Oh fuck. I was already sick to my stomach after lying to Noah's face. Lying to Tiffany's...

"Porter." Her tone was harder now too. "Noah's been acting weird all day, and *you've* been acting kind of weird ever since that talk we had about you and Holden." She narrowed her eyes slightly. "Is something you want to tell me?"

I flinched away from her gaze, which was probably incriminating as all hell. If I hadn't just had that talk with Noah, I probably could've kept my guard up. I probably could've looked her right in the eye and lied through my teeth about my relationship with Holden.

But after that heart-to-heart with Noah, my defenses were shot, and I was worn way too raw to keep my emotions off my sleeve.

"Porter..." The shaky *please tell me I'm wrong* in her voice broke me.

I squeezed my eyes shut and pushed out a resigned breath. "Look, I'm sorry. I—"

"Are you *serious*?" she hissed. "You're sleeping with my ex-husband?"

I winced, but made myself meet her gaze. "We've been seeing each other."

"Seeing each other?" she growled. "What exactly does that mean?"

Instantly, my throat was tight. How was I supposed to answer that? Brush it off and pretend we'd just been screwing behind her back? Or tell her that I'd forged a deep, amazing connection with the man she still stung over? I couldn't think of any answer that wouldn't make this worse, and I really didn't want to hurt her.

"You know what?" She put up her hands. "Forget I asked. I don't want to know."

My stomach dropped. Oh God. She was going to fire me, wasn't she? "Tiffany, we—"

"My kids *need* you, Porter." Her tone was both angry and plaintive. "*I* need you. If you're...doing whatever it is with Holden, that's just going to complicate things, and if there's one thing my children don't need right now, it's more complications. You hear me?"

Swallowing hard, I nodded.

"You just talked to my son and heard how much it worries him to have you dating his father. So don't think for a second I'm saying any of this because I want to dictate your personal life or interfere with Holden's. I just—"

"You're watching out for your kids. I get it. I honestly do."

She nodded. "That's all it is. I mean, I'm sure everything could be just fine while you two are dating. It's the aftermath if you break up that I'm worried about. That kind of thing is hard on kids, and I don't want Holden keeping his distance from his kids—or feeling like he *should* be keeping his distance—because things are awkward between you two. I don't want the kids to lose *you* because of whatever happens between you and Holden." Tiffany glanced toward the house, then up at me, her eyes pleading. "You've already seen how much it hurts them to even think about that. Don't make them live that out for real."

I flinched.

"I'm not doing this for fun." She set her jaw. "But especially now that you've *lied* to them about it, I need you to choose—you either stay with Holden, or you stay with my kids. And don't think for a second that I'll be the one telling them what decision you make."

Just thinking about looking at those three little faces and telling them I'd chosen their dad over them—and that I really was one breakup away from vanishing from their worlds—made me sick to my stomach. Gritting my teeth against the emotions trying to crack free, I nodded. "Okay."

She held my gaze like she was waiting for a decision but then she nodded too. "Okay. Let me know what you decide."

"I will."

We locked eyes for a moment longer before she turned and went back inside, leaving me on the deck with my thoughts, confession, and flailing conscience.

As soon as I was alone, I sighed and wiped a hand over my face. Tiffany wasn't going to force me to make the choice right now, which I appreciated. Then again, if she knew it wasn't an easy decision, then she had to have caught on there was more between Holden and me than sex. But she was still making me choose.

I wanted to be angry at her for that. I wanted to hate her for it. To pack my things, get the fuck out of this house, and go crash at my mom and dad's until I figured out what to do for my next paycheck.

But Noah. But Ethan. But Chloe.

They were the reasons she was drawing a hard line, and they were the reasons I couldn't see any other choice but to *toe* that line. Hadn't they had enough upheaval in their lives over the last couple of years? Hadn't I seen all that fear and hurt in Noah's eyes at the mere suggestion that I might be seeing his dad and thus have one foot out the door?

If I stayed with Holden, Tiffany would fire me, which would make things awkward between us. That would be hard on the kids. If I tried to keep this out of her sight again, and then she found out about us again—or if we broke up and shit got weird—then I'd get fired too. There really wasn't any solution where I could keep Holden and still provide his kids with the stability that they deserved and that I'd been hired to provide. It hurt Noah just to think about me and Holden breaking up. Ethan and Chloe? They'd know something was off. They'd wonder why I was gone. What they'd done wrong. Why I didn't like them anymore.

Holden, Tiffany, and I could be adults about this, and we could keep our emotional shit out of the kids' sight. Holden and I could be amicable and civil, if only for the sake of the kids. They'd been through enough. They deserved better.

Tiffany was putting the kids first. Holden and I needed to do the same.

Which really left me with only one option.

Even if it hurt like hell just thinking about it.

CHAPTER 33

HOLDEN

It had only been an hour or two since Porter left, so I wasn't surprised when he texted me. He usually did once he'd settled back in and had some privacy.

What I wasn't expecting was the message itself:
We need to talk. Tonight.
My heart jumped into my throat. *Okay. What's up?*
Can I come over?
Stomach somersaulting, I replied that he could, and now I had at least fifteen minutes to run through every possible worst-case scenario. What in the world could have come up in the space of two hours?

He wasn't going to keep me waiting, either—twenty minutes after the last text, footsteps came down the hall outside.

I swallowed, making a last-ditch effort to tamp down my nerves, and went to the door. I opened it just as he reached it. Our eyes met across the threshold, but only for a second.

"Come on in," I said quietly and stood aside.

Porter came in, but he couldn't hold my gaze. From the way his jaw was working, he might've been struggling to hold on to his composure too. Those worst-case scenarios banging around in my head were getting a bit too real.

What's happening? Talk to me, Porter.

He rocked on his heels, wringing his hands.

"Come on." I motioned toward the living room. "Let's sit down."

He hesitated, biting his lip hard enough I was surprised he didn't draw blood. Then, without a word, he crossed the narrow stretch of carpet to the couch, and we both sat down. Now he was even twitchier, still wringing his hands and shifting.

"Hey." I put a hand on his shoulder, but he shrank away slightly, so I pulled it back. "What's wrong?"

"I..." Porter sighed, slumping a little, and he raked a hand through his hair. "Tiffany knows about us."

My heart stopped. "What?"

"She..." He exhaled hard, shoulders sagging beneath an unseen weight. "She confronted me again, and I just... I couldn't do it." He finally met my gaze, his eyes full of hurt and fatigue. "I couldn't lie to her."

"You *told* her about us?"

"What was I supposed to do?" He raised his hand like he was trying to wave dismissively, but the movement was heavy and sluggish, as if it drained away what little energy he'd had left. "I told her we weren't dating, but then Noah was acting weird, and... God, Holden. The way he looked at me when he asked if I was going to go away if you and I broke up, I... I mean, what was I supposed to say to that?"

I don't know, because looking at you right now is killing me.

"Do the *kids* know?"

Grimacing as if this was all physically painful, Porter shook his head. "No. Ethan thought we were because of rumors. And Noah... You know how sensitive he is about things."

I flinched. "Yeah. I do."

"So I told him I wasn't going anywhere, and that you and I are just friends. I fucking *lied* to him because it broke my heart to see him like that, and what else could I do? I couldn't tell him the truth." Porter sighed. "Then Tiffany wanted to know what Noah was upset about, and I mean..."

"And you told her."

"I had to," he breathed. "I just couldn't do it. I couldn't lie to both of them."

It was an odd feeling to be relieved that he'd chosen to lie to my son. As much as Tiffany and I had always vowed to be as honest as possible with all the kids, Porter had been trying to spare Noah's feelings. In the moment, I might very well have said the same thing.

"So now she knows," he whispered. "And it's either you or my job."

My teeth snapped together, and fury rose in my chest. "She gave you an ultimatum?"

"What can she do? It isn't like I didn't know where she stood on you and me hooking up, and she's got every right to fire me for whatever reason she wants." His expression and voice turned plaintive. "I can't do that to your kids."

I blinked. "What?"

"Come on, you've seen them with me. I'm something they expect every day. If their mom fires me, don't you think that will stress them out?"

I wanted to argue, but what the hell could I say? He was right. If Tiffany fired him, that would be yet another man—one they adored and trusted and depended on—disappearing from their lives. How much more of that could they handle before they developed trust issues? Or, well, *more* trust issues?

Porter went on, voice shaky. "Don't think for a second I'm doing this because I want to." He held my gaze, though it was obviously a struggle. "But I can't keep... We can't keep seeing each other."

My heart dropped into my stomach. "Porter, we can work this out with Tiffany. We just—"

"Holden." He put up a hand and shook his head. "Please. Don't." As he lowered his hand, he went on. "It's not just because I need to keep my job. The thing is, Tiffany's right. Your kids have been through so much, and what they need more than anything now is stability. If we keep seeing each other, and things fall apart between us, they're going to be caught in the middle just like they were when you and Tiffany separated." Shaking his head again, he broke eye contact. "I can't do that to them."

What the fuck could I say? *No, you* should *do that to them?*

My throat tightened. "Porter..."

"I'm sorry," he whispered. "I, um. I should go."

I didn't know what else to do or say, so I just nodded numbly. If he stayed, I was going to try talk him into staying longer, and the only thing stopping me now were those six heartbreaking words: *I can't do that to them.*

Porter got up. He didn't pause. Didn't speak.

I didn't watch him go. I couldn't. Not that I needed to—I could feel him moving away from me and taking all the air in the room with him. Watching him would just make this hurt more, if that was even possible.

Staring blankly at the wall, I listened.

And then he was gone.

And...fuck.

I'd known since our trip to Leavenworth that I had feelings for Porter, but it wasn't until the door clicked shut behind him tonight that I truly grasped how deep those feelings ran. How much I really had to lose. How much had just slipped out that door, and how little I could do to stop it.

I leaned forward, elbows on my knees, and rubbed my temples. I wouldn't jeopardize my second chance at a relationship with my kids for anything, but there had to be some way to make this work. Some way to be the father they deserved and still hold on to the man who had brought a light into my life that I hadn't even realized was missing. No, I hadn't known him for very long, but there was something more here than just sneaking off and fooling around. There was something here that was worth fighting for. Wasn't there some way we could be together and still do right by my family?

How in the world do I save this?

"We need to talk." I held Tiffany's gaze as she let me into the house the next evening. "Privately."

Her jaw tightened. "You're right. We do." She brushed past me and motioned for me to follow her. As we turned the corner at the top of the stairs, she threw over her shoulder, "Porter, could you get everyone ready to go with their dad?"

Without thinking, I looked, and my gaze landed right on him. For a split second, we both froze, staring at each other in the most painfully awkward silence.

Then he broke eye contact with a quiet cough. "Yeah. On it. Hey, guys. Let's start putting your things together."

I didn't hear anything beyond that because I was following Tiffany down the hall. She stopped at a door and gestured for me to go in.

I didn't spend much energy taking in my surroundings. It was a lot of familiar things—the furniture, the pictures on the wall, the ever-present paperback beside the bed—in an unfamiliar space. Thinking too hard about those would just bring too many feelings about the divorce to the surface. I wasn't here to focus on that.

Tiffany shut the door, and we faced each other beside the bed we used to share.

"All right." Her tone was flat. "Let's talk."

If there was one thing we'd both gained from the dysfunctional latter half of our marriage, it was the ability to fight behind closed doors without anyone in the house hearing us. I wasn't sure if that was a healthy skill to have, but it wasn't one I was going to bitch about tonight.

"Did you really give Porter an ultimatum about us?" I asked through my teeth.

Her jaw clenched. "You two didn't leave me much choice, did you?"

I almost rolled my eyes but stopped myself. That was the quickest way to turn this into the shouting match we were trying to avoid. "We couldn't talk about this before—"

"We did talk about it," she growled. "I asked you—and him—not to get involved with each other. Apparently an ultimatum was the only way I was going to get that point across."

"Or you could have stayed out of it."

"Uh-uh." She shook her head emphatically. "When you're screwing someone, and that threatens to sabotage what I've carefully—"

"I'm not in this to sabotage anything, okay?" My voice

shook, but I forced myself to go on. "We can disagree until the end of time about whether I should be able to date Porter, but don't try to tell me I'm sabotaging anything."

"Maybe it's not your intent, but it's—"

"No, it's not," I said, softer now. "Look, I can't fix what you and I had. I know that. But I do want to fix things between me and the kids. I'm trying to do that without rocking the boat for you any more than I already have. I swear, I am." I swallowed hard, but it didn't do much to steady my voice. "So the last thing I'm going to do is go out of my way to do something that'll cause you more hell than I already have."

"Like screwing the man who's keeping my entire world in order?" she growled through her teeth.

I flinched and broke eye contact. "Tiff, I'm—"

"I don't want your excuses. I don't care why. I don't care how or when or—" She gestured sharply. "For God's sake. Can't you see why I don't want you and him together?" She threw up her hands. "Holden, I *need* Porter."

"So do I." My own words startled me as much as they seemed to startle her, and we stared at each other. As what I'd said echoed in my mind, a lump rose in my throat, and I had to fight hard to force it back as I softly repeated, "So do I."

A million emotions played across my ex-wife's eyes, and for a few hopeful seconds, I thought she might understand.

But that hope was dashed when her features hardened. "Do you think I enjoy this? I don't get some sick thrill out of pushing you two apart." She folded her arms tightly, and her jaw clenched as she glared up at me. "But what am I supposed to do, Holden?"

"Trust us to be adults and put the kids first?" I sighed. "I mean, taking Porter out of the equation for a second—what happens when one of us starts dating, huh? The kids are going to get attached to them too. We might break up with them just like we broke up with exes before we met. Do we just stay with someone because we want to shelter the kids from—"

"This is different, and you know it," she threw back. "Porter isn't some random person who comes into our lives because we're dating, and you knew that before you ever laid a hand on him. Don't you dare pretend otherwise."

"And don't pretend he's going to stick around forever whether I'm in the picture or not. Do you honestly think he's going to keep doing this until they go to college?"

"Of course I know he might quit. I've known that since day one. He could also get hit by a bus tomorrow. There are a million possibilities I can't control." She stepped closer, narrowing her eyes. "But that doesn't mean I shouldn't do what I can to mitigate things where our children are concerned. If he quits, or he's gone for whatever reason, then I'll address it with the kids when the time comes. I'm not going to just throw up my hands and say, 'Eh, whatever' just because something beyond my control could happen."

I gritted my teeth. "I'm glad to know my love life falls under your control."

"For fuck's sake, Holden. You know what I mean." She rolled her eyes. "You know I would never in a million years do anything to keep you from seeing our kids. You know that." She pointed a finger at my chest. "But if you want the relationship with them that you say you want, then you'll stop being a selfish ass, put them first, and don't do anything to screw up the only constant, stable male presence they've ever been able to depend on."

I blinked, then narrowed my eyes. "You make it sound like all that time I spent away from home was because I was shirking my responsibilities. I was trying to *provide* that home and everything you and the kids needed."

"Everything except a husband and a father," she threw back. "They needed more than a bank account and a dental plan, Holden." Voice wavering, she added, "And so did I."

The myriad accusations packed into those four words slammed into my chest, and I had no idea how to respond. My guilty conscience was already on her side, reminding me over and over that all my pain and Porter's could be pinned firmly on me, and the reminder of how much I'd failed my family left me breathless.

Tiffany pushed her shoulders back and looked me in the eye, her tone less hostile but still firm. "Porter isn't just the guy who shuttles them around and makes them lunch. They adore him. He's dependable in ways their father never has been. If you really do care about your children's well-being, then prove it by putting them first. Let *them* have Porter."

"Tiffany, I—"

"I'm not backing down on this, damn it," she snapped. "I hired him so they could have a male role model who wouldn't vanish from their lives the moment I broke up with him. You coming along and dating him throws a pretty big monkey wrench into that."

Part of me wanted to crumble and admit how right she was, but a much bigger part was hurting too much over the divorce and over Porter and over everything I'd seen in the mirror she'd repeatedly held up to my face over the past couple of years.

"Well, congratulations," I growled. "Now you have exactly what you wanted to avoid—Porter and me, broken up, with things unbearably awkward between us."

"Don't you blame me for that," she threw back. "You two can be fucking adults about it now. If one of you had done something or you'd broken up because you couldn't stand each other, then things would get weird. This is two adults doing the right thing, and I would hope you both have enough maturity to suck it up when you have to be around each other, if only for the sake of *your kids, Holden.*"

Flinching, I broke eye contact.

She softened her tone again. "I'm not pretending this is easy for you. You know me better than that. I'm not enjoying this, and I'm not trying to hurt either of you. I'm just asking you and Porter to put this behind you, be adults, and prioritize the kids."

What the hell was I supposed to say to that? If I kept pushing, she was going to let Porter go. I couldn't do that to him. To the kids. To her. If things hurt like hell now, they were only going to get worse unless I took the high road she was begging me to take.

"Fine," I whispered. "All right."

Tiffany exhaled. "Thank you."

I nodded. There really wasn't much left to say.

She took a deep breath. "We should, um, go see if the kids are ready to go."

"Yeah. Good idea."

What else could I do?

I STAYED AWAY FROM THE HOUSE FOR A SOLID WEEK. I needed to, and I was pretty sure Tiffany and Porter needed me to. When I took the kids for the following weekend, Zach picked them up. Maybe that made me a coward, or all of us cowards, but everyone needed a little space right now. If nothing else, it kept the awkwardness out of the kids' sight, and as far as I knew, they had no idea anything had happened between Porter and me.

Porter was probably doing his level best to keep it out of sight too, which made me feel even guiltier. I'd seen the hurt in his eyes, both on the night he called things off and when I'd come over to talk to Tiffany. Hopefully he was calling on all his paramedic poker face training—that training to keep a stoic expression so a patient didn't panic—to keep this off the kids' radars, but I hated that he needed to. And that there was nothing I could do to make this easier for him aside from staying away.

On my way back to my office after a meeting, I checked my phone, and to my surprise, I had a text from Tiffany. To my even greater surprise, it wasn't about my relationship with Porter.

Jay is in town. Ash wants to talk to him, and she wants us all to be there. Are you still in?

Gnawing my lip, I stared at the message. I didn't relish the idea of being in the same room with Tiffany and Porter right now, never mind Tiffany's first husband, but Ashley needed us. If ever there was a moment for the three of us to be adults and put our own feelings aside for the kids, this was it.

So I wrote back, *When & where?*

And I hoped I could still find the restraint not to clock that asshole in the mouth like he so deliciously deserved.

CHAPTER 34

PORTER

To say I was a ball of nerves would be a hell of an understatement.

The thought of seeing Holden for the first time in days had my stomach roiling, but mostly I was worried sick about how things would go down with Ashley's dad.

As part of the custody arrangement, Ashley was to spend Thanksgiving break in Arizona with her dad. She and Tiffany had talked it over, and Ashley had decided she didn't want to wait any longer to come out. So, under the pretense of not being comfortable with Ashley flying alone, Tiffany had arranged for her ex-husband to come to town to pick up their daughter. She had also strategically arranged for Jay to join us for dinner before Ashley left with him. Zach was watching the youngest three tonight—they didn't need to be here for this, and Tiffany and Holden had both promised to make it up to him big time—so it was just Tiffany and Holden along with Ashley and me.

I kept Ashley as busy as possible in the kitchen. Making dinner kept me preoccupied and distracted, and it seemed to be having the same effect on her. Good thing I'd had my mom email me her recipe for manicotti. It wasn't horrendously complicated, but it had enough steps to keep both of us focused on something other than tonight.

At a little after six, Holden arrived. He came into the kitchen, and we glanced at each other and offered quiet nods of acknowledgment. Then he shifted his attention to Ashley. "Hey, kiddo. How you holding up?"

She shuddered, glancing up from the sauce she was stirring. "Okay. I guess."

Holden and I exchanged glances again.

Then he moved a bit closer to her, and his tone was soft as he said, "Hey. Look at me." When she faced him, he put a hand on her shoulder and looked right in her eyes. "I know you're nervous. Believe me, I was too when I came out. But just remember that your mom, Porter, and I are all here, and we support you. No matter what. Okay?"

Her lips tightened, and she nodded but didn't say anything. I wondered if she was trying not to cry. Or throw up. God knew I was familiar with those about-to-come-out feelings.

Holden must have seen it too, because he softly added, "You don't have to do this tonight."

Ashley closed her eyes and took a deep breath. "He's already here. If I don't do it now, it's going to bug me the whole time I'm in Arizona. I just want it done so I don't have to think about it anymore."

Holden and I exchanged glances that screamed *Boy, have I ever been there, done that.*

"Just don't feel like you have to," I said to Ashley. "We've both been there. We'll support you whichever way you go."

Her eyes flicked back and forth between us, and after a

moment, she managed a smile. "Thanks. And, um, thanks for being here."

"Any time." Holden squeezed her shoulder, then let it go. "Like Porter said—we've both been there."

She nodded. "At least I know you guys and my mom are cool with it. It's just Dad I have to—"

A car pulled up outside.

Ashley stiffened. "Oh crap."

I winced. That didn't seem like it should be a kid's first reaction to her dad showing up after she hadn't seen him in a few months. Hopefully it was just nerves over tonight. Given some of the shit I'd heard about the dude, though...

Tiffany appeared in the kitchen. "Come on, Ash. Your dad's here."

Ashley nodded.

As Tiffany gently herded her toward the stairs, she said, "Can you boys finish up in here while we go say hello?"

Holden cut his eyes toward the stairs, his expression dark as if he legitimately wanted to murder Jay with his mind and thought he might pull it off. Then he schooled his face and nodded. "Sure. Yeah."

They left the kitchen, and we were, for the first time, alone.

"So." He swallowed. "Uh, how are you doing?"

"I'm okay. Just...you know." I nodded toward the table that had been set for five. "Worried for Ashley."

Holden grimaced. "Yeah. Me too."

"How do you think it'll go?"

That sigh was not encouraging. "One of the reasons Jay never liked me was because he knows I'm queer. Marrying his ex-wife was my only bigger sin."

"Oh shit. Does Ashley know about that?"

Holden nodded grimly. "Unfortunately, yeah."

"Explains her nerves."

"Uh-huh. Definitely."

We glanced at each other, and I continued finishing up dinner. Food prep had kept me distracted all evening, and now it was *almost* pulling my focus away from Holden standing here in the same room. If my neck would stop prickling with his presence, and my head would stop spinning because I kept forgetting to breathe, and my hands would stay steady enough that I didn't burn myself or something, I'd be good. Really good. I could totally handle this, being in the same room as the man I hadn't been able to stop thinking about since—

The front door opened and snapped my thoughts away from Holden. We both cringed, sighed, and then put on placid expressions a second before Tiffany, Ashley, and a tall, bald dude strolled into the kitchen. He looked pissed off already. I couldn't decide if he was, or if he just had some serious resting bitch face going on.

Or maybe it was because of Holden, who was now wearing a similar expression.

"Jay, you remember Holden." Tiffany's deceptively friendly voice held a note of warning that quite clearly conveyed *if you boys don't get along, I will brain you both*.

Though neither looked particularly happy about it, Holden and Jay shook hands.

"And who's this?" Jay extended his hand to me. "You his new boyfriend or something?"

My stomach dropped into my feet.

"Funny," Holden growled.

"No, Jay," Tiffany said. "This is Porter. He's the nanny I hired to take care of the younger kids while Holden and I are at work. And since he lives here, and he helped Ashley cook, I thought it would be rude to kick him out for dinner." Her tone dared him to have a problem with that.

Jay regarded me suspiciously, then grunted with either resignation or approval. I didn't really care which as long as he wasn't starting a battle about me being here.

"Well, um." I cleared my throat. "Dinner's ready, so if everyone wants to have a seat... Ashley, you want to give me a hand?"

As she helped me serve up plates, she said under her breath, "This is going to suck."

"I know, kiddo." I put some manicotti on a plate and handed it to her so she could add the sauce. "But like Holden said, we support you. Always."

"I know." She flashed me a nervous smile. "Thanks."

I smiled back, hoping it was reassuring and didn't reveal at all that I was almost as nervous as I'd been the first time I'd come out.

We arranged plates on the table, and everyone dug in. Holden sat with Ashley to his left and me to his right. Beside me was Jay, and beside him, Tiffany. I was a little too close to Jay for my comfort, but if it meant putting space between him and his daughter? Fine.

Tiffany and Jay did most of the talking over dinner. Holden, Ashley, and I ate in silence, with him and me exchanging uneasy glances when she wasn't looking and giving her reassuring ones when she was.

"Well." Jay turned to Ashley. "Our flight's early tomorrow morning, so we better head south. I got us a hotel next to the airport."

"Okay." Ashley's eyes flicked toward me, then Holden. We each nodded to her. Then she turned a pleading look on her mom. Tiffany studied her, and finally met her first husband's gaze across the table.

"Listen, Jay." She folded her hands on the table. "Before you and Ashley leave, there's something she'd like to discuss with you."

He shot wary glances at Holden and me before looking at his daughter. "All right."

"So, um." Ashley cleared her throat. She wrung her hands in her lap and bit her lip. "I..."

"It's okay, sweetheart," Tiffany said.

Holden watched Ashley, lips tight and a pained expression on his face. If I knew him, he was fighting hard against the temptation to put a reassuring hand on her shoulder. Knowing what I did about her territorial father, I understood why he was holding back, and it was heartbreaking to see him struggling so hard to withhold that gentle reassurance. It probably would have done Ashley a world of good, but Jay wouldn't take it well, and there was already no telling how he'd take his daughter's news.

Finally, Ashley took a deep breath. "I have a girlfriend."

Jay straightened. "A girlfriend?"

She nodded, cheeks coloring. Her lips bleached as she pressed them together.

"So, what?" he asked. "You're a lesbian now?"

Holden bristled beside me. So did Tiffany. Like me, though, they didn't say anything.

Ashley set her jaw and looked her dad in the eye. "Yeah. I am."

Silence. Tense, impenetrable silence. Nobody moved. Everybody waited.

Jay looked at each of us in turn, stopping when his gaze landed on Tiffany. "And you're okay with this." It wasn't a question.

"Why wouldn't I be?"

He opened his mouth to speak, but then he glanced at us again as we watched him, waiting for his answer.

Yeah, Jay? Why wouldn't *she be okay with it?*

Finally, he fixed his glare on Tiffany. "This is your fault, you know."

"How's that?" She glared right back at him. "Because I let my child be who she is instead of making her feel like crap so she stays in the closet? Hmm. Yeah. Guilty."

Despite wanting to choke Jay, I had to suppress a smile. After seeing her with both her ex-husbands, I decided Tiffany could definitely teach me a thing or two about not taking shit from anyone.

"So you're just letting this happen," Jay said.

"Yes, just like I let her grow to five foot two." Tiffany shrugged dismissively. "You want me to tell her she's not allowed to grow?"

Jay was not amused. "You encouraged her. I mean, for God's sake, you've got *these two* hanging around her." He gestured at Holden and me. "A couple of queers instead of a real man, no wonder she's—"

"I was a lesbian before I even knew Holden was bi," Ashley snapped.

Everyone at the table froze.

"God, Dad." She fixed a look of pure teenage disgust on her father. "They didn't make me gay and you're not going to make me straight. Get over it."

The surprise in Jay's expression shifted to anger. "Don't you talk to me like that, young lady." He turned that anger on Tiffany. "Is this how you let her talk to you? Didn't we agree we'd teach our kid some damn manners?"

"She's one of the politest teenagers I've ever met." My own words came out before I could think twice, and all eyes were suddenly on me. I kind of wanted to cringe and maybe slide under the table and die—I was supposed to be here as a silent show of support, after all—but Christ on a cracker, I was just done with this asshole.

"Excuse me?" Jay growled. "Did I ask your opinion?"

"No." I sat up straighter and raised my chin despite still wishing the floor would open up and swallow me. "But if you're going to try to blame me for influencing your daughter and making her gay, you're going to get my opinion." I waited a beat, thinking he'd have some kind of retort, but he just stared at me in stunned silence, so I kept going. "Ashley never mouths off to adults, but her mother did teach her to have a backbone. And part of having that backbone is knowing that just because someone is a grownup doesn't mean she has to quietly put up with whatever bullshit comes out of their mouths." I shrugged as flippantly as I could. "So if you want some respect from your incredibly respectful daughter, maybe start by respecting who she is."

Everyone at the table was suddenly very, very still. My heart pounded, and the longer the silence dragged on, the more horror crept in. Had I just... *Christ*. How many more fireable offenses could I rack up before the end of the year? Assuming I didn't actually get fired before the ball dropped?

Jay narrowed his eyes at Tiffany. "There a reason you brought an army to give their two cents about our daughter?"

"It's called supporting our daughter," she said coolly. "I recommend trying it sometime."

His lips pulled so tight they nearly disappeared. Finally he huffed and put his napkin on the table. "I'm done here. Ashley, let's go."

She didn't move.

He took a step toward the doorway, but stopped. "Are

you coming or not?"

Ashley didn't budge. "Are you going to be nice about me being lesbian?"

"You're fourteen. You're not—"

"I'm not going."

He sighed loudly. "Ashley, get in the car."

"No." She folded her arms and lifted her chin. "Not until you accept that I'm a lesbian."

"I'll accept that you need some counseling and—"

"Over my dead body," Tiffany said in the most murderous tone I'd ever heard from her. "I'm not opposed to a therapist if she wants one, but if you think you're going to hire someone to shrink the gay out of her, think again."

Jay blinked. Then the surprise vanished. "Fine. I'm going to back to Arizona, then." To Ashley he muttered, "We're not done talking about this," before he stabbed a finger at Tiffany. "And you're reimbursing me for the plane tickets, you manipulative bitch."

"Hey!" Holden snarled, half-rising from his chair. "Don't you come in here and talk to her like that."

"Stay out of this," Jay snapped back.

"Then show some respect before—"

"Both of you," Tiffany growled. "*Stop.*"

They did and faced her.

With a look, she told Holden to take his seat, and he did.

Then she turned her glare on Jay. "I'll be happy to pay you back for the tickets. If you're going to treat our daughter like this, you can get the hell out of my house."

"You'll be hearing from my attorney," he ground out as he started to leave.

"Bring it," she fired at his back. "I've got two witnesses who will testify that you're a toxic parent to a gay child."

She glanced at us as if to confirm we'd testify, and we both nodded without hesitation.

Whatever Jay said next, I didn't catch it over his stomping feet going down the stairs. There was some rustling as he put his shoes back on. A moment later, the door slammed shut behind him, making all of us jump and rattling the entire house.

As one, the three of us looked at Ashley. She was still watching the doorway he'd gone through, and I was pretty sure Tiffany and Holden were holding their breath like I was.

And then, right before our eyes, the defiant teenager crumbled into the devastated little girl. She let her face fall into her hand, and before Ashley had even let go of that first heartbreaking sob, Tiffany wrapped her arms around her and hugged her tight.

"I'm sorry, baby," she whispered, and kissed Ashley's forehead. Over Ashley's head, Tiffany and Holden exchanged something unspoken. Then he turned to me and made a *let's go* gesture. When I met Tiffany's eyes, she nodded as she stroked Ashley's hair.

We got up and left the dining room. The deck would've been the quickest escape, but late November had firmly dug its claws into the area, so we went downstairs instead. A little too close to my bedroom for comfort, but at least it was warm and gave Ashley and Tiffany some space.

There was a rec room off to the left, and we went in there. I was too restless to sit, so I leaned against the wet bar. Holden leaned on the back of the couch.

"Think she's okay?" I asked.

He nodded. "She just needs a minute."

"I figured. God. Poor kid."

"No kidding." He scowled and muttered, "Can't

fucking *stand* that asshole."

I laughed dryly. "Yeah, I got the impression you two aren't exactly friends."

"No. Definitely not."

I chuckled, but quickly sobered. "I hope Tiffany doesn't think I was too far out of line with what I said."

Holden's expression softened. "No, I don't think she will."

"Really? I mean, it wasn't exactly my place."

"Maybe not, but Ashley's always intimidated by standing up to her dad. It probably took everything she had to do it, and I think having you back her up like that was exactly what she needed."

"You do?"

He held my gaze, and he smiled as he nodded. "Yeah. You were focused on Jay, but I was watching Ashley. If I was reading her right, you spoke up exactly when she needed you to."

I released a breath, swaying a little on my feet. "Oh, thank God. I didn't want to steal her thunder or make her think she couldn't handle this on her own, but I—"

"She shouldn't *have* to handle it on her own. She's fourteen. I mean, that's why we were here tonight. So she didn't have to."

"Still. You know what I mean, right?"

Holden nodded again. "Yeah. And I don't think you have anything to worry about."

"Okay. Good."

Silence fell between us. To my surprise, it wasn't... Well, it wasn't comfortable, but wasn't as painfully awkward as I'd expected.

"So. Um." I cleared my throat. "I guess we really can do this. Function like adults without..." I didn't know how to finish that. Without visibly pining for each other? Without acting like a couple of bitter exes, even though we weren't?

Holden smiled, but it was obviously forced. "Tiffany wanted us to put the kids first. I think we can do that." He gestured at the floor above us. "I think we *did* that tonight."

"Yeah. We did. So now we just keep doing it, right?"

He nodded. "Exactly."

Our eyes locked.

Is it just me, or is this easier said than done?

Are you struggling as hard as I am?

Do you have any idea how much I still want you?

Holden broke eye contact. I looked away. The silence lingered for a moment before he motioned toward the sliding glass door leading out to the backyard. "Think it'll snow?"

The weather. Awesome. We were down to talking about the fucking *weather*.

I pressed my elbow onto the wet bar and looked outside. "Don't know. Sometimes we get a little, but it doesn't stick. Sometimes we get a blizzard and the whole area shuts down."

Holden laughed so softly I barely heard him at all. "Is it true what they say? People in Seattle can't drive in the snow?"

I chuckled. "You try driving in wet snow on near vertical streets, and then tell me how bad we are at it."

"Fair enough."

Silence fell again. Slightly less uncomfortable than before, so there was that. We passed the time with small talk that was so not us, but at least it filled the space between us and made this seem marginally less miserable.

All the while, I was torn over how to feel about how we'd handled tonight. I was glad we'd been a united front for Ashley. Putting the kids first was a no-brainer regardless of my relationship with Holden.

But how long was I supposed to hide how much everything about this was killing me?

After Holden left for the night, and Ashley had gone to her room to Facetime with her girlfriend, Tiffany and I finally started cleaning up the kitchen. Neither of us said much. She was probably still fuming over her ex-husband being a douche canoe. I was still jittery over the confrontation with Jay, and of course there were my ever-present feelings about Holden. I had plenty on my mind, that was for sure.

After we'd finished with the kitchen, Tiffany dried her hands on a dishtowel and faced me. "Thank you for being there tonight. And for standing up for Ashley."

"That wasn't out of line? What I said?"

"Oh hell no." She gestured dismissively, and as she hung the towel on the oven handle, added, "He needed to hear it. Ashley was thrilled that you did it, too."

I exhaled, letting my shoulders sag. "Thank God. I was afraid I'd overstepped or—"

"Porter. Honey." Tiffany shook her head. "You were there to support my daughter while she went through something you understand more than I ever will. It means you're off Jay's Christmas card list until the end of time, but I think you pretty much won Ashley's heart forever."

I laughed softly. "I can live with that tradeoff."

"I figured you could." She smiled, though it was short-lived. "And, um, thanks for... You know. You and Holden. Being..."

"Civil?"

"Yeah."

"Of course we were." I shifted my weight, stomach twisting. "Tonight was about Ashley. Not us."

"Still. I know it couldn't have been easy. So, I appreciate it."

I just nodded.

She studied me, and her brow creased. "You're having a really hard time with this, aren't you? Not being with Holden?"

I released a long breath and leaned hard against the counter. "Am I that transparent?"

"Yeah." She grimaced. "You kind of are."

Sighing, I ran a hand through my hair. "Listen, I'm sorry I lied to you about seeing him, and I'm sorry I started seeing him when you made it clear you didn't want us together." I fought back the lump in my throat. "But yeah, this is hard. Because I really do have feelings for him."

"I can see that." Her tone was soft and resigned. "I'm sorry."

"I know. Me too." The conversation threatened to get supremely awkward, and my emotions were threatening to make a very unwelcome appearance, so I decided now was the best time to bow out. "I'm, uh, going to call it a night. Unless you need me for anything else?"

"No. I've got it all under control." She smiled, a hint of sadness in her eyes. "Good night, Porter."

"G'night."

Downstairs, I took out my contacts and got ready for bed. Wrung out as I was, I should have been out like a light the second my head hit the pillow, but not surprisingly, I wasn't. My mind was too active to be clouded over by exhaustion.

Lying back on the pillows, I stared up at the ceiling. In my mind's eye, I saw that mirrored ceiling in Leavenworth, and the two of us tangled up in the sheets. How we had just looked so perfect together. Like we were exactly where we were supposed to be in that moment.

How could any of that be wrong?

I tried to think of ways to tell Tiffany that Holden and I could make this work. Ways to apologize to him and take back my goodbye. Ways to explain how things like tonight made it a hundred times harder to let go of Holden. Jay was an intimidating fucker, and I had a feeling he wasn't the type who was above throwing a punch, especially at the queer man who'd married his ex-wife. But Holden had still stood up for Tiffany and Ashley. Any other man could have washed his hands of this situation and bailed. Ashley wasn't his kid, Tiffany wasn't his problem anymore, and Jay's bullshit wasn't his business.

But his ex-stepdaughter and ex-wife had asked him, and he'd come through. He'd been there. He'd stood up and demanded respect for both of them, despite probably inviting one of those big fists right to the face for his trouble. It had been startling in the moment, but it wasn't surprising now. Of course Holden had been there. Of course he'd gone toe to toe with Jay. He wasn't a violent man, but he didn't hesitate to get between someone who was and someone he loved.

Exhaling into the silence of my room, I scrubbed a hand over my face. Shit like that just made me fall harder and harder for him. In the beginning, it had been his earnestness at making up for lost time with his kids and restoring the relationship he'd neglected. How he'd swallowed his pride and followed my lead because doing right by them meant *that* much to him. The little moments where he was sweet or silly with them. How he'd been a saint when the kids—and eventually Tiffany and I—were sick. And tonight, how he'd voluntarily been in the same room as both me and Jay—neither of whom he probably wanted to see right now—in the name of supporting a queer child for whom he had no obligation anymore.

What was I supposed to do? *Not* fall irretrievably in love with him?

Tiffany, can't you see how perfect we are together?

But every time I convinced myself that I wanted to go marching in and say something to Tiffany, a different train of thought kept me still. My mind kept circling back to sitting on Noah's bedroom floor, watching him struggle to tell me how much it worried him that his dad and I were hypothetically dating. I couldn't stop hearing the waver in his voice as he told me how afraid he was of his dad or me going away, and I couldn't stop feeling the guilt and heartbreak over doing that to him.

I sighed and rubbed my eyes.

Holden's utter devotion to the people he loved made me love him so much it hurt, but I couldn't ask him to love me if it meant hurting them. And I couldn't let myself be with him if it meant risking three little broken hearts who wouldn't understand.

It was my own damn fault for getting in too deep with Holden. The pain would go away eventually. Even the worst breakup didn't last forever. I'd move on. He'd move on.

And I'd keep my promise to Noah that I wouldn't let this send me out the door. Holden and I had both put his kids first because there was simply no other option.

But God, what I wouldn't have done for the chance to really love that man.

CHAPTER 35

HOLDEN

WE NEED TO TALK.

That was an ominous text under the best of circumstances. After everything that had happened lately, getting those four words from my ex-wife didn't bode well at all.

With no small amount of trepidation, I replied, *Okay?*

Can you meet me for a drink ASAP? The message was followed by the address of a restaurant that was roughly halfway between our houses.

It wasn't like her to ask me drop everything and meet her on a moment's notice, and the conversation had me both alarmed and wary. As it happened, I'd just gotten home from work, and I had nothing on my agenda for the evening because I was still getting used to post-Porter life and hadn't quite found that groove yet.

So I agreed to meet her, and twenty minutes later, walked in to find her waiting at a table with a coffee cup in front of her.

"Hey." I pulled out the chair opposite her. "I'm here. What's up?" Screw greetings and small talk. It was time to get to the point.

She took a deep breath. As I sat down, I realized she had her phone in her hands, and she was turning it over and over, staring intently at it as if she were waiting for it to give her some kind of cue. Finally, before I could prod her to say what she wanted to say, she tapped the screen and brought up a photo. "I took this last night." She handed it to me.

It was a picture of Porter on a recliner in the living room with Chloe cuddled against his side. The image had frozen with him rubbing his eye like his contacts were bothering him like they sometimes did in the evening. He had his other arm around Chloe, and she had a handful of his shirt. The scene was adorable and heartbreaking all at once. I missed Porter. I wished I was around for my kid to cuddle up with me like that. The picture was beautiful, but it was hard to look at.

I sighed, holding the phone out for Tiffany. "I'm glad they're—"

"Look closer, Holden."

I hesitated, then brought the phone up again. "What am—"

The waiter picked just that moment to appear, coffeepot in hand. "Can I get you some coffee? Something to eat?"

"Just coffee is fine. Thanks." I slid the empty cup in front of me toward him. He filled it, then left, and I shifted my attention to the phone in my hand again. "Okay, so what am I looking at?"

But then it jumped out at me. Porter wasn't rubbing his eye. He was wiping it. Head tilted slightly, jaw set, he was probably trying to be slick about it, but he was definitely wiping his eye

I gave the phone back. "So...?"

Tiffany inhaled. "Last night, Chloe climbed up on him and said he looked sad. Like he needed a hug."

My heart. Jesus.

"He tried to play it cool," she went on, "and just let her sit with him while they were watching TV, but..." All at once, the breath rushed out of her, and her shoulders sank. "He's been trying to hide it, but every now and then, the cracks show." She gestured with the darkened phone. "Last night they showed enough that Chloe caught on. There've been three separate occasions this past week where I've caught him with red eyes, and even though he insists it's his contacts..." She shook her head. "He's fucking miserable."

"I know the feeling," I whispered. "But why are you telling me this? I get it that you didn't want us to be together, and so we split up, but then we—"

"Because I think I fucked up."

I blinked. "What?"

She put the phone aside and folded her hands in her lap. "I think... I think it was a mistake. Making you two split up. I see it in him every single day, and I can see it in you now that being apart is killing you both." Tiffany's shoulders dropped. "Maybe... Maybe I shouldn't have given Porter that ultimatum."

"I get why you did, though. I should have just been upfront with you about things with Porter. I'm sorry."

"Except I told you both up front that I didn't want you dating. So it wasn't like it would've gone well if you'd told me."

I hesitated, tapping my nails on the table beside my untouched coffee. "But what about everything you said? The kids?"

Tiffany was already shaking her head. "Honestly, I think I'm just being overly protective of them because of everything we all went through with the divorce. They've been so resilient and handled it all so well, and I guess I'm just afraid to push that, you know? Like how many more times can we run them through the emotional wringer without doing some real damage? But then I look at Zach and Ashley, and how they've been through so much more than the little ones, and I think... I mean, let's not be reckless with them, and let's be considerate of them, but maybe I'm sheltering them too much."

"Maybe," I said quietly.

"And hell." She laughed halfheartedly. "Maybe I'm just jealous that you found someone."

"Give it time. After Jay and me, there's gotta be a good guy coming up for you."

Another laugh, but with a little more feeling. "Don't put yourself in the same breath as him. Things didn't work out between you and me, but you're not an asshole."

"Sometimes I wonder. The last couple of years would be a lot different if I'd—"

"Don't do that to yourself, Holden." She shook her head. "None of us can change the past. If anything, you've proven you're committed to being their dad now, and that's what matters."

"I guess." I paused, then took a deep breath. "Listen, I know this doesn't change anything. And there's no going back." Swallowing hard, I met her eyes. "But for the record, you know I tried, right? With us? I failed miserably, but it wasn't—"

"Holden." She put her hand over mine on the table and squeezed gently. "I've never doubted that. Good intentions weren't enough to keep us afloat, but don't doubt for a second that I ever believed you had anything *other* than good intentions."

I had to grit my teeth against the sudden ache in my throat, but it didn't do much for the sting in my eyes. "You're right that I really am committed to being their dad. But..." My voice wavered, and I cleared my throat, but it didn't help much. Neither did a swallow of coffee. "But you're also right that it's killing me to be away from Porter."

"I figured." She studied me, her expression soft. "You've really got it bad for him, don't you?"

"*Oh*, yeah. I mean, he's hot and all—"

"Won't argue with you there," she said under her breath.

I chuckled. "Right? But it's not just that. The more I got to know him, I just..." I couldn't find the words. "And then seeing him with the kids... I mean, is that not every single parent's dream? Someone who's that devoted to your kids?"

"I hadn't thought of that, but...yeah. And not having to introduce him to the kids, or worrying about them being defiant because he's a stepparent." Tiffany exhaled. "Do they make straight guys like him? Or bi guys? I hear bi guys are, you know, kind of all right sometimes if you squint hard enough."

"Hey!" I laughed and playfully bumped my foot against hers. "Kind of all right sometimes. Pfft."

She laughed too, though it didn't last. "Honestly, I don't know if this is the right thing. I don't know if it's a huge mistake to have the man taking care of our children dating their father. I don't know how to explain that to them, and I..." She rubbed her eyes, then dropped her hand into her lap and met my gaze across the table, fatigue written all over her face. "I just know that Porter's miserable, and you're miserable, and if it's hurting you both this much, enough that the kids are picking up on it, then forcing you two to stay apart can't be the right thing either. So I don't know what else to do here except trust you and Porter. You're both good men. You both have your hearts in the right place and prioritize the kids. If the two of you want to be together, then..." She inhaled slowly and set her shoulders back. "Then all I can do is trust you and Porter to keep being who I already know you are."

It was getting really hard to breathe, and speaking was almost impossible, but I managed to whisper, "Thank you." Forcing back the lump in my throat—trying to, anyway—I reached across the table and squeezed her hand. "The kids come first. Always."

"I know." Tiffany turned her hand over beneath mine. "If, um, you want to go talk to him, he's home now." She smiled faintly. "He'll be happy to see you."

Porter was obviously not expecting me.

When Tiffany and I walked into the house, he was in the dining room, helping the boys with their homework. He looked up like he was about to say something to her, but his eyes went right to me, and his spine straightened.

"Hey, um." I cleared my throat. "Do you mind if we talk for a minute? Downstairs?"

Porter glanced at the boys and their homework. Then at Tiffany. "Uh..."

"I can take it from here, hon," Tiffany said. "Go ahead."

"Oh. Okay. Um." Porter pushed his chair back. The boys looked at him curiously, but as their mom joined them at the table, returned their attention to their homework. As he crossed the living room toward me, Porter hesitated, glancing back at Ethan. To Tiffany he said, "Before I forget

—have you heard back from his teacher yet? About the email you sent?"

"Not yet." She glanced at me. "Porter mentioned what you told me. About him maybe being dyslexic."

I nodded, relieved that in the recent chaos, Porter had apparently had the presence of mind to talk to Tiffany about the concerns I'd had while helping Ethan with his homework. As if I needed anything to drive home all the feelings I had for this man—while I'd been licking my wounds and wallowing in self-pity, he'd been doing exactly what he'd done from the start: focusing on my kids.

"I'll follow up with him tomorrow." Tiffany made a *go on* gesture. "You two go talk."

Porter's expression still registered nothing but confusion and a hint of wariness, but he followed me out of the room.

All the way down to the rec room, my heart thumped with preemptive relief. I had to struggle to hold back all the emotions I'd been trying to hide from myself since Porter had left. We didn't have to hide anymore. Not us. Not our feelings. All we had to do was talk, and we could go back to the way things were before, minus the secrecy.

In the rec room, Porter shut the door, and he eyed me uncertainly. It was hard not to throw my arms around him and tell him the good news, but his guard was up. Of course it was. Things had been awkward between us, and he had no idea what Tiffany and I had discussed. Break the news first, then celebrate.

"So, um." I was smiling like an idiot, but I didn't care. "Tiffany and I had a good long talk. About us."

Porter gulped. "Yeah?"

"Yeah. She's..." I couldn't help laughing with relief. "She's okay with us seeing each other."

"She is?"

I nodded. "That's why I'm here."

"Oh. Wow." He leaned against the door and ran a hand through his hair. "So we can..."

"Yes. We can do exactly what we were doing before. Just without keeping it a secret."

It seemed to take a moment for everything I'd said to register. When it finally did, I wasn't sure which hit me harder—the fact that he was shaking his head, or the pain in his eyes.

"I'm sorry," he whispered. "I can't."

"What?" My heart dropped into my feet. "But why not?"

"You guys might've talked, but all the reasons she didn't want us to see each other?" He looked in my eyes. "Those reasons still exist. And two of them are upstairs doing their homework."

"But that's just it—we can make this work. We can—"

"No, we can't." He wasn't just leaning against the door now. It was like nothing else was holding him upright. "If things go bad between us, one way or another I'm out of a job. Either because we can't stand being around each other, or because Tiffany decides she's had it with the tension." He swallowed like he was forcing back a hell of a lot of emotions. "And if that happens, I mean... Jesus, Holden. Losing my job isn't as simple as just needing a new paycheck and a place to live. Those kids are attached to me, and to be honest, I'm attached to them."

The rejection had caught me so off guard, it was a struggle to absorb everything he was saying. "Do you really think things would end that badly with us?" Assuming they ended at all?

"That's the thing—I don't know. And neither do you." He sighed, rubbing his neck like it was suddenly getting stiff. "Everyone goes into a relationship thinking they can make it work, and how many end with both people wondering why the hell they ever got together in the first place?"

I winced.

"I'm sorry." Porter shook his head slowly. "I want to. Jesus, I do. But... I'm sorry. I don't want to hurt you, but I *can't* hurt those kids, Holden. I just can't."

"Oh." It sounded so stupid, but he'd caught me so off guard, I was nearly speechless.

"I'm sorry," he said again.

We stood there for a moment, avoiding eye contact in the most awkward silence I'd experienced in ages. Then he pushed himself off the door and opened it. He met my gaze, eyebrows raised in an unspoken, *"Unless there's anything else?"*

I made a *go ahead* gesture at the open doorway, and we both left the rec room.

Porter disappeared into his bedroom and quietly closed the door behind him. I glanced at it but then continued up the stairs, numbly trudging up one step after another.

Tiffany was in the kitchen, and she turned to me with a bright smile on her lips, but it vanished the instant she saw me. She looked past me, and her lips parted. "Where's..."

I motioned toward the deck. Without a word, she followed me outside. As soon as the sliding glass door was shut behind her, cutting off our conversation from the boys, who were still doing their homework at the table, I pressed my palms onto the railing and pushed out a long breath

"Holden? Did you talk to him?"

"Yeah."

I faced her, and her eyes were wide with concern. "What did he say?"

"He said..." I swallowed, still dazed from my conversation with Porter. "He said no."

"What?"

"This is all backwards." I threw up a hand. "He's telling me we can't date because he needs to put the kids first. My kids."

"Who are his responsibility." Her voice was soft and resigned.

"And mine! I'm..." I pressed my elbows onto the railing and kneaded my temples. "Damn it. Maybe he's right. Maybe we..." I stared out at the yard and gave a humorless laugh. "And here I was, afraid he'd replace me in their lives." My heart sank along with my shoulders, and I exhaled. "Now I don't want to lose him, but I don't know how to keep him." I turned to my ex-wife. "What do I do?"

Shaking her head, she sighed. "I don't know, hon. I didn't see things playing out this way either." She stepped closer and lowered her voice. "Listen. Let's give you and him a couple of days. Just let the dust settle. Catch your breath. And then..." Her eyes darted toward the house before meeting mine again. "Then let's talk to him together."

"Together?"

Tiffany nodded. "The relationship is between you two, but everything else? The job? The kids?" She tapped her chest. "So maybe he needs to hear from both of us that he's an important part of our kids' lives and that neither of us wants him to go anywhere. Then you and he can figure out where you stand."

I was dubious, and I didn't want to get my hopes up, but I also *needed* to cling to that hope.

She'd always been able to read me like a book, and she must have seen right through me this time because she smiled and said, "It's not over yet, okay?" She closed the last bit of space between us and hugged me. "Just hang in there, and don't give up on him."

I hugged her tight, and my eyes stung as I squeezed them shut and fought back a fresh flurry of emotions. I was scared to death I wasn't going to be able to convince Porter to give this another try, but there was also relief in my ex-wife's embrace. The last couple of years had been rough as hell for us. I'd considered myself fortunate that we'd come out of it all on good terms, even if our marriage couldn't be saved. Tonight, after convincing myself I'd screwed up that hard-won civility by seeing Porter behind her back, she was exactly what she'd been during the best years we'd had together—a rock. A calm, rational presence who wasn't going to fight my battles for me but wasn't going to leave me floundering either.

Everything seemed fucked-up tonight, but at least I could find comfort in knowing I still had Tiffany. Not as my wife or partner anymore, but as my co-parent, and—thank God—my friend.

Now I just hoped like hell that Porter hadn't slipped through my fingers for good.

CHAPTER 36
PORTER

I was on autopilot at the grocery store. Tiffany had asked me to make a last-minute run to grab a few things for everyone's lunches, and thank God she'd written it all down. Normally I had both the kitchen inventory and supermarket layout memorized, but tonight I could barely remember which aisle to go down for the fruit snacks the boys liked. And hadn't I picked those up like two days ago? Well, whatever. I trusted Tiffany's grasp on things better than mine right now.

It had been a few days since I'd last talked to Holden, and I still felt like shit. I could focus enough to take care of the kids and do my job, but any time I wasn't concentrating on them, my mind went right back to him. Every time it did, it was only a matter of time before I started second-guessing my decision to let him go.

One look at Noah, Ethan, or Chloe, though, and my resolve would return. They needed consistency and stability. It wouldn't be fair to them if they got attached to me and then I vanished because their father and I broke up. They deserved better than that. Tiffany deserved better than having to explain to those three heartbroken faces why I was gone and some new random stranger—who they wouldn't trust because of me—came along to fill in the gap.

It didn't matter what I felt for Holden. I couldn't do that to his kids.

And eventually, somehow, I'd get over him.

When I pulled in the driveway, I grumbled "fuck" to the steering wheel—I'd have recognized that blue Nissan from a mile away. What was Holden even doing here? Was tonight when he was supposed to come take the kids? Because I could have sworn that was tomorrow. I wasn't ready for it to be tonight, damn it.

Well, whatever. I'd probably read the calendar wrong. After all, I was the guy who'd wandered up four aisles in search of lunch meat before I remembered it was in the back of the store. At the deli. Like it always was.

With a sigh, I shut off the car, grabbed the handful of bags from the passenger seat, and headed inside. I pretended not to notice the spike in my own pulse or the queasy, jittery feeling roiling in my stomach.

It's just Holden. Nothing to stress myself into knots over. Get a grip, dipshit.

Of course I dropped my keys when I was trying to unlock the door. Yay, unsteady hands.

"Damn it." I leaned down to the pick them up, ideally without dropping the groceries I had in my other hand. At least I pulled that off, and with another second or two of fumbling, I managed to unlock the stupid door and let myself in.

"Hey, Tiff?" I called up the stairs. "I forgot to take in the reusable bags." I toed off my shoes and nudged them up against the rack. "Should we just use the paper ones as trash bags?"

"Yeah. Sure." Her voice came from the kitchen, and sounded disinterested but...not. She was probably cooking or something and wasn't going to spare energy worrying about what to do with some grocery bags.

I went upstairs and stepped into the kitchen, and halted.

Tiffany and Holden were both there, leaning against the counters and watching me.

I glanced back and forth between them. "What?"

"We need to talk, sweetie." She gestured at him. "All of us."

Oh, that sounded like a fun way to spend the evening.

"Um." I turned away and put the bags on an empty stretch of countertop. As I started unpacking them, I asked, "Shouldn't I get something started for the kids?"

"They're out with Zach." Holden's voice was soft. "Ashley's at a friend's house. It's just the three of us."

I froze, one hand still hovering in midair with the thin-sliced turkey that the boys liked. Slowly, I set it down, then faced Holden and Tiffany. "Uh, what's going on?" Then my heart dropped into my feet. My stomach somersaulted. "Am I getting fired? Because if I am—"

"No!" they both said, shaking their heads.

"Oh my God, no," Tiffany said. "Don't worry about that. If either of us have any say, we don't want you going anywhere."

"Oh." I relaxed a little, but I was still on edge. I still had my job—good. But...?

"This is about us." Holden's voice was soft and filled with more uncertainty than I'd thought he was capable of. "About you and me."

I gulped. I wanted to say there wasn't a *"you and me,"* but just thinking the words hurt like hell.

"We've talked about everything," Tiffany said. "And I think I made a huge mistake, telling you guys to stay apart."

"You...what?" I shook myself. "But the kids. And...I mean..." I leaned against the counter and stared at both of them. "I don't understand."

They exchanged glances.

Tiffany swallowed. "Look, Holden and I worked hard to minimize the impact of the divorce on the kids, and there's no reason to believe you and Holden couldn't or wouldn't do the same if things don't work out between you." She glanced at him again, something unspoken passing between them before she returned her gaze to me. "In fact, that's exactly what you've *been* doing since you split up. I know it's been killing both of you, but you've kept it out of the kids' sight as much as possible. So there's no reason we can't all be adults about this. About the two of you dating and, God forbid, if it comes to it, breaking up."

I blinked, struggling to comprehend literally anything. "What? Are you... Do... Are you saying you *want* us to date now?"

"I want you to be happy." She glanced at Holden, a fond smile on her lips. "Both of you. And if you're happy together, especially if you're this miserable apart, then what kind of person would I be if I kept standing in your way?"

I wiped a hand over my face and exhaled, still not sure I was hearing her right.

"You don't have to make a decision right this minute," Holden said. "We just wanted you to know the door is open."

My throat tightened. Make a decision? He made it sound like it wasn't the easiest decision ever to say *"Yes, oh my God, yes, I want to be with you,"* and at the same time the hardest fucking thing in the world to accept that we just couldn't do this. Except now they were saying we could? Tiffany was on board? Holden was here? I... What the hell?

I swallowed past the ache in my throat and met Holden's eyes. "Do you want this? Me?"

"Of course I do," he said without hesitation. "I told you in Leavenworth I wanted to be open about us with Tiffany. I wouldn't have done that if I didn't think we have staying power." He glanced at her, and subtle smiles played at both their lips before he turned to me again. "I've never stopped wanting that or wanting you, and now that there's a solution, a way to make things work with us and my family? I'm in if you are."

I could barely breathe. My heart was doing so many things I couldn't begin to describe even one of them. I had no idea what I felt, or what to say, or how in the world this was really happening.

Holden must have taken my silence for being unconvinced, and he went on. "Listen, you've been amazing for the kids. And for Tiffany. Whatever's going on between us isn't going to take away from that. I..." He paused and cleared his throat, but his voice was still faintly unsteady as he whispered, "To be honest, I think it's a huge part of why I fell in love with you."

I stared at him. So did Tiffany.

Holden took a deep breath. "When Tiffany and I started dating, she said there was nothing that made her heart melt more than watching a man with his kids. And I never quite got that. But then I saw you with *my* kids. I've seen how completely focused you are on them, and how you talk to them and interact with them like they're the only people in the world. I've seen you taking care of them when they're hurt or sick, and you're..." His voice was faltering a bit, and he cleared his throat. It didn't seem to help, but he pressed on anyway. "To tell you the truth, you've been a better dad to those kids than I've ever aspired to be. There's no way in hell I would take that away from them. Or from you. And you better believe..." He swallowed hard. "You better believe that played a role in me falling this hard for you."

I had to blink away tears. My pulse was going wild right then, and I was more speechless than I'd ever been in my life.

"He's right you know," Tiffany said softly. We both turned to her. "Porter, I hired you because I needed help, but you've been so much more to these kids than just someone to ferry them around and make their lunches. When I realized you and Holden had something going on, I think I freaked out because I was afraid that if it ended, you'd leave." Now *her* voice was wavering. "It feels like you're part of this family, and I don't want to lose that."

"I'm not going anywhere," I whispered. "Even when things have been weird with..." I glanced at Holden. "When things have been weird with us. I never *wanted* to leave."

"You wanted to put the kids first," Holden said.

I nodded.

"I think I would've fallen for you sooner or later no matter what, but that?" He smiled, eyes shining a bit more than they had a moment ago. "It definitely sealed the deal. You're an amazing man. You're sweet, and funny, and just fun. And on top of that, you already love my kids. All I want is the chance to see if we can make this work."

My eyes were welling up, and I was pretty sure Tiffany and Holden wouldn't buy it if I blamed it on my contacts this time, so I didn't bother. I swiped at my eyes. "I... don't even know what to say."

Holden took a cautious step closer. "Just say yes."

If I said one more word, I was seriously going to crack, so I just nodded.

Holden pulled me into his arms, and I buried my face against his neck. The first time I'd caught a whiff of his aftershave, I'd been so turned on I couldn't see straight. This time, that same familiar, masculine scent filled me with relief and made this moment *real*, and I held him tighter.

"I love you, Holden," I whispered.

He tensed a little, and I had a fleeting second to panic that I'd overstepped even though he'd already said he'd fallen for me. Holden drew back enough to look in my eyes, and with a smile, he said, "I love you too."

I grinned and lifted my chin for a kiss. My knees almost dropped out from under me—I'd never imagined I could find so much release in the softness of someone's lips, or the brush of a goatee against my chin.

You're back. I missed you so much, and now...you're back.

Behind me, Tiffany cleared her throat. "Listen, I think I can bow out of this. Why don't you two go spend some time together?"

That sounded fucking amazing, and I turned to say so, but then the bags I'd put on the counter caught my eye. "Oh wait, crap, I haven't even put the groceries—"

"Porter." Tiffany's voice stopped me dead, and when I looked at her, she smiled. "I'll take care of it. Go."

"Are you—"

"*Go.*"

Holden smirked. "You really want to argue with the boss lady?"

"Uh, not if doing what I'm told means going with you."

"Well, then..." He jerked his head toward the stairs. "What are you waiting for?"

"Okay. Okay. I'm going." I took a step but paused. Then I turned and wrapped Tiffany up in a bear hug. "You're the best, you know that?"

"Honey." She hugged me back and gave my shoulder a firm pat. "I can't keep the two of you apart. I won't." As she let me go, she wagged a finger at Holden and looked pointedly in my eyes. "And if you break that man's heart, you're answering to me."

"Oh. Shit. Uh." I nodded. "Got it."

She turned to Holden. "That goes for you too."

He saluted playfully. "Pretty sure you won't have to worry about anything."

"Good. Now get out of here, you two."

He gave her a quick hug, and then we got out of there, and all the way out to Holden's car, all I could think was thank God he lived close by.

CHAPTER 37

HOLDEN

We got the hell out of the house, but after I'd started the car, I hesitated. "Crap. We can't go to my place—Zach's there with the kids."

Porter buckled his seat belt. "I suppose just going and keeping quiet isn't an option."

I slid my hand over his thigh. "I don't think I'm going to be able to stay quiet this time."

Porter bit his lip and squirmed, the muscles in his leg quivering under my hand.

I pulled my hand back and shifted into Reverse. "Fuck it. Let's get a room."

"Long as there's a horizontal surface, count me in."

We exchanged glances, and damn, but it took all the restraint I had not to drive like a bat out of hell to the freeway. Or pull over and have him right here in the car.

Once I was on the freeway on-ramp, I accelerated hard. Beside me, Porter squirmed.

Okay. Hotel. Someplace with a horizontal surface. Everett wasn't exactly a tourist destination as far as I knew, but fortunately, there were a few hotels around. Neither of us was picky—first place that came along with a *Vacancy* sign would be the winner.

"Before we find a place," he said, sounding a tad out of breath, "do you still have lube?"

I tightened my grip on the wheel. "Crap. I don't know. Check the glove box."

Porter opened it, looked around a bit, and closed it again. "Nope. None."

"Damn it."

"Let's stop at a Walgreens, then." He turned to me, and I glanced over in time to catch a glimpse of the smoldering lust in his eyes. "Because I have a feeling we're gonna need it."

I tapped my left heel on the floor board. I needed to get this man behind closed doors, but he was right—we needed some lube. I could wait a few more minutes. Right?

Thank God, it didn't take long to find a Walgreens, and while Porter went inside, I searched for hotels on my phone. By the time he came out with a bottle of AstroGlide, I had a reservation at a place five minutes down the road.

And after what seemed like goddamned *days*, we had lube and a keycard for room twenty-two, and so help me if anyone or anything got between us and that door…

Porter unlocked the door, and he flashed me a wicked grin as he grabbed my belt and shirt and hauled me into the room. Oh fuck yes. As soon as we were across the threshold, I wrapped an arm around his waist and pushed him up against the door, both to make sure it was closed and so I could—yes. Oh, God, yes. Pinning him there with my hips, I kissed him hard, and Porter whimpered as he kneaded my ass and kissed me right back.

The first time we'd touched like this, when we'd finally been behind closed doors and fully intended to get each other naked, it had been exhilarating and hot. He was someone new. I was breaking a long dry spell.

That night didn't hold a candle to this one. My mind still wasn't fully convinced that we were back in each other's arms, that I hadn't lost him, and my need for him tonight went so much deeper than the primal hunger for friction and orgasms. I didn't want to be able to move tomorrow without feeling everything we did tonight. Throbbing bruises, aching muscles, burning scratches— I wanted to wake up knowing in no uncertain terms that this man really had taken me back and wasn't letting me go. I needed him so hot and so close that his touch branded my skin.

He broke the kiss with a ragged sigh, and he dug his nails into my back. "God, Holden..."

I tried to speak, but...fuck it. I could barely think. Talking was out of the question. Instead, I kissed him again, and we both moaned as I ground against him. We weren't anywhere near the bed, and we didn't even have our pants off yet, and I was already rutting against him, keeping his body pinned to the door and rubbing our hard cocks together through our clothes.

Porter shuddered. "We should...at least get naked before you make me come."

I groaned and dug my fingers into his hips. "Like I'm ever going to say no to being naked with you."

His lips curved into a grin, and he murmured, "Ditto."

I didn't step back from the door, though. Instead, I slid a hand between us, and Porter whimpered as I cupped his rock-hard erection.

"I want to rip your clothes off," I growled between kisses, kneading him through his pants, "and I want to fuck you until neither of us can move, and then have you fuck me."

"Oh God," Porter whispered shakily.

"I *want* to," I went on as I started drawing down his zipper, "but it feels like it's been ages since I've heard you come..." We both gasped as my fingertips grazed his cock, and he arched off the door as I started stroking him. "We'll get to fucking and...and everything else...after..."

I went to my knees, and Porter groaned as I took his cock deep in my mouth.

"Oh...fuck." The words came out as a ragged breath, and we both moaned as I teased his cock and he slid his hands into my hair. He gripped it tight enough to sting, and when he started rocking his hips and fucking my mouth, I had to reach down and unzip my own pants before my restrained hard-on drove me insane.

"Oh God, yeah," he breathed. "Baby, yeah, I'm almost there."

I groaned and egged him on, squeezing with my lips and fluttering my tongue.

"Fuck, Holden..." Porter's hips jerked, and he grabbed the doorknob and the back of a chair as if he were afraid he might drop to the floor. With the way his knees were trembling, that might have been a valid concern.

Go ahead and collapse, baby. I've got you.

He gasped, and his hips jerked again, pushing his cock into my throat. It was thicker and harder now, like he was right there, *right there*, and all it would take was a few good, fast strokes, and—

"Fuck!" He bucked between me and the door, and I almost came myself as he shot his load in my mouth. His breathy cries and sharp gasps had me dizzy with arousal, and *how* had I gone more than a damn day without touching this man?

When he couldn't take anymore, I sat back on my heels

and gazed up at him. He was a shaky, sweaty, breathless mess, and I didn't think I'd ever seen anything sexier in my life.

He blinked a few times, then looked down at me, eyes smoldering with need. "B-bed. C'mon. I want..." His fingers raked through my hair, and he shuddered as he whispered, "Want you naked."

I licked my lips and grinned up at him. "So you're saying I haven't worn you out?"

"Worn me out?" He swayed a little but shook his head. "Just need to catch my breath and get hard again. You, however"—he pointed a finger at me—"have something that needs attention."

Couldn't argue with that, could I?

He helped me to my feet, which I appreciated since everything from the knees down had started going to sleep. Once I was upright, we both shed our remaining clothes, and finally—*finally*—I had him right where I'd ached to have him: naked and tangled up with me beneath the covers.

Though he'd just come, that didn't stop him from kissing me and touching me as if he were still rock hard and ready to fuck. We were as frantic and needy as we'd been the very first time, and somehow still as sensual and sweet as that night we'd slowed things down in Leavenworth. As if we were both needy, hungry, but also holding on tight to make sure this was real and we were really here and there really was nothing left between us.

This was a level of need I'd never experienced before. He'd very nearly slipped through my fingers. I'd nearly lost this for good. But he hadn't, and I hadn't, and I didn't care if tonight left bruises as long as I couldn't move, breathe, *exist* without feeling Porter.

I'm here, baby, I tried to tell him with every kiss and touch. *I'm not going anywhere.*

Don't you dare let go, I heard every time his lips or hands brushed my skin.

Porter was on top, and he broke the kiss to reach for something. I was so turned on, my brain took a second to catch up. By the time it did, he was already sitting over me, lube bottle in hand, and my toes curled with anticipation.

"There's no way I can fuck you right now," I murmured. "You just came. I want it too hard to—"

"I know." He grinned down at me as he poured some lube in his palm. "I had something else in mind."

"Yeah?"

"Yeah." He capped the bottle and put it aside. Then he rolled onto his back and gestured for me to get on top. As I did, he parted his legs for me, and I shivered as he closed a lube-slicked hand around my cock.

"Oh...fuck..." I rocked my hips, pushing into his tight fist.

"Like that?" His grin said he knew damn well I did.

"Uh-huh."

"Thought so." He curved one hand behind my neck and pulled me down to kiss him. He kept the other firmly around my cock, and we both moaned as we made out and I fucked into his fist. He had the most amazing hands. Holy fuck. It was like he knew exactly when and how to loosen or tighten his grasp, to pump faster or slower.

I broke the kiss with a gasp and pressed my forehead to his. "Oh God, baby. Just...that. Yes."

Pumping me faster, he tightened his grip, and my toes curled as he brought me right to the edge. Then, his hand twisted subtly, and I sucked in a breath, shuddered, and came on both of us. "Oh God..."

He slowed, then stopped. As I slumped over him, Porter wrapped his arms around me, and I closed my eyes and sank all the way down onto his hot, sweaty body.

"If that's how makeup sex is gonna be," he murmured against my neck, "feel free to pick a fight any time."

I laughed and nipped his shoulder. "How about we skip the fights and go straight to the sex?"

"Hmm, I think I can live with that." His fingers carded through my hair, and he sighed as we just held each other. "Thanks for not giving up on us."

"Not a chance of that." I pressed a kiss to his feverish skin. "I love you."

"I love you too."

And I kind of wanted to cry as I just held him and trembled and caught my breath. Every time his hand stroked my hair or my skin, or I trailed my fingertips over his mountain lion tattoo, this became more real. Porter was really here. He was naked in my arms, and what we were wasn't a secret anymore, and there was no earthly reason for me to let go of this sweet, beautiful man.

So I didn't.

CHAPTER 38

PORTER

The room didn't have a luxurious California king with a mirrored ceiling and a heart-shaped Jacuzzi tub, but Holden was naked in the middle of the bed with me, so it was a five-star honeymoon suite as far as I was concerned.

Had this really happened? We'd finally had some of the sex I'd thought I'd never have again, and now we weren't just back together, we were *openly* back together? This was real? And for that matter, Tiffany wasn't just on board. She'd all but shoved me into his arms and begged me to take him back. Which in and of itself was a bit surreal.

"Okay, I gotta say." I pushed myself up on my elbow and looked into Holden's gorgeous blue eyes. "Getting your ex-wife to play your makeup wingman is definitely an unorthodox approach."

Holden laughed, sliding his hand up my chest. "Well, I figured if that didn't work, I could stand outside with a boombox and blast Ty Herndon until you caved."

"Oh, now that's not playing fair."

"So you're saying it would've worked?"

"Uh. Yeah?" I sobered and caressed his cheek. "But in

all seriousness, hearing it from both of you..." I didn't know how to finish the thought.

Holden lifted his head and kissed me softly. "You already knew how I felt." He sank back to the pillow, but kept a hand on my arm. "We needed you to know we'd come to a consensus as parents. Since this affects our kids and your job."

"How did you come to that consensus? I didn't think she'd budge."

"I didn't either. She's actually the one who came to me."

I blinked. "Really?"

Holden nodded. "She said she could see that it was killing both of us, and she decided that in the name of being too protective of the kids, she was hurting us."

"I can see why she did it, though. I was trying to protect them, too."

That sweet smile melted my heart all over again. "I know you were. And so did she. That's... I meant what I said in the kitchen. You being so invested in protecting them, even at your own expense, was a big part of what made us both realize this"—he gestured at himself, then me—"isn't such a gamble. Whatever happens, even if things don't work out between us, the kids are still a priority for both of us." He reached up and curved his hand behind my neck. "Can't really ask for much more than that. I mean, I should have known you were perfect when you were willing to put my kids above everything. Including me."

I laughed softly. "I'm not perfect."

"No." He caressed my cheek. 'But you're perfect for me."

"Likewise." I grinned. "I just hope that thing with the kids isn't the only reason you're with me."

"Not even close, baby." He drew me down for a kiss.

Barely breaking that kiss, he murmured, "I'm in it for the housekeeping, too."

I snorted. "Shut up." We both laughed, and then sank into another kiss, one that went on for a long, long time, and left no doubt that he was in this for more than just my nanny or housekeeping skills. Not that I'd actually been concerned, but the reassurance was nice.

After a while, I drew back enough to meet his gaze. "So how do we do this, anyway?"

"What do you mean?"

"Well, like, what happens if we split up? With your kids?"

"I'm still their dad. You're still their nanny." Holden shrugged. "No reason it can't stay like that."

"You don't think it'll get weird?"

"I'm sure it will." He smoothed my hair and smiled. "But as long as we can be adults about it like we've done the last couple of weeks, there's no reason we can't keep things as normal as possible for them."

"True. And I'm sorry I—"

He kissed me gently. "Don't. You were right. Everything you said. Tiffany and I needed to sort our shit out and realize what we both had before we lost you completely." He shifted onto one arm and ran the backs of his fingers down my cheek. "I'm just glad we didn't wait too long."

"So am I." I smoothed his salt-and-pepper hair. "I think I was going to lose my mind without you."

"Same." He caressed my cheek. "So now we have a shot at it, and if things don't work out, we can all be adults about it."

I swallowed. "Yeah. I think we can."

"We were this time." He smiled. "And hopefully that's a bridge we won't have to cross."

My heart fluttered. "I really hope it isn't. Because I like this. A lot."

"Me too." He kissed me gently. "I love you, Porter."

"I love you, too."

We cuddled together and just let the stillness linger.

Then a thought crossed my mind, and I chuckled.

Holden eyed me. "What?"

"Nothing. Just..." I slid my palm up his chest. "When Tiffany told me you were moving up to Washington, I asked her if things would be weird. You know, having her ex-husband so close by. She said no, and..." I laughed again. "She said, quote, 'Honestly, I think you'll love him.' Guess she was righter than she thought."

Smiling, Holden stroked my hair. "Yeah. I guess she was."

I studied him. "You really think we can do this?"

"Do you think we can't?"

"I'm...cautiously optimistic?"

"That sounds pessimistic to me." His brow furrowed with a hint of concern. "You having second thoughts or—"

"No, no." I shook my head. "I guess I was just so resigned to the idea of not being able to do this, I still haven't wrapped my brain around, well, this."

"Well, you have plenty of time to get used to it." He pressed a kiss to my forehead. "And we'll take it a day at a time. Things between us, logistics with Tiffany and the kids, *explaining* it to the kids—all of it." He ran his warm palm up my side. "Whatever it takes for this to work, I'm in."

My heart went wild, and I grinned playfully. "You know, you're hot when you're all snarly and annoyed, but this sappy romantic side is fucking adorable."

Holden laughed, which did nothing to bring my pulse

back down. He really was sexy as hell. Good God. Still laughing, he pulled me closer. "I'm not *that* snarly."

"No, but when you are..." I winked.

He chuckled and rolled his eyes. "Come here, you."

Like he had to tell me twice.

As we tangled up again, I couldn't remember the name of this motel to save my life and wasn't even sure what street we were on, but I was absolutely home. Lying here, wrapped up in sheets and Holden, getting him hot and breathless all over again, I was exactly where I wanted to be and where I needed to be.

A lifetime ago, I'd been nervous as hell over Tiffany's ex-husband coming into the picture.

Now I couldn't wait to see where Holden and I went from here.

EPILOGUE

HOLDEN

Almost two years later.

"Ugh." Zach wiped sweat off his forehead. "What's up with this *heat*?"

"It's your second summer here," Porter said with a laugh. "You're not used to it yet?"

"It's just bullshit, that's all," Zach grumbled. "I thought Washington was supposed to be *cold*."

"Welcome to August in the Pacific Northwest," Tiffany said.

"But it's September."

"Barely."

"You know it's about thirty degrees hotter in Arizona, right?" I said. "Don't complain, kid."

He muttered something I didn't understand.

Mark, Tiffany's boyfriend, laughed. "Good thing we won't be outside the whole time, right?"

None of us argued with that.

We'd been at the Puyallup Fair for the last hour or so, and thank God for barns, awnings, and the occasional blessedly air-conditioned exhibition hall to get us out of the blazing sun from time to time. The late summer heat wasn't the kind of blistering misery we'd been used to in Phoenix, but it definitely wasn't one of those chilly gray days I'd expected when we'd moved up here. Good thing we all had hats and sunscreen—no one needed a sunburn to cap off a day at the fair.

Tiffany had told me for years that the Puyallup Fair was legendary, and Porter had been coming every year for as long as he could remember. We hadn't made it last year, but this year? Once the kids found out about the rides, scones, petting zoos, and games? Like I was going to say no.

So, today we'd made the hour and a half—more like two-hour, thanks to fair traffic— trek down from Everett, dividing our small army between three vehicles since we had the three younger kids plus Zach, Ashley and her latest girlfriend, Porter (who was here in both nanny and boyfriend capacity), Mark, Tiffany, and me.

And now, here we were.

As we wandered throughout the enormous event, I honestly had to marvel at how well our huge group functioned, and not just here at the fair. My ex-wife and I probably had a better relationship now than we'd had while we were married, and I got along as well with her boyfriend as she did with mine. Mark had been a little uncertain about the arrangement when he'd come into the picture a year ago, but once he'd spent some time with all of us, he'd relaxed. Plus, he was great with the kids. It didn't hurt that he had horses, and he'd been teaching Chloe and the boys to ride, which he'd jokingly told us made him the favorite.

Given the nonstop chatter around both houses these days about horses, lessons, saddles, and jumping, he might have been right. And since he was planning on sticking around— he'd confided in me the other night that he was going to propose to Tiffany on her birthday next week—I decided I was okay with that.

He wasn't the only one who'd seamlessly joined this unorthodox family. The transition from Porter being the nanny to being my partner had been a lot easier than any of us had anticipated. The kids had been kind of nervous at first, but they'd adjusted to the idea. It had especially grown on them when they realized that Porter being both nanny and Dad's boyfriend meant they had Porter at Mom's house *and* Dad's place.

Even after he'd moved in with me three months ago, he still took care of the kids the same as he had all along. He was kind of an odd hybrid of hired childcare provider and stay-at-home dad. Tiffany and I had adjusted our child support agreement and worked out a way for both of us to contribute to his salary. On paper, it *was* kind of weird for all of us, the idea of me dating the man being paid to take care of our kids. In practice, though, it worked. And he didn't exactly complain about the utter travesty of being forced to drive the kids to the barn for their lessons twice a week.

"Oh no," he'd melodramatically sighed a while back. *"Please don't add 'visit a barn full of horses' to my job description. No, no, anything but that."*

And he wasn't just happier these days because he "had to" spend time around animals. Not long after we'd started openly dating, Porter had had his first appointment with the therapist who specialized in first responders, and holy crap, she was a godsend. The first visit had been so cathartic for him—just talking to someone who understood and had laid out some ideas for ways she could help—he'd come home afterward and slept for hours.

These days, sirens still made him twitchy but didn't make him jump out of his skin quite so much anymore. The real test, however, had come a couple of months ago when Chloe and a bigger child had collided at the park, and she'd hit her head on the concrete when she'd fallen. There was some concern she might've had a concussion, so Porter had texted Tiffany and me to let us know he was taking the kids to the ER. I'd been a nervous wreck when I'd met them at the ER, both because I was terrified Chloe had been badly hurt and because I was worried about Porter.

Chloe was fine—the concussion was very, very mild, and she was more unhappy than anything.

When Tiffany had arrived, I'd stepped outside with Porter, bracing for him to fall apart like he had after Noah's trip to Urgent Care. The post-emergency crash still hit him, but not as hard this time. We walked around the parking lot to keep him moving, and we talked about everything we'd do after we got home. Simple things discussed in detail—what we'd make for dinner for us and the kids, what TV shows we'd watch once we'd settled in on the couch, whether we'd do the dishes before or after we sat down.

According to his therapist, that would serve to tell his brain that there wouldn't be another emergency call. That there was no need to be poised and ready for the next unknown emergency. Once it was all over, we'd have a perfectly boring, routine evening, so there was no need to preemptively panic about what the next alarm, siren, or ringing phone would bring.

It worked. He was still more jittery than most people

would be after a situation like that, but the panic had never taken hold. We went home, and while I was making dinner, he and Chloe had fallen asleep together on the couch, him stretched out on the recliner with her clinging to his side and his arm protectively around her. I still had that picture as the lock screen on my phone.

Porter's therapist had been straight with him from the start, telling him he would probably always have at least some PTSD. Time and therapy and the odd Xanax would help, but it was entirely possible that he'd always have nightmares and he might never completely shake the conditioning to jump at sirens or shake apart after an emergency. She'd teach him how to cope with what lingered but made sure he understood it would never magically go away. I swear, hearing that had been one of the best things for him. He'd been so hard on himself for not getting over it and letting go of the past, and now he had permission to still be affected.

As I stole glances at him and the rest of our motley crew, it was hard to imagine how chaotic things had been when I'd first come to Everett to be closer to the kids. How uncertain I'd been about Porter, about myself, and about the future of my relationships with my kids and ex-wife.

Now Tiffany and I were both happily with new partners. The kids were all thriving. Ashley was still estranged from her father, but everyone agreed that was for the best. If he couldn't accept his daughter now that she was out as a lesbian, then the rest of us were more than happy to pick up the slack. Maybe the three of us didn't share DNA with her, but Porter, Mark, and I all treated her like she was ours, and though she was still sad about her soured relationship with her father, she seemed to like the three dads she had instead.

In the midst of the chaos of Tiffany, Porter, and me getting on the same page, we'd worked with Ethan's teachers to get him tested for learning disabilities. Not surprisingly, he was dyslexic just like his brother. His teachers and school counselors had been excellent about working with him, and it had turned out to be an unexpected bonding opportunity for Ethan and Zach. Since Zach remembered all too well how frustrating it had been before he'd learned some coping methods, he jumped at the chance to teach those methods to Ethan, along with some he'd developed himself over time. My youngest son still struggled, like Zach would likely always struggle to some degree, but it looked like he was in for a smoother ride through school.

My family and I continued walking through the fair, and as we passed by a poster for tonight's sold-out Ty Herndon concert, Porter made a plaintive noise. "Damn it. I can't *believe* I didn't get tickets to that."

I gave his shoulder a sympathetic pat. "I know. Next time, baby."

He huffed, and we kept going.

Unbeknownst to Porter, he and I had plans tonight. After Zach, Tiffany, and Mark left with the kids, we were going to that sold-out Ty Herndon concert. I'd watched the ticket website like a hawk and snagged a pair the instant they went on sale. Seriously good seats, too—I couldn't wait to see the look on his face when he realized we were not only going to the show, we'd be sitting in the middle of the third row.

And after the show, well...

For the millionth time, I checked my pocket. Yep. Still there.

Fresh jitters went through me. It was a good thing we

were all walking instead of sitting still, because I was way too restless, and I'd give myself away in a heartbeat. I was excited and nervous and admittedly regretted planning it the way I had because I couldn't focus as much as I wanted to on the present. I couldn't even go on the rides with the kids like I usually would because my stomach was already queasy.

They didn't mind. Tiffany, Porter, Zach, and Ashley had *no* problem going on rides with them. That left me and Mark—who had some back problems—to keep an eye on any of the kids who weren't currently riding, and everyone was happy.

We finally found the petting zoo, and thank God, it was indoors. The barn was still warm, but it was out of the blazing sun and had some huge fans to keep the air moving.

In a big straw-filled corral in the middle of the barn, kids wandered in amongst goats, sheep, and a couple of alpacas. For a dollar, they could each buy an ice cream cone full of grain and seeds to feed the animals, and Tiffany and I suddenly had several sets of puppy dog eyes fixed on us, asking if we could get cones and go in with the animals. "Several" meaning all five kids—including the oldest who could buy his own damn cone but knew I'd never say no—and the boyfriend-slash-nanny who was clearly trying to let my ex and me call the shots but was *really* hoping we'd say yes because petting zoos were his kryptonite.

Like I could say no to my kids or my boyfriend. What could I say? I still loved the fact that he was such a sucker for animals. Visit a petting zoo with him? Hell yeah. One look at a baby goat or a bunny, and he was going to melt, which would in turn make me melt.

Tiffany and I bought enough grain-filled cones for each

of the kids and adults in the group, and we stepped into the corral.

And yep...melting.

Porter was instantly enthralled with the baby goats. They were smaller than house cats and bouncy as all hell, tearing around the straw-covered ground, jumping over and under the larger animals. Porter and Ethan laughed their heads off watching them.

Chloe loved the baby goats, but she'd never seen an alpaca up close before. She wanted to pet them, so I hoisted her onto my hip to bring her more to their eye level. There were two—a white one and a black one—and she giggled as she petted their soft, curly coats. They gently took food from her hand and nibbled at her clothes, and she was in seventh heaven.

Something tugged at my shorts. I glanced down, figuring one of the boys was trying to get my attention, but—

"Hey!" I tried to shoo away the goat that had been nosing around, and I realized a second too late that it had pulled something out of my pocket. "Get back here!"

Of course, chasing after a determined goat was easier said than done, especially with a five-year-old perched on my hip.

Porter was faster. He lunged toward the goat. It dropped what was in its mouth and shook its head like a dog. Porter pointed at it and sternly said, "Don't you dare."

The goat took a step back and shook its head again.

"I mean it." Porter kept his gaze fixed on the goat as he crouched. "Don't—"

The goat reared up, then came at him and butted him hard in the thigh.

"Hey!"

Of course everyone in the corral laughed, especially the

kids, which mostly drowned out his muttered, "Jackass." Gingerly rubbing his leg, Porter leaned down to pick up what the goat had dropped. "Got it!" He held his hand up triumphantly, but then he froze when he'd retrieved from the ground. And I froze, because there was no pretending he didn't know what it was.

Carefully, I eased Chloe down to her feet. As I straightened, Porter's wide eyes shifted from the ring box in his hand to me.

"Is this...' He glanced at it, then back at me. "Holden..."

"Um." I held out my hand, and he placed the box in my palm. "Uh. Well." I looked at the box, pretending my heart wasn't suddenly racing in a way that had nothing to do with chasing down the klepto-goat. "I guess since I can't surprise you with it anymore..." I met his gaze and, right there on the straw, went to one knee. "Porter, will—"

Something thumped against my back, then onto my shoulder. For a second I thought one of the kids was goofing around, but then I realized it was a kid, just not one of mine. Turning my head carefully, I looked into the wide eyes of a tiny four-hooved, pointy-eared kid who'd perched on my shoulder, and was looking very pleased with itself.

"Seriously?" I said to the baby pygmy goat. "I'm trying to propose to my boyfriend here."

It responded by trying to eat my hair.

All around us, people laughed hysterically, and I was pretty sure several were filming.

"Uh...a little help here?"

Tiffany carefully lifted the goat off my shoulder.

"Thanks." Laughing, I brushed a few pieces of straw off my shirt. Then I looked up, and the instant I met Porter's eyes again, I stopped laughing and started fighting back tears. This was real. I was really doing this. There was no turning back and no pretending he didn't know what was happening. I'd meant to do this after the concert, but it was happening now, and suddenly I couldn't wait anyway.

I swallowed the lump in my throat and squeezed his hand. "Would you...consider a promotion from nanny to stepdad?"

Porter laughed as some tears slid free, and he nodded. "Definitely."

I rose and, as everyone around us *aww*ed, slid the ring onto his finger. Porter cupped my face and kissed me softly. "I have to say, this was the most adorable proposal I—hey!" He stumbled sideways and glared at a goat. The same goat that had butted him earlier and was now shaking its head and ready to butt him again. "Dude, what the hell?"

I snorted. "Maybe we should take this out of their pen?"

"Yeah, maybe." Porter rubbed his hip, shooting another glare at the goat. "Asshole."

Chuckling, I wrapped my arm around his waist, and we left the corral as people around us clapped and snapped photos.

Safely out of the corral and away from any more goats who might try to interrupt us, Porter wrapped his arms around my neck and smiled at me. "I definitely wasn't expecting that."

"To be fair, I wasn't planning it this way." I slid my arms around his waist. "Maybe a petting zoo wasn't the best place for a proposal."

He laughed, lighting up the whole barn. "Are you kidding? We're going to have the best proposal story *ever*."

"Yeah, we are." I glanced back at the corral. "No goats at the wedding, though, okay?"

His expression shifted to puppy dog eyes. "Well, I

hadn't thought of that, but now that you mention it, you can't just veto it without discussion."

I groaned. "Oh God."

Laughing, he pulled me closer, letting me rest my forehead on his shoulder. As he stroked my hair, he said, "It's okay. We'll just have a *few* goats."

"Great." I lifted my head again and cupped his face. "So, if we're getting married—you know what that means, right?"

He looked in my eyes. "What?"

I grinned. "Now you have carte blanche to make all the dad jokes you want."

Porter burst out laughing, which almost hid the way his eyes were suddenly welling up. Except they were really welling up, and he had to swipe at them with an unsteady hand.

"Hey." I touched his shoulder. "That wasn't supposed to make you cry."

"I know." He laughed as he wiped his eyes. "I just... I mean, when I first met you, I knew you didn't want me trying to replace you as their dad. So asking me to be their... kind of their second dad, it's..."

Well shit. Now he was going to make *me* cry.

I wrapped my arms around him and held him tight. "I never thought I'd want someone to be a stepdad to them, and now I can't imagine anyone else filling those shoes."

He returned my embrace. "Man, I don't know where you learned to be all romantic, but please do keep it up."

I chuckled and kissed his cheek. "You mean like having my proposal interrupted by livestock?"

"I'm telling you." Porter drew back and met my gaze, eyes sparkling with both tears and mischief. "Best proposal story ever."

"Yeah, yeah."

"And the perfect excuse to have—"

"*No* goats at the wedding."

He sighed dramatically and was about to say something, but then he looked down. I did too, and saw Chloe tugging at Porter's hand.

"You got a new ring?" she said. "Can I see?"

"Of course, kiddo." Porter hoisted her up onto his hip, then held up his free hand so she could inspect the ring. "What do you think?"

She smiled. "It's pretty."

"Yeah, it is. I like it." He glanced at me. "And since it means your dad and I are getting married, now I have to find a ring for him."

Her eyes lit up. "Can I help pick it out?"

Porter grinned. "Do you want to do that?"

She nodded vigorously, her smile huge. "Yeah!"

"Okay. We will." He kissed her cheek and eased her down onto her feet. Before he rose, though, he said, "And hey, guess what?"

"What?"

He flashed a wicked grin and said in a stage whisper, "Your dad says we can have goats at the wedding."

Chloe squealed with glee. I groaned, and Porter snickered.

"Do I even want to know?" Tiffany asked.

I gave an exasperated sigh and turned to her. "Someone just promised our daughter goats at the wedding."

Her eyebrows quirked. "Okay. I'm gonna take that as 'no, Tiffany, you don't want to know.'"

"Probably a good idea."

She laughed. Then she hugged us each in turn. "Congratulations, guys."

"Thanks." Cupping Porter's face, I glanced at Tiffany. "By the way, in case I hadn't mentioned it? I'm really glad you hired him."

"Yeah?" Tiffany laughed again. "You don't say."

Porter chuckled too and kissed my palm. Then he sobered. "Uh, how is this going to work going forward? Do I need to look into getting a job, or...?"

"That depends," I said. "How much do you like being a stay-at-home dad?"

"Well, I mean, I love it. But I still need money for things, and I want to contribute."

"We'll figure something out," Tiffany said. "It isn't something we have to iron out this minute, but we'll come up with a solution that makes everyone happy."

He glanced back and forth between us as if he were uneasy leaving it unresolved, but then he relaxed. "Okay. We'll sit down and talk about it and go from there."

"Sounds like a plan." She gestured at the kids, then turned to me. "Okay, well, I think Mark and I can wrangle the troops with Zach and Ashley's help." She winked. "You two have fun."

Porter looked at me, brow furrowed as if he knew he was missing something.

"We will." I grinned. "Thanks for taking over for us."

"Don't mention it. See you guys later."

She left to rejoin her boyfriend and our army of kids, and Porter turned to me. "So, are we going back to the petting zoo by ourselves or something?"

I laughed. "We can if you want to. Or..." I took out my wallet and slid the tickets free. "We could use these?"

Porter took them, and instantly, his eyes were huge. "No way." He met my gaze. "Are these real? Are you serious?"

I nodded. "They're real, and I'm serious."

"We're...going to see..."

"Ty Herndon." I gestured at the tickets. "Third row, too."

"Oh my *God*." Porter threw his arms around me so hard he nearly knocked me off my feet. "You're amazing! How did you get these?"

"You'd be amazed what a good blowjob can—"

"Oh shut up." He kissed my cheek and pulled back, still smiling. "Thank you. This is... This whole *day* has been amazing."

"Even the part where you got attacked by a goat?"

"Well, yeah. Because that gave me the idea for—"

"No. Goats. At the wedding."

He batted his eyes. "But Chloe has her heart set on it now."

I plucked the tickets out of his hand. "So you're saying you don't want—"

"Hey! Gimme!"

"I don't know." I held them just out of his reach. "You did promise my kid goats."

"Uh-huh. And I intend to deliver." He jumped, grabbed the tickets, and pulled them away triumphantly. "Ha! Now I have tickets, a ring, and goats for the wedding."

I rolled my eyes and laughed as I wrapped my arm around his waist. "We'll discuss the goats. But yes, you have tickets and a ring."

"Yeah, I do." He leaned into me and looked down at the tickets in his hand. "I swear, this is the best day *ever*."

"Oh, I see. You're excited about the ring, but it's the concert tickets that are the highlight of your day."

"Yes, baby." He straightened and laced our fingers together. "The concert is definitely higher on my list than the ring." Porter tsked and rolled his eyes. "Shut up."

I just laughed, and we kept walking.

When we finally took our seats, even I was pretty awestruck by how close we were to the front. The concert was in the fairgrounds' stadium, but about two dozen rows of folding chairs had been set up right in front of the stage. From our seats in the third row, I could read the writing on a stage tech's T-shirt. We were *close*.

"Fair warning." Porter turned a sheepish look on me. "This is Ty Herndon, and we're practically in his lap. So I might go total screaming fanboy and let go of any dignity I have left."

"So, what you're saying is"—I held up my phone—"make sure I'm ready to film?"

Porter face-palmed, almost muffling an exasperated groan, and I laughed.

"I'm sure it'll be the most adorable thing I've ever seen."

Porter blushed. "You are such a sap, you know that?"

"Hey, is that any way to talk to the man who got climbed on by a goat while he was trying to propose to you?"

He snorted, elbowing me playfully. "*That* was the most adorable thing ever. And besides, its mom came and attacked me while I was trying to say yes, so..."

"Good God. Goats and marriage proposals just do not mix."

"I don't know." He met my eyes and smiled so sweetly I almost melted right then and there. "I thought it was pretty cute, and we really do have a totally unique proposal story to tell until we die."

"Yeah. We do." I squeezed his hand. We exchanged a long look, and had we not been quite so out in the open, I'd have stolen a kiss.

That could wait until we got home, though.

The concert finally kicked off. The opening act did their set, and when they were finished, Ty Herndon took the stage.

Yeah, my new fiancé did turn into a total screaming fanboy.

And yeah, it was one of the most adorable things I'd ever seen.

ABOUT THE AUTHOR

L.A. Witt and her husband have been exiled from Spain and sent to live in Maine because rhymes are fun. She now divides her time between writing, assuring people she is aware that Maine is cold, wondering where to put her next tattoo, and trying to reason with a surly Maine coon. Rumor has it her arch nemesis, Lauren Gallagher, is also somewhere in the wilds of New England, which is why L.A. is also spending a portion of her time training a team of spec ops lobsters. Authors Ann Gallagher and Lori A. Witt have been asked to assist in lobster training, but they "have books to write" and "need to focus on our careers" and "don't you think this rivalry has gotten a little out of hand?" They're probably just helping Lauren raise her army of squirrels trained to ride moose into battle.

Website: www.gallagherwitt.com
    Email: gallagherwitt@gmail.com
    Twitter: @GallagherWitt

Manufactured by Amazon.ca
Bolton, ON